"This is a lovely story that captures so well the mystery, as well as the inspiration, of the musical autistic savant. It is an astonishing, extraordinary condition explored in this tale in an intriguing, exceptional manner."

DAROLD A. TREFFERT, MD
Agnesian HealthCare Treffert Center, A Member of SSM Health
Fond du Lac, WI
Author of *Islands of Genius: The Bountiful Mind of the Autistic, Acquired, and Sudden Savant*

RETURN
of the
Song

Also by Phyllis Clark Nichols

Christmas at Grey Sage
Silent Days, Holy Night (October 2018)

RETURN
of the
Song

The ROCKWATER Suite

———

Book One

Phyllis Clark Nichols

Return of the Song: Book #1 in The Rockwater Suite
Copyright © 2018 by Phyllis Clark Nichols

 GILEAD
PUBLISHING

Published by Gilead Publishing, LLC
Wheaton, Illinois, USA.
www.gileadpublishing.com

ISBN: 978-1-68370-145-3 (printed softcover)
ISBN: 978-1-68370-146-0 (ebook)

Cover design by Jeff Gifford, www.gradientidea.com
Interior design by Beth Shagene
Ebook production by Book Genesis, Inc.

Printed in the United States of America.

18 19 20 21 22 23 24 / 5 4 3 2 1

For Mama,
who patiently listened to every sour note,
who proudly attended every recital,
and who lovingly and diligently gave me
every opportunity to learn the melodies,
the harmonies, and the rhythms of my song of faith.

Prelude

HIGHLANDS OF GUATEMALA

Sinister clouds hung over the mountain peaks like a faded gray curtain and obscured the volcanoes in the distance. David spent his last few minutes with Ovispo and Sarita while Dr. Morris hauled the gear to the back of the pickup. The truck bed had been loaded with medical supplies when they left Guatemala City six days ago, but three villages and seventy-eight patients later, they were left with only their personal duffel bags and a six-hour drive back to the city.

David knew what mountain storms could do in the tablelands, and he was anxious to get out of these mountains before the afternoon rains started. He couldn't afford to miss his flight back to Atlanta tomorrow.

He heard Josh slam the truck door. "Come on, David. I have your bag. It's best if we make it to Solola before the weather sets in. Say your goodbyes and let's get going."

Their final stop was here at El Tablon, a primitive village in the highlands of Guatemala. With the last of the medicine dispensed, their work was complete, and the villagers now gathered to see them off. David did not speak Cakchiquel, but speech was unnecessary to communicate the displeasure of parting.

Sarita, the tribal matriarch, wordlessly spoke for all the women as she handed David a compactly folded bundle of white woven fabric secured with a handmade ribbon of braided thread. He untied the braid and unfolded the fabric in one brisk motion to reveal sprays of embroidered flowers around the hem of the cloth. Sarita had deliberately folded the piece to conceal the surprise and to protect the stitching.

For a tourist who collected the needlework of the Mayan artisans, this tablecloth was a work of art. For David, it was a gift of great sacrifice. He knew the sale of this piece in the city would have fed Sarita's village for a month. He held it to his face, inhaling the smell of smoke left from the open fire where the women gathered in the evenings to stitch by the firelight, just as women had done for centuries in this place.

"Gracias. Gracias, Hermana Sarita." David hugged her and wanted to tell her how much this wedding present would mean to Caroline and how it would grace their table for years to come.

Sarita blushed at David's attention and smiled broadly, exposing her broken and decaying teeth.

He heard Josh calling again. "David Summers, if we don't get down this mountain, Caroline's trip to the airport to pick you up tomorrow will be in vain."

"I'm coming." David turned to six-year-old Blanca hiding in Sarita's shadow. Hatefully aimed bullets of rebels had robbed Blanca of her father three months before she was born, and an untreated infection sucked the life from her seventeen-year-old mother only days after Blanca's birth. Sarita and Ovispo's childless hut had become Blanca's home. Blanca's story—and countless other stories like hers—still ate at David and motivated his return to El Tablon with medical aid three times a year. She was his favorite village child, although he tried not to show it.

Blanca walked shyly toward him, head down and hands behind her back. He knelt and reached out to her. She lifted her head, fixing her brown eyes on his, and not a muscle in her face moved as she took his right hand and turned it palm up. She relaxed the fingers in her doll-like fist, and placed a small, cloth bag in David's palm. "*Carolina*," she whispered.

"For Caroline?"

"*Sí. Carolina.*"

Treasure in hand, David embraced her tightly. He could hear the truck's motor running and thunder rumbling through the mountains as he held her at arm's length, then blessed her with a kiss on her forehead, as was the Mayan tradition. At last he rose and stumbled back to the truck.

"One of these trips, you're going to decide this is home, Summers. Or maybe you'll just take Blanca home with you, now that you're getting married and she'd have a mother," Josh said.

Still clutching the small bag, David climbed into the truck, trying not to soil the tablecloth. "Maybe, but the decision's not mine alone."

"Hey, man. If you can persuade that beauty to marry the likes of you, surely you can persuade her to take in a Guatemalan orphan."

"Perhaps I could. Time will tell. But for now I'll settle for being a blissfully married professor."

Josh revved the engine, priming it for the bumpy ride along the ridge. He gave an inquiring glance at David.

"Do it. You know how the kids love it."

Josh blew his horn until he rounded the curve and they drove out of sight.

The ramshackle truck bounced over the rocks and gullies across the ridge. David scanned the patchwork quilt of small garden plots across the mountainsides. A year-round growing season kept these poor inhabitants in their staple corn and beans. Some patches were green and ready for harvest, and others lay dormant brown waiting to be planted. Although he daydreamed about living in this Land of Eternal Spring, he'd miss fall and winter.

"Those guys must have legs like mountain goats," David said as they passed farmers hoeing rows of corn.

"If they don't start home, they'll need webbed feet or hides like elephants when that storm washes them down this mountain. The volcanic ash in this soil makes it slick before you can say 'slick.'"

David didn't need to turn around to know the sky was growing blacker. The mist had thickened, and he noticed Josh's frequent glances at the rearview mirror.

"Hey, what time is it?" Josh's fingers strummed the steering wheel.

"About four thirty. Why?"

"I was figuring. We have another hour along the ridge, then an hour to get down the mountain, and half an hour into Solola. I think we'd better stay the night there and drive into the city in the morning."

The sprinkles turned to rivulets down the dirty windshield.

"Sounds like a plan to me." David opened the drawstring bag in his palm and guided its contents onto the white tablecloth spread across his knees. A beaded bracelet. He held it up for Josh to see. "A bracelet for Caroline. This must have taken Blanca days to make. Hey, look! She worked Caroline's name into the beading."

In the few seconds that Josh glanced at the bracelet, the truck veered from the safe ruts. He jerked the steering wheel, nearly losing control of the vehicle. Last night's rain had made syrup of this narrow road. The altitude would have turned it to dust again by now had the morning brought sun instead of heavy mist and the promise of more rain.

"Whoa, that was close! Best to keep your eyes on this goat path," David said.

"Man, I'd prefer it if this truck bed was loaded right now. Would help hold us on the road. Guess I might as well slow down. The road's too slick, and we can't outrun this rain anyway. We should have left sooner."

"Sorry. My fault."

The drizzle turned into a battering assault on the cornfields and the jungle below. David could hardly see the hood ornament through the pelting rain. There was no break in the intensity for the next half hour as they traversed the ridge, leading to the turn that would start their sixty-five-hundred-foot descent down the mountain.

Riding through the jungle was always cool and dark, but the storm, showing no mercy, brought a menacing darkness and an unusual chill as they descended. David knew Josh's muscles must be tense from steering the hairpin turns. Water gushing through the crags on the hillsides had cut deep horizontal trenches across the ruts, which had all but disappeared.

"Boy, these super-sized philodendron leaves are a gift. They usually swat me in the face when I come down this mountain with my window down, but they're swiping my window now, and I'm glad," Josh said.

"Me too. That way we know we're not too close to this ledge I can't see over here."

The water bombarded the truck and drowned out their conversation. David sat quietly and fingered the yellows and reds and greens of the embroidered flowers on the tablecloth. Envisioning Caroline's delight put a secret smile on his face.

He glanced up.

"Josh, look out!"

The avalanche of water and mud gushed down the mountainside just in front of them. As David instinctively tried to open his door to escape, the wall of watery debris hit them broadside. He saw the splintered limbs of an avocado tree crashing through the windshield, striking Josh as the truck plunged from the ledge. In less time than it took to inhale and exhale, the violent torrent surged through the shattered glass, washing away all life and hope.

The truck plummeted—the water's force tumbling it like a tin can, flipping it over and over and slamming it into trees until it became lodged. His battered body now helpless, David clutched the beaded bracelet as the current propelled him from the truck.

The flood-waters ran blood-red as time lost its meaning and a quiet peace silenced the thunderous roars of the rushing water engulfing him. The last thing David saw was the white tablecloth floating away as the cold river ushered him into a warm tunnel of light.

Chapter One

Picture Windows

———— ♦ ————

SIX YEARS LATER
MOSS POINT, GEORGIA

The pendulum clock in the studio struck two. Caroline wished it were six. Painful memories and the dread of another anniversary had robbed her of sleep. She should have been lying next to David, wisps of his breath brushing her neck like a moth's wings and an occasional audible sigh interrupting the night's hush. Instead, the night's silence shouted, "David is gone, and you are alone."

Six years of life without him. Six years of unanswered questions. Why, God, didn't You hold back one thunderstorm for one hour—or maybe even a few seconds? Why did David have to be in Guatemala on that ridge that morning? Why didn't I give in and go with him? He begged me to go. If I had, I wouldn't be lying here by myself still longing for him.

Tears of loneliness moistened her pillow. She untangled her feet from the crumpled sheet, rolled over, and sat on the edge of the bed, rubbing her eyes and pulling the scrunchie from her ponytail. Her thick, dark hair fell loose and free to her shoulders. Cradling her head in her hands, she stared at the floor and watched the moving shadows of the ceiling fan blades.

Why do I keep up this act, trying to make everyone think I'm fine, that I'm no longer grieving for David, that my music and my students make my life complete? They don't know that the music isn't really music anymore. They don't know the piano is where I hide. They think I have it all together. Why should they think otherwise? What would it help if they knew that my ordered, predictable life makes me feel safe? Not alive—just safe.

Caroline stood up, brushed her hair back with her fingers, and twined the scrunchie around her ponytail again. The full moon seeping through the studio windows created a luminescence, making lamplight unnecessary for her trip to the kitchen for a cup of tea. She filled the kettle and turned to look out the window into the cottage garden. The air was still. Not even the plumes on the ornamental grass moved. She stood, twirling the string of the tea bag around her finger as she waited for the water to boil. Thinking herself the only mortal awake in Moss Point at such an hour, she longed for the familiar whistle of the teakettle to shatter the overwhelming silence.

That was her life: still and quiet.

She allowed the kettle to whistle two seconds before pouring the water over her tea bag and slumping over the sink to wait.

Waiting. That's what I do. I wait for the water to boil and for the tea to steep. I wait for the sun to rise. I wait for the summer. When will I quit waiting?

She pulled the tea bag from the cup and squeezed it against her spoon, then fumbled everything and dropped the spoon, splattering tea on the floor. She stared at it. Normally she would have wiped it up immediately. Tonight she didn't.

Teacup in hand, she wandered into the great room where her grand piano reigned in the alcove surrounded by three twelve-foot walls of glass. The painted wooden floor felt cool to her bare feet as she walked across the room. In April she often opened the French doors to the terrace, and the fragrance of spring's first roses drifted in on the sultry night air to mingle with the sounds from her piano before floating back out again. But not tonight. The doors remained closed as she sat at the piano, sipping tea and looking at the water garden. After a few minutes she set her cup down on the marble-topped table where she kept her appointment book and student files.

The moonlight's illumination of the keys was more than sufficient for her hands, so at home on the keyboard. Thoughts of David brought a familiar melody to her fingers: "David's Song," the most beautiful melody she ever conceived and yet never finished. She had written songs since childhood. She was trained to compose. She knew the fundamentals. When she'd begun this composition six years ago, the passionate rush of melody and lyrics had come together so quickly she could hardly record them fast enough. More than a song or a melody, this duet of voice and piano, capturing the essence of David and their passion, would have been her wedding gift to him.

It had been exactly three hundred and sixty-five days since she had allowed herself to play this melody. At least outside her head.

Caroline gazed out the window as she played its same notes over and over again. In six years she had not been able to get beyond this one unresolved phrase. Clenched fists finally replaced her nimble fingers, and a strident, dissonant pounding arrested the melody like David's death had halted her life.

At that moment, a shadow on the pond and a hasty movement across the water's edge caught her eye. She stepped to the window. The tea olives next to the glass still shuddered. Her discordant pounding must have startled some creature.

She turned to pick up her tea. Standing so near that the warmth from her cup fogged the pane, Caroline wondered how many more nights she would find herself here gazing through this glass. That was her life: looking through windows. Windows where she had glimpses of good things, then goodbyes.

Twenty-one years ago she'd stood in Ferngrove, looking out the picture window in her parents' living room, observing the delivery of her 1902 Hazelton Brothers piano: a seven-foot Victorian grand made of burled wood and accented with hand-carved scrolling.

This piano had become her emotional vehicle, defining her and filling her hours. It had become her safest place. Her love affair with that instrument had charted the course of her life.

Nine years later, she'd stood at that same picture window as three movers, like pallbearers, removed her piano. The sale of it paid her college tuition. Often, over the years, she had imagined that piano, her first love, sitting in someone else's living room and responding to a stranger's touch. Even now she longed for the familiarity of those ivory keys.

Windows. She'd been standing at a picture window when she first saw David. He had stepped through the door—and quite unexpectedly into her heart—at her best friend's wedding.

Her pulse still quickened when she thought of watching him walk up the sidewalk of the Baker house.

Oh, David, we were so different, but we fit like the last two pieces of a puzzle. You were so full of life and so spontaneous. And your laugh . . . Your laugh could fill up a room. Me? I was more soulful, always analyzing things, and all I had to bring to a room was my music.

You lived on the edge. I lived safely behind my keyboard. You wanted to teach the world to think and ponder life and its meaning. I just wanted to instill a love of music in one student at a time. You were bold and adventurous, and I was cautious. And look where it got us. You're gone, and I'm alone. How could you just walk in and through my life like that?

She had said goodbye to him at the Atlanta airport six weeks before their wedding. Standing at the terminal window, she'd watched him board his plane for Guatemala. A week later, she had stood at the same window awaiting his arrival as planned. He didn't come. It was days before they knew what had happened. No David, no goodbye, no closure. Only days and nights of looking through windows, hoping he'd come walking up again.

Her own life had been swept into a deep gorge like David's vehicle, never to be recovered. Her faith told her he was in heaven, but her doubt asked, "Where is heaven? What's it really like? Can he see me? Does he know how much I need him?"

Six years in this studio apartment of longtime family friends Sam and Angel Meadows had only numbed the pain. Coming to Moss Point and living at Twin Oaks provided privacy, a place to teach piano, and the nearness of two friends who had loved her all her life, but her wound was still fresh and deep, oozing with despair and loneliness. She kept it bandaged well so no one would notice.

But lately her life dangled like the dominant seventh chord or the unfinished scale she used to play at the end of her piano lesson as a prank on Mrs. Cummings, her childhood piano teacher. Countless times Caroline had run her fingers up the scale—*do, re, mi, fa, so, la, ti* . . .—stopping just shy of the last *do*. She would run out the door and wait for Mrs. Cummings to play the last note of the scale. Mrs. Cummings always did. That was resolution, the kind Caroline longed for now.

The pendulum clock struck three. Her tea no longer fogged up the window, and the darkness remained. Memories absorbed her when she needed to think about her future. Nothing and no one would appear through this window to change the course of her life again. And important issues were converging in the next few days: her twenty-ninth birthday, the end of another year of piano teaching, and the deadline for a decision that could take her from Moss Point and from this studio that had become her glass cocoon.

She moved back to the piano, sat in the deafening silence, and remembered other windows and unfinished songs. *Oh, that morning would come and drown this darkness and the quiet that screams of my solitary existence.*

But for now it was still night. She was alone with her piano, and she looked through this window where the night lights danced on the pond's surface amid the silhouettes of magnolia leaves.

She set her teacup down and started to "doodle," conjuring up a melody to accompany the moonlight's waltz across the water. She instinctively darkened the melody when she noticed a shadow moving at the water's edge and she heard the rustling tea olives outside her window. Nighttime shadows nor stirring shrubs frightened her, for playing her piano ushered her into another reality where she was safe.

Chapter Two

Breakfast with the Meadows

———— • ————

*A*PRIL MORNINGS IN MOSS POINT, GEORGIA, WERE GOD'S peace offering for the long January nights and early March's blustery breezes. With a steaming cup of coffee in hand, Caroline sauntered through the garden and took her seat on the bench at the pond's edge. Fingers of morning light stretched through the weeping willow and played on the water. She measured each morning's unfurling of the fiddlehead ferns and watched the rosebuds swell until color peaked through the green cradles of leaves.

She sipped her coffee. *There really is life after a cold, dark winter. Wish there could be a million April mornings. The irises will disappear in June, and the roses will wilt in July's blistering sun. The ferns will curl crispy brown in August. Then it'll be winter again.*

Caroline returned to the kitchen for her second cup. The phone rang, and before the receiver ever reached her ear, she heard, "You are my sunshine, my only sunshine. You make me happy when—"

She didn't let him finish. "Good morning, Sam."

"'Good morning, Sam'? How'd you know it was me?"

"There are only two people in the world who'd be singing to me at seven o'clock in the morning. One's my daddy, and he's a tenor who can sing. That leaves you, my friend."

"Well, if you're going to be that way, I won't tell you that Angel is flipping flapjacks over here, and yours are almost ready. The bacon's crisp, the maple syrup's heating, and how do you want your eggs?"

"I'll pass on the eggs this morning, but I can't resist Angel's pancakes. Give me five minutes to get presentable. Oh, and, Sam, I'll bring my coffee, and tell Angel I'll bring her a cup too. She doesn't like that swamp water you drink any more than I do."

Sam broke into song again. "You'll never know, dear, how much I love you—"

"Five minutes, Sam!"

The morning sun, blasting through the east windows, spotlighted tea stains on the floor in front of the sink. A reminder of last night's restlessness. She knelt to wipe the stains with a damp sponge. These pine floors were from the elementary schoolhouse Sam had attended seventy-five years ago. He'd acquired the yellow pine before the building was demolished and used it to build this art studio for Angel for their twenty-fifth wedding anniversary. Floors, walls, ceilings, doors—everything but the twelve-foot walls of glass was white. The studio had been Angel's unblemished canvas where she painted until a few years before Caroline moved in. Now Caroline, grateful to call it home and her piano studio, kept it spotless like her mama had taught her.

A short hallway led to the bathroom. She brushed her long, wavy dark hair, inherited from her father, and pulled it away from her face into a ponytail. Gray sweats were fine for her trip to the big house. They'd be having breakfast on the back screened porch, and it was still cool.

She returned to the kitchen, poured coffee into a carafe, grabbed her own cup, and started over. It was this stone path, laid thirty years ago and worn smooth by Angel's trips to the studio, that led to the main house about a hundred yards away. Just this winding through the garden usually lifted Caroline's spirits, but her sleepless night had taken the spring out of her step.

She climbed the steps and opened the screen door with her one available finger, angling her body through the doorway as she heard Sam's trumpetlike voice from the kitchen.

"Caroline, don't—"

"I know, Sam. Don't slam the door. You tell me that every time I come in. It would have taken you less time to get the spring on the door fixed."

Angel's "Amen!" came from the kitchen.

Caroline set the coffee down on the white wicker table already set for breakfast. Sam, holding the platter of crisp bacon in one hand and a pitcher of warm maple syrup in the other, came through the kitchen door. He leaned down and kissed her on the forehead. "I always liked my women short. Makes me feel so tall." At eighty-four, Sam was still a solidly strong man with a six-foot-two-inch frame that had not yet given in to the weight of his years. Balding with only a few wrinkles in his tanned face, he could easily pass for mid-sixties. In his youth he had been an athlete, and he'd continued his workouts at the YMCA on almost a daily basis up until a few months ago. Now his morning jogs had turned into afternoon walks, and his workouts were in the garden.

Caroline stepped into the kitchen and pecked Angel on the cheek. "Angel, you are a wonder woman, flipping pancakes with one hand and eggs over easy with the other."

"Yep, don't know if it's my cookin' or something else that keeps Sam around." Angel winked at Caroline. "Thought he might decide to dump me for Evelyn Masters when my waistline disappeared and I traded in my belted slacks for floral muumuus."

"Sam crossed Evelyn off his list sixty years ago. Oh, he just thinks of you as his floating flower garden."

"Guess that's better than a floral fire hydrant." Angel flipped another pancake.

Caroline giggled. "I'd say it's those quick brown eyes and that feisty disposition of yours that keep him around. Here, let me help you."

"Gladly, my dear. Put that spatula to those pancakes. I'll do the rest. You know how Sam is about his eggs. Did you bring me some coffee?"

"Would I show up for breakfast without it? Still can't figure how Sam drinks that stuff."

"He's been doing it for years, and it's too late to change him now." Angel patted Sam's eggs with paper towel to remove the grease as Caroline put the last pancakes on the platter. She followed Angel step for step out the kitchen doorway onto the porch.

Sam seated them both and proceeded with the blessing. With oratorical voice and King James English, he prayed as though God was high in His heavens and might have trouble hearing him.

Their food—and possibly the neighbors' too—blessed, Angel looked at Caroline. "Oh, honey! I always said when God was passing out eyes, His basket was empty when He got to you, and He just decided to put in sapphires instead. So tell me, sweetie, why are those pools of blue surrounded by pink this morning?"

"Just a bit of trouble sleeping last night." Caroline took some butter and passed it to Sam.

"I know you. Normal people have nightmares, but you have 'songmares.' Too many tunes echoing in your head again?"

"Not only can you put pancakes, eggs, and bacon all hot on the table at the same time, now you're into mind reading." Caroline hoped that Angel wouldn't require further explanation.

"If she can read minds, then I'm in for some trouble," Sam said.

"You've been in trouble for the last sixty years, but right now I want to hear from Blue Eyes over here."

"You mean a song? Or what?" Caroline skirted the issue again.

"I mean 'what.'"

Caroline stared at her plate, stirring the melted butter into the syrup. "Well, it's an anniversary of sorts. Six years today David didn't return home from Guatemala. The what-might-have-beens always steal my sleep."

Sam dabbed his mouth with his napkin. "So that's why we didn't see you all day yesterday."

Caroline jumped at the chance to change the subject. "You did see me yesterday, Sam. I played for Ross Abner's funeral and sat there trying to figure out whose eulogy you were giving. You couldn't have been talking about the man in the casket, dressed in his bowling shirt with his bowling ball beside him."

"Sam's been here so long he's done more eulogies than all the preachers in town. He's got a file drawer full of them. Just reaches in, pulls one out, and hopes it fits. You know Sam—he won't speak ill of the living, much less the dead, even if they do deserve it."

Butter and maple syrup oozed from the short stack as Caroline cut into the pancakes. She paused before taking a bite. "That was another thing I couldn't understand. I heard GiGi Nelson say you put Ross in jail three times. Why in the world would the family ask you to do the eulogy?"

"So you heard it from old GiGi, did you?" Sam put his knife down so hard it jarred his plate. "She thinks everybody in town calls her GiGi because she's cute. I guess I'll let the truth be known when I deliver her eulogy, if I live long enough. And by the way, whoever saw a cute orange-haired prune?"

"Sam, I just got through telling Caroline you wouldn't speak ill of anybody, living or dead."

"Well, I didn't think it was ill or gossip if I'm just telling the truth. Besides, GiGi's not just anybody. And to answer your question, Miss Caroline, no, I did not put old Ross in jail three times. He put himself in jail. When you break a man's jaw with your elbow, shoot your neighbor's dog lying on her back porch, and get caught for driving under the influence as many times as Ross did, the jury tends to find you guilty of something. I just told them which thing it was this time. How about passing the syrup pitcher?"

"Seems you knew as much about Ross Abner as anyone else in town, and his family hedged their bets you wouldn't mention most of it."

Sam drained the syrup pitcher. "There's some good in most everybody. But for some, like ol' Ross, you just have to look maybe a little harder . . . like how hard I'm looking for the last drop of maple syrup in this pitcher. Angel, are you rationing this syrup with that last can of macadamia nuts you thought I didn't know about?"

"Sam Meadows, that sugar must have already gone to your head. *You* poured the syrup in the pitcher this morning. And, no, I am not rationing the macadamia nuts." Angel turned and whispered to Caroline, "Guess I'll have to find a new hiding place."

As they finished breakfast, two men dressed in overalls and plaid shirts and carrying homemade toolboxes approached the screened door. They stood side by side at attention as though awaiting orders. Sam looked at his watch, got up from the table, and greeted them with a booming voice. "Good morning, gentlemen. You're right on time."

Angel leaned over and quietly said to Caroline, "After all these years, he still can't call them 'Ned and Fred' with a straight face."

Caroline had become fond of these identical twins who had proudly taken care of Twin Oaks for the last forty years. Ned and Fred were in their early sixties, still single, and living together at their old home place just outside town. There was a certain goodness and honest simplicity about them that made them vulnerable to a few reprehensible townspeople who took advantage of them on occasion.

The twins stood together on the doorsteps, but only Ned did the talking. "Good mornin' yourself, Mr. Sam. We're here just like you asked us. We come to fix the fence again. We keep thinkin' it's about time you got rid of that ol' thing and put in a new one. We kinda hate takin' your money for fixin' something that ought not to be fixed again."

"I hear you, Ned. But I'm determined that fence'll last as long as I do. Jake noticed when he was pruning the roses on the back side that some of the boards need replacing."

"Now, Mr. Sam, that's another thing. You know them climbin'

roses ain't no good for wooden fences. You want us to take 'em down when we fix the fence?"

Caroline waited for what was coming.

Angel was the Pendergrass brothers' strongest advocate, but she had seen too often what they inflicted on her flowers. "Ned Pendergrass, if you cut one stem of anything that even looks like a climbing rose, I'll paint pink polka dots on that green truck of yours before you leave today."

Caroline watched Ned chortle and Fred gasp. She knew Angel was teasing about the paint job, but she imagined thoughts of pink polka dots on his papa's old Ford truck would indeed catapult Fred into panic mode. Fred, the silent twin who had a passion for anything with a motor, had kept the unmistakable truck's engine tuned up for the last three decades. He'd painted the truck a shiny pea green and proudly lettered the sign on both doors himself: *NED & FRED PENDERGRASS—WE CAN FIX ANYTHING.* The truck bed had long since rusted out, and Fred had designed and built a new one out of wood, using picket fencing for the side bodies. The tailgate resembled a garden gate but was adequate for keeping their tools from leaving a trail down Moss Point's avenues.

"Not to worry, Miss Angel," Ned said. "The only thing I might do is pick you one of them good-smellin' roses. But I know Mr. Sam would chase me off this property with that twenty-gauge shotgun of his if I come awalkin' up to this door with a rose for you—even if it was one of your roses to begin with."

"You're a smart man, Ned," Sam said. "I don't think I'd bother with those roses if I were you. Just go get what you need to do the job, and I'll pay you for your time and the materials at the end of the day."

As the twins started to their truck, Caroline said, "Oh, Ned?"

Ned and Fred both turned like mirror images of each other as the talking one said, "Yes, ma'am, Miss Caroline?"

"Best be careful if you're working in the area of the tea olives.

There was some creature stirring around out there last night. I'd hate for you to scare up a raccoon, or worse yet, a skunk."

"Thank you for them words of wisdom, ma'am. You gonna be playin' that pretty music while we're workin'? We don't even bring our radio when we come to Mr. Sam's place. We like your music."

"Why, thank you, Ned. I'll be practicing later."

Angel got up from the table. "We'd best hurry. May'll be here before long. She's doing a good job of keeping up things around here even if she is like a drill sergeant about dust and grime. But she can't cook like Hattie. I know she's aiming for the job when Hattie retires, but I'm used to Hattie, and after forty years she's used to me."

Caroline asked, "When will Hattie be home?"

"She won't be back until early July. We gave her the vacation to see all of her kids. She deserves it." Angel began to clear the table. "Well, my dear, I hope you have some time to rest those pretty eyes before you start your teaching schedule today. I can just imagine that 'The Indian War Dance' and even 'Fur Elise' will make your eyes glaze over when you haven't had a good night's sleep."

"Oh, Angel, you just haven't heard Eric Morgan play 'The Indian War Dance.' According to his mother, he would thrill recital-hall audiences everywhere with his prodigious rendition of anything."

"It's Mrs. Morgan again, is it?" Sam pointed his index finger at Caroline. "Now, Miss Blue Eyes, you know I'm proud of you, but frankly, I cannot believe you're still taking her money for that boy's piano lessons."

"I know, Sam. Sometimes it really bothers me, but I've had two very straight conversations with her about Eric's lack of interest and talent. She simply won't hear it. She says, 'If you don't teach him, then I'll drive him over to Pine Hill for lessons.'"

"And you've decided to save her the gas money?"

"No, I've just decided to take her money and use it for my own gas. Speaking of gas money, I'm going to Fernwood this weekend.

Mama arranged for me to meet with the family who bought my childhood piano. Daddy sold it to the Whitmans, and they gave it to their daughter when she married. Unfortunately, she moved to Atlanta, and the piano went with her."

"Caroline, you have a fine piano," Sam said. "And I enjoy sitting out here on the porch with my cup of coffee and listening to you play, especially on April mornings when your windows are open. Why in the world would you go looking for that old piano?"

Angel stood in the kitchen doorway. "Because she's a determined woman, and you should know something by now about determined women. She wants her piano, and that's that."

"I've dreamed about it for years, and it's time to start the quest and see where it leads. I'm afraid the trail is getting colder and the price tag's getting higher. Daddy bought that piano for six hundred dollars and sold it nine years later to pay for my college education. It's probably worth forty-five thousand now—way out of my range, but I just have to know where it is and who's playing it."

"You can't always put a price tag on what's yours," Angel said. "Somebody else may own that piano, but it'll always be yours, Caroline."

Sam walked over to Caroline and took both her hands in his. "Little one, you've had two great loves in your young life: that old piano and your David. Lord knows I wish I could bring both of them back, but I can't. Just be grateful you had them. Loving's always worth the pain." He hugged her and held her at arm's length. "You think finding that old piano will bring your music back, but it won't. You're playing another piano now, and when the time's right someone's going to walk right up to you and pluck your heartstrings again. You just remember ol' Sam said that, okay?"

Caroline choked back her tears and put on the smile she was accustomed to wearing. "You're right. I have a very fine instrument, and I have some practicing to do this morning before the steady stream of students this afternoon."

Caroline retrieved her carafe from the kitchen and headed

toward the door. "Chat later." She paused in her tracks. "I know, Sam—don't slam the door." With a last wave, she walked the stone path, careful not to bruise the creeping thyme growing between the stones. She spied the pair of cardinals in the forsythia bush. She paused to watch the lovebirds.

As she rounded the curve of the daylily bed, what she heard halted her steps. The sudden sound of her piano disturbed the morning's silence.

Who's playing my piano? She stood rigid, not even wanting to breathe or bat her eyes. *That . . . That's "David's Song."*

Her thoughts tumbled. *This cannot be. No one's ever heard that piece. I've never played it for anyone. It's not written down or recorded. This isn't possible.*

But there was no mistaking what she heard. The melody abruptly stopped . . . and then a pounding and the melody started again.

This is not happening. Should I go in . . . I have to know.

She resumed breathing and walking, but more slowly and deliberately. The hinges squeaked as she opened the garden gate. She tiptoed to the back door and turned the knob slowly to enter the kitchen, wishing she could see around walls.

She had taken two steps into the kitchen when the phone rang. Immediately the music stopped. She froze.

Oh, no, does he know I'm here? Maybe I shouldn't go any farther. Maybe I should just scream or run. For only a second she deliberated, hands clenched, before she mentally shook her head. *No, I must see.*

She took a deep breath and two more steps. The phone continued to ring as she calculated every movement, slowly making her way through her kitchen into the great room.

"Wha—"

There was only the sudden slamming of the door to the terrace to assure her someone had been there.

Chapter Three

Unexpected Events

———— ◆ ————

*T*HE RING OF THE PHONE WAS THE ONLY THING THAT KEPT Caroline from running out the door for a glimpse of the intruder. Taking a shaky breath, she pulled herself together and answered. "Oh, hi, Mama." *I can't let her know what just happened.*

"Good morning, sweetie. Just checking to see if you're still coming home tomorrow."

"Yes, ma'am. I finish teaching at five, and I'll have the car packed." She stretched to look out the alcove window for any sign of her intruder.

"So, we should see you around seven?"

"See you then. Got to go. The teakettle is whistling." *A white lie now will keep Mama from worrying.*

"Okay, sweetie. I love you."

"Love you, too, Mama. Bye."

She never cut her mother this short, but she needed to get off the phone before her mother's sixth sense intuited her mood. She hung up the phone and sat down at her desk.

The shock of hearing "David's Song" had leeched the blood from her head. She was dizzy, and her hands felt cold. She dropped her head into her folded arms on her desktop to keep from fainting. She didn't know what to do. She wanted to call the police but hesitated.

What would I tell them? That someone sneaked into my house and was playing the piano but ran away when I came in? That someone was playing a song only I know? This makes no sense to me, let alone to the sheriff. Maybe I should tell Sam. But what would he do but worry?

The blood returned to her head, and the room stopped spinning. She looked around. Her purse and keys lay undisturbed on the counter. Her computer was exactly as she had left it. She went into her bedroom. Nothing out of place. She opened her jewelry box to find her pearls, the engagement ring David had given her, and her blue topaz pieces.

Neither robbery nor vandalism had been the intruder's motive.

Caroline returned to the great room. The terrace door swung wide open. She had unlocked the door when she went into the garden earlier, but she was certain she'd closed it before she left for breakfast. She turned and scanned the entire room once more.

This room was the reason she had never looked for a place of her own. Sam's design for this studio included a twelve-by-twelve alcove adjacent to the main room. Angel had painted in the natural light of this alcove, glassed in on three sides with double French doors opening to the garden. When Caroline moved in, this space had become the perfect spot for her baby grand. The view was picturesque, and the resonance in this room could be reproduced only in a recital hall. She often opened the doors when she played. Neighbors never complained, and Sam and Angel seemed to enjoy it.

But someone else had been secretly listening to her. Listening very carefully.

Caroline sat down at the piano and ran her hands across the keys, wondering whose hands had just played "David's Song" exactly as she played it. *No one in Moss Point can play the piano like that. Who could have heard enough to remember every note, including the unfinished phrase where I always stop?*

But then she remembered the rustling tea olives last night. Perhaps the creature had been of the two-legged kind . . .

"What should I do?" she asked her piano. No answer was forthcoming.

After a moment of reflection, Caroline shrugged. For the time being, she would tell no one until after her visit to Fernwood. As strange as it seemed, she did not feel threatened by what had just happened. Yes, someone had broken into her home. But something told her whoever had been there had been more interested in the piano than in harming her. And besides, she was looking forward to Friday's two-hour drive. She had not seen her parents since their Valentine's Day anniversary, and her visit meant a family gathering with her brothers and their families for dinner. Martha Carlyle was Fernwood's finest cook, according to her pastor, and she still looked for every opportunity to have her children's feet under her table.

The real purpose of Caroline's visit, of course, was to see the Whitmans. She was hopeful they would have information to launch her quest for her 1902 Hazelton Brothers piano.

If she told anyone about what had just happened, she'd see neither her family nor the Whitmans. It was settled, then. She wasn't saying a word. Not yet.

—·—

The late breakfast with Sam and Angel and the unexpected intruder had robbed her of practice time before her meeting with Tandy Yarbrough. Caroline dreaded her ten o'clock appointment with Tandy and Gertie, the church organist. Mrs. Yarbrough was planning Moss Point's next wedding of the century.

She had alienated just about everyone in town at her oldest daughter's marriage three years ago. As flawless as it was, the church wedding had played second fiddle to the lavish reception held in the east garden of the town's library. Some ladies speculated that Tandy had wormed her way onto the library board just so the gardens could be designed for her daughter's wedding reception. Those same ladies secretly prayed for rain on Rachel's wedding day, but their prayers went unanswered. The day had been perfect and come close to fulfilling the dream of any doting mother trying to impress the town's blue bloods—until time for the wedding couple's getaway.

The escape car had been parked on Townsend Street right outside the library gate. Tandy, still shouting instructions to her now-married daughter, had led the brigade of guests following the bride and groom through the rose-covered gate to the street. In the excitement, no one noticed the two rear tires nestled in the plump flesh of two ripe July watermelon halves.

Only fate could have placed Tandy where she stood when the groom cranked the car and floored the accelerator. Rear tires spun, and the flesh of that juicy melon flew. Tandy's pink dress might as well have been the bull's-eye for her son-in-law's escape efforts. Dripping in watermelon seeds, she'd stood speechless while the whole town cheered.

Tandy had had her comeuppance and the town mothers their vengeance. They were truly convinced God had given them even more than they asked for. If God had answered their prayers for rain, all the guests would have been wet. But instead—so they determined—God had provided one fresh, sufficient watermelon.

Caroline's recall of this event was a welcome distraction. As she carefully locked all the doors on her way out, she hoped this morning's meeting would be more productive.

Ned and Fred, back with the materials, pulled in the driveway as she was leaving. "I'll be back after lunch."

Ned waved. "Well, thank goodness. We thought for a minute we'd missed that piano playin' you do. You gonna play this afternoon?"

Caroline nodded, smiled, and was glad someone, even if it was just Ned or Fred, enjoyed hearing her play.

—·—

The twins had worked about half an hour when Ned, the older brother by only three minutes, called his younger twin. "Come here, Fred."

"What do you want? I'm trying to fit this board in this hole, and it don't want to go." Fred rose from his knees, squeezing his finger, freshly wounded by a rose thorn. He mumbled as he walked toward his brother. "Dadblasted roses! Dadburned thorns. I've got a mind to just—"

"Who you cussin' now, Fred?"

"I ain't cussin' nobody, and if these bloomin' roses was anybody's but Miss Angel's, I would already done cut 'em down. Can't get to nothing, and the fence is fallin' down."

"Well, look here, would you? Somebody 'round here don't give a rip about Miss Angel's roses. What do you make of this?"

Fred looked to where Ned pointed at the base of the fence. Several boards had been torn loose and partly removed. Both recognized this was not just normal wear and tear on the old fence, not even with the climbing roses. Besides, several limbs of the rose bush had been broken around the opening so that someone could come through without even a scratch. This was deliberate.

Ned pointed to the shrubbery. "And look over there. Somebody's done made 'em a path through the tea olives." They looked more closely as they walked single file down the well-worn space between the bushes and the outside studio wall. "Would you look at that?"

"Why, it looks like a chicken done come in here and feathered her nest right here next to that window."

"Roosters don't sit on nests, and this ain't no hen's doings."

Fred paused. "This is bad, Ned. I mean with that pretty Miss Caroline livin' out here all by herself. Somebody's been comin' right through that fence and sittin' right here in this spot for quite a spell. You better tell her what's been goin' on."

"We can't do that. Come on. We gotta go tell Mr. Sam."

Ned and his brother lived peaceful, simple lives, and they usually ran from trouble. But this was trouble that couldn't be avoided. They approached the back steps to the main house. Early afternoon sun warmed the back porch, and Sam, with an open book in his lap, napped in his wicker rocker.

Ned didn't want to embarrass Mr. Sam by catching him asleep, but neither did he want to do anything to bring Miss Angel to the porch. He tried clearing his throat, hoping Mr. Sam would wake up. It didn't work, so he tried a muffled cough followed by more throat clearing. He was about to knock on the screen door when Sam roused.

"Oh, good afternoon, gentlemen. Appears you've caught me asleep on the job."

"Sorry, Mr. Sam. Hate to bother you and all that."

Sam sat up and put the book on the side table. "No bother. Got to finish this book today so I'll be ready to review it next week for Angel's study club. Why, you can tell just how interesting it is."

Ned had no idea about how interesting or boring a book could be. The closest thing to a book he'd ever read was the stack of out-dated *Popular Mechanics* magazines the librarian gave him years ago. No time for reading. He worked in the daytime and watched television with Fred every night. They never disagreed about books or the night's TV lineup.

Ned took off his John Deere cap and wiped the sweat from his brow with a white, freshly ironed handkerchief. He was anxious for Mr. Sam to know about their discovery, but he didn't want to tell him.

Fred nudged him.

"Mr. Sam, I hate to bother you with this. I mean I hate it even happened so as I have to tell you this, but, uh . . ." Ned looked at his twin for help.

Fred stood silent and sweating.

Ned started again. "Mr. Sam, we was workin' back there on the fence and uh . . . uh . . ."

"Just spit it out, Ned. What did you do? Tear down the fence or disturb some of Angel's roses?"

"No, sir, we was mighty careful not to do that, but, uh . . ."

"But somebody else did," Fred blurted loudly, surprising his brother and Sam.

Fred's announcement bolstered Ned's courage. "Yessiree, Mr. Sam. Somebody's done taken some boards offen the fence, cut an openin' in them roses, and they been comin' through there what appears to be quite regular."

Sam stood up and walked to the door. "What are you saying, Ned?"

"I'm sayin' somebody's been snoopin', Mr. Sam. That snooper made 'im a path right behind them tea olives, and he's been sittin' next to that window where Miss Caroline's piano is—sittin' where nobody can see 'im."

"Are you sure?" Sam asked.

"Yes, sir, just as sure as I am that Bobby Mayfield didn't win that turkey shoot fair and square last year. They ain't no mistakin' what we found. You want to see for yourself?"

"I think I do. Let me get my hat and cane."

"Oh, and, Mr. Sam? I wouldn't bother Miss Angel with this if I was you."

"That's a good idea. No need to frighten her."

———

Sam got his hat and walked with Ned and Fred down the stone path to the studio. They showed him the fence and where the climbing roses had been broken off in several places to allow a body to slip through. Then they showed him the well-worn trail behind the shrubs and the spot where someone had gathered a bed of pine needles.

Sam cringed at what he saw, his protective instincts surfacing. Caroline was young, alone, beautiful, and trusting—not a good combination. Her gift of mercy made her especially kind to people who were shunned by most folks, and it also made her a target.

And yet . . . nothing had happened. Her Peeping Tom had kept his distance, it seemed.

He tapped on the fence with his cane. "Well, I'd appreciate it if you gentlemen would secure that fence so that our snooper can't come back through. I'll check it for the next few days to make certain it stays fixed."

Pondering when, what, and how much to tell Caroline, Sam surveyed the situation while the twins started to work. He made a split-second decision as Caroline pulled into the driveway: he'd hold off on mentioning anything. No harm had been done as far as he knew, other than to the fence and flowers. And her leaving town would give him the time he needed to thoroughly check the situation out. Best not to worry her unduly, he decided.

Caroline smiled as she walked over. "I see your straw boss showed up to make sure you don't disturb the roses," she said to the twins.

"Yes, ma'am," Ned said. Neither twin raised his eyes to look at her. They worked quietly, listening for what Sam would tell her. Instead he made small talk about her morning meeting and her upcoming trip to Fernwood before she went inside to prepare for her afternoon students. Then he started up the path to the main house. He needed to think and make a phone call.

———·———

Caroline was setting up the computer and the tape recorder for her afternoon students when the phone rang.

It was Betsy, her best friend since they'd first shared crayons in Mrs. Haylock's kindergarten class. "Hi, Caroline. Your mom called and said you'd be home tomorrow."

"I will be, and please, pretty please, tell me you have some time for me Saturday afternoon. I'd love to see you and Josefina. Oh, and Mason if I have to."

"You know I'll make time for you. Josefina just squealed when she overheard my conversation with your mother. That little one can put two and two together and come up with five."

"Well, you tell Josefina that her godmother is coming to visit her little princess."

"Oh, she'll love that. She's just about out of chocolate kisses."

Caroline always brought Josefina a bag of candy with instructions to eat one a day to help her count the days until Caroline returned. "On the drive, I'll be listening to the Horowitz CD you sent me. I've been saving it for this trip. It'll be the calm before the storm. The Carlyles are gathering for dinner tomorrow night."

"Hope you'll recover before Saturday morning. There'll be a tornado when you get to my house. I have a surprise for you."

"You do remember I love surprises like you love liver and onions, don't you?"

"Don't remind me of liver and onions."

"Okay. Just remember I won't be able to stay too long. I need to get back to Moss Point before dark."

"My surprise won't take long. Later . . ."

"See you Saturday about two, and hug the princess for me."

Caroline was grateful for Betsy. They could not have been more different, but their bond was tight, and their differences had matured with them. The normal growing-up, knickers-in-a-twist girlish disputes had never found a way into their friendship. The closest thing to a breach in relationship had come at thirteen when Betsy quickly outgrew Caroline by eight inches and refused to walk with her in the school hallways. They had been through life's lulls and lessons together.

——•——

Caroline watched the clock all through her afternoon lessons. "You had an exceptionally fine lesson today, Nicole. It's so much more fun when you're prepared. Could you get all my students to work as hard as you do?" Caroline rose and closed the piano lid.

"Oh, playing the piano's not work, Miss Caroline. I really like these pieces you gave me. They're fun, and my little sister likes them too."

"Perhaps you're right, little Miss Nicole. Piano playing should be fun. After all, we do say 'playing the piano,' not 'working the piano.'" Caroline saw her to the door, turned on the porch light, and watched to see that she made it safely to her father's car. She stood at the door and looked out at the fading sky as they left. It was dusk—that dreary part of the day when the sky lost its color before the darkness set in. The gray was too much the color of her loneliness.

She was tidying up around the computer when Sam appeared at the kitchen door. He was usually done with dinner and sitting in his lounge chair watching the news by seven o'clock. She wondered what had brought him down to the studio at this hour.

"Caroline? Caroline." His baritone voice was almost musical when he called her name.

"Coming, Sam." Usually the door was unlocked and she would just tell him to come in, but she had been careful to keep things locked since this morning. She opened the door and invited him in.

"Are you done with the piano prodigies for the day?"

"Well, seems neither the prodigies nor the protégés showed up today, and I'm not expecting them tomorrow either. What are you doing walking around this time of the evening in your slippers?"

"Angel sent me down to see if you wanted a bowl of soup. She knew you'd be busy getting ready for your trip tomorrow. Want to come eat? Fresh vegetable soup—your favorite."

"That's tempting. And you did walk all the way down here to invite me. How could I refuse?"

Sam scanned the room. "Didn't figure you would."

"Okay, let me get the ice cream, and I think I have a few of my homemade cookies left." She always kept cookies baked for special treats for her students.

"Sounds good. I think I'll just go over and lock the French doors while you do that."

Caroline knew Sam had made a promise to her father to look after her, but this seemed odd. "No need to do that, Sam."

"Well, you can't be too careful these days." He was already on his way through the room to the doors.

"I am careful. They're already locked."

He checked the doors anyway while Caroline got the cookie tin and a half gallon of peach ice cream from the freezer. She saw him staring out the window.

"Ready, Sam? You know how Angel is about cold soup."

"I'm right behind you. Come to think of it, I don't like cold soup either." He walked across the great room toward the kitchen door.

"Here, you're in charge of this. I don't trust you with the cookies." She handed Sam the carton of ice cream and locked the door. Her habit was to leave windows open and doors unlocked. She hoped Sam wouldn't notice the change.

—.—

Daylight had almost slipped away as they walked up the stone path to the big house. Years ago, Angel had planted creeping thyme between the stones. In the daylight, Sam was always careful to stay on the path. But in the darkness, his steps faltered and bruised the tiny leaves, releasing their fragrance. The thyme was forgiving. In the morning, it would spring to life as fresh as always.

If only life was that way.

On evenings like this he would normally have felt that all was right with his world. He could see his Angel moving about through the kitchen window. The soup pot was on. Caroline was beside him with a tin of snickerdoodles, and dinner conversation would not be lacking. How could a man be so privileged? Not one but two strong-willed, captivating women in his life. Caroline brought such joy to him in his old age, and he loved her as he would have loved a daughter of his own.

Angel turned on the porch light as they stepped up. "I see you brought the cookies." She looked knowingly at Caroline.

"Why, of course, you know Mama taught me never to show up empty-handed. Besides, Sam's much better at carrying ice cream than I am."

Inside, Sam sat quietly at the table watching Angel and Caroline do what they always did in the kitchen when they prepared a meal. How could he have missed the perfect choreography of their movements before? He watched their eyes darting and their mouths moving and their faces breaking out in smiles, but he was so distracted he heard nothing they said—like a scene out of a silent movie. He wondered if this was what the interloper had experienced while watching Caroline.

How would he tell her what the Pendergrass twins had found today?

Table conversation was a lot like the soup bowl, a pinch of this and a little of that. They laughed about Caroline's morning meeting with Tandy Yarbrough and talked about her trip to Fernwood tomorrow and what she hoped to find out from the Whitmans. An appropriate time for Sam to interrupt their conversation with his secret never presented itself. Perhaps new information would come to light before he was forced tell them. After all, postponement had saved him more than once in a court case. He would wait for her return from Fernwood before giving her this news.

Caroline finished her last bite of ice cream. "Hey, Judge, you've been mighty quiet tonight."

"Just thinking about that book review next week. And besides, getting a word in at this table is like jumping between two moving boxcars."

"Well, I'd say that stopped the train. Time to clear the table." Angel rose from her chair.

When the kitchen was clean, they said their usual good nights and Sam walked Caroline out. He latched the screen door and stood on the porch, watching her walk the stone path back to the studio, and wondered if the fragrance of thyme still permeated the night air. He waited until she went in and closed her kitchen door. She didn't turn out her porch light.

Sam would manufacture a reason later to call and check on her. He closed and locked the door and pecked Angel on the cheek on his way through the kitchen. She put away the cookies and turned out the kitchen light.

"Sam Meadows, you forgot to turn off the porch light."

"It's okay, Angel, I'll get it later."

He lied. He had no intention of turning off the light until daylight.

Chapter Four

Secrets and Siblings

———◆———

FTER SUPPER, CAROLINE CAUTIOUSLY RETURNED TO THE studio and locked the door. Although still edgy about the day's events, she felt keeping her secret had been the right thing to do.

She put down the cookie tin and headed for her CD cabinet to replace Mozart with Mendelssohn. Not a Mozart evening. She was so tired and sleepy, and she hoped the lyrical melodies and intricate phrases of Mendelssohn's *Songs Without Words* would calm her and cloak the silence. Curled up on the sofa, calendar in hand, she began her list-making while she listened.

Somewhere between the packing list and notes from today's piano lessons, the familiar melody of "The Fleecy Clouds" gently resonated through the room. She put her pencil down, rested her head on the back of the sofa, and closed her eyes. She had introduced David to Mendelssohn, and this piece had been one of his favorites.

The music transported her to an afternoon seven years ago when the music of Mendelssohn had filled her car as she drove to the university to meet David. On her walk to the library, an eight-foot banner suspended from the crosswalk had stunned her. Three-foot-high letters painted sloppily in bright red and yellow had announced *I LOVE YOU, CAROLINE*. This was David: bold, daring, passionate, and colorful.

She remembered staring at the banner and searching the grounds for him. She knew he'd be near observing her reaction. So she'd sat down in the middle of the walkway underneath the crosswalk and waited for him to appear. How like him to be sitting in a big oak tree. She never saw him until she heard the rustling leaves behind her and turned to see him climbing down limb to limb. Her eyes never left his until he approached, pulled her up from where she sat, and kissed her. "I do love you, Caroline."

Nothing else had existed for that moment in time—just David and their love.

Why hadn't she done something pertinently clever like pulling paper out of her briefcase and creating a sign that said *I'M CAROLINE* and positioning herself like a statue until he appeared? She always seemed to think of these things later, never at the appropriate time.

Why didn't she say, "I love you, too, David"? Instead, her first words had been "David, you could have broken your neck hanging up that sign." That was her—so cautious. But somehow, in love's unexplainable way, they had completed each other. Perhaps he had known what no one else would guess: that underneath her thick layer of precaution was a mysterious woman of depth who longed for adventure. And perhaps Caroline knew that behind his bold passion was a man who needed an anchor. Life with David would have been an adventure, and she would have kept them safe.

The last cadence of "The Fleecy Clouds" ended her recollection of that fall afternoon. Caroline lifted her head from the back of the sofa. The remembering was so real she had felt the crunch of the fall leaves as she walked across the campus. Music could transport her to different realities. She wished it would transport her to wherever David was and leave her there. She knew it couldn't, though, so instead she longed for something to fill the cracks left in her heart.

Her heart convulsed when she thought of how David had died so violently and alone in the jungle.

She moved to the edge of the sofa and put her calendar on

the coffee table. Before getting up, she put her head in her hands. "Why, God?" she whispered. "Why would You bring David into my life, give us such a rare love, and snatch him away?" A tear rolled off her cheek and hit the painted wooden floor. She left it there.

She moved down the hall to her bedroom and pulled the covers back on her bed. Moments later, she crawled in and pulled the sheet tight around her shoulders. "Please, please, Mr. Sandman, sultan of sweet sleep, please visit me tonight."

—·—

Friday was a full day. After the last student had left, Caroline grabbed her purse, keys, the new Horowitz CD, and a bottle of water. She called to say goodbye to Sam and Angel from her cell phone as she locked the doors and headed to the car.

The road home could seem so long. Somewhere along this two-hour ribbon of highway through middle Georgia, the moss-laden oak trees were replaced by tall, stately pines. Nineteenth-century plantations had been carved into smaller farms, and Caroline could almost smell the freshly plowed earth. The late afternoon sun piercing the driver's window for the last hour now slipped beneath the horizon, leaving its trail of corals and lavenders. Debussy filled the car like an orchestral accompaniment to the changing afternoon skies, and Caroline had a front-row seat.

Her cell phone rang. *Not now, not in the middle of the Adagio section.* She hit the speakerphone button. No surprise, it was her mother.

"Hi, Caroline, where are you?"

"Oh, hello, Mama. I'm about twenty miles out and should be there at the time I told you if not before."

"That's good. James and the girls are here. Callie's here with Sarah, but Thomas and TJ are running late. TJ's ball practice. It's that time of year, you know. Sounds like you'll be here before them."

"I'm sure they'll be there as soon as they can. Those two don't miss many meals, especially when you're cooking."

"Oh, there'll be plenty. All right, then. Let me get back to the biscuits. We'll see you when you get here."

"Bye, Mama."

Caroline closed her phone. She smiled, knowing the biscuits would be going into the oven in exactly ten minutes. All of her growing-up years, she'd watched her mother scoop out flour into the sifter and turn the crank until the flour mounded up in the yellow crock reserved for biscuit making. Then her mother would use the back of her spoon to carefully flatten the mound's peak into a well that would hold the buttermilk and cooking oil. Mama never measured anything. She gently stirred so the flour would fall into the pool of buttermilk and oil, her spoon never penetrating the flour basin to scrape the bottom of the bowl. She always cautioned Caroline, "Too much stirring and kneading make for tough biscuits and a hard life."

Caroline knew the pride in her mother's face when the hot biscuits were delivered to the table. The scene had been well rehearsed over decades of meals at the Carlyle table.

——•——

Caroline expected to smell the hot biscuits as she made the right turn onto Fifth Street. Pulling into the driveway, she heard FoPaw yelping. FoPaw was her dad's dog, aptly named because he was black with four white paws. His barking alerted the family, and they all rushed out to help her bring in her one overnight bag.

Thomas and TJ arrived just as the tea was poured, and the family moved toward the dining table. Caroline hugged her freckle-faced nephew and followed him out of the kitchen. "Why the frown, TJ? Did you lose the game?"

"No, ma'am. Just practice." He looked at his dad, already standing at the table.

Thomas chuckled. "I'm the coach, sis. No way they could lose.

They even win when they practice." He pulled out the chair for his mother and took his seat next to Julia.

Caroline's father always asked the blessing at family meals, and that never changed. After everyone's plate was served, Mama rose quietly and left the dining room. Everyone knew this meant the arrival of the biscuits. James, Caroline's older brother, spoke. "What I've been waiting on all day: Mama's biscuits."

Caroline knew the grilling would start momentarily—always the same questions, and she'd give the same answers. She tried to head it off. "Okay, my brilliant niece and nephew, how are your grades? And, Callie, how are your parents?" She smiled at her sister-in-law.

Thomas interrupted. "Grades are fine. Callie's parents are doing great, and not one thing around here has changed since your last visit." He elbowed Caroline. "Tell me, sis, dating anybody lately?"

Caroline hated that question. It was always Thomas's first and only. "No, little brother, no dates. No time."

"Don't tell me that. You have time. There's just no one in that one-horse town to date. You need to get out more before you get frumpy."

Callie swiped her husband with her napkin. "Frumpy? Thomas, what does that mean? Be kind to your sister."

Thomas wiped the biscuit crumb from his mouth. "I am kind to her. Nobody else around here will push her, and she needs pushing out of that boring life of hers."

"Don't mind Thomas, Callie. I don't. He'll grow up one day." She rolled her eyes at her little brother and wanted to tell them that her boredom had been severely encroached upon, but she kept her secret of yesterday's intruder. She hoped for a chance to speak with James. She trusted him to keep her secret and to give her good advice.

Caroline tried to keep up with the three different conversations going on around the table, but she felt like a spectator. She quietly stared at the one empty chair—the tenth chair at the table. *David sat there. If David was here, he'd challenge Thomas and get into some philosophical discussion with James. He would be hugging Mama and asking for another biscuit. He'd squeeze my arm and kiss my cheek, and later he'd tell me he loved my loud family.*

The food disappeared, and the family members began their departures. She heard James tell her dad he'd be at the office writing briefs Saturday morning—her chance to talk with him alone.

Caroline and Mama caught up with all the news while they washed the dishes. With good nights said, Caroline found her overnight bag on the bed in the lavender room of her childhood. Lying in her white French provincial bed was truly coming home for Caroline. She had moved to college and then to Moss Point. Her life had taken unexpected turns, but her bed was still here, unchanged and unmoved.

She picked up the picture frame off the nightstand. There they were—those Carlyle kids, twenty years ago, wet from swimming, arm in arm and smiling. They lived different lives now, but at gatherings like this Friday night, they were still the same kids who'd made their parents proud.

Caroline had always found security in James, the oldest. He was forty and had the brains in the family. She accused him of being born fifty. He was serious, self-disciplined, and could be depended upon for anything except fun. During his second year in law school he'd married Julia, the tightly wound social climber from a tobacco-growing family in North Carolina. The family accepted Julia simply because James loved her, and now their daughter, Laura, was becoming more like Julia.

Caroline was more like James but wished she could be more like Thomas. He was thirty-seven and the fun one in the family. He equaled James in mental abilities but was more relaxed than driven. Thomas had become his own person at age five and had never been referred to as James Carlyle's little brother. He had a superb baritone voice, a gift which he had not developed because no one in Fernwood could imagine a singing shortstop. Instead, Thomas played ball, hunted and fished his way through college, and barely got his degree. But he didn't need a degree to open the local sporting goods store. He'd married Callie, his high school sweetheart.

When Caroline needed a laugh, she called Thomas, but when she needed sound advice, she called James.

—·—

Caroline treasured Saturday mornings with her parents. It was customarily just the three of them, with FoPaw circling the breakfast table for any bit of bacon he might beg. Today her father lingered briefly to hear her latest stories about her students and to catch up on how Sam and Angel were doing.

Caroline was more interested this morning in her ten o'clock meeting. "Dad, fill me in on the Whitmans."

"Well, all I know is they had the piano until their daughter graduated from college."

"But didn't they give the piano to her when she married and moved to Atlanta?"

Mama put down the dish towel. "Yes, they did, but there was talk that the Whitman girl and her husband divorced not long after they married. Keep that in mind before you go bringing up things that are best not talked about."

"Why is this so important to you, Caroline?" her dad asked. "I thought you were happy with the instrument we bought you. You picked it out. Just what are you planning to do if you find the piano?"

Caroline noted the disappointment in his voice. "I wish I had an answer. I don't have a plan. It's just something I have to do. That piano was such a part of me for so long, and to think that it's somewhere on this planet, and I don't know where . . . I just have to know, Dad."

"I suppose that's reasonable." He emptied his coffee cup.

"There's one thing for sure. I won't be buying it, not if its owner has any knowledge of its value. Could be well worth anywhere from forty to forty-eight thousand dollars depending upon its condition."

"We'd buy it if we could," her mama said. "But don't count on your dear old dad and mama this time."

"Do you mean I can mark that one off my Christmas list?"

Her dad rose from his chair. "Good luck, little one. You're so much like your mother. No doubt you'll find your piano, and only the Lord knows what you'll do then." He walked to the sink with his cup. "Well, I'd love to hang around for another cup of coffee, but there's a project calling me to the shop."

She knew her dad was heading to the shop to give her time alone with her mom. She asked, "Hey, Dad, is this project your reason or your excuse for leaving the table?"

He hastily turned to look at her. "Aha, you caught me, didn't you? I'll confess. This one's an excuse—but it's for a good reason." They smiled in silent agreement, and he closed the door.

Excuses were never allowed in the Carlyle household. An excuse, according to her dad, was only the skin of a reason stuffed with a lie. And a lie, or something even akin to a lie, was not acceptable under the Carlyle roof. Caroline might have hesitated to answer, but the question "Is this a reason or an excuse?" always brought the truth.

"Is Dad okay? He seems a little distracted."

"Oh, he's fine. He's just wishing we'd never had to sell your piano so you wouldn't be looking for it. He hurts for you, Caroline. He knows how you loved your piano and how much you loved David, and how they both disappeared from your life. We're both hoping you find it and that somehow it will bring you some closure. We just want you to be happy."

"I know, Mama, and I don't want you to worry. If I find the piano, great! If I don't, at least I tried."

Caroline squeezed her mother's hand and started to talk about family things—Julia's latest purchase, her father's health, church matters, and a bit of town gossip. They chatted about Caroline's upcoming student recital in May—when she would have it, what she would wear, and the refreshments she would serve.

"You know I'll be there to help do the baking and decorating as always."

Then came the question about Caroline's summer plans. "I'm planning to continue my private study at the university, teach some master classes in Moss Point, attend a conference, and then do some writing for a professional journal. But I promise I'll spend several days here with you."

—·—

Caroline loaded the car, said goodbye to her parents, and left for her meeting with the Whitmans. She drove down the street, stopped in the shade, and dialed James's number.

No answer. Had James changed his mind about going to the office? Had she lost her chance to unload her secret on someone? The phone rang eight times before he answered.

"Hey, Julia."

"No, James, it's Caroline, and I'm so glad you picked up."

"What's up, sis?"

"Something important, I think, but I'm not sure. I don't want it to be important, but . . ."

"You're talking in circles, Caroline. Just tell me what it is. I'll help you decide whether or not it's important."

"Okay, but you must promise you won't say anything to Mama or Dad. It would just cause them to worry, and it may be nothing."

"Now you have me worried. Where are you? You want me to meet you somewhere?"

"No, I'm on my cell phone a few blocks from the house. I'm on my way to see the Whitmans, and I really didn't want to talk at the house." Her fingers strummed the steering wheel.

"Caroline, I'm really getting worried."

"Okay, here goes. But I don't want you to think I'm losing it. I'm telling you the facts as methodically as I can. I know you don't like all that emotional stuff, so I'm telling you straight. Thursday morning I had breakfast with Sam and Angel up at the big house. After breakfast, as I walked back to the studio, I . . . I heard something very unusual." She paused.

"What do you mean 'unusual'?"

"I could hear someone playing my piano in the studio."

"That's not so strange. You are a piano teacher."

Caroline lowered her voice as though someone might overhear her. "But whoever was playing it was playing a song that only I know. Let me back up. I wasn't able to sleep Wednesday night, so I got up to play the piano. I worked on this song maybe for an hour or more. I got frustrated and just struck the piano keys with the palms of my hands, got up, and went to the window . . ." Her voice trailed off as she remembered.

"Can you speak up? I'm having trouble hearing you."

"Okay. Well, when I looked out, I saw a shadow moving and heard the bushes rustling next to the window, but I didn't think too much about it then. I figured it was a cat or the wind blowing the shrubs."

"Sounds possible."

"But when I heard someone playing that same song yesterday morning, my heart nearly stopped. I came through the front door of the studio and whoever was playing ran out the terrace door. James, I did not imagine this."

"No one said you're imagining this, sis, but let me ask you . . ."

Caroline rolled her window down a bit. "I don't have time for your lawyer's interrogation. I just need you to help me think through this."

"You're sure about the shadow in the middle of the night?"

"Yes, I'm sure. I'm sure there was a shadow, but a shadow of what, I don't know. I wouldn't have given it another thought if it hadn't been for what happened the next morning."

"Did you tell Sam and Angel or call the police?"

"Nope, no one. I didn't know what to say. It makes no sense, and I didn't know how to explain it. It was 'David's Song,' and no one knows it but me. It's not even finished. But what I heard coming from the piano in the studio was exactly as I played it Wednesday night. I mean right down to slamming my palms down on the keyboard. It's just too bizarre."

"And you're certain that someone ran out of the studio when you came in?"

"Yes, the piano playing stopped. And when I entered the room, the terrace door was still moving from someone's hasty exit."

"Did you see anyone?"

She imagined James making notes on his yellow legal pad. "Well, no. It all happened so fast. The phone was ringing. I was frightened, and I wasn't thinking very rationally at that point."

"If someone had meant you harm, the phone might have frightened him. Did he take anything?"

Caroline rolled her window down a bit more. The humidity and the tension caused her to perspire. "No, nothing. My purse and keys were right there on the counter. My laptop was on the desk. Nothing was disturbed. I really don't think anyone meant me harm."

"I think you're right, but it still leaves a lot of questions."

"Yes, and I think I've considered them all. I don't know what to do now. Do I keep my secret or what? Any advice, big brother?" Caroline was ready for his answer.

"Well, it's time to make Sam aware of what happened. He's a wise man. He knows the town, and he'll know what to do. But, Caroline, you need to be cautious for a while. Lock your doors; be aware that someone may be watching you. Vary your comings and goings."

"I am neurotically careful, but my schedule is so set and predictable that it's difficult to vary my routine."

"I'll be thinking, and let me know the minute that anything out of the ordinary happens."

"I will, and remember I'll play the Georgia Tech fight song at your funeral if you tell Mama and Dad," Caroline said. She knew that mentioning the university's archrival would change the tone of this conversation.

"You do, and I'll sit straight up out of my coffin and tell the entire congregation you tried to pay the filling-station attendant for the air he put in your tire."

"Seriously, you can't tell."

"I promise. Bye, sis. Keep me informed."

"Thanks, James. Love you. Bye."

—·—

Caroline drove across town to the Whitmans'. The neighborhoods had changed so little, she decided, as she parked and rang the bell.

Harriet Whitman greeted Caroline cordially and invited her into the kitchen before she called her husband in from the garden. "It's really good to see you, Caroline," she said as the two women sat at the breakfast table. "Carl and I were trying to recall how long it's been."

Caroline hoped Harriet didn't offer coffee. "I'm not able to get home as much as I'd like, but I visit every chance I get. So, how have you and Mr. Whitman been?"

Carl Whitman slammed the back door as if on cue.

"You can see that Carl's doing just fine," Harriet said. "He retired last year from thirty-eight years at the post office, and I haven't been able to keep him out of the garden since."

"After nearly forty years of shuffling envelopes and selling stamps, pulling weeds seems like a vacation," Carl said while washing his hands and grabbing for the dish towel.

Harriet jumped up and snatched it away. "How many times do I have to tell you, Carl? Don't dry your hands on the kitchen towel."

Carl snickered, dried his hands on a paper towel, and sat down at the table.

Hoping to change the mood, Caroline jumped in. "I suppose my mother told you why I wanted to come by to see you."

"Yes, she did," Harriet said.

"Lately, I've just been so curious about this piano. I remembered you bought it for your daughter when she started piano lessons." Caroline took out a pad and pencil from her bag.

"It was such a beautiful piano, and Kelly did take lessons, but I'm sorry to say she never really excelled the way you did. Oh, she learned to play a little bit, just enough to play what she liked. And since no one else around here played the piano, we just gave it to her when she got married. That was almost two years ago."

"Does she still play?" Caroline asked, trying to find out if she still had the piano.

"I'm sure she would if she had a chance, but she no longer owns the piano. You see, when she got married, she and her husband moved to Atlanta. But they were only married about a year and then got a divorce."

"I'm so sorry."

"No need to be sorry," Carl said. "The worst thing she ever did was marry that good-for-nothing, lying—"

"Carl." Harriet reached across the table and touched Carl's arm.

"And the best thing she ever did was to leave him."

Harriet patted Carl's arm. "It was most unfortunate, but she's getting on with her life now. We're just so grateful there weren't any children involved."

"He was such an irresponsible, smooth-talking scoundrel that it'll take Kelly years to get over the financial problems he left sitting on her lap. He should be in jail. Now he's moved on to dazzle some other poor girl." Carl seemed unable to stop himself.

"Well, you didn't come to hear about all our problems, Caroline. The truth is we don't have such good news for you."

"I'm so sorry about all this, but any bit of information might be helpful."

"Kelly was left with such tremendous debt after the divorce that she had to sell the piano along with her house and some other possessions. I called to tell her you were coming so I could get as much information as possible."

"Thank you. Is the piano still in Atlanta?"

"When I talked to Kelly, she was unsure. She sold it about a year ago to a dealership in the metro area. She needed the cash and sold it for half its worth. She naturally lost track of it after that."

Caroline grimaced.

"But I do have the number of the dealership and the name of the man who purchased it from Kelly. She was certain the man would remember the piano. Seems he was quite enchanted with it. I have the information for you here on this card." Harriet handed it to Caroline.

"Oh, thank you, Mrs. Whitman. I'm sorry to bother you with this, and I hope it didn't bring up too many bad memories."

"You're welcome, Caroline, and I wish you luck. Would you mind letting me know if you find it?"

"I'll be certain to do that, and thank you so much for your time." Caroline noticed that Carl remained quiet and never rose from the table to see her out.

———•———

Caroline dialed Betsy's number as she drove away. "Hey, I was hoping you'd be home. I just left the Whitmans'. Is it too early to come on over?"

"No, it's not too early, but your meeting didn't take long. Did you find out about the piano?"

"Not much. I'll tell you about it when I get there. Is Mason at home?"

"No, he and Josefina are at his parents' house. He's helping his dad with some outside painting, and his mom wanted to see Josefina. So it'll just be you and me for lunch. I'll fix us a sandwich."

"See you shortly. Want me to stop at the store for anything?"

"Pickled okra, maybe."

"Are you serious?"

"I'm kidding you, CC. Just come on over." Betsy had stopped calling Caroline "CC" at Caroline's request when they entered junior high. But once Josefina came along, CC returned.

Caroline was disappointed that she might miss Josefina. Three years ago, she had gone with Betsy and Mason to Guatemala to start adoption proceedings. During a previous trip to Guatemala with David, she had met three nuns who ran an orphanage. Somehow, staying in touch with these nuns and Reyna Morris, Dr. Morris's widow, had been important to her after David was killed. Caroline had actually made two trips to Guatemala with Betsy and Mason. Reyna hosted them both times and served as interpreter with the nuns.

All three of them had bonded with Baby Josefina on the first trip. Even Caroline ached when they returned to the States without the brown-eyed baby girl. Weeks later, with thirty thousand dollars in hand, the three of them had returned to bring little Josefina home.

Caroline pulled into the driveway and reached in the back seat for the bag of candy she always brought her godchild. Betsy met her at the door and led her to the patio. "It's a perfect day for lunch around the pool, don't you think?"

Caroline agreed. They chatted over sandwiches. They didn't have much catching up to do since they talked a couple of times a week. Caroline told her about her visit with the Whitmans, and Betsy told her the scuttlebutt about Kelly's divorce.

"What's the deal? Am I going to see my godchild or not? I brought a whole bag full of candy kisses." Caroline reached for the bag.

"Sorry, I called Mason right after you called. His mom took Josefina with her out to the lake and won't be back until early afternoon. Didn't know you'd be here so early."

"Oops, sorry for the change in plans. I'll see her next month when you come with Mama for my student recital."

"Sounds good. Just give me that bag of chocolate. I need it."
Betsy grabbed the bag of candy and ripped open the top.

"Wow, what is it with you? You ate your sandwich, half of mine, nearly a whole bag of potato chips, and now you're wrestling me for chocolate?"

"I can't believe you, Caroline Carlyle. You're really out of it today."

"What do you mean?"

"I mean, I tell you on the phone I have a surprise. You don't even ask, like you forgot or something. That's not like you. Then I ask you to bring a jar of pickled okra on the way over. I'm eating like there's no tomorrow, and you don't get it."

"Betsy, you're not . . . ?"

"Yes, I am, so mark your calendar for late October."

Chapter Five

Two Preachers and a Hobo

———— • ————

CAROLINE TREASURED APRIL SUNDAY MORNINGS. SHE POURED her second cup of coffee and headed for the garden just to sit a spell. She thought every soul had a home on this earth—a place to rest and experience true beauty. Her soul had two homes: the piano stool and her garden bench.

The garden was her cathedral, and the white wrought-iron bench was her pew. Here she sat and watched water trickle over the rocks and fall into a pool exploding with life. The seasons brought change. Wild irises, hoarding their yellow blooms till April, fringed the pond. May's black tadpoles—like wriggling musical notes, her father always kidded her—would grow legs, lose their tails, and become green bullfrogs. Water lily leaves became parasols for the goldfish in June. July sun would squeeze the color from the roses as if to punish them for their spring flamboyance, but their life and color would return with the cool mornings of October.

This garden was her wondering place, where she could imagine what happened to ladybugs in the winter and where butterflies hid in a thunderstorm. Where life was ephemeral. She might take her doubts and fears to church, but not to the garden. Here she read poetry and hummed arias. Here she created lyrics and composed melodies. It was her place, and she would not miss it on this last Sabbath in April.

Still, she had an internal sense about time—too many years with a metronome ticking. So she whispered an "Amen" and went inside to dress for church. That done, she put on her smile. She would hide all that was bothering her and try her best to concentrate and worship.

——·——

Caroline finished the postlude. She gathered her music and reached for her bag as the pastor came through the sanctuary. Reverend Andrew Bixley had pastored the Moss Point Methodist Church for three years as a young minister two decades ago and then moved on as ministers do. His children grew up, his hair disappeared, but his fondness for Moss Point never waned. Although it was highly unusual for the bishop to permit such a thing, he'd allowed Reverend Bixley to come back to Moss Point thirteen years ago. As Brother Andy liked to say, "I'm here till the Glory Train picks me up," and the whole community was pleased about it.

"Your offertory was like salve to my soul this morning, Caroline." Reverend Bixley picked up his Bible from the pulpit and headed toward his office. "And I heard several other folks say something similar on their way out of church. Just can't figure what we did to deserve you."

"You're too kind, and I thank you, Brother Andy. I wish I could say the same of your sermon, but it made me squirm a bit this morning. I'm quite fond of my creature comforts."

"I'm sorry, but squirming is only good if it gets you off your . . . uhum . . . seat."

"I'll confess that expressing my gratitude for my creature comforts hasn't kept up with my growing attachment to them. My dad always said that ingratitude was a prideful laziness. You said basically the same thing, only in different words this morning."

"Oh, how I wish I were as quotable as your father. I hope to goodness my own children don't quote me."

"I think your son probably used your words in his sermon this morning and was grateful he had a father who gave him something worthwhile to say. Goodbye, Brother Andy."

Caroline closed the church door and headed to lunch at Sam and Angel's. She planned not to spoil the meal by telling them her secret. Instead, she would return after Sam's nap and fulfill the promise she'd made to her brother.

——.——

Sam and Angel hurried out of church. The fourth-Sunday-of-the-month pot roast was nearly done, and Angel's yeast rolls were begging to be baked. Over the years, Sunday lunches became tradition. Caroline and Angel alternated the cooking, but Angel had made it a point to prepare everything this Sunday. She knew Sam wanted to talk to Caroline.

"We could eat at the Café on the Square today, you know," Sam said as he opened the car door for Angel.

"Why in the world would I want to do that when I have a roast in the oven and you need to talk to Caroline? Of course, we're early enough today to beat the church crowd."

Sam loosened his tie and pulled out of the church parking lot. "Yep, most church folks rarely get to taste Mabel's coconut cake. Only the first twenty to arrive get cake. The rest of them are out of luck and get banana pudding. But it's good banana pudding."

Angel fanned herself with the church bulletin. "You'd think she'd make more than one cake."

"Those poor folks from that New Life Bible Church don't even try the Café anymore because Mabel's cleaning up the kitchen by the time they get out of church."

"Guess we should be more grateful for Brother Andy."

Sam pulled into the driveway. "Maybe he likes coconut cake."

Angel giggled. "Sam Meadows, sixty years, and you still make me laugh. Well, I think Brother Andy's wise. He knows our minds cannot comprehend more than our fannies can endure."

She fumbled with her seat belt, got out of the car, and went straight to the kitchen to take the roast out of the oven, replacing it with her homemade yeast rolls. The dishes were stacked for serving, and the meal was just about ready. She took advantage of every April opportunity to have meals on the back porch. The need to impress anyone with fine bone china, white linens, and a mahogany dining table had long gone.

Angel heard Caroline coming in through the back-porch door and invited her to join the assembly line of empty plates and over-laden platters on the kitchen counter. Soon talk of the week's changes in the stock market, the upcoming school board election, and Caroline's trip to Ferngrove ricocheted around the table as they ate. They saved room for Angel's peach cobbler with cream.

After eating, Sam went into the library and made himself comfortable in his lounge chair while the ladies finished the kitchen duties. Angel stopped Caroline on her way out the kitchen door. "Don't go yet, Caroline. I think Sam wanted to talk to you about something."

"You mean now? I thought he was already napping."

"No, I think he's been waiting on us to finish the dishes." Angel knew Sam had never been one to put off a difficult assignment. She watched him always tackle the toughest jobs first, but he had postponed this bad job since last Thursday.

———•———

They walked into the library where Sam was waiting and took their seats. Caroline realized something of a serious nature was up. *Is Sam ill? Or is it Angel?* She didn't like the feel of things.

Sam assumed his judge role. "Caroline, I've been waiting to tell you something until you got back from Ferngrove. I've already told Angel, and now it's time to tell you. Before I say anything, I don't want you to worry, because everything's going to be just fine. But there's no way to tell you this except to just tell you."

Caroline could almost hear her pulse, and she felt that uncomfortable swirling in her stomach that made her mouth sweat.

"You know last Thursday when Ned and Fred were here to repair the fence?" Sam asked.

"Yes."

"When you were over at the church meeting with Tandy Yarbrough, Ned and Fred showed me where the bottom boards of about a three-foot section of the fence had been removed. Looked like the boards had been knocked loose and then someone had broken them off. Limbs from the rosebushes had also been broken off."

Caroline's thoughts were far ahead of Sam now, but oh, how she did not want her incident and what Sam was describing to be related. "Do you suppose it could have been a large dog? You know the Sheffields down the street have three huge dogs, and they're always getting loose."

"No, Caroline. What we saw was the work of human hands. There was a well-worn path behind the tea olives there next to the studio too. Someone gathered up some straw and made himself a comfortable place to sit right next to the studio window."

Caroline was certain her heartbeat was visible through her white blouse. The possibility of coincidence flew out the window. She would let Sam finish before she revealed her secret.

Sam continued as Angel sat without saying a word. "It appears someone's been slipping in through the fence and watching you through the bay window. And from the looks of things, it could have been going on for a while."

"You really think so?"

"I do, and I know this must frighten you, but I've been thinking about this since Thursday. I really don't think whoever it is means you harm. Oh, seems like every town has a Peeping Tom on occasion, and I think that's what this is."

"A Peeping Tom? In Moss Point?"

"Well, I've sent a few of them to jail over the years, but not a one of them ever harmed anyone. And we're going to catch this one. But until then I want you to be extra careful."

Caroline interrupted. "Sam, do any of your Peeping Toms play the piano?"

"Play the piano? Now, that's a bizarre question," Angel interjected.

"This whole thing is bizarre." Caroline went on to reveal Thursday morning's events.

"Why in the world didn't you tell me about this?" Sam asked.

"Probably for the same reason you didn't tell me. I didn't see any need in worrying you until I knew more. I told James when I was at home, and he made me promise to tell you as soon as I got back. I was planning to tell you later this afternoon."

Sam got up from his chair, walked over to the fireplace, and propped his elbow on the mantel. He looked directly at Caroline. "Oh, this puts a whole new spin on the situation. Peeping is one thing, but breaking and entering is another." Sam began to twist his wedding ring.

"But playing the piano as you described? There's no one I know in this town capable of that. You're right, Caroline. This is bizarre." Angel looked at Sam. "Well, this blows your theory to where it's too hot for polar bears, Sam Meadows."

Sam rubbed his forehead. "I thought our Peeping Tom just might be Bo Blossom."

"Bo Blossom?" Caroline could not entertain that idea. Bo had been a character around town since he jumped off a train passing through Moss Point about twenty years ago. No one knew his real name, but everyone called him Bo, which was short for "hobo." They gave him his last name from the Orange Blossom Special, the train he was riding when he decided to make Moss Point his home. No one knew where or how he lived.

The furrow in Sam's brow deepened. "Well, this doesn't sound like Bo. He's never broken into anyone's house. I know once in a while he steals a lawn mower or a yard tool from somebody's garage. But he just walks down the street a block or two, rings the doorbell, and sells it to the owner's neighbor. Most of us have played that game with Bo."

"Moss Point folks just take care of him like we did when he stole my gazing ball out of the butterfly garden. He took it to Herman down at the Emporium. Herman gave him five dollars and called me," Angel said.

Sam returned to his chair. "He's never done harm to anyone's property, and it seemed to me a logical conclusion. But this piano-playing business? Now, that's a real mystery."

"We know next to nothing about Bo. For all we do know, he was a concert pianist."

"Now, Angel, why in the world would a concert pianist give up a career to steal lawn mowers?" Sam asked.

Angel reached for a tissue on the table beside her chair. "Who knows? I was just trying to make some sense out of this."

"Well, Bo being a concert pianist certainly does not fit into the category of making sense."

Caroline had listened to this volley long enough. "None of this does. Sam, do you have another theory?"

"No, I don't at the present time. But the fence has been repaired. And my guess is that our mystery man will know he's been found out, and he probably won't come back sneaking around here. Just in case, I think I'll ask Caleb to keep his eye on Bo for a few days."

Caroline knew that Caleb Mullins, the town sheriff, would do whatever Sam asked of him. He had come to Caleb's rescue too many times for him to ever refuse Sam. "Do you think Caleb will keep this to himself? I'd hate for the word to get out around town."

"Of course he will. No need in the town knowing about this. We want to catch this fellow."

Caroline rose from her chair. "Thanks, Sam. I feel better now that you know."

Angel walked Caroline to the back door. "Don't you worry, sweetie. Sam and Caleb will take care of this. You're safe." Angel hugged her.

"You're right, and I'll just stop worrying right this minute. Can't worry and nap at the same time. You and Sam rest."

She smiled, squeezed Angel's hand, and started her walk to the studio. Along the way she took the time to study the familiar lane. The path wasn't straight. She knew its every curve like her hands knew the piano keyboard. The flagstones veered around the daylilies and back around the bed of caladiums and through the shade garden. Her walk would have been quite different if the path had been straight.

She had been walking a straight, dull path the last six years, living on level ground in a valley of monotony void of mountain peaks. She had found comfort in the simmering state of her daily days; but from somewhere deep inside herself, a place she could not describe or explain, came the unsettling sense her path was about to take a turn.

Chapter Six

A Living Still Life

———•———

$\mathcal{G}$OOD MORNING, MY NAME IS CAROLINE CARLYLE, AND I'M calling from Moss Point. I'm trying to reach Mr. Patrick Verran."

"Could you hold, please?"

"Yes, I'll hold." She'd always wanted to say no to that question.

"Good morning, Ms. Carlyle. I'm Patrick Verran. How may I help you?"

"Well, I'm not sure. I'm mainly calling for information. I'm a piano teacher down in Moss Point, and I'm trying to locate a particular piano that you purchased from a Ms. Kelly Whitman a year or so ago."

He hesitated. "Kelly Whitman . . . I think I recall that name."

"I think you'd more likely remember the piano she sold you. It was a 1902 Hazelton Brothers grand."

"Oh, yes, how right you are! That was one very fine instrument, and in mint condition. You know they just don't make pianos like that one anymore."

"I agree. Would you happen to still have the piano?" Caroline almost feared the answer. If he said yes, at least she would know where her piano was even if she could not afford it. If he said no, she would be bound to continue the search. Either way the piano was out of her reach.

"Let me think. No, I had a buyer for that piano right away. Yes,

I remember it well now. A man from Kentucky, looking for a piano of that period, wanted a Victorian. Yep, he saw it posted on the internet, flew down here, and bought it on the spot. Paid forty-two thousand dollars for that piano. We shipped it to him the very next week."

"An astute buyer. He knew what he wanted." Caroline made a note of the price.

"For sure, and he didn't question the cost. But I must say the piano was worth every penny of what he paid for it."

"He must be a really fine pianist."

"Now, that was the oddest thing. Said he didn't play the piano at all. No one in his family plays anymore. He'd just always wanted a grand piano like this one and said he'd pay someone to come and play it for him."

"To think of having that piano and be unable to play it! Would it be possible for you to give me the buyer's name and contact information?"

He paused. "Ma'am, I don't think that I can do that. We have a reputation for integrity and professionalism, and that also goes for maintaining our clients' privacy."

"Oh, how insensitive of me. I understand, and I certainly appreciate that, Mr. Verran."

He must have heard the disappointment in her voice. "If it's a fine piano you're looking for, Ms. Carlyle, I assure you we can provide one," he said in his most accommodating sales voice.

"I have no doubts about that, but it's this particular piano that has my interest at the moment."

"I hope I'm not being too nosy, but why this particular piano?"

"It may sound a bit strange to you, but the piano belonged to me when I was a young girl. My parents sold it when I went away to college. I've played many fine instruments since that time, but never one like this one. I'd just like to see it and play it one more time."

"Now I understand. Perhaps there is one thing that I could do to help you."

She wanted to jump up and down. "Oh, I'd be so appreciative, Mr. Verran. But I certainly don't want to be a bother."

"This would bring me great joy, Ms. Carlyle. We do keep records on our clients, especially those who buy such fine instruments. I'd be happy to give this gentleman a call, tell him your story, and give him your contact information. And maybe, if the stars are lined up just right, he might contact you and invite you to come and play your piano again."

"That would really be very kind of you. I'd be happy to pay you for your time and trouble."

"Just making your wish come true would be more than enough payment, Ms. Carlyle."

Caroline gave him her phone number and address and expressed her gratitude again before saying goodbye.

—·—

Irises were forsythia's strongest competitor as heralds of spring, and they were Caroline's favorite. She always began watching in mid-March for green shoots pushing through the mulch, searching for sunshine. Years of observing this phenomenon never dulled her amazement at how something so fragile could demonstrate such strength.

The green blades appeared first, and long slender foliage could be measured daily. She watched for the first signs of the iris's bud. The birth was like a butterfly emerging from its cocoon, the struggle giving its delicate wings strength to fly. During the short season, she would cut a few flawless blossoms to fill a special vase in the studio, always leaving blooms to enjoy from her favorite garden bench.

Caroline walked in the door with her garden shears and one iris stem. The phone rang. Probably Sam checking on her.

She was wrong. It was James. "Good morning, older brother."

"Morning, sis. Guess you made it back to Moss Point without incident?"

"Yes, without incident or accident. Everything here was just as I had left it."

"Good." James, true to his personality and his profession, went straight to the point. "I'm calling to see if you did what you promised."

"Oh, let me think. Was that to drive the speed limit, not to pick up any hitchhikers, or not to pass go and collect my two hundred dollars?"

"No time for folly this morning. I'm due in court in fifteen minutes. Did you talk to Sam?"

"If I didn't know better, I'd think you were a lawyer." Caroline attempted to lighten this conversation. "Yes, I told Sam and Angel yesterday at lunch."

"What'd he think?"

"Well, it seems I wasn't the only one keeping a secret. Sam had one too. He was waiting until I got back from Ferngrove to tell me what the gardeners found: someone had cut a hole in the fence and through a century-old climbing rosebush."

"Does Sam think this is related to your intruder?"

"Yes. Especially since they found a path through the shrubs and a bed of pine needles where someone's been sitting next to the window out of sight."

"This plot's getting thicker."

Caroline imagined the worry lines in James's forehead were probably twitching. "Sam thinks it might be a local hobo, a mysterious character who's been around here for years. No one seems to know anything about his life before he got here. The townspeople just either ignore him or look out for him. Never caused any trouble before."

"Do you think it could be the same person who was in your studio?"

"Only if Bo plays the piano."

"This is beginning to sound like a made-for-television movie: a beautiful, single piano teacher stalked by a hobo who's a former concert pianist."

"Don't worry, older brother. Sam's looking out for me, and he asked the sheriff to keep his eye on the hobo. You'd better get to court. Oh, and make sure the jury finds him guilty."

"In this case, they're both guilty. A nasty divorce."

"Oops, sorry. Didn't mean to make light of something so serious. By the way, I kept my promise and told Sam. Now you keep your promise not to tell Mama and Dad. No use in worrying them."

"I've not broken a promise to you yet, little sis."

"Yeah, I know, except the ones you made with your fingers crossed behind your back. And don't you dare tell Thomas. I mean it, James. Just don't. Go . . . and goodbye."

Caroline picked up the crystal vase from her desk and walked to the kitchen. She filled it with fresh water and arranged the iris and a sprig of maidenhair fern into a living still life. She understood that one iris was a sufficient thing of beauty.

———•———

"Again. The pickup is on the 'and' of the third beat, not the second beat." Caroline tapped the beat on the piano stool. "Here's the tempo. One and two and three and . . ."

Jay hesitated this time. Last time he'd been a beat early; now he was a beat late.

"Jay, if you're going to play the piano, you must learn to count."

"I know, Miss Caroline. I'm tryin'."

Caroline agreed with the "trying" part. The more talented students always seemed to be more frustrating. Jay Johnson had a good ear and considerable talent, and once he learned a piece, no one in Moss Point could play it better. He was eleven and small for his age. His size kept him from playing sports, but he compensated with a zany sense of humor. He was quick-witted and quite capable of becoming a fine pianist.

"Stop. Jay, why do you want to learn to play the piano?" It was a question she asked her students on occasion, and this was a most appropriate time.

"Ummh, I just like to play it."

"Why do you like to play it?"

"I don't know. I just do."

"Jay, it's important—no, it's necessary—for you to know why you want to play the piano. And just liking to play it isn't enough. It's something you must figure out for yourself."

Jay removed his hands from the keyboard. "You mean like right now I have to figure it out?"

"No. I think it's better for you to think about it when your mother isn't paying me by the minute to teach you how to play the piano. Did you do your theory lesson on the computer when you came in?"

His pause answered her question. Jay was actually one of her favorite students. After four years, Caroline was certain of two things: Jay would not lie to her, and he would likely try right now to distract her with his humor.

"Jay, I asked you a question."

"I'm trying to think."

"Trying to think of what? The answer seems very simple to me. It's either yes or no. You either did or you didn't, and it's not been so long ago that you'd have a memory lapse."

"That's it—I had a brain freeze, like when you eat ice cream real fast." Jay beamed with the pride of answering so cleverly.

Caroline raised her right eyebrow.

Jay knew the look, decided his time was up, and answered quickly, "No, ma'am."

"Oh, so your brain freeze thawed out."

His irresistible grin returned. "Hey, that's good. I'll have to remember that."

The right eyebrow again.

"Oh, yes, ma'am. I know I should have, but when I sat down to the computer, it was like something just came over me and the computer, and all of a sudden a computer game appeared on the screen."

"A computer game. You wouldn't be talking about one of the computer games you get to play as a reward for an excellent lesson, would you?"

Jay's eyes shifted.

"How would you like me to take the games off my computer and tell all my students that I did so because Jay Johnson would not play by the rules?"

"Oh, please, Miss Caroline, don't do that. I promise I won't do it again. I'll follow the rules."

"Do you know how much of your lesson time you have wasted this week? I think I'll just tell your mother and have her take it out of your allowance."

"Oh, please don't do that either. I owe Craig Weaver some money, and if I don't pay him back, he may crush my fingers or do something worse so that I couldn't ever come back to piano lessons."

"Is that so?" Caroline tried not to grin. "Well, then, let's start this piece again and you play it so that I'll not have a reason for Craig to break your fingers. Or better yet, that I don't break them myself." Jay was Caroline's only student to whom she would speak in this manner. Somehow, his impishness summoned her own playful streak. "Once more, one and two and three and . . ."

He missed it again.

"Move over, Jay. Look at the music and count and listen." Caroline started the piece and played the first section. "Now you play it."

Jay played the first section flawlessly, just as she had.

———•———

The next several days were a return to normal. No more signs of the intruder. Caroline prepared for the spring recital. She knew some of the students counted the days in anticipation of a new dress and loads of attention, but others numbered the days in dread of sweaty palms and upset stomachs. She busied herself with sending personal invitations, printing programs, and talking to her mother about plans for her upcoming visit. She had placed a call to Delia Mullins, the *Moss Point Messenger*'s society editor, to give her the date and the time. Delia would fill up a whole page with pictures and more information about composers and compositions than most Moss Point folks wanted to know.

Recital activities were welcome distractions. With the fence repaired and no further sign of an intruder, Caroline's evenings became more relaxed, and her comfort in playing the piano at two in the morning returned. Life was daily again.

———·———

"Mr. Sam. Mr. Sam," Ned hollered as he banged on the back door. "Mr. Sam."

"I'm coming, Ned. Hang on to your John Deere cap. I'm coming," Sam said as Angel followed him step for step through the kitchen to the back-porch door.

"What in the world, Ned?" Angel asked. "Are you okay? Is anyone bleeding?"

Sam noticed Ned was close to breathlessness and Fred's face was as white as an Easter lily on Resurrection morning.

"Yes, ma'am. I mean, no, ma'am, Miss Angel. But I need to talk to Mr. Sam."

"Okay, Ned. You're not bleeding, and I haven't heard the town siren, so what's this emergency?"

"Mr. Sam, the fence is tore up ag'in. Somebody's done come back. It's in a differ'nt place this time, not where we fixed it before. He's back, Mr. Sam. He's back."

"He's back," Fred repeated in his rarely used monotone voice.

"Okay, would you gentlemen secure the fence? I'll be down in a minute. I need to make a phone call."

The twins left, and Sam walked back into his study. He sat, thinking for a few minutes. He didn't like this.

He knew Caleb had been watching Bo. Bo's daylight activities were predictable. Dressed in worn-out khakis and a blue flannel shirt with hands stuffed deep in his pockets, Bo probably walked ten or twelve miles a day. Everyone in town recognized his stooped silhouette and his gait and knew how Bo spent his days, but no one was certain of where he spent his nights. As a judge, Sam had held at least a dozen come-to-Jesus meetings with teenagers who taunted and teased Bo and made a game of following him late in the day to find where he would spend the night. Their stories of huts in the woods, old barns, vacant houses, caves, and the riverbank floated through the air around Moss Point just like the chimes from the Methodist church steeple.

Sam picked up the phone and called Caleb.

"Hello, Caleb, this is Sam. Any news on Bo?"

"Nothing except I think we're wasting our time watching him. His comings and goings haven't raised any of the few suspicious hairs left on my head."

"So, you've seen nothing?"

"Not a thing. He did come one night a few days ago. It was that night of thunderstorms that took Henry Carter's barn down. You know I leave the jail open so he can spend the night here when the weather's bad."

"Did you get a look at his hands?"

"Yep, and I don't know as I'd call 'em piano-playing hands, Sam."

"Well, just keep watching, and have your deputy drive by in the evenings. Our intruder has returned. Later, Caleb."

Sam didn't know if Caleb's report was good news or bad news. He'd hoped the interloper was Bo, because he thought Bo harmless. And days without a recurrence of the unseen watcher had been welcomed. But fresh thoughts of a stranger chilled Sam.

He walked through the house and grabbed his cane. "Angel, I'm headed out to check the fence."

"Wait a minute. I'm coming too."

Sam and Angel made their way to where Ned and Fred were working. "All right, all right, gentlemen. I'm here. Ned, is Caroline at home?" Sam asked.

"Her car's gone, and we ain't heard no piano playing this morning, so I think she's gone, Mr. Sam."

"Good. Let's see what's going on before we tell her."

Fred led them to the spot where once again the old boards were pulled away. Sam's years as an attorney had given him an acute sense of details and summations. He surmised the intruder was using crude tools and deliberately choosing weak areas in the fence. A fresh path was worn through the shrubs lining the fence. He checked the path behind the tea olives and found fresh tracks made by athletic shoes. The tracks led straight to the studio window just as before.

Sam, Angel, Ned, and Fred made their observations in silence, each quiet with individual concerns. Sam was appalled with thoughts of an intruder's violating the security and sanctity of Twin Oaks. He broke the silence. "Ned, you think you can get this repaired today?"

Ned looked at Fred, and Fred nodded. "Yes, sir, Mr. Sam, we'll git the stuff we need and git right to work."

Sam and Angel started back up the path home. They stopped at the pond. Caroline's favorite coffee cup sat on the arm of the garden bench. Caroline's sacred place.

Next to the waterfall in the boggy area, Sam saw one lone purple iris—the last iris of spring.

Chapter Seven

That's What Heroes Do

———◆———

CAROLINE SAT AT ANOTHER MEETING WITH TANDY YARBROUGH. She knew she'd do good to make minimum wage for this wedding if she considered her time.

The plans were set. The wedding would be in Tandy's backyard. A string quartet would play on the patio, and Caroline would play a piano under a white tent about thirty yards away. Tandy had put Caroline in charge and dismissed Gertie—a plan that Caroline did not like. Gertie, the organist at the Methodist church for forty-three years, knew everyone in town and could untangle the vines in all the family trees even when they turned to bushes. Caroline had been grateful for Gertie's guidance through many ticklish weddings and awkward funerals.

As professional musicians, Caroline and Gertie had come to an agreement four years ago on a fee structure for weddings. They'd decided if the mechanics down at Snake's Garage made good livings, then it was time they should be compensated fairly too. No more linen handkerchiefs and brass picture frames. However, they had not factored Tandy Yarbrough into their calculations.

———◆———

Caroline rushed home after the meeting to find a sawhorse in front of her garage door and the Pendergrass brothers' pea-green truck in the driveway. She parked along the street.

"Howdy there, Miss Caroline." Ned met her in the driveway.

"Good morning, Ned. I see you parked your horse in the driveway."

"Yes, ma'am. Another job for Mr. Sam. We tryin' to finish today, so that ol' sawhorse'll be outta your way before long."

"It's really not a problem. I guess Mr. Sam is getting things all spiffed up for our recital next weekend."

"Well, you might say that." He shuffled a moment. "We'll be finished before long. I gotta git back to work, Miss Caroline."

Inside, Caroline was welcomed with the answering machine's beep. Three calls. She stood at her desk, punched the message button, and picked up a pencil to take down the numbers. As she listened, her fingers traced the velvety petals of the iris on her desk. Only a few more irises this year and she would put her grand-mother's cut-glass vase back in the curio.

First message: Megan was ill and would not be at her 4:30 piano lesson. Delete button. Second message: her mother had new ideas about a color scheme, which would mean a change in the punch ingredients for the recital. Delete button. Third message: an unfamiliar voice introducing himself as Roderick Adair.

Listening now more intently, she picked up her pencil once again.

"I apologize for the delay in getting back to you. I've been out of the country. Patrick Verran gave me your message. You may reach me at . . . ."

She listened to the message three times, making certain she wrote down the correct numbers. The edgy baritone voice with the southern-gentleman-from-Kentucky accent ignited her imagination. Was he a singer? Would he allow her to see her piano? What had Patrick Verran told him exactly? There was only one way to find out.

She picked up the receiver and punched each number very intently, thinking of what she might say if he answered the phone.

"Hello, this is Mr. Adair's office," said a strong-voiced female.

"Ah, yes. This is Caroline Carlyle calling from Moss Point, Georgia. I am calling for Mr. Adair. That is, I'm returning his call. No, actually, his call to me was in response to a message left by Patrick Verran on my behalf." This nervous jabbering was unlike her. "This must sound strange, Miss . . . I'm sorry, I didn't get your name."

"You're correct, this does sound strange, and you didn't get my name because I did not give it to you."

Caroline was certain she had not made a good first impression. "Well, again, my name is Caroline Carlyle, and I'd like to speak to Mr. Adair if it is convenient."

"Is he expecting your call?"

"I think so. He just called and left a message about half an hour ago."

"Will Mr. Adair know the purpose of this call?" the woman asked, demonstrating her skill in interrogating solicitous callers.

"Yes, I think he will."

There was a long pause. Perhaps she was connecting Mr. Adair. The woman finally broke the silence. "Would you like to tell me what this call is about?"

Caroline realized she might never get through this brick wall without revealing the nature of her interest. "Yes, I'm calling about the grand piano."

"The piano is not for sale."

"Oh, I would just like to speak with Mr. Adair about the piano. I'm not trying to buy it." Caroline twirled several strands of her hair around her finger. A nervous habit left over from childhood.

"One moment."

Another long pause.

"Good morning, Miss Carlyle."

Caroline released the strands of her hair. "Good morning, Mr. Adair, and thank you so very much for taking my call."

"You're most welcome. I'm sorry it took me so long to contact you. My business took me out of the country for several weeks, and I'm now catching up on my correspondence. How might I help you?"

"Well, I don't know how much Patrick Verran told you, but I have interest in the grand piano you purchased from him."

"Yes, Patrick told me this fine instrument may have belonged to your family at one point."

"It did. My father purchased it for me when I was eight years old. When I went away to college, my parents sold it to a family in my hometown. It may seem a bit strange to you that I would have such an attachment to this instrument. Most people assume all pianos are the same."

"One has only to look at this piano to know that it's not just any piano."

"Do you play, Mr. Adair?"

"Ah, no." He cleared his throat. "And please call me Roderick. I purchased the piano to fulfill my childhood dream."

"I hope your dream includes learning to play. It would be a shame for this piano not to be played. Oh, forgive me. I seem to be out of line here. After all, it is yours."

"I understand perfectly, Miss Carlyle—"

"Oh, please call me Caroline."

"Thank you . . . Caroline. As I was saying, I do understand. Having this piano sit in the music room without someone to play it is like having a Rolls-Royce in the garage and no one around to drive it."

"I think that is a perfect analogy, Mr. A—I mean, Roderick. It pleases me you would classify this instrument in the same league as a Rolls-Royce."

"I take that to mean that you would have taken offense had I said Volkswagen."

"Well, maybe not 'offense,' but it certainly would have indicated you're unaware of what you possess."

"I've been accused of that before. Now, I understand from Mr. Verran that you would be interested in playing the piano again. How would you like to pay a visit to Kentucky?"

"Oh, my . . . . But I didn't expect to be invited. I mean, I am a perfect stranger. You know nothing about me."

"Quite the contrary, Miss Carlyle."

Caroline began to twirl her hair again. So now, it was back to "Miss Carlyle."

"I would never have made the call without knowing something about you. Perhaps I should get to the point. I understand you are a teacher and recitalist, and I'd like you to come and perform for a few of my friends. We'll call it a parlor concert. Does that interest you, Miss Carlyle?"

"I . . . think it does." She stopped twisting her hair and sat perfectly still. "Yes. Why, yes, it does."

"Then it's done. This plan satisfies your desire to play the piano and my delight in having guests over to hear it played. I understand you play Chopin, Debussy, Mendelssohn, and Brahms."

"Yes."

"And what about Rachmaninoff?"

Caroline stretched her fingers and looked at her hand. "Oh, I'm sorry. I have the heart but not the hands for Rachmaninoff."

"That's too bad. But I'm certain you'll put together a fine program. How does sometime in June sound to you? The June nights in Kentucky are like none other."

"June sounds just fine. I have a few commitments, but I will check my calendar."

"Why don't you talk with Liz? Give her some available dates. We'll settle on one, and she'll make all the travel arrangements. And please let her know what your fee is for such an engagement."

"My goodness, this is moving so fast and is so much more than I expected. There'll be no charge. I think I would pay *you* just for the opportunity to play this piano one more time. Now, who is Liz?"

"She's the woman who answered the phone. She did not identify herself?"

Being friendly with Liz was more important than ever. "I'm sure she did and I just missed it. But I'll check my calendar and get back with her in the next few days. Thank you so very much, Mr. Adair."

"That's Roderick, remember?"

"Yes, I do remember, Roderick. But you seemed to forget it's Caroline."

"You're quite right. I look forward with great pleasure to meeting you, Caroline Carlyle. Good day, now."

He was gone before Caroline could respond. She hung up the phone slowly and took a seat in her desk chair.

What did Patrick Verran tell him? What does Roderick Adair know about me, and how did he find out? Why would he ask me to perform a recital when he's never heard me play?

One conversation and she was halfway to Kentucky. These things didn't happen to her.

———•———

April, Caroline's favorite month of the year, was history. But summer was coming with a recital in Kentucky, master classes, some journal writing assignments, and constructing her teaching schedule. May and her student recital were upon her.

Caroline lived to teach piano lessons, and nothing pleased her more than seeing the measurable progress of her students as they performed for recital. This May afternoon was different. At dusk she practically kicked her last student out the door and only waved at Ned and Fred as they carried their tools to the truck, which was probably glowing neon green in the twilight.

She made herself a cup of tea and stood at the kitchen sink drinking it while she watched the sun slide behind Angel and Sam's rooftop. Then she went to the piano and sat down as if she'd been standing for days and could finally rest. She ran her fingers over the keyboard, closed her eyes, inhaled deeply, and started to play. Her body became one with the instrument, and she moved into a familiar world, one of her soul's homes, an inexplicable place where time stood still and all was well.

Caroline played for a while before remembering she was to call Betsy. On her way to the phone, she grabbed a box of crackers, an apple, and a cheese stick from the refrigerator, then dialed Betsy's number.

"Hello," growled Mason.

"Hi, Mason. It's Caroline. What's happening?"

"We're having a baby."

"I know, but what's new?"

"Nothing. We're having a baby."

"You sound . . . well, focused."

"I may be focused, but everybody else around here is obsessed. You'd think Betsy is the only woman in the world who ever gave birth. She's obsessed. Her mother's obsessed. My mother's obsessed. Betsy's hardly showing, and she's buying maternity clothes, picking out paint, wallpaper, furniture . . . And she goes to bed every night poring over a book trying to come up with a name for this little booger."

"You think I could speak to the little booger's mother?"

"Sure, let me see if I can find her. I'm in the workshop studying plans for building a cradle."

"The baby's due in October, it's Thursday evening in May, you're in the shop looking at cradle plans, and you're not obsessed?"

"No, it's the only thing to get me out of the house before I'm attacked with the catalogs and the baby-names book again." Mason hollered for Betsy. "It's CC. Pick up the phone." He held on until Betsy had connected, then said his goodbyes.

"Hey, CC."

"Hey, yourself, little mama. Mason said you're focused on getting ready for the baby. Oops, I mean this little booger."

"Shut up, Caroline. Would you believe he had a red T-shirt made for me? A red shirt with *HERE'S BOOGER* on the front. Then he got mad when I wouldn't wear it. He has the whole town calling our baby Booger."

"Tell him he'd best be careful about this name. You know what they say about kids living up to labels. Hey, have you worked things out for a visit?"

"Yes, Josefina and I'll be coming with your mom for the recital. I can't wait to get out of this town and away from our parents and Mason for a few days. I don't know if you can stand me, though. My moods blast from red to blue all in about five seconds."

"I'll put up with you. Not the first time in your life I've had to put up with your hormones. Hope you can stay a few days after the recital."

"I'll see. I'll work that out with Miss Martha."

Caroline never could keep anything significant from Betsy. "I have news about my piano. Just when I thought it was a dead issue, I got this call today from a man named Roderick Adair. He has this deep, luscious baritone voice, and his speech is very refined. We had quite a chat this afternoon. He's been out of the country on business."

"Is he the man at the piano store in Atlanta?"

"Nope. He's the gentleman from Kentucky who purchased the piano for forty-two thousand dollars from the piano dealer in Atlanta. He paid cash, had it delivered to his home in Kentucky, and has had it ever since. And he doesn't even play the piano."

"Sounds interesting."

"And . . . he's invited me to come to Kentucky in June to do a recital for some of his friends."

"Sounds *very* interesting. Does this Roderick Adair have a wife and children?"

"I don't know. How would I know that? Why would I even want to know?"

"Sounds even more interesting. I haven't heard that excited lilt in your voice in years."

"What are you talking about?"

"'A deep' . . . Let's see, I think 'luscious' is the word you used to describe his voice."

"Oh, no. I know nothing about this man, and that's exactly what you hear in my voice. Nothing."

"You know nothing? Is that what you said? You know he lives in Kentucky, that he does business out of the country, that he has the money to spend on a grand piano he does not play, and that he must love music or have friends who do."

"Well, that's not much to know about someone."

"Did you say yes?"

"Yes to what?"

"Why, Caroline Carlyle, you are befuzzled! Did you say yes to his invitation to do the recital?"

"Oh, that. Yes, I did."

"Cautious Caroline accepting an invitation from a man she doesn't even know? Sounds pretty intriguing to me."

"You're just way off base, Betsy. And besides, you seem to forget my interest is in the piano."

"I don't recall saying anything about your interest. I'll ask you about your interest after the recital in Kentucky. But I'll remind you: women fall in love with what they hear, and men fall in love with what they see. And I can imagine he's been going through university archives of Caroline Carlyle recitals. A man like that? Oh, no—he's not taking a chance on something like this."

"Okay, that's it. Time to say good night. I'll see you next week. And give Josefina a hug from CC."

"See you, friend, and sweet dreams."

Caroline put down the phone. She was grateful for Betsy, a childhood friend who would grow old with her.

She finished her apple and went back to the piano. Sitting down, she closed her eyes and started to play again, back to her place where she was surrounded by music and good things. She played for a long time, hardly ever opening her eyes.

A solid loud thump followed by a crash and a distinct holler startled Caroline from her musical trance. She stopped playing and sat motionless. There was movement in the shrubbery near the fence.

The pendulum clock her father made for her had just chimed the midnight hour a few minutes ago. She slipped from the piano bench to the floor and crawled down the hallway to her bedroom where she could not be seen. She locked the door, checked the latch on the window, and grabbed the phone. Her hands trembled as she dialed Sam's number.

The intruder is back, and he knows I heard him. What'll I do if he breaks in? The window. Maybe I should climb out now.

Her heart palpitated as she waited for Sam to answer.

"Hello, who is this, and what do you want this time of the night?"

Caroline feared that his booming voice could be heard all the way from the big house. "Sam, it's Caroline."

"What? Speak up! I can't hear you."

"Sam, it's me, Caroline."

It took him a few seconds to speak. "Caroline, what's wrong? Are you all right?"

"I'm all right, Sam, but I just heard some strange noises out by the fence. I was playing the piano. There was a loud thump and a crash, and then someone screamed. I'm in the bedroom now. The doors are locked, but I'm really scared."

"Stay right there, Caroline. I'm calling Caleb, and I'm on my way."

"No, Sam, don't come. Just call Caleb and turn on your outside lights."

He was no longer on the phone. She waited. Nothing. No sounds. Just Moss Point quiet.

She went to the bedroom door, quietly turned the lock, and tiptoed back out to the great room, where she stood silently listening. Still no sound. She went to the terrace door. A café curtain covered the window, and she pulled it slightly to the side, enabling her to peep out without being seen. She stood waiting, watching intently, still able to hear her own heart beating. If Sam was out there, he was moving quietly, and he wasn't known to do anything quietly.

She strained her eyes as a faint light coming through the alcove window grew stronger. It had to be Sam coming down the stone path with a flashlight.

Why didn't Sam wait for Caleb? He doesn't need this, not at his age. And what'll I do if something happens to Sam? I'll never forgive myself. Why didn't I just call Caleb?

In such thick silence, she heard the constant ticking of the clock on the table behind her. Streaks of light flashed in the room as the clock's brass pendulum reflected the beams coming closer and closer through the window. Her pulse was like the pounding of a bass drum.

I just want to run, but where?

It all happened very fast. A bright shaft of light shone toward the shrubbery along the fence as Sam's voice boomed. "I don't know who you are, but my double-barreled shotgun is aimed just above your shoes."

Another voice. "Don't shoot! Please don't shoot!" Bright lights revealed a male dressed in camouflage clothes stepping cautiously out of the shrubbery.

Yet another voice. "Sam, it's Caleb over here. Don't shoot. Keep your light shining on the suspect's feet. I got him in my sight."

"Mr. Sam, Mr. Sam, please don't shoot." Another man in camouflage clothes came out of the bushes.

A third man appeared out of nowhere right in front of Caroline's eyes. Only the pane of glass on the terrace door separated their breaths. He knocked on the glass. "Miss Carlyle, you in there? You okay?" It was the deputy.

"Yes, I'm here, and I'm fine."

"Would you mind turning on your porch lights?"

Caroline reached for the light switch and the doorknob at the same time. She came out onto the terrace, and the deputy grabbed her arm and pulled her behind him. Sam stood to her left with his flashlight and his shotgun aimed at the perpetrators. Caleb, poised with pistol ready to shoot, was to her right.

Before them, shaking like wet dogs, appeared Ned and Fred.

Sam growled. "What in the . . . ? Ned, what in tarnation are you and Fred doing out here in the middle of the night?" Sam propped his shotgun against the wrought-iron patio chair and scowled at his two handymen.

The deputy, paralyzed in his stance, kept Caroline behind him.

Caleb put his gun in its holster and pulled out his handcuffs. Just as he approached Ned and Fred, there came a jolting clunk followed by the loud blast of a gun and shattering glass.

Someone screamed.

"Angel! Is that you?" Caroline saw Angel running toward Sam. She freed herself from the deputy and ran toward her neighbors. The terrace lamps provided enough light for her to know they were both still standing.

Angel embraced Caroline. "Yes, child, I'm here. But I thought you were screaming."

Sam bent over to pick up his gun. "It's all right, Deputy. The shoot-out's over. Everything's under control. My gun just slipped off this chair and fired. Guess that hair trigger still works."

Angel had to sit down in the chair. "Sam Meadows, I ought to shoot you myself. You have nearly scared us all to death."

"Caroline, you take Angel back to the house. We'll have this conversation later. I have other business to tend to right this minute."

Angel pulled her robe around herself more tightly. "We're not going anywhere. Why, the whole neighborhood will show up any moment, and I'll not have them knowing things going on right here in my own backyard before I even know about them."

"Then you sit quietly while Caleb and I take care of this matter."

Caleb moved to handcuff Fred, who was whimpering like a scolded child.

"No need for handcuffs, boys," Sam said.

The quivering deputy had put his gun away and walked over with his handcuffs for Ned, the talking twin who now stood utterly speechless. Both officers put their cuffs away as Sam turned to Ned.

"Ned, none of this makes any sense. You men would have been the last on my list. What in the world are you up to?"

"Mr. Sam, we just come back to take care of Miss Caroline."

"What does that mean?" Caleb said.

"Well, today we was fixin' the fence where somebody's done come in ag'in, and we got to thinkin' that we oughta just catch this feller and be done with it. That way Miss Caroline would be safe and we wouldn't have to keep fixin' this dadblasted fence."

Caleb led the twins into the terrace light. "You mean you're not the Peeping Toms?"

"You ought to know better than that," Sam said. "There's not a hurtful bone in these men's bodies, but there's a stupid one or two."

Fred, the silent twin, whispered, "He was here." Caroline was the only one aware that he had spoken, but she was too rattled to interrupt the interrogation.

Sam sat down in the chair next to Angel. "Ned, do you know that I could have very well shot the both of you and asked questions later?"

"Yessir, Mr. Sam. But we was plannin' on doin' the catchin' our-selves, not gittin' caught."

"The snooper was here," Fred said a bit louder this time. Caroline stared at him, wide-eyed.

"Well, you nearly scared Caroline to death and got your body parts full of buckshot. Why in the world didn't you call me and let me know what you were doing?"

"Mr. Sam, we just wanted to do it ourselves, kinda like bein' heroes," Ned said sheepishly.

"*I said he was here!*" Fred shouted.

All eyes turned to the usually silent twin.

"What?" Sam rose from his chair. "What do you mean he was here?"

Fred stood now like the statue of the Confederate soldier in the town square, with his head down to avoid eye contact.

Ned stepped forward. "Mr. Sam, whoever's been doin' this was tryin' to git back through the fence ag'in. You see, we finished our work and went home to eat. Fred just had this feelin' that we ought to be heroes. We talked it over, and we decided to do it. He made us some banana sandwiches, and I rounded up our huntin' stools and some rope. We got all dressed in our huntin' clothes like Pa showed us when we was boys. You know they're green and brown, and Pa said the animals couldn't see if us if we would wear 'em."

The sheriff took off his cap and ran his fingers through his hair. "Do you mind getting on with the story?"

"Well, we figgered nobody could see us in the bushes if we wore our huntin' clothes. So we come back about nine o'clock. We just been sittin' out here in the bushes waitin'."

"You've been out here for the last three and a half hours?" Sam asked.

"Yessir. It was kinda nice. We missed the reruns of *Hawaii Five-O*, but it was worth it. Why, we ain't had this kind of excitement since Pa caught them escaped convicts while we was coon huntin'."

"Ned," the sheriff said. "We don't care about no coon huntin' or escaped convicts. That was forty years ago."

"Well, we was hidin' over there in them bushes. And it was nice 'cause we could hear Miss Caroline playin' that piano. She was just serenadin' the whole neighborhood. And 'long about midnight—you know what they say about that midnight hour. Well, it was 'long about then that we heared somebody on the other side of the fence right down there where we fixed it today. We stayed real quiet. Pa taught us to do that when we was deer huntin'."

Ned squirmed a bit and started again. "Well, then, whoever it was got real quiet, too, and we thought he was gone. But it wasn't long before we heared somebody, what sounded like knockin' on the fence. We knowed he was tryin' to tear that fence down ag'in, so we was goin' to follow our plan.

"Fred had the rope in his bucket, and we was goin' to wait till the feller came through the fence. I'd be on one side of him with my end of the rope, and Fred would be on the other side with his end of the rope. When the snooper came through, we'd trip him up and hog-tie him to the ground. We was just goin' to haul him right down to the jailhouse. That way, it wouldn't upset Miss Caroline."

Sam pounded the patio table with his fist. "You mean he was here, and you let him get away?"

"Well, yes and no. He was here. But here's what happened. Fred got the rope out of the bucket and handed me my end. I crawled down the fence line real quiet like where I could see the boards about to give way to this knockin'. But when Fred got his end of the rope and started comin' toward me, he tripped over my bucket, hit his head on the fence, and hollered. You ever heared what a tin bucket full of RC Colas sounds like when it's knocked over at midnight?"

Caroline finally broke her silence "I know what it sounds like. That was the sound that startled me."

"Well, it's been a long night, boys, and we all need some sleep. Caroline, you're coming with us to the big house tonight," Sam said, continuing to give orders.

"That's a good idea. 'Specially since you done blowed a hole through her window." Ned moved toward the broken glass. "We'll board it up for the night, and I s'pose you want us to come back and fix it tomorrow."

"You mean you'd do that after I said you had a few stupid bones in your body?"

"Yessir, Mr. Sam, we would. That's what heroes do."

Chapter Eight

Peach Brandy and Thoughts of Blue Grass

———◆———

*A*NGEL HELD CAROLINE'S HAND AS THEY WALKED THE STONE path up to the main house. Sam carried his shotgun. They'd left Ned and Fred securing the broken window with plywood, all the while grumbling about missing their opportunity to nab the snooper. Plywood might secure the window for the night, but Angel knew it didn't solve the problem.

"Angel, would you just look at yourself? I cannot believe you've been traipsing around in your gown and that bathrobe and your old house slippers. That's not like you," Sam said.

"Well, what did you expect? I wasn't planning on entertaining the sheriff and Ned and Fred after midnight."

Sam opened the back door. "How about entertaining us with a cup of chamomile tea? I could use something to settle my nerves."

"Cuppa chamomile tea? My hind leg. I have just the thing." Angel pulled her step stool to the refrigerator and started to climb.

"What in the world are you doing, woman?" Sam headed toward her. "We've had enough excitement for one night. We don't need you tumbling off this stool and breaking something." Sam steadied her and stood ready to break her fall.

Angel stood on her tiptoes and stretched to open the cabinet atop the refrigerator. She pulled out a brown bottle. "Oh, hold your tongue and take this bottle," she muttered as she held on to Sam's shoulder and stepped down from the stool. She grabbed three glasses and went to the table. "Sit. Tonight's no night for tea. We're having peach brandy."

Caroline raised her eyebrows. "You mean *the* peach brandy I tasted at your fifty-fifth anniversary party?"

"Yes, *the* peach brandy." Angel opened the decanter and poured a respectable amount into each glass. "Why, we could have all been killed, and there's still peach brandy in the cupboard. A lot of good it'll do me dead."

Angel always enjoyed telling the story of how she came to have the recipe. Her aunt Alice had lived in the Texas hill country during hard times nearly a century ago. She'd provided the nuns in a local monastery with beef and homegrown vegetables for years. The nuns returned the favor with bottles of peach brandy. After years of deliveries, the nuns finally gave Alice the recipe with the understanding she could only share it with one trusted family member. Angel had been the anointed niece in her generation. The recipe involved fresh peaches, sugar, a large jar, a dark closet, a secret ingredient, and six months' time. But that's as much as Angel had ever shared, and she only made the brandy when the peach crop was exceptional.

"Well, dear ones, this is it. The last bottle. We'd better pray for the best peach crop ever." Angel swirled the brandy in the glass, held it to the light, and sipped it. Sam and Caroline observed the ritual too. The brandy was sweet and smooth, and only a few seconds after swallowing it, Angel felt the warmth in her throat. "Oh, this will do better than a cuppa tea."

"You're mighty right, but I'm not so sure this is such a special occasion," Sam growled.

"When you're as old as dirt, you can't expect too many more special occasions. At our age, every day is a special occasion, and

I guess it took nearly getting my head blown off to remind me of that."

Caroline put her glass down. "Angel, don't say things like that."

"But it's true. No reason not to drink peach brandy every day."

"Sounds like a mighty fine idea to me." Sam drank the last drop. "Now, don't you go climbing up on that stool to put the bottle up, especially if your head is spinning like mine is." Sam got up from his chair.

"Brandy always goes to his head." Angel turned to Caroline. "Why in the thunder would I want to put the bottle up? Climbing to the top of the refrigerator is not near the top of my list of favorite things to do. I'll leave it right here on the counter tonight. Then tomorrow I'll pour it into that crystal decanter Aunt Alice left me, and it'll be on the counter when I want a little sip."

"Well, sounds like you're dead serious about this." Sam rinsed his glass.

"Surely just as serious as I am about getting back to bed. It's nearly one thirty in the morning, and a girl needs her beauty rest. Caroline, you take the bridal suite." Angel had decorated the upstairs guest room in shades of white and lace a number of years ago. Another of her canvases. Occasionally she changed the curtains or the pillows to add a bit of color or seasonal décor. "You know where everything is. Hope you rest well, and I'll see you in the morning."

"Thanks, Angel. I hope the brandy does the trick for all three of us. After all, we've had quite a night."

"Well, I think those Texas nuns and Aunt Alice would be happy to know their peach brandy had settled our nerves," said Angel as she left the kitchen. "Sam, is your head still spinning? You need my help?"

Sam's voice trailed as he walked down the hall. "I can see it now—nuns sitting around a long table passing the bottle for a sip just after they fought off a whole tribe of Indians and saved the orphan children."

"Shootin' Indians makes a better story than blowing up a flowerpot when you drop your shotgun."

———•———

This was Caroline's final teaching day and the last day to get things ready before her Ferngrove crowd arrived, so she rose early and tiptoed out, trying not to wake Sam and Angel. She left a note for them in front of the coffeepot, which would be Angel's first stop after her feet hit the floor, and walked the garden path to the studio, tiptoeing into the great room to avoid the broken glass of the shotgun's blast. The buckshot had shattered a large ceramic planter on the terrace and broken the bottom panes of glass in the alcove's bay window. The piano had been spared.

Ned and Fred would return early to finish their job, but she swept up as much glass as she could before getting the vacuum cleaner. Vacuum cleaners were wonderful contraptions in spite of the noise. They sucked up all the dirt and debris and evidence of disaster, making it safe to walk barefoot again. She wished her problems could so magically disappear, leaving no trace of trauma.

The cleanup taken care of, Caroline tidied herself and went to the grocery store early. A quick trip dressed in sweats without makeup was not an option, because anonymity did not exist at the market or the post office in Moss Point. Women gossiped over the grapefruit and planned parties over the pears, and someone always engaged her in conversation.

She looked over the list as she placed the whipping cream—her last item—in the grocery cart. She was home free and on her way to the checkout counter in record time when she heard an unfamiliar voice calling her name weakly.

"Miss Carlyle?"

Caroline turned to see a woman in the aisle behind her. She had seen the woman before but did not know who she was.

"Miss Carlyle? Aren't you Miss Carlyle?"

"Yes, I'm Caroline Carlyle."

"And you live at Twin Oaks and teach piano lessons?" She pushed her cart nearer Caroline.

Caroline studied the woman's face. "Yes. I don't believe we have met." She extended her hand.

The woman kept her grip on the grocery cart and only nodded her head, keeping a safe distance. She was fiftyish and slight of stature with silver hair pulled back severely. Only when she turned her head slightly could Caroline see the bun of braided hair wrapped and secured at the nape of her neck. She was struck by the woman's porcelain skin, which gave no evidence of having seen much of the southern sun. Silver-green eyes were like none Caroline had ever seen. The absence of a smile hinted at previous pain, but the stillness in her eyes suggested a resigned peace.

Beside the woman was a striking girl, perhaps twelve or thirteen. Caroline observed the adolescent had the same unblemished, pale skin, platinum hair falling in curls below her shoulders, and silver-green eyes—which were also still and fixed on Caroline's face.

"No, ma'am, we have never met," the woman said. "I'm Gretchen Silva, and this is Bella. We live not far from Twin Oaks, and we hear you play the piano on occasion. You play so beautifully."

"Thank you, Mrs. Silva. That's very kind of you."

"I love the music of the piano. I grew up listening to my grandmammá play, and I miss it so much."

"Yes, there is nothing quite like the piano and its music. Do you play?"

Mrs. Silva lowered her head. "Oh, no. No. I only wish to hear it."

"Bella, what about you? Do you play?"

Bella stood reticent and motionless. Caroline found her silence intimidating.

Mrs. Silva quickly answered, "Oh, yes, she loves the piano. Do you think you could teach Bella to play the piano?"

"Well, we could set up a time to get together next week. The spring recital is this weekend, and I'll be putting together my fall schedule next week. I don't teach during the summer." Caroline's eyes darted to see Bella's expression. Neither Bella's eyes nor any facial muscles ever moved.

"I see. I know so little about piano lessons."

"Perhaps you and Bella would like to come to the recital Saturday afternoon. You would enjoy it, and it might inspire Bella."

"Oh, I don't think it would be possible." She paused. "No, that would not be possible at all."

Caroline observed the immediate tension in Mrs. Silva's face. "Well, then, maybe it would fit your schedule better if you and Bella came to my studio next week, and we could talk about lessons in the fall."

Mrs. Silva's face softened.

"I'll brew a pot of tea, and we can get acquainted." She reached into her bag for her card. As Caroline neared their cart and extended her card, Bella moved quickly behind Mrs. Silva and hid her face.

Mrs. Silva took the card. "Thank you, Miss Carlyle. I'll try to call next week. I hope we were not too much of a bother today."

"Heavens, no. I'll see you next week." Caroline started toward the checkout counter.

"Miss Carlyle?"

Caroline turned to answer.

Mrs. Silva hesitated. "Oh—I'm so sorry. Not to bother . . . God bless you, Miss Carlyle." She and Bella turned and walked away.

———·———

Caroline had put away her groceries and started on some baking when she heard the knock at the door. She had already glimpsed the pea-green truck through the kitchen window.

"Good morning, Ned." Caroline opened the door to Ned and Fred standing in their usual stances in overalls, plaid shirts, and caps in hand.

"And to you, Miss Caroline. We didn't rightly tell you how sorry we were 'bout last night. We didn't mean to upset nobody. We just thought we would take care of the problem and catch that snooper. Then you wouldn't have to give it not one more thought."

"And I don't think I rightly told you how grateful I am that you would even attempt such a thing. Why, both of you could have been injured!"

"I guess we been watchin' too much TV, and we decided there wasn't nothin' keepin' us from bein' heroes except our own selves. It's hard to be a hero when you just sit and watch 'em on TV. At least that's what Papa woulda said."

"Well, thank you both. You're certainly heroes to me." She watched Ned and Fred redden simultaneously.

"Well, now, Miss Caroline, whoever that snooper is, he's still out there, and you gotta be careful."

Fred elbowed Ned.

"You gotta keep your doors locked, and I'll be talking to Mr. Sam about nailin' your windows shut so nobody can break in 'em. Why, it might be a purty good idea to put some curtains over them windows."

Fred elbowed Ned again.

"In fact, you might want to talk to Mr. Sam about some wood shutters."

Fred tugged on the hammer hanging from the loop on Ned's overalls. "Shut up, Ned," he said and turned to walk off.

"Excuse me, Miss Caroline. Better git my tools and start to work. We'll be done in a little while, and we'll try not to be much bother."

"I'll be baking cookies, so you gentlemen do whatever you need to do."

Ned picked up his toolbox and joined his brother on the terrace as she closed the door. Through the open window she could hear them talking as they walked away.

"Did you hear her, Fred? She called us gentlemen. Now, ain't that a lady for you? Nobody ever calls us gentlemen."

"Hmmph, you ain't no gentleman, Ned, so just git that outta

your head. Ain't no gentleman in the whole wide world, and then some, woulda kept on talkin' about things that scare ladies to death. Lockin' doors, nailin' the windows shut. Now, what kinda gentleman talks to a lady about things like that?"

With a grin, Caroline went back to her work and soon had the cookies finished. She packaged up a few for Ned and Fred and began working down her to-do list, adding items as she checked others off. She looked at her schedule. She really needed to choose a date for her recital in Kentucky.

Okay, June. What have we got going? she asked herself as she perused the squares of her calendar. She was dismayed to realize the answer was quite a lot. With a grimace, she flipped the page to July. After some consideration and counting, she chose a date later in July. That would give her a few weeks to prepare and schedule at least two lessons at the university for critique.

Caroline was looking up Roderick Adair's number when the phone rang.

"Hey, Caroline, hate to bother you. I know you're busy."

"Why, Angel, I'm surprised. I haven't heard from you all morning. I just figured you had a hangover."

"No hangover, but I slept like a baby. Got your note earlier, so I know you have a full day. Sam and I've been talking. We think it best if you stayed up here for a few days. Your mom and Betsy and Josefina are coming, and I know that you were planning on Betsy staying with you, but we just don't think that's wise right now."

"Oh, Angel, that's so much trouble, and with all of us, your inn will be full."

"The more the merrier. Do your parents know about this intruder?"

"Not unless James has broken his promise to me. Oops, that reminds me. I promised James I'd call him if anything new developed. But maybe I'll wait until next week."

"I still think you should stay with us for a few days anyway. We have plenty of room, and when Martha gets here, she can do all her cooking in my big kitchen. You could share the bridal suite with her, and Betsy and Josefina could stay in the blue room down the hall."

"Angel, did I ever tell you that your mother surely named you right?"

"Oh, just about four hundred and ninety-two times."

"What would I ever do without you and Sam? Thanks. I'll take the bridal suite, and you won't even have to change the sheets."

"Good. Will you be here for supper? Creole casserole."

"The one with all the bacon and green peas?"

"The very one."

"I'll be there with fresh cookies."

"See you then."

———·———

Caroline reached for her day planner for Roderick Adair's number and took a deep breath. Talking to Liz equaled making a dental appointment, she decided. She slowly dialed the number, thinking of how she would begin the conversation. After several rings, however, she heard a click and assumed the machine would answer. She tapped her pencil on the tile counter and hummed while she waited for the beep.

"Good morning, Caroline. Ah, 'Plaisir d'amour'! I believe that's 'The Joy of Love' you're humming. A very romantic melody coming from a lovely voice, I might add."

Caroline was stunned. "'Plaisir d'amour' it is, and thank you, Roderick." She wondered how he knew such and why he'd answered the phone.

"Giovanni Martini?"

"Right again. You seem to know your music and your composers."

"Perhaps it was a fortuitous guess. Make my day and tell me you're calling to accept my invitation to play this lovely piano sitting in my parlor."

"Yes, I am, but I'm surprised to hear your voice. I expected to speak with Liz."

"She must have stepped away from her desk, and the marvels of modern technology flashed your name on my caller ID." Roderick paused. "I hope you prefer me to some computerized voice asking you to leave your name and number."

"Well, actually—" Caroline was about to respond when she heard a loud click and another voice on the line.

"I'm back at my desk now. I'll handle this call," Liz said.

"That's quite all right, Liz. Just carry on. I'm speaking with Miss Carlyle."

"But I can handle—"

"I'm sure you have other things to do, Liz."

A pause as Caroline held her breath. Then another click.

"And you were saying, Caroline?"

Interesting interchange. "I'm not sure what I was saying. But I did call to accept your invitation."

"Oh, that is splendid. Do you have a date in mind?"

"Yes, I do, and hopefully it will fit with your July schedule. My June schedule is so hectic, and then I start teaching again in August."

"I certainly hope you build in some time for fun and maybe something quite frivolous on occasion."

"Yes, I've scheduled some time to play in early August. What would the summer be without a vacation?" She wished her plans included some exotic beach, but Ferngrove was it.

"So, it's playtime in August. Now, about July?"

"I wasn't certain if you preferred a weekend afternoon recital or a weekday evening, but Thursday evening July twenty-first is best for me, as long as I get back Saturday evening to be here for Sunday morning church services."

"Wonderful timing. You'll fly up on Monday, the eighteenth. That'll give you a couple of days of rest and rehearsal. We'll plan the event for Thursday evening and your return flight for Saturday in time for your Sunday responsibilities. How does that sound?"

She was taken aback. Roderick Adair had taken complete control, and her two-day trip had turned into almost a week. "Let's see, that's almost a week I'll be gone. I had only planned on a couple of days."

"Are there commitments that would keep you from being away during that week?"

She looked at her calendar. "Nothing here, only some writing I need to do to meet a journal deadline."

"Well, then, it's settled. I'll set you up in a suite here where you can work and rehearse, and maybe the Kentucky bluegrass won't tempt you to look away from your computer screen too often. You might even take time for a few long walks. Do you like to fish?"

"Do I like to fish?" Caroline had grown up fishing with her brothers and missed it.

"There's a great little trout stream here on the property, and the trout fishing is better than average. Lilah will prepare what we catch."

"My goodness! Trout fishing, Kentucky bluegrass, and the piano. Doesn't sound much like work."

"Good, we'll make it a pleasurable time. I'll have Liz send the details of when and where the plane will be."

"Do you mean the plane ticket?"

"No ticket's necessary. I'll be sending my plane for you."

Caroline's jaw dropped. He was sending a private plane for her?

"Oh, would it be agreeable with you if I made a couple of requests for your program?"

She struggled to pull herself together. "That . . . that would be fine, as long as it's not Rachmaninoff. Remember?"

"I remember well—big heart, little hands. You'll know these pieces. They're standard repertoire. I'll call you in a few days."

"That's good. I'll look forward to that."

"Till then, 'Plaisir d'mour.'"

"Yes, joy and . . . Goodbye, Mr. Adair."
"Goodbye, Miss Carlyle."

—·—

Roderick put down the phone, walked to his window, and stared into a blue sky. After a second or two of contemplation, he huffed out a laugh. He was actually going to see Caroline Carlyle.

He had surprised himself. Ever since their phone call and his subsequent checking into her background, he'd found himself just a tiny bit enthralled with her. He'd received video recordings of two of her recitals and had found himself watching them repeatedly and thinking of her throughout the day. She was strikingly lovely, and her music reached him in places that had been untouched for years. She was so much like his mother . . .

He'd found himself pretty much determined he would get Caroline here and playing the piano. Her piano. What he thought he'd accomplish by that, he had no idea. But something had drawn him to her like a moth to a flame.

He shook his head. *I need to get a grip on reality. I don't know all I'd like to know about this woman, and I'd better be cautious. Well, July is coming, and you, Miss Caroline Carlyle, will be visiting Rockwater. I'll see if you're real or some made-up image I've concocted.*

And "Plaisir d'mour"? Another song about the pain of love. Pain or not, at least your music will be beautiful.

With a deep breath and a nod to himself, he turned his thoughts away from Caroline and back to work.

Chapter Nine

When Words Aren't Enough

———— ◆ ————

CAROLINE HAD ONLY A COUPLE OF HOURS TO WORK DOWN HER list before the entourage from Ferngrove arrived. She grabbed her purse and sailed out the studio door for Pollyana's Florist. The smell of carnations slapped her in the face as she opened the door to the business.

Why can't florist shops smell like roses? These carnations reek of funerals. "Good morning, Polly. I'm here to place the order."

"Must be recital time again." Polly stopped arranging the funeral spray, wiped her hands on her apron, and picked up pad and pencil.

"You're right. Don't know where the year went. But here I am again. I need a bundle of yellow daisies, two bundles of pink snapdragons, white irises, and one bundle of baby's breath. Could I pick those up in the morning around ten o'clock?"

"Sure. I'll have them ready for you by nine. You sure you don't want me to arrange them for you? Or is your mama coming again?"

Caroline knew Polly would turn as green as the leather-leaf fern thinking of what Delia Mullins would write in the *Moss Point Messenger* about Martha Carlyle's flowers and tea table. "Mama wouldn't miss the recital. She's convinced I couldn't pull it off without her. But we'll surprise her one of these years, won't we, Polly?"

Caroline quickly wrote a check, handed it to Polly, and bounced out the door for her next stop. She picked up Angel's laundry and stopped at the printers for the recital programs. Last stop: the Emporium for film. Then home.

She and the Pendergrass twins entered her driveway at the same time. They had the borrowed folding chairs from the Methodist church.

"Good morning, gentlemen. I didn't get back any too soon, did I?"

"No matter when you get here, Miss Caroline, you'd just be right on time. We got the chairs. We'll get 'em set up and then get outta your hair."

Caroline unlocked the studio door and put her purse on the desk as Ned and Fred trudged to the terrace with a double armload of chairs and stacked them against the wall. She followed them back to Ned's truck and reached for a folding chair on the truck bed.

Ned, standing behind her, took off his cap and scratched his head. "I don't mean to be nosy, but what'n the world you think you're doing?"

"I'm helping unload the chairs."

Fred took the folding chair from her and nodded to Ned.

"Now, Miss Caroline, that just ain't gonna happen today or no other day when me and Fred are around. Why, we cain't take no chances on mashing one of them pretty little fingers. You just go on inside and do your job. This job's for Fred and me. We'll have this done afore you can say 'scat.'"

She obliged them and headed to the studio. Before she reached the door, however, a blaring car horn announced the arrival of her mother, Betsy, and Josefina. Hugs and kisses were followed by a parade of coolers carrying homemade bread and Martha's pimiento cheese, carefully packed boxes of serving trays, and the punch bowl that had floated half a ton of ice rings and hundreds of gallons of Martha's punch over the last thirty-five years.

When the last box was unpacked and the food refrigerated, Caroline called the Café on the Square and ordered hamburgers for takeout. All day she had looked forward to a brown, greasy bag of Mabel's cheeseburgers and onion rings. Onion rings were one of several items not on the menu because Mabel cooked them only when she was in the mood.

"Hi, Mabel, it's Caroline, and I have company from Ferngrove. We're dying for your hamburgers and onion rings. Are you making onion rings tonight?"

"You say they're just dying for them?"

"Surely are. Sam and Angel are too."

"Well, I wasn't planning on frying onion rings tonight, but since you did so good playing for my cousin's funeral last month, I guess I'll fry some. How many hamburgers?"

But Caroline's thoughts had betrayed her and flashed back to Betsy's wedding—the day she had met David. After the late afternoon reception, he had asked her to join him for hamburgers at Chester's, a local hamburger shack down by the town lake. She'd known him only hours, but she didn't hesitate a moment in accepting his offer. They'd eaten hamburgers, greasy onion rings, and chocolate malts.

She had never met anyone else who shared her passion for chocolate malts.

Hours later, they'd accepted coffee from the manager and his invitation for them to continue their evening at the picnic tables down by the lake because it was well past closing time. They'd talked until two o'clock in the morning.

They had not known then that the evening would change their lives. Down by the lake, with hamburgers and greasy onion rings, had become their Ferngrove place.

Mabel was repeating herself. "Caroline? How many hamburgers? Or do you just want a bagful?"

Caroline jolted back to reality. Taking a slightly shaky breath, she counted silently. "I—I think about eight ought to do it?"

"That's a bagful. Eight it is, and two bags of onion rings. Guess since you got company, I'll just send my grandson over there when I get things ready."

"That's not necessary. I'll be glad to pick them up." Caroline had planned to take Betsy with her for the cultural experience. Athletic shoes, black spandex bike shorts stretched over narrow hips and muscular thighs, and an XX-Large orange T-shirt for her broad shoulders and overgrown bosom were Mabel's standard uniform, whether it was Friday night or Sunday lunch.

"Nope, I insist. He'll be there in about thirty minutes."

"Thanks, Mabel. You're the best."

———·———

Hamburgers delivered and eaten, the women held Sam to his promise of entertaining Josefina while the ladies played a game of cards—an annual event Angel and Martha had won for the last five years. Caroline waited for a while before breaking the news about her July trip to Kentucky. She hoped her mother's game concentration might squelch the inquisition.

She discarded the queen of spades. "Oh, Mama, did I tell you that I've been in touch with the man who owns my old piano?"

"No, you didn't, and why would you discard that queen when you could play it?"

"Oops, guess I missed that one," Caroline said, thinking her plan was working until she looked at Betsy.

Betsy lowered her reading glasses and looked at Caroline. "What's with you? We're never going to beat this duo if your mind's not on the game."

"Sorry, Betsy, I'll try to do better."

"Good. I'd really like to win."

Caroline continued. "Yes, this gentleman lives near Lexington. He purchased the piano from the dealer in Atlanta for forty-two thousand dollars. Slightly more than you and Dad paid, right, Mama?"

"Slightly." Martha never moved her eyes from her cards.

Caroline dropped the bomb. "I'm planning to go there in July."

Betsy's eyes flared. "You mean to Kentucky?"

"That would seem reasonable since that's where the piano is."

"So he's invited you to come and play?" Betsy inquired further.

"You might say that." Caroline gave Betsy the raised right eyebrow.

"Oh, that's quite nice. I know how much you want to play your piano again," Martha said, still studying the card game while Angel sat noticeably quiet during the whole interchange.

The plan worked. This kind of news needed to be delivered in stages.

"Hey, Angel, you want to go out?" Martha asked.

"Yeah, now's the time to go out. Caroline just picked up her foot, and Betsy's still playing her hand. That'll gig 'em." Angel didn't bother to count her cards.

"That's it! I'm done! You two have something shady going on here. What are the odds you'd win this game every time?" Caroline cared nothing for the game but enjoyed seeing Martha and Angel so happy.

"So, are we ready for the second part of the Friday-night-before-the-recital ritual?" Angel headed to the freezer. "Caroline, get out the bowls and get out the good stuff."

"You mean the stuff in the decanter that will make us sleep like Josefina?"

"Yeah, that stuff."

"I'm for it. Hey, Mama, you like peach brandy, don't you?"

"Sounds good to me."

"I'm not sure about you, Betsy. This stuff is potent and not what your doctor ordered." Caroline brought the bowls and decanter to the table.

"Well, let's see . . . If I can't have the good stuff, then I get double ice cream, right?"

"Any way you want it, little mama." Angel dipped the last scoop and held the decanter high before dousing the ice cream.

Saturday morning was a whirlwind with three generations of women involved in the recital bustle. Even Josefina helped by placing the printed programs on the chairs. At one o'clock, the preparations were done. All but Caroline went to the big house to dress for the three o'clock recital. She wanted a few minutes of quiet before the guests arrived.

On their way out the door, Betsy stopped. "Caroline, what are you wearing?"

"My navy suit and white blouse."

"Oh, how absolutely charming." Betsy rolled her eyes and motioned for Martha and Angel to follow her to Caroline's bedroom. "Would you ladies vote 'No' with me on the navy-blue suit?"

They raised their right hands and agreed.

Betsy opened the closet door and walked in. "You've got to be kidding. Everything in this closet is either navy or black."

After looking through her closet, they changed their votes. At least navy was brighter than black.

"Would you ladies join me in another vote? I think we should award Caroline the prize for having the neatest and most boring closet in the county, maybe even the state."

Again they raised hands in agreement.

Betsy thoughtfully rubbed her pregnant stomach. "Caroline, what size do you wear?"

"Six petite. Why?" Caroline was perplexed by all of this attention to her clothes.

"Six petite? Do you ladies think your closet would look like this if you were a six petite?"

"Not on your life." Angel twirled in her hibiscus-covered muumuu.

Martha said, "That's it. Angel, you're in charge. Next week, you are to take Caroline shopping. She needs some new summer clothes, something more colorful and more feminine."

"Yeah, something that a man would take a second look at." Betsy elbowed Caroline.

"Who wants a man who's only attracted to colorful clothes?" Caroline closed the closet door.

"It's packaging, Caroline . . . packaging."

"Why don't you package yourself and get out of here so that I can shower?" Caroline shooed them out the door and locked it.

———·———

Caroline entered the great room in a navy suit with her long dark hair pulled up and pinned loosely on top of her head. To calm and center herself, she went to the piano. It was another twenty or thirty minutes before her guests would start arriving. She had reached the middle section of Debussy's Arabesque no. 1, an old favorite, when the phone rang. She answered to a familiar voice.

"Caroline, this is Roderick Adair. I hope I'm not calling at a bad time."

"Oh, hello, Roderick. I was just playing the piano."

"It must be such a joy to just sit down and play."

"It is for me."

"Would you play if no one ever listened?"

What an odd question. "Why, yes, I would. I mean . . . I do. Most of my playing is done when no one is listening, when all of Moss Point is asleep."

"Oh, what a waste."

"It's not a waste if I enjoy what I'm doing or if it calms my nerves. That's why I was playing when you called. My spring recital starts in about twenty minutes, and I'm a bit uneasy until it's all over."

"I understand that, and I also understand that I've reached you at a rather inconvenient time. I called to make only two requests for your program here. Would you please play Debussy's Arabesque no. 1? It has always been a favorite of mine."

"I'd be pleased to honor your request, sir," Caroline responded without telling him it was one of her favorites and that she'd been playing it before she answered his call. "I've made note of that, but what about your second request?"

"Yes, I'd like you to sing 'Plaisir d'amour.'"

"Oh, I must think about that. Playing and singing? I either play well or I sing well, and if I try to do both, both will suffer."

"I hardly think that anyone would suffer listening to you, Caroline."

Not knowing how to respond, she bluffed. "Oh, I'm so sorry, but my doorbell is ringing. I'll think about your request."

"Good, that will give me another reason to call you."

"Goodbye, Roderick."

Well, that should help him peg me as an emotionally clumsy school-girl, she thought with a sigh. *I should have told him straight up I won't play and sing.*

She unplugged the phone and went back to the piano and finished the arabesque. This time the doorbell really did ring, and hand-wringing students and parents started trickling in. Guests took their seats, and students took their usual places in a section of chairs at the end of the room. Her mother, Betsy and Josefina, and Sam and Angel had their own little gallery on the opposite end of the room near the entrance to the kitchen.

She checked off the students and their families as they arrived and noted that Jay Johnson was not present.

Just as she was about to take her position in the curve of the piano for her traditional welcome and acknowledgments, the doorbell rang again. She opened the door to Polly, peeking between the stems of purple and yellow irises in a large crystal bowl draped with yellow silk ribbon. Assuming the florist was vying for equal space in Delia's column next week, she ignored the gift card nestled in the greenery and placed them on her desk. She was thanking Polly and seeing her to the door when two more guests arrived dressed in simple, homemade cotton dresses.

"Oh, hello, Mrs. Silva, I'm so glad you decided to come."

Gretchen whispered her apologies. "We're so sorry. We did not know there would be so many people. Maybe we should leave."

"Please come in. You'll enjoy the music and refreshments. And it's Bella, isn't it?"

"Yes, it is Bella," Mrs. Silva responded.

Caroline embarrassed herself by looking too long into the silvery green eyes of her new guests. "Bella, come, sit right here. They're almost front-row seats."

Gretchen grabbed Bella's arm. "Oh, no, we could not do that. Please. No, we would like to sit in the back."

"But Bella could see better up front."

"No, no." Gretchen led Bella to the very back row. Bella never spoke and clung to Gretchen until they took their seats.

With a smile, Caroline returned to the piano and made her welcoming speech. The program started with the youngest students. Except . . . Will Peterson, the first pianist, could not be found. His younger sister took pleasure in announcing to the crowd that her brother was in the bathroom. As if that pronouncement had called him, Will, with tie askew and white shirttail poking through his partially zipped fly, appeared and hurriedly slipped to the piano. He looked at the keyboard and moved not a muscle.

Caroline waited.

Will looked at her and got the raised right eyebrow in return. He looked back at the piano and still did not move a muscle.

Caroline approached the piano to rescue the seven-year-old boy. She rarely taught students under third grade but had made an exception in Will's case. All year long, his performance and progress had made her proud of her decision. As she stood next to him and shielded him from the eyes of the audience—mostly parents holding their breath and realizing this could be their child—Will poked his shirt inside his pants and zipped his fly.

Caroline reached over and straightened his tie. "You look great, Will, and your playing will be even better."

Will never looked up and sat frozen with his hands in his lap.

"Will, are you all right?" she whispered.

He gazed at her with flushed cheeks and big brown eyes fringed with lashes that a teenage girl would pay for. "Miss Caroline, where is middle C?"

Caroline disguised her chuckle and pointed out the key in question. As she walked to her seat, Will was playing at a lightning speed, finishing almost before she could sit down. He took his bow and, at the same tempo he had played his piece, sprinted to his seat next to his mother. The crowd applauded loudly to drown out their laughter, and Caroline called up the next student.

Before she knew it, the last student had played, and the race to the tea table began. The adults admired the display while the kids were quite taken with the fruit tray. Martha had cut a pineapple in half lengthwise, scooping out the flesh to create a bowl and leaving the greenery to become plumage. To the other end of the pineapple, she'd attached a peeled potato that had been soaked in yellow food coloring and carved to look like the head of a tropical bird. The adults thought it too beautiful to eat, but the boys delighted in spearing the melon balls, grapes, and strawberries with the fancy toothpicks and eating the entrails of this pineapple parrot.

As the party wound down and guests departed, Linda Johnson appeared in the middle of the room. Caroline had worried that Jay did not show, so seeing Linda was a relief. "Linda, we missed Jay. Is everything all right?"

"Caroline, I am so sorry. I don't know what to say. We just couldn't get Jay to come. I don't know what's going on with him! We seem to have lost control."

"It's not so uncommon for students to get last-minute jitters, but Jay knew his piece so well. He would have made himself and me look good."

"I don't know. It's more than jitters. He's a good kid, but lately he's turned into a little monster. He's not doing well in school, he's started lying, and lately he's been slipping out of the house at night."

"I had no idea things were so serious."

"Serious enough we're looking for a child psychologist. I've told Jay he will not be allowed to continue his piano lessons until he apologizes to you himself."

"Oh, I'm sure he'll do better over the summer. He'll be ready to start back in the fall."

"I hope so, for all our sakes. Anyway, I just had to come and tell you what happened and tell you again how sorry we are."

"Apology accepted, and I'm glad you came. Stay and make my mother happy by having something to eat."

The crowd dwindled. Gretchen and Bella were the last to leave. Caroline kept her eye on them and realized they'd had no interchange with anyone else in the room. She was standing at the door when they approached with Bella still clinging to Gretchen's arm and standing slightly behind her. Gretchen graciously and articulately thanked Caroline for allowing them to come. She mentioned many of the names of the pieces and recalled growing up listening to her grandmammá play them in the old country. Bella never spoke.

Watching as they walked silently away together, Caroline sensed a real story behind those silvery green eyes, their meekness, and Gretchen's obvious knowledge and appreciation of music.

Caroline sent Sam and Josefina to the big house to finish watching *The Jungle Book* while the cleanup started. Ned and Fred, arriving like clockwork, removed the chairs and returned them to the church. They didn't refuse to take Martha's platter of goodies with them.

Another Saturday-afternoon spring recital. Students wringing their hands, mothers holding their breaths, and fathers wishing they'd been fishing. She had seen her mother glowing from the compliments. Caroline realized once again why she spent her time teaching.

Caroline's mother, Betsy, and Josefina accompanied her to church, followed by lunch at Café on the Square. Mabel had promised to hold them a table and plenty of fried chicken.

Sam sat at the head of the table. "Well, I do believe that was the best recital yet."

Angel swallowed her bit of macaroni and cheese before agreeing. "Yep, another fine one. And you girls remember, Martha and I are still the 'Hand and Foot' champions, and we're a bit disappointed you didn't provide a trophy or something. I think we need to up the stakes next year. It's high time the losers pay."

"Just get 'em a plaque, would you?" Sam pointed his knife at Martha. "All right, Martha. I'm taking a right turn in this conversation, but I think it's an appropriate question for a cook with a biscuit pan no one is allowed to touch. What do you think of Mabel's fried chicken?"

"Well, let me put it like this, Sam: Mabel's fried chicken would make you slap your own grandma. And from the looks of that chicken leg in Josefina's hand, I think she would agree."

"That good, huh?"

"Her fried chicken is up to par—par being my fried chicken, of course. But I'd like to challenge her chicken and dumplings."

"Sounds like a trial to me, and consider me the self-appointed judge," Sam said.

They finished their meal, and Sam grabbed the check from Caroline.

"No, Sam, this is my party."

"You're wrong, dear. It *was* your party, but now it's mine."

"Thank you, Sam." Caroline hugged him, knowing that arguing with Sam was like arm-wrestling with Mabel.

As they walked to their cars, Betsy said, "Before we get away, Angel, remember that you promised to take Caroline shopping. You won't forget our discussion, will you?"

"What discussion?" Caroline raised her right eyebrow.

"In due time, Caroline, in due time." Angel grinned at Martha and Betsy as they took their seats in the car. They drove to the studio, and Caroline helped load Betsy's car with silver trays, leftovers, luggage, and the not-to-be-forgotten punch bowl. She waved goodbye, glad they had come and grateful now to be alone. Almost before they'd pulled out, she'd undressed and put on her robe to nap for a couple of hours on the sofa.

She woke to the comfort of her quiet studio. Needing a lift, she headed for the kitchen to put on the teakettle. She dropped a teabag of Darjeeling into her favorite cup and headed to the desk for her day planner.

The irises—she had forgotten the irises Polly delivered yesterday. She laughed to herself. *Got to give it to Polly. She's counting on free advertising.*

Caroline parted the stems to remove the card and take it from its envelope. It read "Music . . .when words aren't enough. Enjoy what you have created in your students. Roderick Adair."

She sat down at her desk, running her fingers over the card and savoring the irises. *How did he know? And how did he get them delivered before the recital?*

"'When words aren't enough'?" She was smiling when the teakettle whistled.

Chapter Ten

Deductions, Drapes,
and Dresses

———————•———————

S AM KNEW HOW TO TAKE HIS SABBATH: HIBERNATING IN THE library napping and reading the paper. Still, he heard Angel walk down the hall toward the kitchen. "Did you talk to Caroline this afternoon?"

"Was I supposed to?"

"Well, yes. I don't think she should stay in the studio this evening."

"Oh, that's right. I'll give her a call. Would you like something to drink?"

"What about a tall glass of water with a big bowl of ice cream? Maybe Caroline would join us."

Angel called Caroline from the kitchen phone. "Hey, sweetie, Sam and I are about to have a scoop of ice cream with the peach brandy. How about joining us?"

"Sounds great. I'll bring the cookie tin."

"You mean you still have cookies?"

"Angel, I'll have cookies until GiGi Nelson lets her red hair go gray."

Angel chuckled. "That long, huh? Bring your nightgown, and you and I'll play Scrabble when Sam turns in early tonight."

"Would you like me to bring some pimiento cheese sandwiches?"

"Mabel's fried chicken is still clucking for Sam and me, so we're eating light. Besides, we're old enough to have ice cream for supper. I'm dipping it now."

"I'm on my way."

"Sam, get yourself in here. I've dipped the ice cream and Caroline's on her way," Angel yelled after she hung up, not realizing that Sam was standing in the kitchen.

"This fast enough?"

She squeaked as she whirled around. "Sam Meadows, I do hope you enjoyed turning my one last gray hair white. I didn't hear you come in here."

"You mean after all these years, you can't sense my presence when I enter the room?"

"I've never had to do that. Your voice generally precedes you. Put the ice cream on the table, and I'll get the ice water."

"You know, with all the excitement, we haven't been thinking too much about this intruder problem. I've had conversation with Caleb, and we need to talk seriously with Caroline. I promised Rogers Carlyle that I would take care of Caroline, and I intend to keep my word."

———•———

Caroline hoped Sam was up for a conversation. She had some ideas about this intruder, and holding them inside was like holding her breath. She popped through the kitchen door about the time Angel grabbed the decanter of peach brandy.

"Just in time," Angel said.

"Didn't want to keep Sam waiting. He gets fussy when he has to wait for his ice cream." Caroline took her place at the breakfast table.

Angel shook out her napkin. "Seems like we need to have a blessing or something. I mean, this is your supper, Sam."

Sam prayed his usual prayer in oratorical King James English, and before the "n" on "Amen" had stopped resonating, he asked, "Where's your bag? Didn't see it when you came in."

"I didn't bring it."

"Now, Caroline, I just think you're much safer up here. Why, Angel and I'd hear the chimes from the grandfather clock every half hour wondering if you're safe."

"Then you'll sleep much better tonight because I know who this Peeping Tom is, and I can assure you I'm in no danger."

Sam put down his spoon. "I'm all ears."

"I learned a very interesting bit of information Saturday afternoon. You remember Jay Johnson didn't show."

"I remember, but I saw his mother there." Angel rationed drops of peach brandy over the ice cream.

"Yeah, Linda came late and sat out on the terrace until the recital was over, and then she came in to explain that Jay refused to come."

"What do you mean 'he refused to come'? He's eleven years old. The way I look at it is eleven-year-olds don't have refusing privileges. That's what's wrong with this country—unruly children controlling things. Seen enough of those in my courtroom to prove my point."

"Sam, shush and let Caroline finish."

"Linda says Jay's been giving them a hard time. Getting in trouble at school. He's started lying to them, and they think he's been slipping out at night."

"So, you think that Jay is our culprit?"

"He could be. Jay's a gifted musician with a good ear. He'll struggle to learn a new piece until I play it for him. But once I play it for him, he plays it near perfectly. And then Linda said they've caught him slipping out at night, and they don't know where he goes."

"Adolescent boys are curious, all right, but I can't quite figure why he'd come through the fence and just sit there," Sam said. "Maybe he has a crush on you."

Caroline reached for a cookie. "Well, I've thought about it. I think it's just a safe place for him to come and hide when he slips out at night. Jay may be curious, but he's not the bravest kid I know."

"Pass me a cookie please." Sam took one out of the tin. "Okay, I might buy this theory, but answer this: why did he come into your studio in the middle of the morning, play your piano, and then run out when you came home?"

"I think he was skipping school and needed a place to hide. Then he ran out to keep from getting into trouble."

"I don't know." Sam hem-hawed. "I'm not sure I buy all of this. Does he really play the piano that well?"

"Yes, he plays well—maybe well enough to play what I heard."

Angel swallowed her last bite of ice cream. "You would be the only one to know that. So what do we do?"

"Don't move so fast down that track, Angel. I'm not convinced. Caleb still has his eye on Bo Blossom."

"But what makes Caleb think it might be Bo?" Caroline asked.

"The same things that made us suspicious from the beginning. Bo's lived here for years, and no one knows his real name or anything about his background. Not one person in this town has ever had a meaningful conversation with him. Caleb had the deputy keep an eye on him for a few evenings, but Bo gave the deputy the slip every time. It's like he disappears into thin air come dark."

Angel pointed her spoon at Caroline. "So, here's where we are. Caroline, you think it's an eleven-year-old student." She pointed at Sam. "And Sam, you think it's the hobo from only God knows where. But we do know a few things about this intruder."

"Would you listen to that approach? My wife should have been the judge. She's right. So, what do we know?"

Caroline perked up. "We do know he's caused no one harm, and he's not destroyed or stolen any property. He plays the piano very well, and it seems he's very persistent."

Sam piped in. "We also know he's strong enough to rip boards off the fence, and that he's not afraid of the dark."

"And don't forget, we know that Ned and Fred scared the living daylights out of him last week," Angel said.

Caroline looked at Sam. "I think I was in more danger with you and the deputy and the Pendergrass twins than I am with this Peeping Tom."

"Can't argue with that, can you, Your Honor?" Angel shook her finger at Sam.

"Sustained."

They stacked the ice cream bowls, and Caroline convinced Sam and Angel she'd be safe in the studio. She promised to lock the doors—and no playing the piano after dark.

———.———

The last thing Caroline and Angel had done before Caroline left was make plans to go shopping this coming week. Monday was good, so Monday it was. They'd look at some window coverings for the studio. But Angel was really making good on her promise to shop for new clothes for Caroline.

She stood at the back-porch door and watched Caroline until she made the curve around the daylilies. She looked forward to the shopping trip. Caroline was the daughter she had always wanted.

Her eyes brimmed with tears and she gave a shaky sigh. She hadn't expected to still be grieving over her barrenness when she was eighty-four.

Sam joined her on the porch, standing silently beside her. He slipped his arm around her shoulder. Angel moved closer in a familiar way and looked up at him.

"Now, what's behind those tears, my love?"

"Oh, just thinking about the children we couldn't have." The spit-and-polished veneer of her smiling face could not cover her wounded heart all the time.

Sam put both arms around her and pulled her even closer so

that her soft white hair brushed his chin. "I'm so sorry, my Angel, but God took our sadness to heart and brought us Caroline."

"Yes, He did."

Angel kept her thoughts of Caroline's future to herself. Holding Caroline here in Moss Point was like holding a breeze in a bag. She wanted Caroline to be happy, even if it meant moving away. After all, how many more years could she and Sam have?

———·———

Monday morning's visit to her closet for something to wear confirmed Betsy was right: her wardrobe was as bland as unsalted grits. She was glad for the shopping trip, even if Angel's interest was in curtains to cover the studio windows. She couldn't imagine looking at floral draperies instead of the light coming through the garden. Maybe she could distract Angel with clothes shopping and lunch until their time ran out.

Clothes had long lost their place on Caroline's want list. Dress slacks and cotton blouses were her teaching uniform and her out-and-about clothes. Her black and navy suits clothed her for church services and funerals. Her black formal wear was standard for performances. A couple pairs of jeans and sweaters for the winter and some shorts and T-shirts for the summertime rounded out her wardrobe.

The time had come. After all, she couldn't embarrass a man who would send her yellow irises, and she had no clothes for fishing in a trout stream. Her problem was she had no idea what to buy. Where was Betsy when she needed her?

Absurd. She didn't need Betsy. After all, this wasn't the prom.

———·———

Angel surveyed the mall parking lot. "Oh, let's park at the south entrance."

"But the fabric store and the other places where we can look at window coverings are at the other end of the mall." Here was

Caroline's chance to avoid the dreaded drapes, and she was about to miss it.

"That's okay. The walking will do us good."

Caroline parked, and they walked to the entrance. They would pass at least ten dress shops walking through the mall. Game playing was against Caroline's nature, and her guilt was growing.

"Let's stop here. How convenient! A coffee shop next to the bathroom," Angel said. "The cookies look good. Let's get us a couple—energy for shopping. Shopping's hard work, you know."

"Oooo, those chocolate ones with the coconut look good. I can take or leave the pies and cakes, but cookies . . . no, ma'am." Caroline purchased the cookies, and they found a table and sat down.

Angel took a bite. "It's just not fair. You eat cookies, and you wear a six. I eat cookies? I wear a sixteen."

"Oh, Angel, but that sixteen looks so good on you. I mean, you have style, flair. You still turn heads."

"Muumuus with bright yellow parrots on a white-haired fire hydrant will make heads turn." They both laughed. "I had so much fun buying clothes back when I was your size. And I truly was about your size until I hit fifty. Enjoy it, girl."

"So, let's see, you're saying I'm good for another twenty years?" She licked the melted chocolate from her finger.

"Yep, after that you'd be on a fool's errand to reach for leather belts and blue jeans. Elastic takes care of the belts, and large gray sweat suits replace the jeans. And muumuus are my favorite. You'd better get busy and enjoy it while you can." Angel folded the tissue away from the rest of her cookie.

"You know, I think you're right. Maybe we could dart into one of these dress shops."

"Sounds like just what we ought to do. I think I could locate something that's calling your name. Anything in particular you're looking for?"

"Well, I have this trip to Kentucky coming up." She wiped the last crumb from her mouth.

"Seems like I remember you saying something about that. A recital on your piano you haven't seen in years. Well, now, that certainly calls for a new dress."

"Among other things," Caroline said under her breath, wading in a bit deeper.

"What did you say?"

"I said, 'Among other things.'" Caroline paused. "Angel, I think I've lost my mind."

"What in the world are you talking about, child? We're just talking about buying a dress, and now you've lost your mind?"

"I think I have. I've been dying to tell someone, but the time hasn't been right. Roderick Adair is sending his plane to get me. I'm doing the recital. Oh, and I'm staying at Rockwater and going trout fishing. And by the way, he sent yellow irises."

"Whoa, slow down, now. Wait a minute. You're right, either you're losing your mind or I'm losing my hearing. Run that by me again, a bit slower this time."

"Okay, I'll start again. You know I called the Atlanta dealer who purchased my piano from Kelly Whitman. He sold the piano to a man who lives in Kentucky, but he couldn't give me the man's name and contact information because of privacy issues."

"Aha, I get that part. Go on."

"Well, the dealer offered to help by giving the purchaser my name and contact information and by telling him my story. I didn't hear a word for a few weeks, and then I got a call from this Roderick Adair. He left a message and apologized for not calling sooner. He had been out of the country on business."

"Out of the country?" Angel caught herself. "I'm sorry. I'm interrupting your story."

"Well, I returned his call, and he invited me to come and play the piano. It's sitting in the parlor of his home in Lexington, Kentucky, and no one plays it."

"No one? Does that mean this Roderick Adair doesn't have a family?"

"Don't know. But anyway, he invited me to do a recital while I'm there, and I said I would. He asked me to call Liz back with some possible dates."

"Liz? Who is this Liz?"

Caroline frowned. "I thought she might be his wife, but now I think it's his secretary or assistant or housekeeper. Oh, Angel, I don't know who she is, but she's arrogant and unpleasant. And he instructed me to call her back to make the arrangements."

"So, did you call?"

"Yes, but he answered the phone. And before I hung up, we had set a date, and he was making plans to send the plane after me."

"What do you mean he's sending a plane?"

"Yeah, my question too. At first I thought he meant plane tickets, but it's his plane. And not only that, but he's insisting I stay longer. Now my overnight trip has turned into a week."

"A week? You mean seven days?"

"Yes, nearly. I'll be staying in his house so that I'll have adequate practice time. He said to bring riding clothes and that if I liked to fish, there was a trout stream on the property."

"Horseback riding, trout fishing, a recital? Sounds like something I read in a romance novel. And you're not kidding, are you, sweetie?"

"No, Angel, this is for real. He even called back and asked if he could make a couple of suggestions for my program, and of course I agreed."

"Well, certainly, if the man is sending his plane, the least you can do is to play his favorite song." Angel played with the corner of her napkin and smiled like a woman who'd lived a long time and knew things. "Let's see. You're going to fly to Kentucky in a private plane. You're doing a recital on a piano you haven't played in years. You're spending a week with a man in his home, neither of which you've ever seen. You'll be riding horses and trout fishing in a Kentucky stream. Why, Caroline, your adventurous streak is returning! I'm proud of you."

"You don't think I'm crazy?"

"Why, no, I don't think you're crazy. Especially after I get Sam to check him out."

"Can Sam do that?" Caroline propped her elbows on the Formica tabletop.

"Of course, and he will. He'll find out if what this man is telling you is the truth. Then we'll all feel better that he's not a pervert who lures beautiful pianists to his lair."

"Oh, Angel, what in the world would Mama and Dad say?"

Angel shook her head. "You don't want to hear it, so don't tell them yet. Not until Sam checks him out. Besides, you are a full-grown woman, capable of making good choices."

"You're so wise." Caroline was relieved that she might find out something about Mr. Adair and that she didn't need to tell her parents yet. "Come to think of it, he knows about me. I wonder how he did that."

"Haven't you heard of the telephone and the internet?"

"Guess it's not that hard."

"Of course. If he is a man of means, as it appears that he is, he wouldn't think of inviting you into his home and risking embarrassment in front of his friends if he didn't know something about you. Only a fruitcake or a psychopath would do that. So that's why we have to tell Sam."

"No argument from me. Oh, I almost forgot. He called about half an hour before the recital. I explained it wasn't a good time to talk because of arriving guests. Then just as the recital started, the yellow and purple irises arrived with a card that read 'Music. . . when words aren't enough.' How did he get that done so quickly?"

"Girl, I know Moss Point is slightly south of a city, but there are ways." Angel shook her head. "Polly."

"Yes, but flowers within half an hour? And I don't even want to consider what Polly thinks and what she'll be telling everyone in town."

"Too late for worrying about that. How old do you think this Roderick Adair is?"

"Can't tell. But he has a baritone voice and speaks like a southern gentleman."

"Well, I'll assume he's just the right age, single, loves music, handsome as the devil, and has his values, purpose in life, and priorities all lined up like my kitchen canisters."

Caroline raised her right eyebrow. "And just what does that have to do with anything?"

"If all that's true, then I think you need a recital gown that'll make you look like you just floated in from some distant star, and a few new dresses for dinner in the evenings, maybe a red strapless with a sheer shawl. Come on, I know just the place to find a dress with your name on it."

Undeterred, Angel was on a roll. "Let's see, you'll need a pair of jeans for riding, a pair of khaki shorts and a fishing vest, and maybe a department store makeup makeover, and—"

"Wait just a minute. I'm not so sure about all this. I do have clothes, remember."

"Yes, I've seen them. Come on, Caroline; let's go find the dress with your name on it."

They walked arm in arm, chattering all the while, as Angel led them into her favorite shop. Angel stopped to greet a sales clerk. "So good to see you, Mrs. Kramer. You always knew exactly the dress I needed, whether it was for a ball or a political event or a cruise vacation."

"Oh, I remember, Mrs. Meadows. I dressed you for years, and you were always a joy."

"Thank you. Now my friend, Caroline, needs a showstopper of a dress for a piano recital."

"Come with me. I have several for such an occasion."

They followed Mrs. Kramer to the back room. The room's

furnishings communicated class: fresh flowers, peach-colored walls to warm pasty complexions, floral-patterned upholstered chairs, mirrored walls, and coffee and cookies served on a Queen Anne's table.

Mrs. Kramer seated Angel. She took Caroline's hand, led her up the riser in front of the mirror, and twirled her around studying her body shape and size.

"Six? Or six petite?"

"Six petite."

"Oh, that's too bad. I have just the gown for you, but it's not a petite. Let me bring a few for you to see." She disappeared through a rear door.

Angel grinned looking at Caroline's raised right eyebrow. Caroline took the chair next to Angel and eyed the cookies.

Mrs. Kramer returned with a black gown that Angel quickly nixed, a blue gown with beading that was a possibility, a red gown Angel knew would be a knockout but Caroline dismissed, and an emerald green that got the let's-try-on-the-blue-one-first response.

Caroline tried on the blue. "With this, I could wear the blue topaz necklace and earrings David gave me."

"No, Caroline, this dress won't do even if it is the color of your eyes." She didn't want Caroline thinking about jewelry that David had given her.

"What about the emerald-green one?"

Mrs. Kramer quickly stepped in. "Well, no doubt that color would be striking on you with your dark hair, but I think it's one of those dresses that looks better on the hanger."

"What she's trying to say, sweetie, is that this dress is not one of those dresses you wear. It wears you."

"Oh, Mrs. Meadows, you always did have that eye," Mrs. Kramer said. Then turning to Caroline, she explained, "You really want the people to see you first, not the dress. You want people to say, 'Isn't she absolutely stunning?' not 'Would you look at that gorgeous dress?'"

"Oh." Caroline stepped down from the riser feeling like a schoolgirl who had just been scolded.

"Mrs. Kramer, what about the first one that came to your mind, the perfect dress that's not a petite? Do you still have that miracle-working alterations lady?"

"Oh, yes, she's still here and still working miracles."

"Lord knows she had to alter everything I ever bought in here. They don't make gowns for five-foot barrels."

Mrs. Kramer smiled and sailed through the rear door again. In moments she returned with the dress. It was icy pink, the color of cotton candy. The bodice, with a scooped neck, was fitted and covered with delicate swirls of tiny seed pearls. The long, full, and flowing sleeves of a sheer icy-pink georgette crepe fell to the pearl-laden cuffs. Multiple layers of the same sheer fabric oozed from the waistline and draped to perfection.

Angel broke the silence. "She'll try it on."

Caroline raised her right eyebrow again but followed Mrs. Kramer to the fitting room. In a few minutes she returned and stepped up on the riser in front of the mirrors.

"See, it's just like I told you. You'll look like you've floated into the room from some distant rosy star. I can only imagine what you'll look like, sitting at the piano with puddles of pink rippling around you and those sleeves swaying as you play. It's your dress, Caroline."

"But, Angel, the sleeves, and it's too long."

"Mrs. Kramer, get the seamstress."

The clerk slipped once again through the rear door and reappeared with Matilda. Matilda adjusted and pinned the sleeves and the skirt's hem and commented on how lucky she was the bodice didn't need altering.

Mrs. Kramer patted the seamstress on the back. "Hemming the sleeves and the skirt will be a snap for Matilda. Don't worry."

"This is it. The color is perfect. Shows off your blue eyes. Oh, and the contrast with your hair. Oh . . . hair. Why, we have to get

Gracie to give you a new 'do, and we have to shop for a push-up bra."

"Angel, this is all a bit much, don't you think?" Caroline stepped down from the riser.

"Nope, I'd say it's a bit perfect."

Caroline started toward the dressing room.

"Caroline?"

Caroline stopped, turning her head to look at Angel over her left shoulder.

"Caroline, the dress truly is yours, just like your Hazelton Brothers piano."

As Caroline went to change, she couldn't help but wonder what Roderick Adair might think when he saw her sitting in this pink gown at her piano—his piano.

Chapter Eleven

A Melody of Change in the Air

———— • ————

CAROLINE AND ANGEL RETURNED HOME WITH A CAR FILLED with boxes and bags, none of which contained window coverings. Caroline was secretly glad. But she noticed Angel was unusually tired and a bit winded as she climbed the porch steps. "Let me go to the studio and grab the pimiento cheese and toss a quick salad. You don't need to be making supper."

Angel gratefully accepted. She was pouring the iced tea when Caroline stepped through the kitchen door. Angel's animated spirit returned during table conversation when she began to tell Sam about the upcoming trip to Kentucky.

Caroline couldn't judge Sam's reaction about Roderick Adair. Years on the courtroom bench had trained him to conceal his feelings. But he agreed to do a check on Mr. Adair and would start the process tomorrow.

"Caroline, we didn't finish our conversation last night," he said.

"Which one?"

"We all laid our suspicions about your intruder on the table, and then we made no decisions about what to do with the information."

"I don't think we can do anything right now, Sam. I certainly can't speak with Linda Johnson about this and imply that Jay may be involved."

Sam nodded in agreement. "And it's not wise to involve Caleb in that scenario either. We're talking about a child here. I'll just ask Caleb to continue keeping his eye on Bo. Maybe it's time to consider clearing that land on the other side of the fence, Angel."

Caroline wiped her mouth and spoke with the last bite of pimiento cheese sandwich in her mouth. "Oh, Sam, you don't want to do that." She quickly swallowed. "It's a haven for birds and ducks and rabbits and an occasional deer and such beautiful trees. That land's been in your family for nearly two centuries, and it's the only wooded area left inside the city limits. I really hate to see you do that."

"And it's become a perfect hiding place for someone up to no good. Caleb looked over the area and found lots of beer cans and liquor bottles and a makeshift little shack down next to a ravine in the thickest part of the woods."

Caroline raised both eyebrows. "A shack?"

"Yep, and the deputy found the remains of some campfires. Fires get to be dangerous."

"Probably teenagers. They must have somewhere to do their mischief," Angel said.

"We've thought for years about turning it into a park. Clean up the underbrush, create hiking and biking trails, put in some picnic tables, and turn it into a place for good use by good folks. Of course, it would have to be rezoned, and that process could take a while."

"The surrounding neighbors would have to agree," Angel said.

"I don't think that'll be a problem. Mrs. Hendricks would be elated. She's been fussing about the deer wandering onto her property and eating her flowers for years. The Morgans wouldn't mind. They'd probably be glad Eric could ride his bicycle through the park to his piano lessons. Old man Silva might give us a problem."

"Ernesto Silva? He's mad with the world. Just ignore him," Angel said.

"You can tell a fool by the big, fat lumps on his head. Do you see lumps on my head? You can't just ignore him. He's just the kind waiting to sue somebody."

"Silva. Does he have a wife named Gretchen and a daughter named Bella?" Caroline asked.

"I don't know," Sam said. "He had a wife, but I don't know how he could have kept her, and I don't know about any children. They stick pretty much to themselves."

"Yes, I think they have a daughter, but she should be grown by now. I remember seeing her years ago when she was younger. An absolutely beautiful child—got all her mother's coloring," Angel said.

"Hmm, I have an appointment on Wednesday with Gretchen Silva. She has a young girl named Bella who wants to study piano with me."

Sam got up for the tea pitcher. "Just hope Ernesto doesn't come with them."

"Mrs. Silva brought Bella to the recital."

"Were they the pair who came in late and sat on the back row?" Angel said.

"Yep, dressed in cotton dresses almost alike."

"So that was Gretchen Silva. My, she's aged since I saw her last. I remember when she came to town."

Sam sat back down with the tea pitcher. "Talk about an unlikely pair. Ernesto's as rough as a cob, and his wife was a beautiful blonde, seemingly more refined. She spoke very little English. I think maybe she was German."

"Good eye for details there, Judge," Angel added.

Sam winked at Angel. "And blondes."

"That makes sense. She told me that her grandmammá used to play the piano in the old country."

"Let's see, we've talked about private-eye work, park-building issues, and now we've gone to Europe. You ladies are as hard to keep on track as Uncle Ross's old mule."

Angel looked at him over the top of her glasses. "You'd better quit right there, sir. Mules don't fix your dinner and wash the dishes."

"Excuse me, ladies. I don't know what gets into me sometimes."

"I do, but I dare not say," Angel said.

"All right. Let's agree on a few things here. I need to know what my assignments are. Now, Caroline, you want me to do some checking on Roderick Adair?"

"Only if it's not too much trouble."

"And if I understood you, neither of us is going to mention to anyone the possibility that Jay Johnson is our intruder—or our snooper, as Ned says."

"That's right. I just don't think I'm ready to take that step," Caroline said.

"Well, you're probably right. Heading down that path, especially if it's the wrong one, could be like tapping a beehive with my walking stick. All we'll do at this point is to have Caleb continue to keep an eye on Bo."

Caroline nodded. "Agreed."

"Now, about this park idea. I'd like you both to think about what I said. I like the idea myself, but I know sometimes my ideas are like a whole armload of nothing. But what I like better is keeping you two ladies happy."

"Sam Meadows, you should have been a politician. I don't have to think about it. I'm already planning the landscaping. A park would be something quite nice to leave the town."

"Leave the town?" Caroline didn't like the sound of that. "You're not going anywhere."

"Now, Caroline, when you're eighty-four, you'll understand."

"I don't like the tone of this conversation, so I think it's time to wash the dishes and head to the studio." Caroline cleaned up quickly, gave Sam a hug and kissed Angel on the cheek, and headed down the stone path to the studio.

As usual, she had several phone messages. Tandy Yarbrough was frantic. Betsy was curious about Kentucky. Mrs. Silva confirmed their appointment on Wednesday. And Patricia Cunningham left her number. Caroline hadn't heard from Patricia in a couple of years.

Caroline dialed Mrs. Silva's number first. It rang several times before she answered with a weak hello.

"Hi, Mrs. Silva. This is Caroline Carlyle returning your call."

"Oh, yes, hello, Miss Carlyle. Thank you," Mrs. Silva whispered.

Caroline heard a gruff voice in the background.

"Who the hell is that calling this late?"

Caroline quickly looked at the clock. It was only ten after eight.

"It's a telemarketer. I'll get rid of him."

"Well, just tell that telemarketer where to stick that telephone."

"I'm sorry, Miss Carlyle, could I call you back tomorrow? I just want to confirm our Wednesday morning appointment time at ten o'clock."

"I'll see you and Bella at ten on Wednesday. No need to call back."

"Thank you and good night."

She was getting a clearer picture of the Silvas. She dialed Betsy next, and Mason answered.

"Hi, Mason, it's Caroline."

"Is this the old CC who tickles the ivories and sings sad love songs?"

"Yes, would you like me to sing you one?" Before he could answer, she sang the beginning phrase of "Plaisir d'amour."

"Stop, stop, please. I'll get Betsy."

"Thought that would get you moving."

"It may take a minute; she and Josefina and Booger were just about to go swimming."

"Swimming? Isn't it a bit cool?" Caroline twirled the pencil between her fingers.

"Are you kidding? No, and besides, it's the best way to get Josefina calmed down so she'll go to sleep. And Booger's mama needs the exercise. She's growing a baby and an acre of butt."

"Mason, I don't know why Betsy loves you. You are wretched." Caroline sang the second phrase.

"Okay, okay, I'm really going this time. And don't you tell her what I said about her butt."

Caroline could hear him stomping through the house on his way to the pool. "Betsy, it's Caroline."

Betsy persuaded Mason to watch Josefina while she talked to Caroline. "Hi, CC, what are you up to?"

"Oh, just the normal barhopping and mud wrestling."

"Hey, sounds like more fun than you've had in years. Keep it up." Betsy laughed.

"You'll actually be happy to know that I went shopping today. I bought the dress."

"The dress? Would that happen to be the dress for the Kentucky recital?"

"Yep."

"Is it black or navy?"

"Yep."

"Caroline Carlyle, I knew I should never have left Moss Point before taking you shopping. You need me, the professional shopper that I am, 'cause you're clueless."

"Yep, you're right. But Angel went along. And you can thank her. The dress is icy pink, and she insisted on a push-up bra."

"Wow, you're living dangerously, CC."

"And she helped me pick out a couple of cocktail dresses, a pair of tight jeans, and three new shirts. And I bought new makeup, and I'm going for a new 'do."

"I don't believe my ears. Or maybe it's you I don't believe. I won't ask if it's Roderick Adair who might have inspired this change."

"Is that Josefina crying?" Caroline changed the subject.

"Sounds like that man-child I married just splashed our little princess, and she's unhappy. They may need a referee. Got to go, CC. Love you."

"You too, friend."

Next call to make. Caroline did not recognize the area code for Patricia Cunningham's number. Maybe she had moved again. Remembering Patricia was like walking down a long corridor of doors, all of which Caroline had closed. Now she was reopening this one, a room of painful and yet tender memories.

Patricia and her former husband, Robert, had been one of Moss Point's most promising young couples when Caroline moved to town. Robert was a banker, and Patricia was a stay-at-home mom and a professional volunteer for church and community activities. They had a young son, Robbie, who became one of Caroline's first piano students. Robert and Pat had befriended Caroline and introduced her to parents of other potential students.

Robbie was an energetic and bright eight-year-old. She remembered the first time she saw the bruising on his arms and legs. She'd followed him to Patricia's car that fall afternoon and bragged on Robbie's lesson. "Are you beating this child to make him practice?" she teased. "If you are, it's working, but you're leaving lots of bruises."

She'd never forget how embarrassed and ashamed she'd felt about that statement when she learned Robbie had been diagnosed with leukemia and begun months of treatment. She had kept him engaged with the piano by taking a keyboard to his hospital bedside. They worked on songs together. When there was little doubt that Robbie would die, she'd told him about David's death and played what she had written of "David's Song" for him. He was the only person, with the exception of the intruder, who had ever heard this composition.

She was amazed at how Robbie accepted his illness, the medical treatments, and his impending death. He told her that somebody had to be Robbie, and God had chosen him. He grew tired of the needles and the medicine but rarely complained.

Their long talks helped with her own grief. They talked of what heaven must be like. They spoke of dying as another stage of living. She had never had those thoughts before, but they came spontaneously as she talked to Robbie. She told him dying was like passing from infancy into childhood, and from childhood into adolescence, and from adolescence into adulthood. Just another stage of life. She prayed it was so.

She believed in heaven. Yet with her unanswered questions, she'd wondered why she was the one to walk this journey with Robbie.

Robbie died within six months of his diagnosis, and Caroline cried. She wept over David. And for herself.

And the tears flowed for Robbie's grieving family. She had watched the months of treatment and Robbie's death pulling the strings of Robert and Patricia's relationship so taut they finally snapped. Their relationship ended in divorce. Robert stayed in Moss Point until he could be transferred to another bank in Mill Valley. Patricia moved back to her hometown to be with her family. Caroline had talked to her once a couple of years after she moved, and that was the last time she knew of Patricia's whereabouts. She curiously dialed the new number for Patricia. A child answered.

"This is Caroline Carlyle, and I'm returning a call to Patricia." She stopped there, not knowing what her last name might be now.

"Yes, ma'am. She's here. I'll get her for you." This was the voice of a well-mannered young boy.

As she waited, Caroline imagined a whole new life for Patricia.

"Oh, hello, Caroline. Thank you for returning my call. You must be surprised to hear from me."

"I am surprised and so glad. I've often wondered about you. And I apologize for calling so late, but I've been out all day."

"No need for apology. Are you still teaching piano lessons?"

"Yes, what else would I do? Teaching is the bedrock under my feet. I'm right here, and little has changed since you moved. How about with you?"

"Lots of changes. Good changes. I was sad for so long I thought I'd never be happy again. But I am. I've remarried, and I have a family. For two years, I went to grief seminars until I realized I could be helping someone else through their grief because of my own experiences."

"Sounds like you, Patricia."

"This time the volunteering really paid off. A year ago, I met a wonderful man whose wife and infant child had been killed in a car accident. He was attending the seminar to work through his own grief and to help him deal with his two surviving children. Long story short, we got married about three months ago, and we're living in Missouri."

"Congratulations. I'm so happy for you. You're proof that dawn does follow the darkness."

"And I do hope God will be so kind to you, Caroline. He was gracious in providing a fresh start for all of us. Now we're learning how to be family." She paused. "You must be wondering why I'd be calling you after all this time."

"I'll confess I'm a bit curious."

"Do you remember the song that you and Robbie wrote—the one you sang at his funeral?"

"Of course I remember." What she really remembered was how difficult it had been to do.

"Do you still have a copy of it?"

"I'm sure it's in my files. Would you like me to send you a copy?"

"Oh, that would be so good of you, Caroline. I'd like Ron, my husband, and the children to hear it. I want them to know about my Robbie."

"I'll look tonight and get it in the mail to you."

"You know, after Robbie died, things just came apart at the seams. I'm not sure I ever thanked you properly for all you did for us. Robbie loved you so, and he loved your music time together."

"So did I. His influence on me will outlive the sun. I'm sure he's glad you're happy now. He didn't want you to be sad."

"I remember your telling us all about the serious talks you had. I wish we could have held it all together, but life just happens that way sometimes."

"It truly does. Give me your address, and I'll get this copy in the mail to you with my permission to do as you like with the song."

Caroline took down the address, and they said their goodbyes. Caroline turned on the teakettle and went to search her files for "Someday in Heaven." She put her fingers right on the manuscript and made a copy before the water boiled. She was organized to a fault.

She sipped the chamomile tea and went to the piano to play and sing the song before she put it in the envelope.

> *Gazing in the heavens in the dark of night,*
> *Every little twinkle gives hope of morning light.*
> *Heaven must be beautiful, like sunrise all day long.*
> *All the angels singing. Someday I'll join their song.*
> *Father, in heaven, with You I will be,*
> *Someday in heaven eternally.*
> *No more tears, no more fears, and no more night.*
> *Sunlit rays, endless days, living in Your light.*
> *Father, in heaven, with You I will be,*
> *Someday in heaven eternally.*
> *No more hate, no more hurt, all sorrow gone.*
> *Angels sing, praises ring in heavenly song.*
> *Gazing in the heavens in the dark of night,*
> *Every little twinkle gives hope of morning light.*
> *Heaven must be beautiful, like sunrise all day long.*
> *All the angels singing. Someday I'll join their song.*
> *Someday I'll join their song.*

"Someday I'll join their song," she sang. Then she whispered, "Your song, Robbie."

She closed the piano, picked up her tea, and wiped a tear from her cheek. She was glad the music had returned to Patricia's life. She hoped it would return to hers.

May wore on into June and the heat became oppressive. Caroline's days were filled with planning and practice and a couple of short calls a week from Roderick. She was surprised at how comfortable she was becoming in their conversations.

She did research for the journal articles she was writing. She was smart enough to wed her program notes with her articles.

Tuesday was Caroline's lesson day with Dr. Martin. She assumed Dr. Martin would press her for her decision about moving to Athens. The hour's drive to the University of Georgia gave her time to think about her response. She parked in front of the music building and made a quick dash through the drizzle, into the building, and down the long hallway. She removed her raincoat and stared at the brass plate as she opened the studio door. *Dr. Annabelle Martin.*

With polite greetings shared, Caroline started right to work. As she played, Dr. Martin rose from her chair, crossed the room, and stood in front of the window. Caroline glanced at the woman's silhouette against the gray sky. She was tall, slim, and statuesque with deep-set blue eyes and small angular features. Her wavy white hair, held softly back from her face with a tortoiseshell headband, brushed the tops of her shoulders. Her leathery skin suggested she was in her seventies. Her slender fingers were unusually long in proportion to the rest of her hand. Her hands had that fragile look of a grandmother's but were still strong and sure at the piano.

Midway through the lesson, Annabelle walked over and sat in her straight-backed chair next to the piano. She placed her right hand over Caroline's hands and stopped her playing. "You and I must talk. I know you drove over an hour to get here, but we need to have this conversation. And don't worry; you won't have to pay for this. This lesson's on me."

"Any time spent with you is worth paying for, Dr. Martin."

"Let's see, you've been studying with me for the past five years now?"

"That's correct."

"And you've been teaching privately for about six years?"

Caroline nodded in agreement.

"You are a remarkable balance of performer and teacher, and it's time for you to come to the university full time and work on your doctorate."

"I am truly considering it."

"Time's up for consideration. It's time for a decision. You're what? Twenty-nine?"

Caroline again nodded in agreement.

"Yes, the time is now. You could teach undergraduate-level students and become a staff accompanist while you study."

"The university would be quite a change for me. Remember, I live a very simple life in a sleepy little town."

"All the more reason you should be here. You're too young and too gifted to be living in a sleepy little town."

"But I like the people there, and they depend on me."

"Oh, I'm certain they like you, but is this really what you want to be doing ten years from now?" Dr. Martin touched a nerve. "You'd have so many more opportunities here on the university campus—opportunities to teach, to perform, to travel in circles where people would really appreciate your musicianship."

Caroline looked out the window. "But there's no one else in Moss Point to teach piano or voice."

Dr. Martin touched Caroline's chin and gently turned her face until blue eyes met blue eyes. "Well, if you moved, it would give someone else an opportunity to come to Moss Point and open a studio, wouldn't it?"

"I suppose so."

Dr. Martin stood up. "Listen, I've already talked with the head of the department about you. I recorded your lesson today so he can hear you play, and I truly think you may receive an invitation and possibly even an incentive to come here. You certainly will if I have anything to do with it."

"I should be on my knees in gratitude to you, Dr. Martin. I realize that you're sticking your neck out for me, and I'm most grateful, but the only thing harder for me than change is making decisions."

"I'm not asking you to make a decision today, but time is running out. We can talk when you get back from Kentucky."

Caroline gathered her music, putting it in her bag. "I'll think about it seriously and will give you an answer then."

"And Caroline, I know how much you want to play your infamous 1902 Hazelton Brothers instrument again. I only wish I could be there to hear you. Dear one, I hope the experience is all that you want it to be. Enjoy yourself and make beautiful music." Dr. Martin hugged Caroline just the way her grandmother used to.

"I will do my best." Caroline put on her raincoat and picked up her bag. As she closed the studio door, she lifted her eyes to the brass nameplate again. The letters blurred until Caroline imagined it read *Dr. Caroline Carlyle*.

Chapter Twelve

Shatterings

———— • ————

THE MID-JUNE MORNING'S HUMIDITY LEFT NO DOUBT OF summer's arrival. Caroline spent her days reading and practicing and her evenings wrestling with the decision about the university opportunity. Sam and Angel and her parents had all said they supported her decision whatever it might be. She grew sorry she ever mentioned the opportunity to her brothers. They had practically packed her up and moved her already, and she wasn't certain she was ready to go. Unready to make any kind of public announcement yet, she continued to line up her students for the fall just in case she stayed.

Caroline was playing the piano when she saw Gretchen and Bella Silva walking the path up to the terrace.

Mrs. Silva was a striking woman. She had the complexion of a thirty-year-old, but the platinum hair pulled back so severely and the sadness in her eyes suggested an old soul. Her gray sweater covered a simple cotton dress, probably homemade. She held Bella's hand, encouraging her along, but neither of them talked.

Bella also wore a cotton dress of light cream-colored fabric with sprays of tiny roses. Her blonde hair was pulled high on her head in a ponytail with long curls swinging from side to side as she walked.

Caroline observed them as they paused at the door. Mrs. Silva adjusted the ribbon in Bella's hair and brushed the disobedient curls along her hairline away from her face. She said something to Bella but got no verbal response. She took Bella's hand again and reached for the doorbell.

Caroline waited for it to ring before moving from the piano to answer the door. "Good morning, Mrs. Silva, and hello, Bella."

"Hello, Miss Carlyle. It is so lovely to see you again, and thank you so much for seeing us."

"I've been looking forward to your visit." Caroline stretched the truth. "I was so glad you came to the recital. Did you enjoy hearing the children play, Bella?"

"Oh, yes, we both did." Mrs. Silva did not give Bella opportunity to answer. "The selections were so very beautiful and reminded me of my childhood."

Caroline had never seen such silver hair, silvery-green eyes, and flawless fair complexions. "Please forgive me, and come in. I just enjoy looking at the two of you, mother and daughter. You look like spring personified, especially against that bank of climbing yellow roses on the fence." She noticed the blush on Mrs. Silva's face and the slight downward turn of her head.

"Oh, thank you, Miss Carlyle."

Bella never changed expressions.

Caroline closed the door and led them to the two chairs next to the piano bench. It was a comfortable setting and offered a perfect view of the garden through the large windows. She preferred sitting at the piano when she talked with prospective students and parents. Before she sat, she offered to take Mrs. Silva's sweater.

"Thank you, but no, I prefer to wear the sweater."

Caroline noticed the muscles in her face tighten. "Could I offer you a cup of tea, and maybe a glass of lemonade for you, Bella?"

"Oh, we would not like it if we were any trouble to you, Miss Carlyle."

"It's no trouble at all. The water's heating, and the lemonade's already made. Perhaps you'd prefer a glass of lemonade?"

"It would be my pleasure to share a cup of tea with you, and Bella will have the lemonade."

Caroline wondered why Bella never answered for herself. "Would you prefer Earl Grey or Darjeeling or maybe an herbal tea?"

"I'll have what you're having."

"Well, then it will be Darjeeling." Caroline made her way to the kitchen. With only a counter separating the kitchen from the great room, she continued to observe her guests as she poured lemonade and steeped the tea. Mrs. Silva and Bella sat noticeably erect and still. Their simple beauty and unflinching modesty were refreshing.

Mrs. Silva turned toward the kitchen. "They say Darjeeling is the champagne of teas, you know."

"Yes, I know, and I'll confess that I save the Earl Grey for guests who enjoy it. Would you like some cookies, Bella? You'll find I always have cookies."

"No, thank you, I do not think she would like a cookie." Mrs. Silva paused. "It is probably the oil of bergamot."

"I'm sorry, the oil of what?"

"The oil of bergamot in the Earl Grey tea. Usually tea drinkers have a taste for it and prefer it. Or if they are like you—and me, I might add—they just cannot abide it."

She realized Gretchen's meekness and good manners would have forced her to drink the Earl Grey tea had it been Caroline's choice. Guessing it was the same meekness and good manners that denied Bella the cookies, she put a few on a plate anyway.

She returned, set the tray of tea and cookies on the marble-topped table next to the piano, and handed Bella her lemonade. Still no response. "Mrs. Silva, do you prefer milk and sugar in your tea, or maybe lemon?"

"I'll have it just like you."

"Are you sure? I'm a tea sipper who likes just a bit of sugar."

"That is the way I like my tea also. If you have good Darjeeling, it needs only a hint of sweetening."

Caroline served Mrs. Silva her tea with a linen napkin.

"Oh, my, it has been a very long time since someone made me tea and served it in a real china cup."

"That's one of life's pleasures. I only drink tea from china cups. Isn't that absurd?"

"Quite the contrary. Tea just seems to taste better in bone china."

"My friends know how I am about my tea and my teacups, so I have quite a collection of them. I learned years ago not to save them for some special occasion that may never arrive. So I use them every day. And while I'm confessing, I'll admit this cup's my favorite."

Caroline offered the plate of cookies to Bella, whose eyes had followed Caroline's every move since she returned with the tray. Bella quickly looked at Mrs. Silva, whose slight nod sent the girl's hand quickly to the plate. She took one cookie and held it in both hands in her lap. Her eyes moved back to meet Caroline's. Caroline had never seen eyes like hers.

"Bella, I'm crazy about cookies. I like baking them, I like eating them, and I really like rewarding my students with cookies after good lessons. You'll find that my cookie jar is usually full."

Caroline waited for some response from Bella. There was none.

Mrs. Silva responded for them both, "We like cookies too. I have taught Bella how to make the lacy cookies that we made in the old country."

"You mention the old country, and your accent is almost musical. So tell me, where did you grow up, Mrs. Silva?"

Just as Mrs. Silva started to respond, the phone rang.

"Oh, please excuse me; I'll only be a moment." Caroline went to her desk.

"Good morning, sis. You're on my mind this morning, so I just decided to pick up the phone and see what's up."

"Oh, hello, James. I'm actually interviewing a potential new student for the fall term. Could I call you back in a while?" She brushed cookie crumbs from her mouth.

"That won't work. I'm headed to the courthouse, and I don't know when I'll be finished. I know you can't talk, but you could ease my mind if you'd just say yes or no to a few questions."

"That would be fine, I think." She saw Bella take a bite of her cookie.

"You're still interviewing students. What about the university? Never mind. We'll talk about that later. Have you been bothered with the prowler again?"

"Yes, only once. But not for a while now."

"Is Sam staying on top of this?"

"Oh, yes, and generally according to the same plan." She wondered how her part of the conversation must sound to Gretchen.

"You mean the sheriff's still watching the hobo?"

"Yes, as a matter of fact, but I'm thinking it might not be the right one."

"You think you know who it might be?"

"Yes, I do. A student, perhaps."

"A student. Do you think you're in any danger? Is he a pervert or something?"

"Oh, no, everything's fine. You might want to know that Sam and Angel are thinking of making a park out of the undeveloped land next to Twin Oaks."

How thoughtless! When she remembered Sam's concern over getting Mr. Silva to agree to zoning issues for the park, she lowered her voice.

"Does this have anything to do with your prowler?" James continued.

"Well, partly, but there's certainly more to their thinking than that. It's wonderful of you to call, but I really must go now."

"Are you one hundred percent okay?"

"Yes, I'm sure of that, and goodbye."

"Bye, sis, I'll call later."

Caroline returned to the piano and resumed her conversation. "You were about to tell me about the old country."

"Are you certain you have time for this, Miss Carlyle?"

"Yes, I'd find it very interesting."

"Where should I start? I have many ripe remembrances. I was born in Austria and came to the United States after I married Mr. Silva."

She calls her husband Mr. Silva.

"During all my years in my father's house, we were surrounded by beautiful music of the piano. My grandmammá lived with us, and after our evening meals, we gathered in the parlor. Grandmammá would play until her fingers could play not another note. And then we had such wonderful music in our church. It was a cathedral."

"Those must have been memorable times." Caroline remembered her own family gatherings around the piano.

"Oh, they were. They were such sad and yet beautiful times. When Grandpappá died, Grandmammá was never the same. The part of her that did not die with him retreated to a cold corner of her heart."

"They must have had a great love," said Caroline, fully aware of cold corners in one's heart.

"Oh, yes. When she first came to live with us, she told us stories of her life with Grandpappá. They loved each other so much, but her sea of joy turned into a well of despair when he died. And even near the end of her life when she told no more stories and no longer recognized any of us, she still played the piano. Grandmammá had two great loves: my grandpappá and her piano."

"I understand that." Caroline identified with Grandmammá more than Mrs. Silva would ever know. "That's very interesting. There's fascinating research on music and the brain—seems to be a curious connection, especially as we age. But you never learned to play, as I recall."

"Oh, no. I always wished to learn, but there was not money for such things when I was a girl. I had grand hopes that Grandmammá would teach me, and she tried. She was better able to play the songs she had known all her life than to teach them to a silly young girl. Besides, teaching me was like planting an edelweiss with a plow." Mrs. Silva looked straight into Caroline's eyes. "You cannot imagine me a silly young girl, can you, Miss Carlyle?"

"A silly young girl?" Caroline was taken aback. "Oh, I think all women were silly young girls at some point."

"I was a silly young girl, but I grew up quickly."

"That sounds like another interesting story."

"Oh, it is, but I'll not tell it today. I've already taken too much of your time, and I want to speak with you about my Bella. Bella is like Grandmammá. She has real talent."

"Has she studied piano before?"

"No, no, no." Each no got softer.

"But you say she has talent?" Caroline's fascination was growing.

"I fear it is another story," Gretchen said. "I'm so sorry to take so much time."

"We're doing just fine, Mrs. Silva, and I've always been a sucker for a good story."

"Sucker?"

Caroline realized Mrs. Silva wasn't familiar with such slang. "I'm sorry. My seventh-grade English teacher would be appalled at my use of such language. It means that I've always enjoyed listening to a good story."

"Did your mother tell you stories as a child?" Gretchen sipped her tea.

"As a matter of fact, she did. I begged her to read the stories over and over again, especially the fables."

"*Aesop's Fables?*" Gretchen looked at Bella.

"Yes, *Aesop's Fables*. Do you know those?"

"Every one of them. Bella loves them too. And Bible stories. I have read them all hundreds of times to her."

Bella's silence and stillness had not gone unnoticed. Caroline turned to her. "Which one was your favorite?"

"They were all her favorites."

The doorbell rang, and Caroline excused herself once again. She took the package the delivery person handed her and put it on the table. As she turned, she watched Mrs. Silva straighten Bella's ribbon and brush cookie crumbs from her face. Mrs. Silva leaned over and whispered something in Bella's ear and then sat back down in her chair.

Caroline picked up her day planner on her way back to the piano.

"I apologize for the interruptions. Just books I had ordered." She sat down at the piano. "You probably have some questions about my piano instruction."

"I'm so sorry. I've talked very much. But you're right, we should talk about the reasons we are here."

"There's no need to apologize. You were simply answering my questions. So now I'll answer yours." She reached into her day planner for the information. "I have papers for you to take home, but I'd like to talk through some of the items."

"Very well."

"Today's interview is the first step in the process. It is important for the student and the parent to understand what you can expect from me and what I expect from you. It's critical that the student wants to learn to play the piano, and I emphasize *student* here."

"Oh, my Bella wants to learn to play."

"It simply isn't enough that the parent wants the child to study, and I usually discover that fairly quickly. My students have weekly lessons, each being forty-five minutes. The first fifteen minutes are at the computer, where students learn fundamentals and theory at a pace that I design for each student. The last thirty minutes are at the piano. Bella, do you like to use the computer?"

"Bella has never used a computer," Mrs. Silva answered quickly.

"Oh, I see." There were growing reasons this would not work, and Caroline dreaded the answer she would be forced to give them. She took a sheet from her day planner and handed it to Mrs. Silva. She felt very uncomfortable talking about costs. "This sheet will explain the costs and payment plans. It also details how I handle missed lessons."

Mrs. Silva took the paper without looking at it and placed it in her lap. "Bella's never sick, and she would never miss a lesson."

"But sometimes you might be out of town for a holiday, or there could be circumstances."

"Oh, no, we never leave town, and there could be nothing more important than Bella's piano lesson."

"Another requirement is a piano. I'm assuming you have a piano."

Mrs. Silva looked at Bella sadly and then dropped her head. "No, Miss Carlyle, we do not have a piano."

"Do you have access to a piano?"

"Not a real piano."

Mustering up courage to let Mrs. Silva down as gently as possible, Caroline said, "It would not be ethical of me to take your money if she cannot practice."

"Oh, she can practice." Gretchen took Bella's hand.

"But you said you don't have a piano."

"We do not have a real piano, but we have a small keyboard, and that is what she plays."

"A keyboard?"

"Yes, it is small, but it has twenty-two white keys and fifteen black ones. Is that not enough?"

Caroline quickly surmised it was three octaves and tried to be diplomatic without encouraging false hope. "I'm assuming this is a small, battery-operated keyboard with lots of buttons and fun sounds?"

"Yes, but Bella only plays the keys. She never experiments with the buttons."

Mystery heaped upon mystery. "How old are you, Bella?"

"She is twelve."

"Mrs. Silva, I'm not certain this will work. I hear your passion for the piano, but I've not heard this from Bella. Computer skills are necessary for my piano-teaching methods. And as I said, I wouldn't feel comfortable taking your money for lessons when Bella doesn't have access to a piano. In my experience, that will not work."

"Oh, but my Bella must learn to play. God has given her a gift. You must hear her play."

Hear her play? Caroline would be satisfied if she could hear her speak.

"I'm so sorry, Miss Carlyle, to take up so much of your time, but you must teach my Bella. She is a very special child. She can already play the piano. Bella has been denied many things, but she must not be denied playing the piano."

"What does she play?"

"Let us show her, Bella." Mrs. Silva stood and guided Bella to a standing position. "Bella, you have practiced and practiced. Now it's time to show Miss Carlyle what you can play."

Caroline moved from the piano bench and took the chair where Mrs. Silva had been sitting.

Mrs. Silva led Bella to the piano. "Sit here, my beautiful Bella. Sit here and play for Miss Carlyle."

Bella never moved. She could have been a Bernini statue. Flesh-colored marble, silken hair too beautiful to be real, eyes that never moved, and a fragility that said, "Don't touch." Caroline sensed a purity and an innocence in this girl. She also sensed the great love and almost palpable aspirations this mother had for her.

"Please sit and play, Bella." Mrs. Silva coaxed Bella, but not forcefully. Then she turned to Caroline. "I'm so sorry, but she's never played a real piano before, and I think she's very frightened."

"Just take your time." Caroline was intrigued.

"Bella, would you like me to play first and then you will play?" Silvery-green eyes met silvery-green eyes. "Please, Bella, I'll go first." Mrs. Silva sat down to the piano. "Oh, my, Miss Carlyle. I fear I'm like Bella. I haven't touched a real piano since I left the old country."

She ran her hands lightly over the keys, then played a simple melody with her right hand and basic chords with her left. After a few measures, she stopped and turned to Bella. "Oh, Bella, it's a real piano. It's so lovely and so much better than our little keyboard. You must play." Mrs. Silva began the piece again.

Caroline guessed it was from a "Teach Yourself to Play the Piano" instruction book she had seen advertised on television. She listened and watched Bella as Mrs. Silva played. Bella swayed to the music, her knees becoming her own keyboard as her right fingers played the melody and her left hand formed the chords.

"Now it's your turn, Bella. If you don't play now, you may never have the chance again to play such a fine instrument. You must show Miss Carlyle you can play. She must see she would not be wasting her time to teach you."

Caroline knew Bella was not the typical twelve-year old and that her mother's love was genuine. She surmised that Mrs. Silva's life had been plagued with disappointment, and she dreaded adding to that heap. Caroline's father had wanted her to be a doctor. She had the brains, but not the stomach or heart. She could no more deliver bad news to a patient than she could formulate the words she needed to say to Mrs. Silva now, but she knew it was better to say it today than six months after accepting Mrs. Silva's money.

"Mrs. Silva, I can see how much you want Bella to learn, but I don't think she's quite ready. Perhaps after she learns to use the computer you could bring her back and we could try again." Unable to bear the look in Mrs. Silva's eyes, Caroline focused on the Cherokee roses covering the fence. The words "This is never going to work" would not slip past her tongue. She had softened it as much as she could and still be truthful.

Mrs. Silva rose from the piano. "Oh, my beautiful Bella, maybe one day you'll know what playing a real piano is like. We must go now. We have taken enough of Miss Carlyle's time." She took Bella's hands once again and led her to stand.

Bella stood in front of her chair looking at the piano. Mrs. Silva picked up the lemonade glass and napkin and then turned to get her teacup.

"Oh, please, Mrs. Silva, you don't need to do that. I'll take care of it later."

"Please, let me help. We've taken up so much of your time, and a woman with your talents should not be serving someone like me."

Her words pierced Caroline's heart. She had been taught that all persons were of value because God had purposed them to be and they should be treated with equal respect. The thought of disappointing Mrs. Silva and Bella would disturb Caroline's tender spirit for days.

What can I say? I can't have Mrs. Silva leaving this studio thinking that she's lesser than . . . lesser than me? A single, twenty-nine-year-old woman living in somebody else's backyard hiding behind my piano?

Caroline picked up the tray and her teacup, and she and Mrs. Silva walked quietly toward the kitchen. She put the tray beside the sink and turned to take the cup and glass from Mrs. Silva. As she did, she noticed Bella had moved to the curve of the piano. Bella stood with her hands clasped behind her back and studied the strings and hammers.

"Let me show you my favorite teapot." Caroline tried to reconnect with Mrs. Silva. They walked to the glass curio in the breakfast nook. She opened the curio door and removed the teapot carefully, trying not to bump the cup and saucer next to it. Crackled from age, the porcelain teapot was white with sprays of pansies. The rim of the top and the handle were trimmed in gold. "This is my favorite because Grand Ma'am gave it to me. I loved my grand-mother as you loved your grandmammá. We had tea parties, and she always used this teapot." She handed it to Mrs. Silva.

"Oh, my, it is so lovely."

Caroline glanced at Bella, who had made her way to the piano bench and was standing in front of the keyboard sliding her fingers across the keys. "Grand Ma'am always told me that pansies were the symbol of friendship. So the next time you come to visit, I will make us a pot of tea in this teapot to symbolize our new friendship."

Caroline watched Mrs. Silva's cheeks flush. "You would invite me to tea, Miss Carlyle?"

"I would invite you only if you would call me Caroline and you would allow me to call you Gretchen. Friends usually call each other by their first names." Caroline knew this might not be the wisest move, but somehow she had to brighten this woman's spirits.

"Oh, but you and I friends?"

"Of course. I have only one friend who shares my love of tea, and she's heard all my stories. I would love to hear more about your life in the old country and especially about your grandmammá."

"That would be quite nice, Miss Carlyle."

"Remember, it's Caroline and you're Gretchen, if that's okay with you?"

"It is wonderful. I have a new friend who says that friends call each other by their first names." Gretchen spoke as though to her-self. "Would it be permissible for me to bring Bella? She cannot stay alone."

"Having Bella here would be fine. After all, young ladies need to learn the fine art of tea drinking."

Gretchen handed the treasured pot back to Caroline.

Music.

The piano.

Caroline froze. She hadn't felt such shock since she learned of David's death—that feeling when the heart is pumping so hard yet the blood seems to curdle and the body turns icy cold, the hands are sweaty, the room spins, and everything is too much to comprehend.

Caroline dropped the teapot onto the stone floor, shattering it.

With no thought of her treasured teapot, she turned from the curio and looked toward the great room. The bank of yellow climbing roses through the alcove windows framed Bella's silhouette at the piano.

Bella was playing "David's Song."

Chapter Thirteen

A Duet of Intruders

———•———

AROLINE STOOD MOTIONLESS. GRETCHEN STARTED TOWARD the piano, but Caroline took hold of her arm and stopped her. Gretchen remained still.

Caroline deflected her own bombarding thoughts to experience this moment. Bella sat at the piano, rocking back and forth, playing "David's Song." It could have been a recording. Playing it over and over, Bella always stopped at the same place—the place Caroline stopped because there was no more music.

When Bella began the piece for the third time, Caroline and Gretchen started around the counter toward the great room. Bella never stopped even as they approached her. Caroline stood at the curve of the piano to see Bella's face.

Gretchen moved behind Bella and wrapped her arms around the girl's narrow shoulders. They both rocked back and forth as Bella played and as tears filled Gretchen's eyes. "Oh, my beautiful Bella, I knew you could play. I knew you could." She covered Bella's platinum hair with kisses.

At last, Gretchen took Bella's arms to stop her from playing. Bella put her hands in her lap and made some whimpering sounds, and Gretchen sat down beside her. They continued to rock together. "Bella, you have a new song. I've never heard you play that song before. You have a new song."

Caroline knew she must look ashen. *How can she play like that? She has to be the one. Bellas's the Peeping Tom. But this stunning young girl only wanted to play the piano. How do I tell Gretchen?*

"Oh, Gretchen," she whispered. "You were so right about Bella. She does have a gift, and I was wrong in saying that she's not ready to study piano. But we do need to have a talk."

Gretchen looked nervously at the clock on the marble-topped table next to the piano. This clock was kept in plain sight so Caroline could stay on schedule when teaching or practicing. It was eleven twenty.

"Oh, you're right, Miss Carlyle. I mean Caroline. I have much to tell you about Bella, but I'm afraid I must go. My husband sometimes comes home for lunch, and he would be frightfully angry if Bella and I were not there."

"Yes, but I need to spend more time with Bella. When can you come back?" Caroline was anxious to explore this girl's extraordinary abilities. What explanation could there be for this one who didn't speak or use a computer or read music but who could play a piece note for note after hearing it only once?

Gretchen behaved very nervously and tried to move quickly to the door. "I'm not sure, and please don't call me. I'll call you. It's much better that way."

"You promise to call me?"

"I promise. Thank you, Caroline." Gretchen led Bella briskly toward the gate.

"We'll have tea when you come back." Caroline stood at the door.

Gretchen stopped and turned. "Oh, Caroline, your teapot. I should stay and help you pick up the pieces."

"Oh, no, please don't give that another thought."

"But it was your very favorite. I'm so sorry, and I'm so sorry that I must get home." Gretchen picked up her pace on her way out the gate.

"Bye," Caroline said under breath. She remained in the doorway trying to make sense of all this.

Before she picked up the shattered pieces of her teapot, she called Angel. "Hello, Angel, is it too late to make plans for lunch if I'm tossing the salad and bringing the soup?"

"That's a deal. I was about to call you. Sam has news for you."

"Tell Sam I have some news too. This lunch is going to be more than soup and salad. What time?"

"Let's see, it's eleven thirty. Make it noon straight up."

"Bye, Angel."

She looked at her favorite teapot scattered over the kitchen floor. She dreaded the cleanup, not just because the teapot was a treasured heirloom, but because she feared injuring her hands. She cautiously picked up the largest of the shards. Some of the pieces were large enough she could still see the pansies, and the lid was only chipped. But the teapot was destroyed. She was on her way to get the broom and dustpan when the phone rang.

"Caroline, this is Gretchen. Please do not throw the broken pieces of your teapot away."

"Gretchen, you sound out of breath. Are you all right?"

"Yes, I am fine. Just the brisk walk. I have no time to explain. I must not be on the phone. Just do not throw the broken teapot away. Put the pieces in a box. I'll explain later. I must go."

Caroline heard the click before she could even say goodbye.

Sure I will. Broken pieces of my life. Broken pieces of my teapot. I'll just sweep them all up and put them in a box. Guess a box beats a garbage heap.

She found a box and did as Gretchen had requested.

—·—

Sam met Caroline at the back-porch door. "Looks like you could use some help." He opened the door and took the bowl of salad balanced on the top of the soup pot.

"Sorry I'm running late. I had to clean up a mess, and you've

never been more right in your life, Sam. I need help, all right."
They walked to the kitchen, where Angel was pouring tea.

"Did I hear you say you had a mess to clean up? You didn't spill the soup, did you?"

"No, my favorite teapot met your studio's stone floor."

"Sounds like you had an object lesson on what happens when an irresistible force meets an immovable object." Sam sat down to the table.

"Yep, both cannot exist, and my teapot doesn't exist anymore. The one my grandmother gave me." She and Angel took their seats at the breakfast table, and Sam pronounced the blessing.

"I'm so sorry about your teapot, Caroline. I know it was one of your treasures."

"The teapot's in pieces, but I still have my memories."

"That's my girl," Sam said. "I just don't know how you can stay single. I mean a girl with your attitude who can make homemade soup like this? An unclaimed blessing, I'd say."

"I'm not certain I like the idea of being an unclaimed blessing."

"Speaking of that, I have a preliminary report on Mr. Roderick Adair."

"That didn't take long." Caroline felt herself pulled in the direction of Sam's conversation. Years of summations before a jury had enabled him to coax a listener the way a snake charmer brought a cobra out of a basket.

"It's just a preliminary report. I don't have the full dossier yet, but we have enough to know we're not dealing with Ned and Fred Pendergrass here."

Angel slapped his hand. "Sam, you should be ashamed."

"You're right. I am ashamed. Guess it was just my way of saying that your Mr. Adair doesn't drive a pea-green pickup."

Caroline raised her right eyebrow. "What do you mean, 'my Mr. Adair'? I don't even know the man."

"Well, if you must get to know a man, he's certainly the kind to get to know." Sam winked at Angel.

"Just get on with it, Sam. Tell her what you found out."

Caroline continued to eat her soup, trying not to appear too interested.

"Mr. Adair is landed gentry. Comes from old money."

"So, he's a spoiled rich kid." Caroline smeared butter on her corn bread.

"Well, you're right about the rich part, wrong about the kid part, and I don't know about the spoiled part. I'd says he's about thirty-eight based on his schooling. Adair's grandfather amassed quite a fortune in land, and then Adair's father was apparently a very shrewd businessman who leveraged their wealth to acquire companies. Roderick and his sister are the sole heirs."

"He has a sister? Umm, I wonder if this Liz is his sister."

"I can't answer that. Give me a few more days. I do know he doesn't have a wife. Ran across an engagement announcement, but a wedding never took place. He spends his time managing the family's investments."

"Sam, how in the world did you find out all these things?"

"I have my ways. A few phone calls and the internet."

"But you don't even use the computer."

"Don't have to. I know people who do and who can get the information."

"Just don't tell me, Sam. I don't think I want to know."

"Probably not, but there is one thing you do need to know. Mr. Adair is a very sophisticated businessman who has access to information too. What I'm trying to say here is that he's not the kind of man who would invite you into his home if he didn't already have the scoop on you."

"Oh." Caroline swirled the butter on her corn bread with her knife.

"That's not all Sam's trying to say. I think Mr. Adair liked what he found out. He liked it enough to make plans to get acquainted with you."

"Oh, really?" Caroline felt uncomfortable. "Maybe he's just a kind and generous man who thinks he's granting my dying wish to play my piano."

Sam and Angel gave each other their knowing look.

"Let's just hope he's a kind and generous man who doesn't have expectations," Sam said.

"Oh, let's hope he does." Angel giggled.

"Enough about that. You think you have interesting news? Well, I have shocking news. I know who our intruder is. Something happened this morning that would have startled that Civil War statue on the square."

Angel stopped eating and turned to Caroline. "Well, don't stop with that."

"I had an appointment with Gretchen and Bella Silva this morning. You know that Gretchen wants her daughter, Bella, to study with me this fall. This was the first interview."

"Don't tell me it's Ernesto Silva? Why, that skunk! He's been a scamp since the day he showed up in Moss Point."

"Sam Meadows, watch your language and just listen."

"You're right; I shouldn't speak of a man in those terms. I do apologize, but just the thought . . ."

"And when is an apology followed by 'but'? You're either sorry or you're not."

"You're right again, my Angel. I truly am sorry. Go on with your story, Caroline."

"No, Sam, the intruder isn't Mr. Silva, and I'm glad, especially with the impression I have of him. Anyway, Gretchen and Bella came over this morning. I did my usual tea and cookies while we got acquainted. I learned Gretchen was born in Austria and grew up with all the social graces. But apparently that stopped when she got married."

"I can believe that," Sam interjected.

"She has this appreciation for the piano and for music because of her grandmother, and she's convinced that her daughter has talent for the piano."

"Daughter? How old is this Bella?" Angel put her spoon down.

"She's twelve."

"Maybe I shouldn't even bring this up. Oh, fiddlesticks! I'll just say it. There was talk several years ago about the Silva girl. She was maybe fifteen. Well, the town scuttlebutt was that she was pregnant. She dropped out of school, and no one saw her for months. Some of the Pink Lady volunteers at the hospital saw her after she had a baby girl. But once she left the hospital, she disappeared again. Word was she ran away."

Caroline looked puzzled. "Are you saying that Bella might be this child, that she's really Gretchen's granddaughter?"

"Could be. The Silvas stick close to home, and they're not involved in church or the community, so I can't say for sure."

"That's interesting. Gretchen may not attend church, but it's obvious she is a woman of faith. And Bella? Well, I can say Bella is not a normal twelve-year-old. She never spoke a word. Completely detached from the whole scene. Gretchen answered for her when I asked a question."

"If she can't talk, what in the world makes Mrs. Silva think she can learn to play the piano?" Sam asked.

"I didn't say she couldn't talk. I said that she didn't talk. I don't know if she can talk or if she's just too shy."

"That's odd," Angel said.

"Well, it gets a whole lot odder. Apparently Gretchen has a small keyboard that Bella plays, and she was desperate for Bella to show me she could play. So Gretchen tried by going to the piano and playing something herself. She coaxed and begged Bella to play, but Bella sat like a statue, never moving or responding."

"I think a good whack in the right place might have been an encouragement," Sam growled.

"Not in this case, trust me. Gretchen gave up and apologized for wasting my time. We put our teacups in the sink, and I showed her the pansy teapot my grandmother gave me. We were standing in front of the curio with our backs turned to the great room when I heard the piano." She paused, even now disbelieving what she'd seen and heard. "Bella was playing 'David's Song.' I was so shocked I dropped the teapot."

"That's the song you heard someone playing the morning of the break-in?" Angel asked.

"Yes. The same one. Here's this twelve-year-old girl sitting at my piano, rocking back and forth, playing a song note for note the way I play it. She has to be the one. It answers some questions and leaves about a hundred more."

"Has she ever studied piano?" Sam rattled his tea glass.

"Gretchen says not, which means that Bella has some kind of extraordinary gift. It's like—it's like she's this human tape recorder and that playing takes her to some other place."

"What did Gretchen say about all this?" Angel asked.

"She was as shocked as I was. She kept saying 'Bella, you have a new song.' So apparently she's never heard her play this song before."

"But that implies she's heard Bella play something before," Sam analyzed further.

"That's true. I just need more time with Bella. They rushed away before I could ask questions. Frankly, I don't even know where to start. Gretchen's such a sensitive woman, and I don't want to create problems for her. I have this feeling she has more than her share of those."

Sam pronounced his verdict. "You can be assured there's more to this puzzle, and it's going to take time to even get the pieces out of the box to lay on the table to see how they fit together."

"I think you're right about this Mr. Silva, Sam. When Gretchen looked at the clock and found out it was eleven twenty, she nearly panicked. She hurried home to get there before he did. But she promised to call and bring Bella back."

"Today's a red-letter day. Our mystery has been solved." Angel got up from the table.

"One mystery solved and several more surfaced," Caroline said. "This child's the biggest of them all. This rare and mysterious ability. Nothing like I've ever seen, and I want to reach her."

"That should be easy for you. Maybe music is her language," Angel said. "And you're absolutely convinced she's our prowler?"

"I am. I truly am. I know there are big holes in this story, but I have a feeling about all this."

"Is your feeling strong enough that I can call off the posse?"

"Yes."

Angel turned from the sink. "Oh, my, if Bella is the intruder, just think what might have happened if Ned and Fred had actually caught their snooper. Why, all the gunfire must have scared that poor girl out of her wits!"

"Proof again. The good Lord takes care of fools and children. And apparently, He took care of both that night," Sam said. "I can read the headlines of the local paper now: '*Mysterious Musical Genius Child Captured by the Pendergrass Twins.*'"

Caroline hung her head. "This story's like peeling an onion, layer after layer of mystery and intrigue. Oh, and I forgot to tell you. Remember, I was so stunned I dropped the teapot."

"You mean the irresistible force and the immovable object thing?" Angel asked.

Caroline nodded in agreement. "Well, Gretchen apologized all the way out the gate for not staying to help me clean it up. As soon as she got home, she called and made the strangest request. She didn't have time to explain, but she said not to throw the broken pieces away and that she'd call me. So now I just have to wait."

"Another puzzle piece," Sam said.

They managed to finish their meal in the midst of all the news. Sam pushed his chair from the table, folded his arms across his chest, and threw his head back as though he was about to announce his ruling. "Well, it seems to me, Miss Caroline Carlyle, with

Roderick Adair and Bella Silva, two unusual and mysterious persons have walked right into your life. I'm interested to see what you'll be doing with these intruders."

———.———

Caroline stretched out on the sofa with a book and a light blanket. She had the phone next to her. She stared at it as though her vibes would make it ring. She desperately wanted to talk with Gretchen, but what she knew of Mr. Silva dashed those hopes.

I wonder how he makes a living. How and where did they meet? What goes on in that house that would make them such private people? I'm not imagining that pain in Gretchen's eyes.

The phone rang. It was James again. She had forgotten to call him back. She gave him the full story about Bella. "Hey, big brother, do you remember how you would always tell me what to do when we were growing up?"

"Yeah, I remember. But I mostly remember how you hated it."

Caroline put her book down. "I'll let you in on a secret. I just told you I hated it, but I was really relieved. According to this birth-order theory, you're supposed to be the child who has the most problems making decisions. But I think that got pushed off on me."

"Sounds like you are in a decision-making mode, sis."

"Not exactly in the mode, just hovering and considering."

"Just do it?"

"Moving to the university is not that simple."

"What's not simple?"

She fluffed the pillow under her head. "It's a big change. I have a life here. I mean Sam and Angel and the studio. And the church . . . And who'd teach my students? And then there's the whole financial thing."

"You need a reality check, sis. Sam and Angel aren't going to live forever, and then where will you live? There are churches on every street corner in Athens, and someone will show up in Moss

Point to teach your students. You don't owe any of these people anything, Caroline. You're twenty-nine years old, and unless you plan on being Moss Point's old-maid piano teacher for the next forty years, you're going to have to make a change sometime."

"Slow down with the summation, big brother."

"And finances? Seems to me your skills are more marketable in the university setting, especially with a doctorate. Take this opportunity."

"You're talking to my head, James. When's my heart supposed to catch up?"

"What's the real issue? Your heart or the fear in your gut at the thought of change?"

"You always get to the point, don't you?"

"I work at it. Dancing around an issue's a waste of time. Just do it, sis. If you need some financial help for a while, you know you can count on me."

"Thanks, James. Actually, I think I'm really okay in that area, but it might be a good thing for you to review my finances. That would take you all of about ten minutes."

"You got it. Just let me know. Caroline, don't take too long to make this decision."

"Things were simpler when we were growing up and I just listened to you, fussed a bit, and then did what you told me. Why is life so complicated?"

"Life's simple, Caroline. It's the living that gets complicated. Gotta go. I'm glad your prowler is a twelve-year-old girl. I won't have to clean my shotgun and camp out in Moss Point now."

"You're the best, oldest brother. Good night."

Caroline went to the kitchen and made herself a cup of tea, then returned to the great room and turned out all the lights. She instinctively headed toward the piano. Stars embossed the night sky, and a full moon peeped between the limbs of the oak trees. She still had images of Bella rocking back and forth as she played. She sipped her tea, put the teacup down, and began to play. Music was her language, a language that had no requirement to reference anything outside itself. The music itself was enough. It must be the same way for Bella.

Caroline played more freely than she had in weeks. The intruder's threat was gone, and so were the constraints in her playing. One piece flowed into another until the pendulum clock struck eleven, calling her back to real time. She sat for a moment, took the last sip of tea, which had cooled, and put the cup down again. And then she played "David's Song" up to the measure where the music always stopped for her and now for Bella.

On her way to bed, she paused to read the card in the yellow irises again. "Music . . . when words aren't enough."

Chapter Fourteen

Anticipation

———•———

SEVERAL DAYS HAD PASSED SINCE GRETCHEN AND BELLA left the studio in such nervous haste. Caroline's fascination migrated toward worry by Sunday.

Hoping for any sign of them, she drove by the Silvas' house every time she left her studio. She honored Gretchen's request not to call, but wondered . . . What if they were in trouble or need? What was more noble: to honor Gretchen's request or to discreetly do some checking?

Monday morning and Caroline could wait no longer. Mr. Silva would probably be at work. She picked up the phone and dialed the Silvas' number. If he answered, she would apologize for dialing a wrong number. If Gretchen answered the phone, she would quickly inquire about their safety.

Her palms began to sweat as the phone rang for the sixth time. She was about to hang up when she heard Gretchen's voice.

"Hello?"

"Gretchen, it's Caroline. Are you all right?"

"Yes," she said quietly.

Caroline could hear the television in the background. "Can you talk right now?"

"No, but my husband is leaving on a run Wednesday. I'll call you then."

Caroline heard his gruff voice in the background above the television.

"Who's that on the telephone?"

"Just a wrong number." Gretchen answered him and hung up without saying goodbye.

"Well, then," Caroline said to the empty room. She stood a moment, pondering, then sat at her desk and put in a call to Dr. Annabelle Martin.

No answer. She left a message and went to the piano.

Hours of practice passed before the phone rang.

It was Annabelle. "Hello, Caroline. I hope you're calling to tell me you've packed your bags and you're moving to Athens."

"Unfortunately, I'm not calling with an answer. I'm calling with a question."

"Oh, Caroline, be impulsive for once. Don't think about it too long. Well, if it's not about that, did you call to schedule another lesson before your Kentucky recital?"

"Actually, I would like to schedule another lesson, but I'm quite stymied over a situation here in Moss Point, and I really hope you can help me." She told of the mysterious intruder and of her experience with Bella.

"This is extremely interesting." Annabelle revealed an unfamiliar excitement in her voice. "Has the girl studied piano before?"

"No, she's twelve, and she's never had a piano lesson."

"Do you have any indication of her IQ? Do you think maybe she's autistic?"

"I have almost no information about her, only what I've observed."

"Start from the beginning with your observations. They could be very, very important."

Caroline flipped the pages in her day planner. "Well, she's twelve and a strikingly beautiful girl with haunting silvery-green eyes that look beyond what I see. She is nonverbal and almost non-responsive, certainly nonresponsive to me. She responded slightly to the woman who brought her here, and I say 'woman' because there is some question about the relationship between the two. Gretchen could be Bella's mother or her grandmother."

"You mentioned her eyes. Do you think she has visual impairment?"

Caroline hesitated. "I don't think so, but Gretchen does seem to lead her all the time. That's interesting. I'll be more observant."

"Tell me about Bella at the piano—all the details."

"Apparently she's been playing simple songs that Gretchen plays on a small keyboard. When Gretchen tried to get Bella to play my piano, Bella sat like a statue in her chair, but when we went into the kitchen, Bella moved from her chair to the piano. She stood there in the curve of the piano, and I thought she was looking at the strings."

"Did she touch the strings?" One question led to another.

"I don't think so. I wasn't paying attention. But then, the next thing I knew she was playing one of my compositions."

"Could she have had access to a manuscript?"

"Impossible. I've never written it down. But she played it note for note. I guess she has memorized it from hearing me play it. But the way she moved, she played as though she were under a spell. Her body rocked front to back in rhythm with the music."

"Did she play anything else?"

"No. It was close to noon, and Gretchen ran out rather quickly. I think the situation at home is not a pleasant one. She promised to call me on Wednesday, and I hope to see them then."

"This rocking, swaying motion—does she do this all the time?"

"I observed this only when she played the piano."

"And she never spoke?"

"Not in my presence." There was a pause. "Annabelle, are you there?"

"Oh, yes, I'm still here. Just thinking."

"I know what you mean. These thoughts have been rolling around in my head like marbles in a glass jar."

"Caroline, do you know the term *savant?*"

"I think I've heard or read something about that. They're usually very good with numbers, if my memory serves me well." Caroline wrote down *savant* on her notepad.

"Some savants are phenomenal with numbers, but others are near prodigies in music and art. I'd suggest you get online or come to the university library and do some reading."

"Do you think Bella might be a savant?"

"I'm unsure, but she's exhibiting some of their basic characteristics. I'd be most interested in meeting her myself."

"That would be great. Could you come here Wednesday?"

"No, I don't think that's wise. You do this next meeting yourself. They have a rapport with you. Meantime, you begin your research. Don't tell anyone else about this until you and I talk again."

"Agreed. I'll get on with the research, and I'll call you after my next visit with Bella."

"Her name is Bella? Do you know what *bella* means?"

"No, do you?" Caroline asked.

"*Bella* means 'beautiful.' Her name couldn't be more appropriate. Handle her as you would an irreplaceable and fragile piece of art, Caroline."

"I'll do my best. Thanks for your help."

"You're welcome, and thanks for giving me the possibility of this experience. We'll talk soon. Goodbye."

Caroline turned on the teakettle and her computer. Before Wednesday morning she would have a better understanding of what a savant is. Surely there was a key somewhere to unlock the secrets behind those silver eyes.

———

Caroline's last meeting with Tandy was Tuesday morning. If she could make it to Saturday dusk, this wedding would be over and she'd be eternally grateful Tandy Yarbrough had birthed only two children. She still smiled when she thought of Rachel's wedding and Tandy dripping in watermelon from her dyed hair to her dyed satin shoes.

This morning, Tandy was ready to nail everything down, including the groom's mother, who according to Tandy gave new meaning to the word *bodacious*. The wedding would be held outdoors at the Yarbrough residence. Landscapers had installed fountains, flowers, and a reflecting pool—everything Tandy had seen in the last twelve months of her favorite magazines. White tents and white tulle and the smell of gardenias would probably drift all the way down to Mill Valley.

A string quartet was coming in from Atlanta, and Caroline's responsibilities were to play the piano for the reception and to direct the music and musicians for the grand entrances of all the members of the bridal party.

"There will be a special tent for the string quartet on the patio. That way, the bridal party can come from inside the house across the patio. Ned and Fred Pendergrass have built an arch for the bridal party to walk through, and a stage so the bride and groom can be seen.

"My two sisters from Dothan, Alabama, are coming in tomorrow, bringing two hundred more yards of tulle. And poor Polly—she's just got to hire some extra help. She's got gardenias coming from all over, and you know she can't put those out too early or they'll turn brown."

Caroline waited for Tandy to turn blue from lack of oxygen and wondered what the woman would do with a concrete slab covered in parquet flooring in the middle of her yard next November. Thoughts of potential wedding disasters skipped through her mind: slipping on white satin, tumbling into the reflecting pool from the parquet dance floor, rain-soaked tents and wilted tulle. Caroline understood completely why Tandy's eldest daughter, Rebecca, and her husband had moved to Arizona and why Rachel and her groom would be settling down in Alabama.

"And the caterers—I've spent more time with them than I have my family the last two weeks. But I think they finally have it clear. I'll never have it said that anyone goes away from this wedding hungry. Of course, half of the folks around here won't even know what they're eating and couldn't pronounce it if they did. But I'll know, and it's all going to set this town on its heels.

"Now, Caroline, here's the music and the list of all to be escorted in. And don't forget the three flower girls. I think it'll take three to cover that satin aisle in white and pale pink rose petals. You need to know the photographer will have them stop for a photograph as they come through the arch. So now your job is to make sure the string quartet has music enough for everybody to get to the stage.

"Then you'll need to run down to the dance floor to the keyboard and play some kind of trumpet fanfare. Can't you make that thing sound like a trumpet? You may remember my nephew played the trumpet fanfare for Rebecca's wedding, but he can't come this time. Then you'll need to run back to the patio and make sure the string quartet plays the bridal march for Rachel and her daddy to come down the aisle.

"I'm hoping it'll all be over by nine thirty or ten. And you'll probably need a break in there somewhere since I figure you'll start playing about five o'clock. Ray said he'd have a boom box to play while you take a break."

Caroline sat in amazement. She could be replaced by a boom box. She vowed silently to join the rest of the club ladies in town in their fervent prayers for rain on Saturday. Nearby farmers needed a good shower, so it wouldn't be entirely selfish. She hadn't spent her years of training and practice to play dance tunes on some pseudo-piano on a parquet floor where her shoes might stick because the glue wasn't dry.

But Caroline was committed and could not back out now. So she kept her mouth shut. Still, she couldn't recall looking forward to late Saturday evening so much in a long time.

—·—

Gracie snapped the plastic cape around Caroline's neck and spun the chair around to look at Caroline face-to-face. "Why, Caroline Carlyle, you're living proof that wonders never cease! You want to change your hairstyle? I've been trimming the ends of your hair every two months for the last six years, and now you want something different?"

"Not too different, just a bit different. What do you think?"

Gracie was in her early fifties and owned her salon. She'd bought the Weatherlys' filling station two years ago. She replaced the gas pumps with wooden barrels filled with petunias, hung out her *Cuttin' Loose* sign, and did a bit of refurbishing to make it look more like a salon than a gas station—although in an edgier style she hoped her male customers would like. The old gumball machine and the black-and-white tile flooring had stayed. They matched the black bowls she'd purchased for washing hair. She'd then covered all the chair seats with leopard or zebra print, added some African-themed throw pillows, and put artificial palms around to hide the 1940 radiators too costly to remove. The white wicker room dividers had been spray painted a dark green. When the blue-haired matrons who liked a bit more privacy when their hair was wet complained about passersby looking in the windows, Gracie found zebra-print fabric on sale down at Mr. Sumner's Emporium, made drapes to cover the windows, and tied them back with raffia.

Gracie had decided it was high time for Cuttin' Loose to become *the* place in town for all beauty needs, so she'd added two more operators who could do hair and facials, a masseuse, and a nail technician. Now the ladies in town could avoid the drive to Mill Valley to get their nails done or to get a massage.

Gracie herself was a good-natured people person who never tired of her work. A plump woman whose hair was forever changing color and styles, she'd spent her childhood fixing dolls' hair and her adulthood dolling up women. She knew more about what was going on in town than any of the pastors, the policemen, or the politicians. She knew whose marriage was on the skids, who was sleeping with the city manager, who was diagnosed with what, who was mad with the preacher or upset with a teacher, and who was traveling where.

She looked Caroline straight in the face. "Now, Caroline, this new 'do wouldn't have anything to do with a certain man from Kentucky, would it?"

"A man from Kentucky? You must be kidding."

"Yeah, the man from Kentucky who had Polly's knickers in a twist trying to get the biggest bouquet of irises she could gather delivered to your recital all in a matter of fifteen minutes. Of course, Polly said he really made it worth her time."

"Oh, did she say that?" Caroline grew uncomfortable realizing the whole town knew by now about the flower delivery.

"Yeah, said he called and wanted to know if she knew you and what your favorite flowers were. Polly told him you just loved irises and that she had fresh ones from the wholesaler that she got for Tandy Yarbrough's daughter's tea. He paid her double to deliver them all to you. So she called the wholesaler for another delivery before Rebecca's tea." Gracie never stopped combing through Caroline's hair. "Now, what are we going to do with this mane?"

Caroline was almost to the point of hyperventilating. Her hair issue paled in comparison to being Moss Point's latest gossip fodder. "You know, Gracie, the more I think about it, maybe just a trim will do. I'm in a hurry."

"Let me think here a minute. You don't need color on that shiny dark hair. You don't need highlights; they'd just turn to red streaks. You don't need a perm 'cause you got curls already. I don't think you'd be happy going with a short cut. You like your ponytail. Maybe I could layer it a bit or texturize it so it wouldn't be so heavy."

Caroline was sweating underneath the plastic cape. "I don't think I'm ready for that change. Let's just trim the ends again."

"Oh, why didn't I think of this already? I could cut you some bangs."

"Now, that's really an idea, Gracie, and I tried bangs once. Could you just trim the ends?"

"All righty, but Miss Angel's not going to be so happy about this."

"She's not?"

"Nope. She told me last week you were coming in for a new 'do, and she seemed all excited about it."

"I guess I'll just have to give her something else to get excited about, won't I?" Caroline was getting antsy and just wanted to get out of there. Wicker room dividers were far from soundproof.

"Well, let's see . . . If you don't want it layered and you don't want bangs, I could teach you how to pull it up and do something different than that ponytail."

"That'll be fine, Gracie. Just give me a trim and then do what you just said." Maybe this would halt this conversation and satisfy Angel at the same time. "I guess you'll be busy Friday and Saturday doing hair for the Yarbrough wedding." She attempted to change the subject.

"Oh, honey, Tandy's booked the salon for the entire day on Friday for manicures, pedicures, massages, facials, and hair for all the bridesmaids and grandmothers. Now, wouldn't you like to tell Juanita Dalton you're rescheduling her appointment? She's had a standing nine o'clock Friday morning appointment for about three hundred years."

"Bet she wasn't happy."

"Nope. Tandy came in yesterday to make sure I had the new terry cloth robes she wanted for all the girls. Can you believe it? She expected me to order robes for the girls to wear while they're getting their massages, facials, and nails done. Fourteen white bathrobes that I don't need."

"Sounds like they're having the female version of a bachelor's party."

"Yep, a hen party right here while the roosters are out strutting. All I can say is that Tandy's giving the rest of the hens in town plenty to cackle about."

Gracie was snipping and pulling a wide-toothed comb through Caroline's long ebony hair. "Maybe we'll be doing something like that for you before long."

"Doing something like what?"

"Like a wedding party. A man that'll pay twice what he should for flowers has more money than brains. Or maybe he's just trying to impress a certain young lady."

Caroline wanted to run. "Now, Gracie, don't get any ideas. The gentleman owns a piano that is of great interest to me, and I'll be playing a recital on that piano in a few weeks. He is the one making the arrangements." She hoped this would satisfy the stylist and maybe throttle the rumor mill.

"Oh! Arrangements? Yeah, men seem to do that when they're up to something—flower arrangements, dinner arrangements, ar-*range*-ments."

Gracie pulled Caroline's hair loosely on top of her head. "Now watch this, Caroline. Pull out a small section, put your comb about here, and tease slightly. Then take the tail of your comb and your fingers and swirl the hair around like this. You just secure the strands like this and spray the dickens out of 'em. Just keep doing that same thing till all the hair has been teased, curled, pinned, and sprayed."

Caroline imagined she'd look like a cross between Shirley Temple and a 1960s beauty queen contestant, but it was too late to stop Gracie. "Well, I'm certain I won't be able to do it like you, Gracie. But I'll give it a try." This was a trial run, she reasoned to herself. At least her hair would have a few weeks to recover before her trip.

"Women and their hair. Most of 'em pay me seventy-five dollars to curl it. You wear yours long to get rid of the curl. Blondes want to be brunettes, redheads want to be blondes, and brunettes want to be redheads." Gracie was still pinning and spraying.

"I guess it says something about our nature, doesn't it? We just don't seem to be satisfied with the way God made us."

"Well, I guess if we were, then I wouldn't have a job, would I?" Gracie laid the comb and hair spray down, stepped back to look, and then twirled the chair around so Caroline could see herself in the mirror. "Well, now, how's this for perfection?"

As Caroline tried to stifle her gasp, GiGi Nelson walked through the shop with strands of flaming red hair falling out from under the towel wrapped around her head. Her arms and fingers were out-stretched to avoid marring her freshly painted, nearly purple claws. GiGi looked at Caroline and stopped moving. "My God, Gracie, you been sniffing hair spray again? What did you do to Caroline? Oh, how stupid of me. I'll bet this has something to do with those flowers from that Kentucky gentleman." Gigi sashayed through to get her hair rinsed.

"That woman! She's a hundred-and-fifty-pound busybody stuffed into a size-six pair of stretch pants. Why, I hope her hair turns green and falls out and her forehead down to her eyebrows is covered in big red warts," Gracie said when GiGi was safely out of hearing range.

Caroline smiled at the thought as she followed Gracie to the cash register. She bought a rain bonnet and assured Gracie it was to protect her new 'do from the wind until she could get home. Caroline's father had taught her not to lie, but there were circumstances. And this was one of them.

Having happily avoided anybody on the trip home, she entered the studio and removed the rain bonnet, just catching the beep of her answering machine. Two calls. The first from Gretchen saying she'd try to call again tomorrow, and the second from Roderick Adair saying he was sorry he'd missed her and that he was leaving the country and would call when he returned.

Caroline remembered that in spite of multiple chats with Roderick since the recital, she had never acknowledged his flowers.

Chapter Fifteen

A Heart That's Free

———— • ————

CAROLINE TELEPHONED ANGEL. "HI, ANGEL. GOT SUPPER going?"

"It's Tuesday. Sam's picking up barbecue chicken plates from the Eastern Star. They're raising money for something again. Want one?"

"No, thanks. I think I'll stick to my fruit salad this evening. Want to see the new 'do?"

"Oh, that's right, you went to see Gracie this afternoon. Sure, I want to see it."

"Shall I put on the teakettle?"

"To tell you the truth, I don't feel too much like a stroll through the garden this afternoon. What about coming up here, and I'll put on the kettle?"

"Give me a few minutes."

"We'll be here. No place to go, and getting there fast."

Caroline carried her clippers along the path to cut a few roses for Angel. Over the years, Angel had immortalized the roses on her canvases. She held on to their beauty if not their fragrance when they had long ceased to bloom.

Angel met Caroline at the back door. "Come on in."

Like a six-year-old with her freshly picked bouquet, Caroline stepped through the door with both of her hands behind her back and surprised Angel with the blossoms. She noted the stunned look on Angel's face and hoped it was from the roses and not the sight of her hair.

"Oh, roses. Remember, fragrance clings to the hands of the one who brings roses." Angel led her to the kitchen, where Sam was standing at the sink.

"I married a woman with a poet's pen and an artist's eye." Sam slipped his arm around his wife and kissed her on the cheek. "And I'm glad I did." He turned to Caroline, and his eyes immediately widened. "What in the world happened to you?"

"Not what, but who. Gracie happened to my hair. What do you think, Angel?"

Angel took Caroline's arm and walked around her to see the catastrophe from all sides. "Well, it's, ah . . . ah . . . it's . . ."

"It's awful. That's what it is!" Sam didn't waste words or time. "Why in the world did you let Gracie do that to you? Must have been painful."

"Sa-am!" Pause. Angel looked at Caroline. "Sam's right; it's awful." She stepped back, lifted her hands and fingers to frame Caroline's face, and then squinted her eyes. "Turn to the side."

Caroline turned.

"Stop, right there. Yep, just what I thought. Your silhouette looks like a basket of cotton bolls just landed right there." Angel smooshed the curls.

The three of them had a good laugh. "It does feel like I'm walking around with a basket on my head."

"A cyclone would have done a better job. And you paid money to look like that?" Sam shook his head.

"Yes. Gracie earned it, but I'm guessing the hair spray ate up her profits. Angel, I may need your help to get all these pins out."

"I'll get the brush if you want me to do it right now."

"If you have time, that would be great! I'll check the teakettle."

Angel went for the brush, and Sam took his regular seat at the breakfast table. Caroline got out the cups and tea bags. "Sam, watch the kettle. I forgot the new praline bars I made. We'll have them with our tea."

Caroline ran out the porch door holding her hair to keep it from toppling as she sprinted to the studio. Nearing the door, she heard the phone ringing. As she entered, she heard Roderick Adair's voice. "Goodbye, Caroline."

She rushed to pick up the phone, but it was too late. She replayed the tape. *"Hello, Caroline, it's Roderick Adair again. I'm at the airport and thought I would try to reach you once more before I boarded the plane for London. Plans for your visit are developing, and should you need anything in my absence, please call Liz. I'm really looking forward to hearing this piano played by one who knows it well. I wish you joy. Goodbye, Caroline."*

She put a few praline bars on a plate and headed back up the path.

He had called twice.

The teakettle whistled as she climbed the steps to the porch. She was in the kitchen in time to grab it. She set the plate of cookies on the table and poured the water in the teacups.

"Ooh, thanks, sweetie. These look good. New recipe?" Angel took the first bite without waiting for her tea to brew and passed the plate to Sam.

"Old recipe, but first time I tried it. Does that make it new?"

"Well, Miss Caroline No-Middle-Name Carlyle, it doesn't matter. They good."

"You never have gotten over the fact I don't have a middle name, Sam."

"Never heard of a person who doesn't have a middle name. You're a rare one, girl."

"My parents actually couldn't decide on one, so Dad decided 'Caroline' was enough."

"You answered that question. By the way, I got answers to a few more questions about your Kentucky gentleman."

"*My* Kentucky gentleman? He's just *a* Kentucky gentleman."

"Then I guess what I've learned about *a* Kentucky gentleman is of no interest to you?"

Caroline blushed slightly.

Angel got up and went around behind Caroline's chair to start removing hairpins. "You sure you want to do this now?"

Caroline nodded.

"Caroline may not be that interested, but your wife with the—how did you put it? A poet's pen and an artist's eye? Well, she has a mind for mystery. So spit it out!"

"I knew that curiosity would get the best of one of you. Well, let's see, apparently Mr. Adair's parents taught him well how to manage and be responsible for wealth. He's been generous with his contributions to medical research and to the arts. He must lead either a private or a very quiet social life because his name rarely pops up in the society columns. His one sibling, a sister, is a professor in Boston and is married to a professor and physician."

"Criminal record?" Angel pulled the last pin from Caroline's hair and picked up the brush.

"Not a shadow of impropriety. Looks like a clean-living, hardworking man."

Caroline winced while Angel tried to detangle her hair. "The hardworking man's on his way to London."

"You seem to have more current information than I do."

"That's because he's called twice today and left messages. He just wanted me to know he was leaving for London and to call Liz if I had any questions."

"I guess we can add 'thoughtful' to the list of words describing our mysterious gentleman." Angel continued to brush the tangles. "Kentucky gentleman, piano recital, and pink dress or not, don't ever let Gracie do this to you again. Nobody should have this much hair." Beads of perspiration broke out on Angel's face.

"Gracie surely gives new meaning to teasing hair."

"That's what you call what she did to tangle up your hair? Teasing?" Sam asked. "Well, come to think of it, there's not much difference between teasing and tangling. Just depends on how you look at things." He noticed the sheen on Angel's forehead. "Angel, I think you'd better sit down and give Caroline a rest."

Caroline ran her fingers through her hair. "Thanks, Angel. See what I mean about the hair spray eating Gracie's profits? I need to go anyway. I talked to Dr. Martin the other day and told her about my experience with Bella, and she suggested I do some reading on musical savants. Gretchen and Bella may come tomorrow, so I want to know as much as I can before this meeting."

"Savant? Bella may be a savant?" Angel wiped her forehead with her napkin.

"I don't know, but she has typical savant characteristics. The research is fascinating, so I'm anxious to get back to the internet. I checked the local library today, but they didn't seem to have much of anything. Guess I'll do my research online until I can get to the university library."

"Mind telling me what a savant is?"

"Sam, where in the world are you when we're watching those TV magazine shows? They do all kinds of super-human things with numbers and music!" Angel turned to Caroline. "Remember, the only kind of unusual people Sam dealt with were drunks, junkies, and jailbirds."

"Angel's right—savants have phenomenal abilities most often coupled with very severe limitations. They're usually somewhere on the autism spectrum, with very low IQs and difficulty functioning with basic living skills. Yet they have these rare and magnificent abilities. Just like Angel said, some with numbers, some with music and art, and some with languages. Their mental functions can make computers look like mere typewriters."

Sam propped his elbows on the table. "Guess it's true: we are fearfully and wonderfully made. I've been saying it for years to people who think computers are really something. They forget it was a human brain that thought of computers."

"From what I read, the mind of a musical savant is like a

computer storing files, or more like a tape recorder. And oddly enough, of the savants they know about, they're often blind."

"Well, that would explain some things you know about Bella, wouldn't it?" asked Angel.

"It certainly explains how she came to be playing 'David's Song.' I mean, if she's been sitting there listening to my playing at night, her brain recorded the music." Caroline pushed away from the table, picked up the teacups, and took them to the sink. "I must be so careful in explaining things to Gretchen. Maybe I'll get her story before I bring up the issue of the intruder."

"Smart thinking, sweetie. Don't bother with the dishes; I'll do them later."

"I'll get the cookie plate tomorrow." Caroline started toward the porch.

"Oh, by the way, Caroline, Ned and Fred will be here tomorrow. They'll finish up the painting on the studio windows."

"You mean Tandy Yarbrough is giving them a day off? I understand she's had them quite busy out at her place."

"I don't think she's giving them a day off. I think they're taking a day of rest. Seems Tandy's been possessed by an alien species this week."

"Poor Ned and Fred. I'll look for them and stay out of their way. Bye."

Caroline strolled home with her loosed hair floating in the late-afternoon breeze.

————·————

Liz breezed into Roderick's London office without knocking and parked herself in front of his desk. "Conference call in five minutes."

Roderick quickly fumbled around for the remote among the papers. Amid adjusting numbers on spreadsheets and changing the wording in legal documents, he'd been listening to one of Caroline's recitals since lunch. He had hit the rewind button three times.

Liz cleared her throat and leaned over the desk, exposing tanned cleavage. "Looking for this?" She dangled the remote in front of him as she laid a green folder on his desk.

"Yes, thank you." He reached for the device, but she kept it.

She turned and pointed it at the television, which quickly went to black. "Is she the Caroline girl that keeps calling? The one coming to play the recital?"

"Yes, that is Miss Carlyle."

Liz turned back to face Roderick, her face stern. "You have this call and documents to complete before your meeting this afternoon. No more distractions."

"The documents are completed, and I'm ready for the call. And in reality you're my only distraction right now."

"Well, you needed these." She pointed to the green folder. "First draft of closing documents."

"Thank you." He looked at his watch. "And you can leave after you put the call through."

"Are you sure you don't want me to stay in case you need anything?"

"Yes, just put the call through, and you can call it a day. Hopefully, this will be quick, and I'll be able to close this deal. There'll be lots of paperwork exchanged in the weeks ahead." He turned back to his computer.

"I'll be available if you need me. I'm always just a call away." Liz sashayed out the door.

The call lasted only ten minutes, during which Roderick found himself not as focused as usual. The minute he put the phone down, he reached for the remote.

I'm glad she plays Debussy. Soothes my soul like when Mother played.

He studied Caroline's profile on the television screen, then rested his head on the back of his leather chair and closed his eyes.

Why am I so captivated by Caroline? Is it her music? Her beauty? Or her discipline? I don't know. But there's something about her . . . Maybe she's searching for more than her childhood piano. There's depth in her soul. But I've never been afraid of the deep. That's where every-thing is still.

He listened, completely satisfied, as the music swelled and then eased with the classic ritardando before the quiet finish. When he opened his eyes to the video again, it was to see Caroline, still seated at the piano, turning to acknowledge her audience. He smiled back at her.

I'll call you again, Caroline Carlyle. And I'll keep calling until I figure this out.

——•——

Wednesday morning was fair, in spite of the previous night's thunder and lightning. The phone rang as Caroline dried her hair. Gretchen called to say they could come to the studio at nine thirty.

Caroline would simply gather as much information as possible from Gretchen, observe what she could about Bella, and trust that her own good sense would help her navigate the conversation. Telling Gretchen that Bella had been the intruder would not be easy.

She tidied up the studio, hurriedly cut a few roses for the counter, and got out a couple of teacups just as the bell rang.

They're early, she thought as she approached the door. Through the window she saw denim and plaid. Not Gretchen and Bella but Ned and Fred. "Good morning, gentlemen."

"And a good morning back to you, Miss Caroline," Ned said as they both took off their caps, holding them to their chests as though pledging allegiance to the flag.

"Sam told me you'd be here to paint the windows."

"That would be right, ma'am. We told Mr. Sam we would be here at nine o'clock, and we're here just like we said we would be. But Miss Caroline, we have to leave for a little while." They both hung their heads as if the movement had been choreographed.

"Oh, you must be going to Mrs. Yarbrough's house to finish up a project."

"No, ma'am, that ain't exactly it."

Caroline heard Fred mumbling something unintelligible under his breath.

Ned said, "No, ma'am. For real, we have to go back to the barn. We fergot the paint. And besides, it's still too wet out here to paint anyway. So, if that ol' green truck'll crank ag'in, we'll be on our way, and we'll be back by the time that beautiful sunshine's dried up them raindrops."

"That'll be just fine, Ned. I'll be here with some fresh lemonade and cookies when you get back."

"And Miss Caroline, if Mr. Sam comes down here lookin' for us, you tell him we was here on time, and we'll be back later to get our job done."

"I'll tell him. He knows you gentlemen do what you say."

"Yessum, we sure do. That's the way we was raised. A man ain't no better than his word," Ned said.

Fred nudged him and put on his hat. Caroline heard them talking as they checked the windows on the way out.

"Can you believe Miss Caroline's so nice? Cookies and lemonade, and still callin' us gentlemen?"

"She ain't like that yackin' Yarbrough woman orderin' us around like we don't know which end's up. Treatin' us like ol' man Grange treated his mules. Why, just thinkin' 'bout that woman'll keep me single the rest of my born days."

"Fred, you sure don't talk much, but when you do, you speak the truth, for true, for true."

Caroline quietly chuckled. Why weren't there more Neds and Freds in the world and fewer Tandys? Unpretentious, simple people who took pride in their work and spoke the truth. People with pure motives who did what was honorable.

Moments later the doorbell rang a second time. This time there was no denim or plaid, but a gray sweater and cotton floral dresses.

"Good morning. I've been looking forward to your visit." Caroline hugged Gretchen as she came through the door. Gretchen warmly responded to Caroline's gesture. However, when she tried to hug Bella, Bella stiffened and gave no response.

"Good morning, Caroline. We've looked forward to this much more than you have, I'm sure. I felt badly about leaving so abruptly last week, especially with your broken pot. Oh, did you save the broken pieces?"

"Yes, I did. They're in a box in the pantry."

"Oh, I'm so very glad." She reached for Bella's hand. "We must remember to take the box with us when we go home."

"What will you do with them?"

"That is really not for you to know right now. Oh, I'm so sorry. That sounded intolerably rude. Maybe it is better if I say that we do not want to reveal the surprise just yet. And that's enough talk about this. How have you been?"

"I've been very well, thank you." Caroline started around the bar into the kitchen. "A cup of tea for you and lemonade for Bella, and I have some praline bars. They're really very good. First time for this recipe." She lifted the plate of cookies from the countertop to the bar.

"Look, Bella, Miss Carlyle has made more cookies. Bella really enjoyed your cookies the last time we were here."

"I'm so glad. Remember, there are always cookies here, Bella."

Caroline guided them to the chairs, which she had arranged just as they were for their first visit. She served the lemonade, tea, and cookies and continued the small talk until they finished their refreshments.

Caroline then turned to Bella. "Bella, I've been dying to hear you play the piano again. Would you play for me?"

Bella sat motionless until Gretchen took her hand and coaxed her to the piano. Bella followed her, sat down, and immediately started playing "David's Song" accompanied by the rocking-back-and-forth motion.

"I've not been able to get her to play this song on our little keyboard, but she plays lots of other songs."

Caroline stood and moved toward the piano. She gently and deliberately placed her hands over Bella's hands to stop her from playing and guided Bella to put her hands in her lap.

Bella turned her enchanting eyes toward Caroline and followed her lead.

Caroline sat next to her on the piano bench and began to play Bach's Minuet in G an octave above where Bella was seated. She repeated it and then guided Bella's hands toward the keyboard right in front of her.

Bella, without taking her eyes off Caroline, slid her hands up to the octave where Caroline had played and flawlessly repeated Minuet in G. Caroline's insides fluttered with excitement.

Bella continued to play until Caroline stopped her again. Caroline played another of her student's recital pieces. When she finished, Bella lifted her hands and repeated what Caroline had played. This time she continued playing, repeating not this piece but all the pieces she had heard at the recital in the same order as they had been performed.

Caroline sat mesmerized by this child who remained speechless yet could play these pieces with great expression and finesse.

Gretchen was just as shocked as Caroline. "She's been playing these simple pieces since hearing them at your recital."

"What other pieces does she play?"

"She plays the pieces I play on the keyboard. I play them once or twice, and then she plays them. That's why I knew she has a gift."

"You're right. Bella has a very unique and rare gift. Do you suppose we could go out into the garden and talk a bit?"

"Yes, I'd like that."

"Do you think Bella would like to stay here and play?"

Gretchen moved toward the piano, stopped Bella from playing, and spoke softly to her. "Bella, Miss Carlyle and I are going out into the garden. She says it is fine if you would like to stay here and play the piano. We'll bring you a flower."

A slight grin broke the fixed expression on Bella's face. This was the first time Caroline had seen her smile.

Gretchen put Bella's hands back on the keyboard, and Bella started to play. Gretchen and Caroline walked into the garden and sat down on the bench in front of the pond where they could see Bella through the window and hear her play.

"You were so right about Bella. She has a marvelous gift, and I really want to help her develop this gift, but I need to know some things."

Gretchen nodded in agreement. Caroline took that as a sign that Gretchen would cooperate and began with an open-ended question, giving Gretchen opportunity to tell the story the way she would like to tell it. "Would you just tell me about Bella?"

"I hardly know where to start, Caroline. Bella is my beautiful child. *Bella* means 'beautiful,' you know."

"You chose the perfect name for her."

"Thank you. You are so very kind, Caroline. You are such a beautiful woman yourself, and I'm so glad you see the beauty in my Bella. I just knew you would. I have seen the kindness in your eyes, and a bit of sadness too."

Gretchen turned her face from Caroline and stared at the water falling over the rocks into the pond as she began her story. "Bella is my granddaughter. You see, Mr. Silva and I had a daughter. Karina looked just like my Bella. She was smart in school and a very good child. But when she was sixteen, Karina gave her heart to a young man who did not treat it with tenderness. Karina became pregnant, and her young man said very bad things about my Karina. Mr. Silva made serious threats to the young man, and he left town."

Caroline was sympathetic. "Karina's heart must have been broken."

"It was. Mr. Silva wanted Karina to end the pregnancy, but she would not. How could she take the life of the love gift that was growing inside her? He was embarrassed and wanted her to go away out of his sight. I told him I could not bear it if she left. So Karina stayed at home and had the baby."

"And that is Bella?"

Gretchen's eyes met Caroline's, and then she stared at the water again. "Yes. He forced Karina to stop going to school and would not let her out of the house for months. He refused to look at her or talk to her. I do not understand, but that is his way. I tried to make things happy for Karina."

Caroline looked intently at Gretchen's profile. "That was a tough job."

"Oh, she missed her friends and school, but when she was at home with me, we read great books and listened to music all day while we sewed and knitted clothes for the little one. When the little one was born . . . Oh, she looked just like my lovely Karina."

Gretchen's story was so engrossing that Caroline hardly noticed the pea-green truck pulling into the driveway. Gretchen continued.

"We brought the little one home. She was so beautiful and such a peaceful baby. Karina would hold her and look into her eyes for hours, humming little songs that I had taught her, songs from the old country. Oh, but when little Bella cried, Mr. Silva would become so angry, and he would speak in a very loud voice to us. It frightened Karina so much. We tried to keep the little one from crying. Music was the only thing that would quieten her."

"Music, salve for the soul." She wondered how Gretchen possessed the gentle, sweet spirit when she had been living with the devil himself.

"Oh, yes, it would soothe her. But Mr. Silva does not allow music in the house when he is there, so Karina or I would rock the little one and hum softly to silence her cries. One day, when Karina could stand it no more, she told me she must go. She was afraid of her father and afraid of what he might do to Bella in one of his rages. She wanted to take the child and leave."

"To find her young man?" Caroline inquired.

"No, just to get away from her father. Oh, I did not want her to go, and I had no money to help her. Mr. Silva gives me only enough money to buy the groceries, and that's all I had. I persuaded her to leave the baby with me, and I promised her I would protect her from Mr. Silva. I reminded her I had always protected her from his be—" She paused. "From him."

"Beatings? He beats . . . ?"

"Oh, he does not mean to; he cannot help it when he gets really angry. It is just his way. But I never allowed him to touch Karina or Bella. I try to understand him and be patient with him. He has many good qualities."

It was too late to convince Caroline he wasn't a demon. "Does he beat you? Is that why you wear this gray—"

"Oh, please, could we not talk about that? Could we just talk about Bella today?"

Caroline had planned to follow Gretchen's lead in the conversation, but she hadn't known their talk would take this path. While Caroline was forming her response, she noticed Ned and Fred coming up the path with paint and buckets in hand. They stopped just shy of the terrace to open the paint.

"Yes, Gretchen, not because I want to or because I think it's the right thing to do, but because I value your friendship and I trust you."

"Thank you, Caroline. I really do not mean to complain. We have a very good life. We have a house and food, and I have my Bella. And I've always known she is special."

"Does Karina know that Bella is special?"

"I do not know. I think mothers know things, but she has not seen Bella since she was four months old." Gretchen looked again at Caroline.

"Do you know where Karina is?"

"I get a letter from time to time. She mails them to one of her old friends, and Lisa brings the letter when Mr. Silva is out of town. I've not seen my daughter in twelve years, and I am not allowed to speak her name in the house." This was the first time that tears filled Gretchen's eyes.

Caroline put her arm around Gretchen. "I'm so sorry, Gretchen. I can tell how much you love her."

"I do, and I have taken care of Bella for her. Bella went to school for a short while, but she is not like the other children. She is special." A gentle smile replaced Gretchen's tears. "The other children learned to read and write and play games, but my Bella . . . she makes music. Her music will make many people happy."

"Have you taken Bella to a doctor to see why she is so special?" asked Caroline, carefully choosing her words.

"Oh, no. Bella is not sick. She is a happy, healthy child. She loves being with me. We listen to beautiful music all day long, and you should hear her sing."

"She sings?"

"Oh, yes, she makes beautiful songs. She sang first. That's how she talks. She talks with her music. Oh, but when I saved up enough grocery money to buy the keyboard, I learned she can play the piano. God taught her how to play and sing. We make beautiful music when Mr. Silva is not at home, and we have a special place we go sometimes, a beautiful place, and we can sing and make music with hearts that are free."

Caroline had a rush of desire to take Gretchen's hand and promise her a better life, a life filled with music and freedom and laughter. Gretchen had answered many of her questions in the telling of her story, but Caroline knew in her heart she had only waded in ankle deep in this mire of mystery.

"Hi, Ned, I'm enjoying the garden with my friend, Mrs. Silva."

"Oh, good morning ag'in, Miss Caroline. We come back to do the job. Did you tell Mr. Sam what I asked you to?"

"I haven't seen Sam this morning, so all is well."

But all is not well. Here's a woman living a few blocks down the street as a virtual prisoner who has convinced herself she's living a good life. She has lost a daughter and is nurturing an autistic child who is possibly one of a hundred people like herself on the whole earth. All is not well.

"Well, then, that's good. We just gonna start paintin' these here windows. But who in the world's making that beautiful music in there? I thought it was you, Miss Caroline." Ned shielded his eyes from the sunlight and looked in the windows he was about to paint.

The music gave way to a traumatized scream—a scream that Caroline had heard only once before, accompanied by the calamity of an overturned cooler of RC colas.

Gretchen jumped from the bench and ran through the garden, across the terrace, and into the studio. Caroline was right behind her. They found Bella standing rigid in front of the piano, staring at Ned and Fred through the window. Gretchen embraced Bella but could not calm her.

Caroline, acting on a hunch, stepped back onto the terrace and asked Ned and Fred to move away from the window to a place where they couldn't be seen. They were so startled that Fred nearly turned over a bucket of paint trying to escape the screaming.

Bella's cries turned to a whimper. Gretchen held her, rocked back and forth as she hummed a Brahms melody. Bella slowly quieted down and started humming with her.

Caroline stepped back in to see Bella cradled in Gretchen's arms. She knew, in that very real but unexplainable place deep inside herself, that her life was about to change.

Chapter Sixteen

Making Things Right

---•---

CAROLINE WAS CONVINCED HER HUNCH ABOUT NED AND Fred was right, so she did not discourage Gretchen from leaving. She assumed Bella recognized their voices and associated them with screaming and calamity the night the Pendergrass brothers had secretly attempted to catch the snooper.

Gretchen once again left the studio in a hurry, but this time she held a box containing broken pieces of a china teapot along with the hand of a fragile but gifted young girl. And with Mr. Silva on the road for several days, his absence would give Gretchen and Bella more freedom.

Caroline quickly made notes of her morning's observations to go over with Dr. Martin. Her notion was that Annabelle knew much more about savants than she had let on. But that was Annabelle's style—briefly introducing a new piece or a new idea, backing off, and seeing where Caroline would take it.

After lunch, Caroline breezed through the side door of the Moss Point Methodist Church. Preparation for choir rehearsal and Sunday services were regular Wednesday activities, but today she needed an extra hour to experiment with the keyboard for the Yarbrough wedding on Saturday.

Reverend Bixley was leaving as she entered. "Well, hello there, Caroline. Am I going to miss your practice session this afternoon?"

"Yes, unless you're prepared to make a hundred-and-eighty-degree turn toward the sanctuary."

"Oh, dear one, you do make heads spin and turn, but I'm afraid I'd better keep my heading. Must make my hospital rounds and a nursing home visit before the prayer service."

"Guess I'll see you Friday evening for the wedding rehearsal?"

"Oh, yes, the wedding rehearsal." Brother Andy smiled a knowing smile. "I imagine I'll have a few unspoken prayer requests this evening, and my guess is they're all praying for rain."

"Surely you've taught your parishioners not to waste God's time for such. As for myself, I'm praying for sunny skies and dry ground. Have you ever known of anyone getting electrocuted while playing one of these electronic keyboards?"

"Can't say as I have, but I've heard of stranger things. Don't fret. I'll be there to administer the last rites. Tandy Yarbrough didn't rent a grand piano?"

"No, she has string players coming from Atlanta, and her trumpet-playing nephew can't make it this year, so I'm to create a trumpet fanfare on this keyboard. That's why I'm here to practice."

"Well, just play it really loud, and maybe those guys down at the Waterin' Hole will think it's Gabriel's last blast, and they'll clean up their ways. Why, I can see the bartender and J. T. Barns on their knees right now." Brother Andy's chin wiggled when he laughed. "You do it up right, Caroline. I'm counting on you." He left through the side door.

Caroline was grateful for a pastor like Brother Andy. No one laughed and loved life more than him.

She spent the next hour turning dials and knobs on an instrument foreign to her. There would be a trumpet fanfare like none other Saturday evening.

—·—

Sam was determined to have fresh peaches from the first gathering, and he hoped there just might be a homegrown tomato or two at the market. "Angel, are you ready?" His booming voice reached the bedroom. "All the peaches'll be gone if we don't get there before July."

Angel stepped into the hall so he could hear her. "I think I'll be ready by dark."

"Instead of standing here in the kitchen watching the clock, I'm headed down to check on Ned and Fred. I'll meet you at the car, and when I honk, you'd better hop." He loved teasing his Angel.

"Now, Sam Meadows, you know what Mama taught me about running to the car just because a boy honked his horn."

"Yeah, and it didn't stop you sixty years ago."

Sam headed to the studio to see if Ned and Fred had finished the job. He rounded the corner and stepped up on the terrace. "Good afternoon, Ned. I'm glad you're still here. I wanted to talk with you about something." Sam could smell the fresh paint.

Ned stood up from his painting. "We're still here, Mr. Sam, but we're just about done."

"I'd like you and Ned to take a look at these few acres," Sam said, pointing to the wooded area on the other side of the fence. "I need to know what it would take to clean it up, do some landscaping, and make a park."

"You and Miss Angel want a park?" Ned wiped his brow.

"It'll be a park for the city. I've pondered for a long time, and it's the right time to do it. You think you could take a look, and tell me how much of the work the two of you would like to do?"

"Yes, sir, Mr. Sam. We'll take a good look and get back to you. Fred's done gone 'round the corner to the spigot to wash up the paintbrushes, and I'm peelin' the last of this here blue tape off the windows. Looks brand-new, don't it?" Ned pointed to his finished job.

"Just like the way the Pendergrass boys would do it. I would've brought a check if I had known you were finished."

"Now, Mr. Sam, we got to have a talk about that. Me and Fred done decided that, really and truly, we're the ones who caused all this mess, and it's our job to make it right."

"What are you talking about, Ned? It was my gun that blew a hole in this window."

"For true, for true, Mr. Sam. But if Fred and me hadn't decided to be heroes that night, you woulda not been down here with your shotgun, and Miss Angel and Miss Caroline woulda not been scared nearly to death. This was all our doin's, and the only thing to do is to make it right. So, there, you got yourself a new window, and our conscience is clean ag'in."

"Ned, I thought your daddy taught you to respect your elders."

"He did for true, Mr. Sam. And you know we respect you. But sometimes there's right, and then sometimes there's righter. And it's righter for us to fix this window this time."

"You're a good man, Ned. Your daddy would be proud of you." Sam saw Fred coming around the corner drying his hands. "And he'd be proud of you, too, Fred. Ned and I've just had a discussion about my paying for your work today."

"See, Mr. Sam, Fred agrees wi' me."

Fred nodded his head and stood quietly. Finally, he said, "Tell 'im, Ned."

"What Fred wants me to tell you is what happened this mornin'. We brought our paintin' stuff around here to the window, and we thought Miss Caroline was playing the piano. Then she called to us from the garden, and we was talkin' to her. All of a sudden, we heard this screamin' like somebody was crackin' knuckles and pullin' hair. Come to find out, we had scared this little girl nearly to death. She was the one makin' the music. So Miss Caroline and this other pretty lady come runnin' in here like scalded apes . . ."

Fred punched Ned hard in the ribs with his elbow. Ned turned to see the scowl on Fred's face. "You're right, Fred, that wasn't a nice thing to say about Miss Caroline when she's the only one that ever calls us gentlemen."

Sam still was amazed at how these two communicated without words. "Keep going."

"Well, anyways, they come runnin' and grabbed the young lady and finally got her to stop hollerin'. Miss Caroline run out and asked us to move around the terrace so the girl couldn't see us. Fred nearly turned the bucket of paint over tryin' to get outta sight. Fred, he don't like screamin' women."

Sam sized up the situation, explained the possibility that Bella was the snooper, and swore them to secrecy. He knew this secret would go to their graves unless he released them from their promise.

"Seems like we come near killin' a pretty little girl when we was tryin' to be heroes, and then come pert near scaring her to death today. We gotta make that right, too, Fred. I don't know how, but we gotta think of somethin'."

"Well, I'm going to leave it with you boys. I'm taking Miss Angel to get some fresh peaches. Fresh peaches are just like opportunities—you have to grab them when you can."

Sam walked toward the driveway. He got in the car and blew the horn, and they all watched Miss Angel put a skip in her step as she approached the car. Sam leaned over across the front seat to open the door for her and pecked her on the cheek when she got in. He noticed Ned's face turn red at the sight.

"I see you're still not paying attention to what your mama taught you about boys pulling up to the house and honking the horn," Sam said.

"I know. The whole town'll be talking about me. Did you see Caroline?"

"Her car was gone." Sam pulled out of the driveway.

"I forgot. It's Wednesday. She's probably at the church."

"You know, Angel, we've gotten so used to having Caroline around, and we like it. But I've been wondering if we're being selfish."

"I've been thinking the same things. Her whole life revolves around this studio, the church, and an occasional visit to the university. That's a small world for a young woman like Caroline." Angel opened the glove compartment for a tissue.

"We've lived long enough to know that nothing stays the same. There's just something with this Roderick Adair and now Bella entering her life. I have a sense things are about to change."

Angel wiped perspiration from her brow. "Don't think it's a coincidence, huh?"

"No, don't think so. She's been on a sheltered, safe path for the last six years getting her bearings back. Six years is long enough. And besides, you don't want to close up the acorn when the oak tree starts to sprout."

"Oh, Sam, everything you're saying is true, but it doesn't mean I'm ready to talk about it all now. Can we talk about something else?"

"Okay, how about the taste of a plump, fuzzy peach?" Sam smiled at Angel.

"That's much better. After all, a girl my age can't have too many more springs and first crops of peaches. Why, I'm not even going to peel the first one. I want to bite into it just like it came off the tree."

Sam loved this woman. Her joy was his joy. Her delights were his delights, even the ones that came as fuzzy, fresh peaches.

———

Caroline pulled into the driveway just as Sam and Angel returned.

Angel opened the car door. "Hi, sweetie, we have fresh peaches. The first ones arrived at the market today."

"I guess that means summer's officially here even though the calendar says it'll be another week or so."

"It surely feels like summer." Angel wiped her brow. "Why, if this muumuu keeps sticking to me, I'll be the talk of the town for running around in my birthday suit."

They walked up the driveway together. As they neared the path to the studio, Caroline heard her phone and ran to catch it.

"You're running like that ring's from London," Sam called as they watched Caroline disappear around the studio.

He and Angel walked arm in arm on up the path. He helped her up the steps and onto the porch and put the bags of peaches on the table. "Now, Angel, why don't you sit right here and let me get us a glass of that lemonade you made this morning."

"Why, I think that's a fine notion you have there, handsome." Angel sat down in her favorite wicker rocker and fanned herself with the newspaper lying on the table. Sam left her with the hum of the crickets in the late afternoon, the tune from the ice cream truck coming down the street, and the smell of fresh peaches filling the air.

He returned quickly with two tall glasses of lemonade, an idea in mind. "You know what I think I'd really like?"

"You mean more than sitting here in the cool of the late afternoon drinking lemonade with me?"

"Well, the only thing that could improve on that is a sprig of mint in this glass of lemonade." Sam set his glass down on the wicker table next to his rocker.

"That's the second fine notion you've had in less than five minutes. You keep coming up with ideas, and you're going to set a record. Want me to go pick some?"

"No, what about you sitting right here? I'll take Caroline a few peaches and pick a few sprigs of mint on my way back."

"Sam Meadows, you don't give two whits about a sprig of mint. You're just plain nosy. You want to know who called Caroline, don't you?"

"I married a smart woman, and I've been caught again. But you did say on the way home you wanted Caroline to have some peaches, and you know she'll be going back to the church for rehearsal in a little while."

"You're right. Time's wasting. Get gone before my lemonade disappears. Get a basket."

Angel had collected baskets for years. There were two requirements to make it into her collection. First, it had to have a handle, and second, it couldn't be made in China. The back-porch baskets had carried flowers, greenery, fresh vegetables, acorns, and pinecones for decades.

Sam grabbed a basket from the baker's rack, chose a few large peaches to fill it, and started out the door.

"Wait, Sam."

Sam turned quickly to answer her. "Do you need me, my Angel?"

"Of course I need you, but I was mostly interested in one more look at that basket of peaches." Sam, relieved at her playfulness, came back from the door and set the basket of peaches on the table.

Angel stopped rocking and stared at the basket. "Now that's a work of art. Makes me want to get out my brushes and oils again."

Sam had never tired of looking at Angel. He even looked at this basket of peaches differently after he saw how she looked at them.

"You can go now. That weird little camera thing inside my head has done its work."

"Taking pictures again?"

"Click, click, got you too," Angel said, shooing Sam out the door.

———•———

Sam knocked on Caroline's door and shouted as though she wouldn't recognize his knock. "Caroline, it's the judge with a summons."

"Hello, Judge." She opened the door and took the basket from him. "Is this your peace offering for that wisecrack you made when I ran to answer the phone?"

"I guess it is if it needs to be."

"You're just dying to know if that was the Kentucky gentleman, aren't you?" She reached for a fruit bowl and began to remove the peaches from the basket.

"I confess the thought did travel across my mind. Just keep the basket. You can bring it up later."

"I'll not do it. It would embarrass my mother." She lined the bottom of the basket with fresh paper towels. "You know this basket will not be returned empty. How about some tea cakes?" In seconds she had the basket filled with cookies. "And just so you know, the phone call was from Betsy."

"Well, how is Betsy and how is . . . what did she call the baby? Booger?"

"Betsy's fine. And according to the doctor, Mason needs to come up with a new name for this one. You can't call a little girl Booger—not even in South Georgia."

"So, Booger's a girl?" Sam smiled.

"Seems so."

"Ned and Fred told me about your episode with Bella this morning."

"Oh, Sam, she is the most amazing person. She sat at the piano this morning and played for nearly an hour. I played a couple of pieces, and then she repeated them almost perfectly. Then she started playing all my students' recital pieces, which she had heard only once at the recital."

"Really? I wish I could've heard her."

Caroline put away the cookie tin. "No doubt that Bella was our intruder."

"I came to the very same conclusion when Ned told me what happened. I hope it's all right with you that I told them about Bella. I swore them to secrecy in my best judge's voice."

"That's no problem, Sam. After all, if you can't trust those two . . ."

"Yep, they're mighty fine men. Wouldn't even let me pay for repairing and painting the window. Said if they hadn't tried to be heroes, none of this would have happened."

"Speaking of fine, Gretchen is another fine one. She told me this morning that Bella's her grandchild. She told me about Karina and how she had the baby and left home shortly after Bella was born. Gretchen hasn't seen her since. She gets an occasional letter, but one of Karina's high school friends has to deliver it when Mr. Silva is out of town."

Sam hung his head and shook it. "That poor woman. What she must have had to bear!"

"Oh, but it gets worse. Mr. Silva apparently abuses Gretchen. She says he's never touched Karina or Bella."

Sam raised his head. "I knew it. I knew it. That man's just a dump-truck load of devilment. Some of the boys and I need to pay him a visit."

"Now, Sam, don't go and get all worked up over this. He's a truck driver, and he's on a run for a few days. Gretchen and Bella are coming back tomorrow, and I'll get a few more pieces of this puzzle. You know, when I think about it, I can hardly bear the thoughts of what that precious woman and child live in day after day, but she's convinced herself that her life is good."

"I can guarantee you one thing: one way or the other that woman's life is going to get better."

"Gretchen's been entrusted with this rare child. I believe Bella truly is a musical savant. And from what I have read, there are fewer than one hundred savants alive out of billions of people on this planet. That's what I mean by 'rare.' When word gets out, life as Gretchen and Bella know it will be history."

"You really think so?"

"I know so. And I'll need your help and your wisdom. For twelve years, Bella's been a secret. But when this secret becomes news—we're talking national news, psychologists, neurologists crawling all over Moss Point, and who knows what else?"

Sam put his hand in his pocket and started to rattle his change. "Hmm, hadn't even thought about all that."

"I can't even begin to put my mind around all of it yet. But

I know there are some life-changing decisions just around the corner." She handed the basket to Sam. "What bothers me right now is Gretchen's reaction when I tell her about our intruder. She'll need me in the future, and I must be worthy of her trust, Sam."

"So Gretchen was entrusted with this gifted girl. Looks like now you've been entrusted with both of them, and I know of no one more trustworthy and sensible. Your motives are pure, and you'll do what is right."

"I just hope I'll know what is right. I know so little right now, but I know enough to be frightened. Gretchen naively knows that Bella is different but has no clue what could happen very soon. Doctors who want to study her brain . . . There'll be media exploiting her. And people in line on the Silvas' doorsteps—people who've figured some way to profit by using Bella. What's right for Bella and Gretchen? What's right for science and medicine? Oh, Sam, this can get sticky so fast."

"Don't worry, sweetie. When the time comes, you'll know what to do. You'll do what's best. Like old Ned said today, 'Sometimes there's right, and sometimes there's righter.' You'll know what's righter."

"And if I don't, I'll ask you." Caroline hugged Sam.

"I'd best get back up to the house. Angel's lemonade will be gone before I get that sprig of mint she wanted."

"Oh, I'm sorry, I didn't mean to keep you. Guess I didn't want to carry this load by myself."

"Caroline, I'm a little concerned about my Angel. She's been slowing down a bit lately—having these weak spells. When I talk to her about seeing the doctor, she always changes the subject. How about keeping your eye on her when you're around?"

"I've noticed it, too, but I didn't want to say anything." She walked Sam to the door. "But you don't worry either, I'm right here. We'll take care of Angel. After all, the peaches are coming in, and she has cobblers and peach brandy to make."

She stood at the door and watched him pick a few mint leaves and then saunter up the path until he disappeared through the porch door. That heart-wringing dread that had gripped her when Gretchen and Bella left this morning returned.

Chapter Seventeen

Interrobang

———◆———

AROLINE WAS GLAD FOR THE LIGHT OF MORNING. THE night's restlessness was like pushing her mind through a sieve and then pulling it back through, only to start all over again. The heaviness of responsibility and the burden of this secret were weighing on her. Fortunately, yesterday's episode with Ned and Fred opened the door for her talk with Gretchen. She would claim the moment and proceed gently.

Gretchen phoned early to tell Caroline not to eat breakfast. She was bringing homemade pastries. Relieved not to have to wait all day to see them, Caroline turned on the kettle and imagined Gretchen putting on her gray sweater. They lived only a short few blocks away, but there was a great chasm to cross to bring them both to the same side, wherever that might be.

The simultaneous whistle of the teakettle and the doorbell summoned Caroline from the kitchen sink. She removed the kettle and went to the door.

"Good morning, Gretchen, and good morning, beautiful Bella." She hugged Gretchen and turned to Bella, not attempting to hug her today. Instead, she stood near and stroked Bella's silky blonde hair. "Bella, you have the most beautiful hair I've ever seen. It's just as lovely as your grand—"

Bella's penetrating gaze halted her.

Caroline did not know if Bella thought of Gretchen as her grandmother or her mother, and she decided quickly to change the subject. "Now what did the two of you concoct for this charming package?" she exclaimed as she took the pastries Gretchen now handed her. She observed the elegant way the goodies were covered in clear plastic wrap and then covered in wrapped layers of pink netting secured with white ribbon. Nestled in the bow was a delicate bouquet of white wood violets. The package was proof that Gretchen had a gift for making simple things elegant. "This is entirely too lovely to unwrap, but something tells me what's inside is just as delicious as the wrapping is lovely."

Gretchen stood with Caroline at the counter as Bella kept her distance. "Caroline, you've been such a kind hostess to us, always serving tea and cookies. So we wanted to bake you our favorite pastry. It's my grandmammá's recipe from the old country. It's not quite the same as my grandmammá made it. The butter here is a bit different, and so is the milk, but we like it very much, and we want you to like it too."

"Oh, my, this looks like something I'd have to pay lots of money for in a specialty bakery." Caroline pointed to the plaited bread drizzled with icing and sprinkled with nuts.

"My grandmammá used hazelnuts, but they're not so easy to find here. So we use pecans from the tree in our backyard."

"I prefer pecans anyway, especially when they're coated with sugar and butter. Come, let's share this treat."

"No, no, not until you have eaten first. Then Bella and I will have just one slice. The sweets have come to your house to stay, and we return to our house with a clean, empty plate and the joy of knowing you liked them."

Caroline tasted and immediately thought of her own mother's baking skills. "Why, Gretchen, I do believe this is the tastiest treat ever to pass my lips. I can't decide if it's pure heaven or just sin."

"Oh, no, please. Nothing I do can be compared to heaven, and please do not think of them as sin. I think God wants you to enjoy the sweetness of life."

Interesting from a woman who's tasted of so much bitterness.

"I like how you think, and I especially like the way you say things. I'm so glad you're my friend." Caroline turned to Bella, "And Bella, I'm so glad you're my friend too. I've been waiting to hear you play the piano again. We had a grand time yesterday."

Caroline thought she noticed a slight grin as Bella approached the counter. "Bella, do you like chocolate milk? I hope you do. I just made some especially for you."

"Chocolate milk? What a treat! She loves chocolate milk, and we get it only on very special occasions."

"Good, then we'll make today a special occasion. Let's see, is it anyone's birthday?"

Gretchen and Bella shook their heads.

"No? Is it a holiday? No? Well, what about . . . what about if we call it . . . Let's call it 'Interrobang Day.'"

Gretchen straightened the blue ribbon on Bella's ponytail. "That's such an unusual word. It is a new word for me and for you, too, Bella. I know my English could be much better, but I've never heard such a word. What does this word mean? How do you say—in-terro-bang? Is that correct?"

"That is correct. An interrobang is actually a punctuation mark—an exclamation point on top of a question mark. It's like a big surprising question, sort of like our day."

"Interrobang." Gretchen repeated the word deliberately and thoughtfully. "I like that new word, and so we celebrate Interrobang Day."

"Good. Here's the chocolate milk, Bella. I hope you like it. I used my special good chocolate just for you."

They chatted, ate their goodies, sipped tea and chocolate milk. Caroline enticed Bella to play the piano while she and Gretchen went out on the terrace. They took their tea and sat at the patio table so Bella could see them.

"Gretchen, I'm so glad you came early this morning, I have much to ask you and much to tell you."

"Not before I apologize for Bella's behavior. I have searched my thoughts for why she might have misbehaved so yesterday, but I have no answer."

"I think I have an answer, Gretchen, but before I get into that, I need to ask you a few more questions. Did I understand that Bella doesn't go to school?"

"Yes, you understood. I tried sending her to school, but as I told you, she is different than the other children. The teachers did not know what to do with her, so they sent us a letter saying there was nothing they could do to teach her."

"What did they expect you to do? I thought there were laws requiring her to go to school. I'm certain the school has some responsibility to teach her."

Gretchen's face had that faraway look again. "Maybe that is true, but their decision was quite satisfactory to me. They have many children in the classroom, and not much time to be with Bella. And it pleased Mr. Silva, for he does not like Bella to go out in public. He cannot see the beauty in her, and he thinks that Bella is our punishment for Karina's bad behavior."

"Punishment?"

"Yes. He does not look at Bella or speak to her—just as he was with Karina before she went away. But Bella is happy, and I am pleased, for she is with me every moment. She is a gift, a miraculous gift."

Caroline put down her teacup. "Gretchen, I've never heard Bella speak. Does she speak with you?"

"Oh, yes, she speaks mostly through her eyes and her music. She speaks only when she really has something to say or if she's repeating something she hears. She often hums and makes other sounds that let me know she is quite happy or frustrated."

Caroline wished she could memorize Gretchen's answers. "Does Bella think of you as her mother or her grandmother?"

"I do not know how to answer that question or how Bella thinks of me. I only know how she treats me. She is tender with my feelings. She hears my heart. Her spirit is peaceful when I am near her, and somehow she knows when my spirit is not peaceful. I see Bella is the same way with you. She knows that your heart is a good heart. There is much to learn about the mysteries inside her mind, that which is locked behind her beautiful eyes, and I hope you have the key." Gretchen drank the last sip of tea.

"Oh, Gretchen, how I wish I had the key, but maybe we can find it together. Have you tried to teach Bella to read?"

"Yes. When the teachers decided that she could no longer be in the classroom, they gave me books at my request. They told me I would be wasting my time. I tried, but I am not very good at teaching. Bella knows all the books I read to her. I'll show you sometime. Bella knows many things, many things girls her age do not know. She knows how to do stitching, and knitting, and crocheting. And she makes things. You will see one day what she can do. And Caroline, you've heard her music. She makes such beautiful music. Who can do that but my Bella?"

They stopped to listen. Bella was playing "David's Song."

"That song . . . Bella hums that song at home, but she only plays it on your piano. I do not know this song, but it is so beautiful. I think my Bella has created her own song."

Caroline knew it was her time to speak. "Gretchen, you've been open with me, answering my questions, and I'm grateful. That is a sign of our new friendship. Now there are some things I need to tell you; but before I do, you must know that I agree with you about Bella's special abilities and I only want to help her and you." Caroline paused. "So, where do I start?"

"You start at the beginning, my friend."

"That's always a good place to start, but in this case I'm not certain where the beginning is. Let's start with the song Bella is playing. It's 'David's Song,' a song I've been writing for years." She noted the puzzled look on Gretchen's face. "You see, about six years ago, I fell very deeply in love with a young man, and we were to be married." Caroline paused. "Our wedding was only six weeks away when David was killed. He was delivering medical supplies to an Indian tribe in Guatemala, and his vehicle was washed away in a flood and mud slide."

Despite herself, her eyes became glassy with tears. *How long will I feel the freshness of grief when I tell this story?*

"Oh, my precious friend, I am so sorry. Your pain is still great. I only wish I could make it go away. David must have been a rare man to have won your heart and kept it all these years."

"Yes." Caroline wiped a tear from her cheek. "He was a rare man and a gift to me like Bella is to you. His death changed the direction of my life, and I've had many questions about that. Time helps a bit, but the loss is always with me."

"It seems life brings us some . . . in-ter-ro-bangs, but God brings us interrobangs too." Gretchen paused. "But I don't understand about the song. Why does Bella play this song?"

"As I was saying, this is a song I was writing, and it was to be my wedding gift to David. I would have sung it at our wedding had there been one. I've never been able to finish it. Sometimes at night when I can't sleep, I play the piano. The other night, for the first time in a very long time, I played this piece."

Caroline felt the knot in her stomach grow tighter. "One morning, several weeks ago, I had breakfast with the Sam and Angel—that's the Meadowses, the owners of Twin Oaks here—and I was walking home. When I neared the studio, I heard someone playing my piano. I must tell you, it was quite startling, because as I listened, I heard 'David's Song.' I was frightened, but more curious than afraid, so I opened the door. When I did, the intruder ran out the terrace door, leaving it open."

"Someone was in your studio?" Gretchen twisted the napkin in her lap.

"Yes, but no harm was done and nothing was taken. The person only came to play the piano."

"It was Bella? You think it was my Bella?" Gretchen pulled at the napkin in her hand and moved to the edge of her chair.

"I do, Gretchen. But it's okay. Everything's fine. No harm's been done, and the mystery has been solved. But I must finish. I told no one about this, but a few days later, Sam reported that the Pendergrass brothers had found a hole in the fence and signs that someone had been hiding in the bushes next to the studio windows.

"These are the men who were here yesterday?" Gretchen kneaded her knuckles and rocked back and forth in worry—moving much like Bella.

"Yes, Ned and Fred repaired the fence, and a few days later they found the boards were removed from a different spot. We had an incident a few nights later that answers why Bella reacted the way she did yesterday."

"Oh, Caroline, this cannot be. Bella would not do such a thing. I never leave her alone except when she is in her room listening to music or sleeping. She would not go out by herself, not at night."

"Gretchen, please don't fret. No harm has been done."

"No harm? Oh, yes, there's been much harm. She has made damage to your fence. She has frightened you. How can you say there has been no harm? And for Bella, something terrible could have happened to her. It's all my fault, my fault."

"No, Gretchen. It's no one's fault. It's the desire of a young girl who wants to play the piano. That cannot be bad. The incident I want to tell you about involved Ned and Fred Pendergrass." Caroline took a sip of her tea. "They had decided, without telling anyone, to come here late one night and sit in the shrubs waiting for this intruder. They meant well, thinking they were protecting me. They heard the snooper—that's what they called our intruder. Anyway, they heard the intruder coming through the fence and attempted to get to the opening with a rope. Fred fell, making a loud noise, and this frightened the intruder away."

Gretchen leaned over, putting her head in her hands.

Caroline leaned toward her. "I was playing the piano, heard the noise, but I had no idea it was Ned and Fred, so I called Sam. He called the police and came down with his shotgun. They all arrived about the same time only to find out that Ned and Fred had created the disturbance."

Caroline decided not to tell her about Sam's gun going off and breaking the window. It wasn't necessary and would only frighten her more. "Gretchen, our mystery has been solved. Bella heard Ned and Fred's voices yesterday, and I think she associated them with that night when she must have really been frightened."

"This is too much." Gretchen looked at Caroline

"It's truly okay. Now that we know, we can prevent it from happening again. There have been no signs of the intruder since that evening. I felt early on that the intruder meant no harm. There were opportunities to vandalize or to steal, but no harm was done. I'm so glad that it was Bella and that she's safe. I want you to know that I have told only Sam and Angel."

"This is all my fault, Caroline. It's all my fault."

"What do you mean it's your fault? But think, I would never know about Bella and her gifts if she hadn't done this."

"If Mr. Silva knew this, I can only imagine what he might do."

Caroline's thoughts quickly mobilized her anger toward this vicious man, and she tried to hide her emotion lest Gretchen think she was angry with her or Bella. "Then Mr. Silva will never know. There's no need for him to know."

"He's right; I should not take Bella out."

"No, no, Gretchen, he is wrong. You have every right to take her anywhere."

"If I had not taken her out, then this would not have happened. Bella loved to listen to the music. It calmed her. We listened to the records I brought from my grandmammá's collection back home. We listened to them over and over, and Bella would hum the melodies. I had wanted to learn to play the piano, but my life gave me no opportunity, so I wanted Bella to have the opportunity. I told you I saved money to buy this small keyboard. We would play the keyboard at home when Mr. Silva was away."

"Does he know you have the keyboard?"

"No. He would be very angry I spent grocery money on such 'nonsense,' as he would say."

"He would be wrong. Music is the furthest thing from nonsense. I believe it is Bella's language."

Gretchen sat back in her chair with her arms folded and tightly clenched. "The keyboard brings us so much joy. She would not touch it at first. So I studied the book and started playing tunes. Then Bella finally touched the keyboard for the first time and played the tunes she had heard me play. I knew she had a gift. But then one day—it was a beautiful spring day—we took our walk down through the woods." Gretchen pointed to the woods beyond the fence.

"We walked to our favorite spot. There is a small wooden structure in the thickest part of the trees and underbrush. Maybe some young boys built it. It was one room with a door and two openings like windows." She used her hands as she described the opening. "It became our favorite place. Bella and I cleaned it up and gathered scrap wood to create a floor. We made cushions and pillows and curtains, and I was saving money to buy paint. We go there and sit on a quilt we spread over the floor. We do our needlework and sing, and sometimes I read to Bella or tell her stories about the old country."

Caroline noticed the tense muscles in Gretchen's face relax a bit.

"But Caroline, the real reason we go there is because we can hear you playing. It is so quiet, only the sounds of the forest and the birds singing as you play. We call this place our parlor, and we think it the finest parlor in all of Moss Point. There was no way for me to know that our joy in listening to your music could cause such harm."

"Gretchen, please believe me, there has been no harm. Really, only good things will come from this. Trust me, only good." Caroline was glad Gretchen had one peaceful place.

"Bella loves hearing you play. As the melodies float through the trees, she turns to the music. Sometimes she walks out the door as if she were trying to find the source of such beautiful sounds. I have followed her a short distance to bring her back to our parlor."

Gretchen relaxed even more and began to smile as she continued. "One day, her yearning softened my heart as I watched her take one deliberate step after another in her search of the music. She made a few steps, stopped and listened, and started toward the music again. I could not bring myself to stop her. I followed her all the way to the fence. I tried my best to explain this was as far as we could go, that the music was coming from the house on the other side of the fence and that we were not allowed to go there."

Caroline listened to Gretchen's story and to Bella playing the piano, and she imagined floral curtains and lace-trimmed pillows and a homemade quilted floor in their parlor. She envisioned the two of them sitting there with yarn and knitting needles. In her heart, she wept at thoughts of their joy in such simplicity and of Gretchen's grateful spirit in spite of the places she was not allowed to go.

Gretchen continued. "Bella stood and looked through the cracks in the fence, and she rocked back and forth to the music. We did this only once, only once, Caroline. But Bella's yearning was so deep." Gretchen began to cry.

Caroline took her hand. There were no words. For a while, they just sat silently together while the clouds gathered. Not even sparse raindrops broke the spell. Caroline watched the raindrops creating ripples on the pond surface—ripples that could not be stopped, much like the sight of Bella through the window and the sound of her unfinished song.

"Gretchen, I know we're both sitting here wondering about things, maybe about where we go from here. I want desperately for you to know that I'm very grateful you and Bella walked through my studio door and into my life. I want to teach Bella, and I want to be your friend. You probably think that I have a full life and many friends. And in a way, you'd be right. I have my family and friends back home, Sam and Angel right here, my students, my friends at church, and a few friends at the university. But I have very few close friends. I have allowed my pain to separate and protect me from relationships. There's something I know in my heart about you: you know pain, and you love music. We have much in common, and I truly want you to be my friend."

"Caroline, how could you want me to be your friend? You're younger, and you are educated, and you have such beauty and grace. I'm nobody, except Bella's grandmother, and I can't even help her."

"You are wrong, Gretchen. You're a fascinating woman. I know little about your history, but I know you're a woman of great character. You have suffered loss—loss of more than I could even guess. And yet you're a woman of such faith, and you're not filled with anger and questions about the interrobangs in your life. You have such a sweetness and a gentleness and a depth about you that I don't see often. I have so many questions to ask you about how you've stayed so gracious and hopeful even with such loss."

"You, my friend, can ask me anything, but I fear I have nothing to tell you. There is an unexplainable mystery about living, and my faith is simple. I fear we spend too much time pondering the unanswerable questions instead of appreciating what is given. My grandmammá always told me life is all about purpose—finding it and staying true to it."

"But you have found your purpose, have you not?"

"Oh, yes, I have my purpose. I wake every morning and live every day to care for my Bella. She makes me smile, and she makes my heart glad I'm alive."

Caroline could not imagine what Gretchen's life would be without Bella. Neither could she envision what her life was like with Bella—living in a prison, having to watch the man she married treat his own granddaughter as if she did not exist. "Gretchen, I told you before, you have been entrusted with Bella. God knew you would love her and provide for her needs. I have something else I need to tell you about Bella."

Gretchen hung her head. "Please, no. I think I cannot bear hearing more today."

"No, no, this is good, Gretchen. It's something you've known for a long time, but now we have a name for what you know. And please remember, I'm no expert. I know only a little, but I know that Bella is unlike anyone I've ever experienced. When I heard her play 'David's Song' last week, I knew her giftedness was beyond me. So I called my piano instructor at the university."

"She knows about Bella?"

"Yes, she knows what little I've been able to tell her. Her name is Dr. Annabelle Martin. When I told her about Bella, she asked me several questions. You have given me many of those answers today."

"I don't understand what this means," Gretchen said.

"Right now I don't either. When I spoke with Dr. Martin, she asked me if I was familiar with the term *musical savant*. I've heard the term, and I've seen a television documentary about a musical savant, but my knowledge is limited and shallow."

"What is a savant?"

"I don't know that Bella is a musical savant, but I know she has many of the classic characteristics of one. This could be such a good thing. Savants are unusual people who have exceptional abilities in certain areas—like how Bella plays the piano without being taught. There are other types of savants—some gifted with numbers and others with art. Their brains work almost like tape recorders. I've done some reading in the last few days, and I'll be glad for you to take the articles I've printed from the internet to read them for yourself."

"How did Bella get this gift?"

"I don't have the answer to that question, and from my reading, I'm not sure that the experts know for certain either."

"This is rare?"

"Very rare. From what I read, Bella is probably one in less than one hundred people on earth with this gift." Caroline knew that not everyone considered savants gifted persons, as their IQs were frequently under sixty and they might or might not even be able to tie their shoes, but she preferred Gretchen's perspective remained positive.

"I would like very much to read what you have read."

"I'll put the articles in an envelope, and you may take them home. You must have hundreds of questions."

"I would just like to know what other people say."

"Gretchen, there may come a time when we should take Bella to the university and have her play for Dr. Martin." She could see the tension build in Gretchen's facial muscles. "Would you like to do that?"

"I cannot do that, Caroline. I have no vehicle, and I do not think Mr. Silva would allow me to go."

"I'm not asking you to take Bella. I would take you. It's very important for you to be together. Would it help if I spoke with Mr. Silva?"

She watched Gretchen tense even more. "Caroline, you must never speak of any of this with Mr. Silva." Her eyes darted toward Bella inside. "I need to get home. He's been on a road trip and will be back this afternoon, and I must be there. And please do not ever tell him about Bella breaking into your studio and causing damage to your fence. I will save money to pay you for the repairs." She stood to go.

"Wait, Gretchen." Gretchen had started toward the door. "Please wait. You mustn't think that Bella broke in. She did not. I always leave the door unlocked. She did no harm. And the fence—the old fence is about to fall down anyway. Ned and Fred have been repairing that fence for years. Bella just moved some boards. There's no need to repay anything. Why, if Bella hadn't heard the music and come in, I'd never have met her. And to think that I lived just a few blocks from a musical prodigy and had no idea . . . We just need to believe there was some divine intervention here. At least that's what I think."

Gretchen stopped at the door and turned to Caroline. "Do you truly believe that, Caroline?"

"I truly do."

"Then I will believe it too. And I will trust that God will make a way for us and that He will let us know what way that is. But I must warn you, Caroline, that could take time. It has taken me twelve years. For almost twelve years, I have prayed constantly for His way for Bella. I'm beginning to think you are the answer to my prayer. Time will tell."

Caroline stood to join Gretchen, and words would not come. Playing the piano was easier. With music, words were unnecessary, and she found herself often without words.

They went inside. Bella was still playing. She played Gretchen's little tunes only on the keyboard, and on Caroline's grand piano she played only the songs she had heard played there. Conversation with Gretchen had left little time for Caroline to sit with Bella and observe her.

"Come, Bella. It's time to go home."

Bella kept playing as though she heard nothing.

Gretchen walked to the piano and gently moved Bella's hands from the keyboard. "Come, child, we must go. Maybe we'll stop at our parlor on the way home, and maybe we'll hear the music in the trees again."

Bella smiled, and Gretchen looked toward Caroline as though asking her to play once they left.

Caroline smiled and nodded.

"Let me get your plate," said Caroline as she moved toward the kitchen. "I remember. You take home an empty plate and the joy of knowing I liked your pastries." Caroline continued talking as though Bella would understand every word. "We celebrated Interrobang Day today. We're the only people in the whole wide world who were doing that. And who knows? We might be the only ones who even know what an interrobang is."

"Interrobang," Gretchen repeated to remember it.

"Let's see, is it a surprising question or a questioning surprise? I don't know. But thank you, Bella, for bringing the goodies, and thank you for playing my piano. I like it when you play my piano. No one plays it like you—just like your name: beautiful."

She handed Gretchen the clean plate and turned to stroke Bella's hair again. "I have a teacher named Annabelle. I really hope you get to meet her someday. You'd like her, and she would really like you. Her name is like yours—it means 'beautiful gift.'"

"And do you know what your name means, Caroline?" Gretchen asked.

"Not really. I was named for my grandmother."

"What is your middle name?"

"You're the second person who's brought that up in the last few days. I don't have a middle name—just Caroline."

"Well, 'just Caroline,' your name means 'beautiful' too."

Chapter Eighteen

A Muumuu and a Mooning

———— • ————

CAROLINE AND BROTHER ANDY HAD SURVIVED FRIDAY night's rehearsal dinner for the Yarbrough wedding. It appeared Brother Andy had left his servant spirit at home, donning a take-charge attitude like he donned his navy blazer.

Caroline was relieved to know the glue had dried on the parquet floor. Impromptu, she was asked to provide music in place of the string quartet, which would arrive tomorrow. Her trumpet fanfare had startled Grandmother Yarbrough and the guineas down at the barn. Perhaps Brother Andy was right. This trumpet fanfare just might be mistaken for the last blast of Gabriel's trumpet, especially if the guys down at the beer hall had a few drinks under their belts.

Caroline had moved through the evening on autopilot, grateful to get home and into bed. Once there, she hadn't stirred an inch until dawn. As she sat enjoying her coffee, the phone rang.

"Good morning, sunshine!" Sam crowed in his best good-morning voice. "Didn't wake you up, did I?"

"Have you ever awakened me at seven thirty in the morning, Sam?"

"Well, let's see, there was that morning back in—"

"Okay, one time, but being sick doesn't count."

"You want some pancakes? Angel's concocted something special with peaches and some whipped cream. There might be a little of the recipe involved—you know, the peach brandy. Besides, we want to hear all about last night. Angel's just dying to know if your feet stuck to the parquet floor."

"Who could turn down peaches on pancakes? Not me. I'll bring—"

"I know, you'll bring the coffee. Just get yourself and your coffee on up here. Not even fresh peaches can revive cold pancakes."

She poured the carafe of coffee and walked briskly up the path. Sam met her at the back door. "Let me see your shoes."

"My shoes? Oh, they may have wet grass on them. I'll leave them here at the door."

"Caroline No-Middle-Name Carlyle, either you're getting slow, or you're really distracted. I was checking them for glue. You know, the oak flooring out at the Yarbroughs'?"

"You're right, I'm getting slow. No glue. It was dry. In fact, the place was lovely."

"Well, Angel's in the kitchen champing at the bit to hear all the details."

Caroline set her carafe on the breakfast table. "Wow, would you look at her!" She gawked at Angel's new muumuu.

"I already looked at her. I'd say she's a sight for sore eyes."

Angel twirled around, streamers of brightly colored ribbon trailing around her. "You like it? I call it my man-getting muumuu."

"I'd say it's working." She winked at Sam and stepped up for a closer examination. The muumuu was crisp white cotton. Sewn into the front and back yokes were bold-colored buttons securing the ends of yard-long pieces of brightly colored ribbons. The ribbons streamed loosely down to the hem, and at the end of each sat a matching button weighting down the ribbon. "Did you make it?"

"Of course I made it. I had all this ribbon and all these artsy buttons, and I decided it was time to do something with them. Do you know how hard it is to find a plain white muumuu? Nigh on to impossible. I finally found one in a catalog. So while Sam's snoozing when he says he's reading, I've been cutting ribbon and sewing on buttons."

"It's a work of art—just like you, Angel."

Sam chuckled. "I'm just glad she didn't have cowbells she needed to use up. That's my girl, colorful and always on the move. How about moving some of those hot pancakes over my way?"

"Coming right up."

They sat down to eat, and Sam was sure to thank the Lord for peaches when he asked the blessing.

"Now tell me about the peaches, Angel," said Caroline.

"Just fresh Georgia peaches, a tad of sugar, and a splash of peach brandy. Tossed them in the blender until they were pureed. But I confess the cream is the real stuff. None of that fat-free, nondairy whipped topping this morning. You get the first crop of peaches only once during a season, and I figure they deserve the best whipped cream."

Sam surveyed the table. "Where's the maple syrup?"

"It's where it always is."

"It's not where it always is when we're eating pancakes."

Angel put both hands on the table. "Sam Meadows, you're telling me you're going to eat maple syrup on your pancakes when you could eat fresh peaches?"

"Well, I suppose not, now that you put it that way." Sam picked up his fork.

"Sweetie, I'm dying to hear about last night. We saw all the guests arriving at Tandy's when we walked down to the activity center."

Caroline plopped whipped cream atop her pancakes. "There's really not much to tell. Brother Andy took charge and went through the processional and ceremony, and then we left for dinner."

"Brother Andy took charge? Even with Tandy Yarbrough and a professional wedding coordinator?" Sam had a look of surprise.

"He did. I think he feared a repeat of Rachel's rehearsal and wedding."

Sam wiped his mouth with his napkin. "Well, we heard your trumpet fanfare all the way down to the center. The Masons were having their First Friday Fish Fry, and half the town was there eating, and the other half was picking up plates to go. All of a sudden we heard this trumpet blast, and we didn't know whether to stand and salute or run for cover. Why the fish were flying, the hushpuppies started barking, and the ketchup—"

"She gets the picture, Sam. So tell me about the evening." Angel smeared whipped cream over the peaches on her plate.

"It was all rather usual. Not one thing for Delia Mullins to write about."

"Delia Mullins needs something to write about. I always read the *Moss Point Messenger* just before bedtime. That way I'll be sure to go to bed with nothing on my mind."

"I can imagine if Delia went out to the Lawsons' lake house for the bachelor party, or if she'd be invisible at Cuttin' Loose tomorrow, she'd have plenty to write about."

Angel cut into her stack of pancakes with her fork. Butter oozed. "Sounds juicier than these peaches."

"Gracie told me Tandy booked Cuttin' Loose for the entire day yesterday and up until noon today. The girls had pedicures, manicures, and massages yesterday. They're all getting their makeup and hair done this morning."

"Well, that's enough to curl your hair." Sam swallowed his last drop of coffee and smacked his lips.

"I think you're right, Sam. That's why I declined Tandy's invitation, as gracious as it was. Are you all coming to the wedding?"

"Angel's dragging me down there, but you'll find the marks of my fingernails all the way down the sidewalk."

"You'll enjoy it once you get there, just like you always do," Angel said.

"Yeah, like I enjoyed the mumps. But I'll admit I did enjoy the last Yarbrough wedding. It's hard to forget the sight of Tandy covered in watermelon."

"Hey, this is changing the subject, but I wanted you to know I had a long talk with Gretchen Silva yesterday. I told her about the intruder episodes. I think she'll watch Bella more closely. It's not safe for her to be leaving the house in the middle of the night."

"That's for sure, not even in Moss Point," Angel said.

"She told me she and Bella found a small wooden shack down in the middle of the woods beyond the fence, and they cleaned it and decorated it a bit. They call it their parlor. That's how they heard my piano. Bella would follow the sound, and Gretchen allowed her to come all the way to the fence one time to hear me play."

"This all makes sense. Sounds like you were right, Miss Carlyle," Sam said.

"I don't need to be right about that. What I need to be right about is this savant thing. I told Gretchen about that possibility and sent home some material for her to read. She flat-out refused when I told her we should take Bella to the university to play for Dr. Martin."

"But I thought she wanted Bella to develop this talent," Angel said.

"She does. But her fear of Mr. Silva is greater than her desire to help Bella. From what I gather, she has a right to be afraid. This whole thing has me in quite a quandary."

"It'll all work out. You just wait and see." Angel began to stack the dishes. Sam sat silently.

"Hey, I hate to eat and leave, but I need to go. The pancakes and peaches were the best. Ought to hold me until the reception this evening—that is, if I get a chance to eat."

"I'll check on you and bring you a plate."

"What would I ever do without you, Angel?"

"You'd do just fine, just like Sam would do."

Caroline looked at Sam. His eyes were lovingly fixed on Angel, and he said nothing.

"Now scat. Sam will help me do the dishes."

"Thanks, and I'm glad your man-getting muumuu worked. You

got yourself a winner over there," said Caroline on her way out the door.

———.———

The town matrons were disappointed; their prayers for rain had gone unanswered again. The afternoon summer breeze was cooler than usual, and the only clouds in the sky were the big, fluffy, cotton-candy kind that made ten-year-old girls want to lie in the grass and daydream. Caroline's father always said of such a picture-perfect day, "If God made a more beautiful day, then He must have kept it for Himself."

Caroline arrived and had the help of two of the local football stars to help unload the keyboard and stand. Potted ferns and tall palms covered the platform where the actual ceremony would take place. In the center of the platform was the arbor that Ned and Fred had built. Its latticework was covered in green smilax, more gardenias, and acres of baby's breath. Caroline wished Ned and Fred could see the fruit of their labors, but she knew that not in a million years would Tandy invite them to this event.

Folding chairs were arranged in rows on each side of a center aisle. Each chair's back was covered in white tulle and tied with a white ribbon and a gardenia. Caroline saw the head football coach coming through them toward her. "Hi, Coach."

"Hello, Miss Carlyle. Anything else you need, just let me know."

"Thank you. I will. Looks like you brought the team with you."

"You bet. The Yarbroughs offered a hefty gift to the boosters club if the team would move chairs and park cars."

Caroline smiled. "Tandy always thinks of everything."

"You're right about that. Even got somebody to build a peg-board rack so the boys would have a place to put the car keys with name tags."

"What can I say?"

Caroline had fully expected the decorations to be slightly beyond the edge of tasteful, but in looking over the grounds, she decided they were quite elegant. Guests were arriving, and things were going according to schedule. She checked the keyboard for power and proper settings, spoke with the musicians and the wedding director, synchronized their watches, and went inside for one last summit with Tandy.

Tandy was in the back with Rebecca and the bridesmaids making sure the three flower girls had all been to the potty one last time. Caroline found her and assured her that everything was set. The string quartet had started to play. This meant business was about to pick up, and the wedding would begin in exactly twenty minutes.

Satisfied that all was well, Caroline returned to the patio just to sit quietly for a few moments. She sat among the ferns and palms listening to the quartet playing Pachelbel's Canon. It still amazed her that a composer could take such a simple motif and turn it into something so very beautiful and complex.

The patio door opened and the brigade of bridesmaids and grandmothers and mothers summoned her to reality. She looked at her watch—five minutes to go. She moved to the dance floor where the keyboard was located.

It was as if Someone above had orchestrated this event. The moment the string quartet finished the piece, the courthouse clock struck four o'clock. She decided to delay the trumpet fanfare until the clock had finished chiming. One, two, three, four, and finally . . . the sound of trumpets. Her horns vibrated the dance floor, filled the air in Tandy's yard, and startled Mr. Appleby snoring on the fourth row. As she sprinted from the dance floor back to the patio where the string quartet was in position, she imagined the guys down at the pool hall, on their knees about now, confessing their sins.

Seating herself, Caroline looked at the score and gave the wedding director the cue to send in the groom's grandmother as the quartet began to play. Grandma paused for the picture-taking and was escorted to her seat.

Tandy's mother-in-law, Mrs. Yarbrough, was next. At eighty-six, she was decked out in a tea-length blue silk dress with hose to complement and carried an heirloom white-linen handkerchief. Years of eating without exercise had settled in her hips, and she had chosen this dress with a soft gathered skirt to disguise her roundness. As it turned out, with Gracie's dye job, Mrs. Yarbrough's hair nearly matched her dress.

Caroline held her breath as Mrs. Yarbrough took the arm of her escort and started down the steps. When they reached the point where the photographer was kneeling on the ground poised to take her picture, the photographer suddenly stood up and motioned to the wedding director. The wedding director sent Caroline over to see what the photographer needed.

"Stop her. Look." The photographer pointed at Mrs. Yarbrough's ankles.

Caroline looked and saw a puddle of blue silk hose. She quickly stepped over and grabbed the usher's arm, pulling the pair back a few steps to handle the problem. She had no quick and brilliant ideas as to how to fix things and had decided just to point out the problem and let Mrs. Yarbrough help make the decisions. But when Mrs. Yarbrough realized she was not moving forward, she jerked the young man's arm and pronounced to him and all the guests, "Come on, young man, take me down this aisle."

"Wait, Mrs. Yarbrough," Caroline said, stepping in. "Look at your ankles."

Mrs. Yarbrough leaned slightly forward, trying to see her ankles. When that didn't work, she tried lifting one ankle and teetered before the usher and Caroline stabilized her. "Heavenly days, what is that around my ankles?" she asked loudly enough to be heard all the way to the platform.

"I think it's your panty hose, ma'am."

"What? Did you say my panty hose?" The guests were beginning to turn in their seats to see what was happening, and Caroline could already see the town matrons grinning. Mrs. Yarbrough lifted her dress and leaned forward a bit further this time. "My stars, you're right. It is my panty hose. How in the world can that be? They're brand new. Here, honey, take this." She handed Caroline her handkerchief.

Before Caroline, the usher, the entire wedding party, the wedding director, or the string quartet could figure out what was going on, Mrs. Yarbrough had yanked up her skirt, leaned over—exposing her naked derriere to the entire wedding party standing not more than ten feet behind her—and begun trying to pull her panty hose up. She was giving it her all, pinning her skirt tail to her sides with her elbows and attempting to pull up her hose at the same time. She bobbed back and forth like the last standing bowling pin when a strike has been rolled.

It had all happened so fast. Caroline slapped the usher on the arm. "Young man, turn your head, hang on to her, and give me your coat." He twisted and contorted, trying to keep Mrs. Yarbrough from doing a head roll down the aisle while at the same time removing his coat as Caroline requested. She took his jacket and tried to protect what was left of Mrs. Yarbrough's dignity.

Tandy stood ten feet away hyperventilating while the bride, eight bridesmaids and eight groomsmen, and three flower girls tried to control their laughter. The four-year-old ring bearer's curiosity got the best of him, and he threw the ring pillow down and rushed for a closer view. Strange sounds from the string quartet indicated the viola player had lost her place, and the cellist had stopped playing altogether.

Mrs. Yarbrough's son, the father of the bride, moved in to take hold of the situation—mainly his mother's arm to keep her from landing on her head.

"What are you doing, son?"

"I'm trying to cover your backside, Mother. You're mooning the entire wedding party."

"I'm what? What did you say?"

Rumbles and snickers echoed through the crowd, and even

Brother Andy pretended to have a coughing fit to cover his own laughter as Mrs. Yarbrough finally accomplished what she set out to do and wiggled her way back into her hose. She turned to her escort, announcing once again so that all the wedding guests could hear, "Young man, are you going to take me down this aisle, or am I going to have to find someone else to do it?"

Caroline handed him his coat and straightened Mrs. Yarbrough's dress from behind, and the elderly woman started her dignified walk down the aisle, never giving thought to the commotion she had just created. The wedding director yanked the ring bearer's arm, dragging him back to his position as members of the wedding party tried to regain their composure.

Caroline reached for her music to locate where the musicians were. The last thing she noticed before returning her attention to the ceremony was Delia Mullins standing in the bushes with her camera still swinging around her neck.

——•——

The evening finally came to a close as the bride and groom ran down the driveway in a shower of birdseed and bubbles to the white horse-drawn carriage awaiting them on the street. But the real excitement came when the guests lined up for the valet parking service. The football players positioned themselves only to find the pegboard had been emptied of all keys. Discussions of a master ring of thieves with the intent of looting and vandalizing all the guests' homes were dismissed when the ring bearer and his cousin proudly brought two buckets of keys to the football players. They had planned to help.

It took more than an hour to sort the keys and get cars. As guests stood in the driveway awaiting their vehicles, they lamented the fact that the Yarbroughs had only two daughters and took bets on what would appear in Delia Mullins column in the *Moss Point Messenger* next week.

Chapter Nineteen

Step One and Fifteen Minutes

———◆———

THREE DAYS PASSED WITHOUT ANY WORD FROM GRETCHEN. With Bella's entrance into her life and with the offer from the university, Caroline felt as if she were dangling from a rubber band, and just when she felt she could stand on firm ground, someone would yank the elastic again. She'd had no idea her initial call to Dr. Martin would ignite such interest. Dr. Martin had made calls to a professor in the psychology department and to a neighbor who was a neurologist. They all wanted to meet Bella.

Two more days passed and finally the early morning phone call came. Mr. Silva was out of town again, and Gretchen wanted to see her. Caroline volunteered to come to their house, but Gretchen declined, saying it would be better if they came to the studio.

It was a warm, humid morning. The thick air hinted at an afternoon thundershower. Despite the summer morning's temperatures, Gretchen stood silently in a flowered cotton dress and her gray sweater until Caroline answered the door.

Caroline greeted Gretchen, but before she could say good morning to Bella, Bella was on the piano bench. Bella was different today. There was the familiar rocking motion, and the music sounded the same, but there was a slight smile on her face, something Caroline had not seen before. Bella was more comfortable. She was home again—not home in the studio but home at the keyboard.

Gretchen's quiet gentleness was not present this morning. She was more focused and purposeful. It was not long before she asked if she and Caroline could sit in the garden for conversation. Caroline made them a cup of tea and they made their way to the garden bench.

Gretchen clutched her teacup in both hands. "Thank you, Caroline, for allowing us to come for a visit. I must begin by telling you how sorry I am for my behavior. I have been very unfair with you, especially since you have been so helpful to us. We seem to always have such surprising conversations, and then I rush away without explanation and without telling you when you'll hear from me again."

"Oh, you really don't need to apologize. I know you don't have the freedom to contact me. I promise I understand, but I must tell you I do worry about you and Bella, especially when I don't hear from you for a few days." Caroline sipped her tea.

"You need not worry about us."

Caroline turned toward Gretchen. "But Mr. Silva and his anger? I worry for your safety and what he might do to you."

Gretchen sat resolute, staring into her teacup. "Caroline, I've lived with Mr. Silva for nearly twenty-eight years, and I've learned how not to upset him. I want to be honest with you, but I really do not wish to worry you. It would enrage him to know I had brought Bella to see a piano teacher. He does not like her to be out of the house. That is why I must be so secretive. It is not my nature to be dishonest and to hide things from my husband, but somehow, I think God will forgive me. I am only trying to get help for Bella."

"I must ask you this. Has he ever beaten you?"

Gretchen looked away and was hesitant.

Caroline sat in silence, determined to wait for Gretchen's answer.

"Oh, I do not want you to think badly of Mr. Silva. In many ways, he has been good to me."

"I'd really like to hear more about how he's good to you."

"It is a long story that started in the old country. I've told you about my family and my grandmammá's coming to live with us, and how much I loved her. My grandparents and parents were White Russians living in Hungary, then Austria. It was expected of me to marry someone from the White Russian community in our city. It was not an arranged marriage that involved money, but it was expected that all the Russian girls would marry Russian young men."

"Did you have a choice?" She sipped her tea.

"Yes, one always has a choice. But the choice is not always between what is better or best. Sometimes the choice is between what is better or worse. The consequences of disobeying my parents' wishes would have made my life most difficult." Gretchen held her tea, never taking a sip.

"So, you chose to be obedient?"

"Yes, at first." Gretchen paused. "There was a couple who owned a small market two blocks down the street. They lived in a comfortable apartment above the market. The owners were getting old and planned to give the business to their eldest son, Peter. I was nearly seventeen, and Peter was almost thirty. He was shy but a responsible and dutiful son. Peter's parents convinced my parents that I would have a very good life as Peter's wife. So we began the courtship in the way of our people."

"Did you have feelings for Peter?" Caroline studied Gretchen's face. The breeze picked up, whirling petals from nearby rose bushes.

"Yes, I think so. But really, this was not about my feelings. It was about security. Peter and his parents were very kind to me." Gretchen hesitated. "Caroline, this is a very long story, and perhaps I will tell you all the details someday. But what you need to know is there was a dreadful incident that changed everything. This incident shamed me, and I could no longer remain in my parents' home. They did not know of the shame, but I did, and I could not bring it upon them, so I ran away."

"At nineteen?"

"Yes, at nineteen. History has a way of repeating itself, does it not?" Gretchen picked up a rose petal and inhaled its fragrance.

"You're thinking of your daughter, Karina?"

"Yes. Perhaps I brought it upon her."

"I don't think it works that way, Gretchen."

"I must finish my story before I lose my courage to tell you these things." Gretchen bowed her head. "I had no money, so I took some of my grandmammá's jewelry and her silver hand mirror. I knew my mother hid her money in a teapot in our dining room, and I took some of it. I did not take it all—just enough." Gretchen paused to sip her tea.

"Enough for what?"

"I did not know at the time. But I could not bear to think I had taken it all. I packed a small bag and pretended I was going to the market, but instead I went to the train station and bought a ticket to the farthest place my money would take me and still leave me money for food for a couple of days. I got off the train in northern Germany."

"Did you have family there?"

"No. I was alone in my shame. I got a job at a small café. That is where I met Mr. Silva. He was in the US Army and was stationed at the base there. Ernesto rescued me from the trouble I was in and took care of me. He married me and got the papers necessary to bring me to the United States."

"Were you in love?" Caroline noted this was the first time she had heard Gretchen call Mr. Silva "Ernesto."

"What is 'in love,' Caroline? If gratitude is love, then I was in love. I think maybe in the early days, there was infatuation. Ernesto was lonely and homesick and did not get along with the other soldiers. I was lonely and homesick too. So I became his wife and friend. I was his whole world, and he took care of me. Maybe that is love."

A sadness darkened Caroline's thoughts. *I lost David, but I would bear the pain of loss just to know the intensity and the joy of his love. Gretchen has lived more than half her life never knowing this kind of passion.*

"It was only after we came to the States and he finished his tour of duty that we went to his hometown. By that time, Karina was born, and our lives were changing. Ernesto found it difficult to go home again, and he couldn't find work. When he found a job here, we moved to Moss Point. In the early days, our life was good. We had a few friends. We went to church and to the movies and even on picnics down by the lake. But people would stare at me and say things about me, and he became very jealous. So we began staying at home. It was then that his drinking and his rages started. His old demons returned. That's when . . . that's when . . ." Gretchen could not finish.

"Is that when he became abusive to you?"

"Yes. He did not mean to hurt me, and he only hurt me when he was drinking. But he never touched Karina. I always protected her, as I told you before."

"Is he still beating you? Is that why you wear the sweater?"

"No. No, he has not hurt me in a long time. I wear the sweater to cover these." Gretchen set her teacup on the wrought-iron table and slowly pushed the gray sweater up her left forearm. Caroline saw deep-purple scars in contrast to porcelain-white skin—scars from past injuries. Worse than those scars was the pain in Gretchen's eyes as she described what happened.

"Mr. Silva was drinking and became agitated when Bella broke the knob on the television. I feared he might hurt her." Gretchen hung her head. "Oh, I cannot tell you this. I cannot bear for you to think of me this way."

Caroline brushed a rose petal from Gretchen's shoulder. "It's all right. I know whatever you did, it was out of love for Bella."

"Oh, I would have died of sadness had he hurt her. She was only four. I was in the kitchen when I heard him scream at her. I just picked up a knife without thinking about it. I just did it. I ran into the den. Bella was screaming, and he had grabbed her hair. When he saw the knife in my hand, he released Bella. He snatched my arm and took the knife away. I was so afraid and told Bella to run to her room and lock her door, but she would not. She saw it all."

Her trembling caused her teacup to rattle. She set it down and continued. "It was as if someone else had entered his body—someone I did not know. He started flailing his arms with the knife and threatened to kill me. I raised my arms in defense, and he began slashing me. I can still feel the burning blade when I remember." Gretchen rubbed her forearms. "I was bleeding badly. I just fell to the floor unable to defend myself any longer. When he saw all the blood, he came to his senses and became the man I knew. He bathed my arms and bandaged them and took care of me for days."

"You didn't go to the hospital? Or to the doctor?"

"Oh, no. If I had, there would have been questions and an investigation, and Mr. Silva might have gone to jail."

"But from the looks of these scars, you needed stitches." Caroline raised the sweater slightly on Gretchen's right arm.

"My arms healed after several weeks. He bathed the wounds and covered them in salve. He promised if I would stay at home and keep quiet about this that he would never touch me again. I moved into Bella's room, and my arms healed. But my heart for Mr. Silva did not."

"I can certainly understand why." Caroline gently squeezed Gretchen's scarred forearm.

"He still takes care of me. I have food and clothes and someplace to live."

"But you live as his servant and not his wife?"

"It is the way we live, Caroline. I do this for Bella." Gretchen pulled the arm of her sweater back down to her unblemished wrist.

Caroline stared at the Cherokee roses on the fence and sat quietly for a moment. "Gretchen, what if I could make it possible for you and Bella to have a better life? A way for Bella to develop her musical gifts and for you to have freedom to live, freedom to go places and have friends. Would you like that?"

"Oh, this is not possible."

"What if I could make it possible?" Caroline had no clue as to how she would make it possible, but she knew she would try.

"I do not know. I do not know. I have no other family. I fear my parents are dead. I know nothing of my sister. When I took their money the day I boarded the train, I never saw them again. I am dead to them. Mr. Silva has been good to me, and I must not abandon him. That would not be right."

"Gretchen, I really don't know what to say, but this I know: Mr. Silva has not been good to you or good for you. There is more to life than having a roof over your head. You don't owe him for that."

"Caroline, you know not of what you speak. I owe him much."

"From what you've described, you're no more than a slave to him. I'm all for loyalty and keeping families together, but not when there's such violence. And you have Bella, and I don't think you understand about her gift."

"You're wrong, Caroline. I do understand. Bella is God's gift to me. I've known for many years that she is different, and I have prayed for so long that somebody else would know it too."

"If what you're saying is true, and you think I'm the answer you have prayed for, then you must trust me."

There was a long silence. "I do trust you, Caroline. I do. But I do not know what to do."

Suddenly Gretchen's situation made sense to Caroline. She had heard Sam talk about inmates who served long sentences and were finally paroled. He described how many of them violated parole so they could go back to jail. Their prison cell was a safe place, a place where they had to make no decisions. They had lost the ability to live with freedom. This was Gretchen. Living with her husband, as bad as it was, had become a safe place for her.

"Then I'll tell you what to do," Caroline said in a confident manner most unlike her. "The first thing to do is to get Bella to the university. We'll not tell your husband about this. We'll go up and back in one day on a day when he's on the road. That's the first step. Then we will trust God to guide us for the next step after this one. Will you do that?"

Gretchen paused thoughtfully before saying, "Yes, I will do that."

Caroline was satisfied. She knew Gretchen had taken the first step.

They went inside, both smiling and much lighter of heart. Bella had never stopped playing and smiling. Caroline joined her on the piano bench, first playing a song and then Bella repeating it. She believed Bella would have gone on with this for several more hours, but Gretchen once again removed Bella's hands from the keyboard, helped her stand, and said their goodbyes. Caroline walked with them to the street and watched as they went hand in hand with Bella pointing to the woods.

———.———

Summer afternoons in Moss Point were famous for thundershowers. The mornings were hot and humid, and by midday the prelude to the storm began when the sultry, thick clouds gathered, washing the sky with shades of gray. As if on cue, distant thunder alerted farmers to come in from the fields and children to come in from their play. Then the crashing of thunder and lightning bolts began, followed by the downpour, as if someone had punched the release buttons on hundreds of bottom-heavy clouds.

Caroline stood at her window during the prelude, watching the clouds move into position and dreading the storm. When the thunder began, so did her ritual of brewing a cup of tea, turning on a Mendelssohn CD, grabbing a book, and cuddling up in her favorite chair away from the windows. When the afternoon's stormy sonata was over, she returned to the window to watch for the rays of sun coming through the haze and the steam rising from the warm stone on the terrace floor. But soft, misty showers lingered. No streaks of sun piercing the clouds and no rising steam, just a steady drizzle. She had just brewed her second cup of tea when the phone rang.

"Hello, Caroline. This is Roderick Adair."

"Hi, Roderick. Are you on this side of the Atlantic?" She sat down at her desk.

"As a matter of fact, I am. I just arrived at LaGuardia. How are you? Well, I hope."

"I am very well, thank you." She contemplated why he hadn't waited until he got back to Lexington to call her. "And yourself?"

"I, too, am very well and very glad to be home. This trip seemed longer than usual."

"But productive?"

"Yes, productive. That's an appropriate word for an arduous trip that left little time for relaxation." He paused. "But I'll be in my favorite trout stream at sunrise in the morning."

"Let's hope that's productive too. My brother's quite the fisherman, and there's nothing quite like fresh trout, coleslaw, and hushpuppies—my mother's, of course."

"Oh, please tell me you make them too."

"Hushpuppies? I try, but they're never quite like Mama's." Caroline looked at her desk and the photograph of her parents taken at their anniversary party.

"Not much in life is like our mothers."

She noted a bit of melancholy in his voice. "I must ask, why in the world are we talking about hushpuppies when you could be telling me all about London? How was it?"

"It was London. More meetings than I can remember, a few quiet dinners, no fishing, no theater, no music, and lots of rain. Have you been to London?"

"Yes, once, as a college student. I quite liked it. They're such practical people, not overly friendly but practical. My friends think me an Anglophile. I love the British writers, I love the weather, and tea runs in my veins."

"I'll make note of that. What has filled your time since we last talked?"

"Someone extremely interesting." She thought of Bella.

"A young man worthy of you?"

"Oh, no. You misunderstood. There are none of those in Moss Point . . . I'm sorry . . . I didn't mean that like it sounded. I'm no one to require worthiness on a man's part. But I'm not seeing anyone in Moss Point." She was grateful he could not see her scarlet cheeks. "Guess I should follow my grandmother's advice. Grand Ma'am always said to polish your shoes with vanilla flavoring. Tastes better when you stick your foot in your mouth."

She frowned. *How could I have made such a stupid remark?*

"I think I'd like your Grand Ma'am. But perhaps there's a gentleman from somewhere else?" he continued his inquiry.

"Afraid not. My work consumes me. You sound as though you would understand that."

"I do, and I'm intrigued. So, tell me, who is this extremely interesting someone?"

"It's a long but very interesting story, and you're between flights. Perhaps I'll tell you about this person later."

"Would fifteen minutes later be all right?"

"Fifteen minutes, but you'll be in flight."

"Planes do have phones these days, and I'll be all alone with two hours in the air. Give me fifteen minutes to make contact with Acer. He's my pilot. And I'll call you back as soon as we're safely in the air. Fifteen minutes . . ."

Roderick did just as he said, but during that fifteen minutes, Caroline replayed their entire conversation word for word many more times than fifteen. He had cleverly found out she wasn't dating anyone. She would need to be more careful and maintain the same mystery that surrounded him.

When he phoned, they small-talked about flying for a few minutes before Roderick asked her again about the extremely interesting someone. She began with the story of the intruder and ended with Gretchen's last visit and her plans to take Bella to the university. She had intended to omit the part about "David's Song," but somehow it just slipped out as she interrupted Bella's story briefly to explain the song was hers. When she paused, Roderick commented and asked leading questions until she had finished Bella's story. They both agreed she was taking on a rather awesome responsibility.

"You are an excellent listener and such an insightful thinker, and I fear I've done all the talking." She also realized it had been a very long time since she'd had such a comfortable conversation with anyone.

She was nearing the end of the story when Acer announced to Roderick they were fifteen minutes away from landing. "Caroline, may I be so presumptive as to say I'd like to help you? I know you have friends at the university, but I'd like you to know about my sister."

"That's not presumptive, and I'd really like to hear about your sister."

"I have an older sister who is a psychiatrist and is affiliated with Boston University where her husband is also a professor. Dr. Sarah McCollum is her name, and coincidentally, she has done some study and work with autistic children. With your permission, I'd like to tell her what you have told me about Bella this afternoon."

"By all means. I know enough to know that I'm in way over my head. And perhaps my role is only to get Bella and Gretchen out of this dangerous situation and into the hands of people who can help her develop her gifts. I'd be most appreciative of any help at this point."

"I'll give her a call, and she might want to call you directly. May I give her your number?"

"Of course. You know I've talked all this time about Bella and not one word about this upcoming recital in a couple of weeks."

"That was deliberate. It gives me another reason to call you tomorrow. May I?"

"Yes, but this time you must do the talking lest you think I don't know how to listen. I'm normally the quiet one."

"We'll see tomorrow. Good day, Caroline."

"Goodbye, Roderick. Safe landing."

Chapter Twenty

Sink or Swim

———◆———

RODERICK ROSE EARLY ON SATURDAY MORNING, ATE A QUICK bite, and gathered his gear to start his half-mile walk to the stream, his sanctuary—the place he longed for when he was in London or Boston or somewhere in between. A haven where phones did not ring and crystal-clear water washed away the grime of doing business. He could stand knee deep for hours listening to the water rushing over the large smooth stones and the birds chattering overhead.

He controlled the family's fortune, the businesses, and the boardrooms. He did it with polish and with certainty; but here in the middle of the creek, he had no control. He could not stop the water with a suggestion as he could stop a merger with a phone call. He knew not if he would catch a trout or a crappie or anything when he popped his fly into the eddy underneath the overhanging limb. He liked the mystery of not knowing and not controlling.

He saw the light on in the kitchen and stopped at the main house first. "Lilah, are you here? Lilah? I'm home and heading to Blue Hole." He didn't see her in the kitchen, but he heard the hon-eyed tones of her voice in the loggia.

"Sometimes I feel like a motherless child. Sometimes I feel—" Lilah stopped midphrase as she came in. "Well, good morning and welcome home. Are you wanting some breakfast? I can have some toast and eggs in five minutes."

He hugged the woman and kissed her brown cheek. "You're always trying to take care of me, but I've had my coffee, and I'm off to see if the fish are biting."

She poured herself a cup of coffee. "And if I know you, you don't care if they're not biting. Go and make peace with yourself. I'll be leaving shortly. Your lunch is in the refrigerator."

"Thank you, Lilah. You're the best." He left through the kitchen door and grabbed his rod leaning against the wall. As he walked the path to his favorite spot and then spent the morning in the water, he thought of his conversation with Caroline. He had never known a woman who liked to fish. He wondered if he'd have the opportunity to bring her here.

True to his ritual, he ended his fishing about sixty yards downstream from where he'd started, where the water formed a large, deep pool and only a narrow stream trickled next to the bank on the opposite side. He disassembled his fly rod, put it carefully in its case, and perched himself on the rock above Blue Hole. It was quieter there, the water still and deep. He heard the buzzing of the dragonflies and watched the water spiders doing their dance on the glassy surface.

Blue Hole, a reservoir of cool water and warm memories, was where his father had taught him to swim. Roderick remembered as a six-year-old walking with his dad to the stream on a Saturday morning like this one. They were dressed in their swimming trunks and carried only two towels—no fishing gear this time. John Roderick Adair Jr. was of medium build, with deeply tanned skin and graying thin hair, but to young Roderick he was larger than life. His father had climbed atop Beckoning Rock and reached down to pull him up. With legs dangling several feet above the water, they sat on this very boulder.

John said to young Roderick, "Rod, this is where I learned to swim, and today I'm going to teach you to swim. But I'm not going to teach you the way my father taught me."

"Why, not?"

"You see, my father walked this same path with me when I was about your age, and when we got to this very spot on this rock, he told me he wanted to teach me to swim. I was ready. Then Father picked me up and threw me in the water and told me to sink or swim."

"He just threw you in?"

"Yes, he did."

"After I flailed around for a while, I realized he meant what he'd said. I yelled, but he didn't move. I screamed, and he offered no help. I finally gave up my own fight with the water and made it to that rock over there and climbed up. Then I realized I'd have to swim back across to get to Father."

"Did you do it?"

"Yes, I did it because I had no choice. He didn't teach me to swim. I taught myself. He gave me a good talking-to on the walk home. He told me life was a lot like that swimming lesson—sometimes you just had to jump in and sink or swim and not to expect any help from anybody."

"But we have lifeguards at the club pool. They teach swimming," said young Roderick, wondering about his own swimming lesson.

"Yes, and they do it right. Your grandfather was wrong, Rod. Life's not that simple. That's why I have no plans of throwing you in Blue Hole and letting you flop around coughing and spitting till you figure out how not to drown."

Roderick remembered his relief at that moment, and he remembered his father's words.

"I'm getting in first, and I'll be there when you jump in. You remember that. You don't have to jump into anything by yourself, but be sure the people you jump into the water with are interested in keeping your head above water as well as theirs. You remember that, son."

Roderick had learned to swim that day, and he hadn't forgotten the lesson.

——.——

Angel called Caroline early to invite her to breakfast, but Caroline politely declined. She planned to stay in all day in shorts and T-shirt, no makeup, and read and practice.

"Well, how about you let me come over and listen, then?" Angel wheedled. Caroline agreed and invited Angel to come down around ten o'clock.

Angel arrived, on time, at the back door with a pink sweetheart rose fresh from the garden. "Here's a blossom that had your name on it this morning."

"Thanks, Angel." Caroline took the petite flower and added it to the vase of violets on the counter.

They sat down in the chairs next to the piano. "Tell me, sweetie, are you getting anxious about this trip to Kentucky?"

"Maybe, a little. I'm beginning to wonder if I've made a poor decision. Mama thinks I've gone off the deep end. I put off giving her all the details as long as I could, but I had to tell her yesterday. She wasn't really listening when I mentioned it while she was here for the recital."

"Oh, joy!"

"I'm sure my phone will ring several times in the next few days—my family checking on my sanity. Would you like some tea and cookies?"

"No, thanks. Did you tell her that Sam had checked him out?"

"I told her, but I don't think she heard it."

"I'll give her a call. We're due a conversation anyway. So, do I get to hear the whole recital this morning?"

"If you're willing to sit and listen, you'll get the whole dose."

"Lovely. Then I'll get myself all comfy in this chair right here, and I'll tune everything else out and just enjoy what I hear coming from those little hands of yours."

Angel positioned herself in the chair where she could see Caroline's hands and where she could see the Cherokee roses on the fence line. She inhaled the familiar melodies as she thought about this young woman whose dreams had disappeared over a mountainside in Guatemala. She watched Caroline become one with the instrument, never faltering or hesitating. As an artist, Angel understood right-brain activity and knew that about now, Caroline had moved to that place where time does not exist and physical realities are replaced by the act of creating. It was an inde-scribable place, and Angel had been there many times, paintbrush in hand, here in this very studio. She missed painting, but the joy of having Caroline in the studio was greater than her sadness over blank canvases.

As Angel listened, she thought of how the years had passed with only routine activities. Void of major tragedies or much excite-ment, just daily days. Sam called these the "in-between times." He thought if he wasn't dealing with a serious problem, he was just living in between them, for surely they'd return. They had been living in the in-between times for several years, but the scent of change had been in the air the last few weeks. With Bella's entrance and Dr. Martin's invitation to move to the university and Caroline's finding her piano, some kind of change was inevitable, and Angel would embrace it even if she couldn't welcome it.

—·—

The phone rang, heralding them back to present space and time. Caroline stopped playing and went to her desk, and Angel sat a little straighter in her chair. Caroline expected it to be Mother Martha. "Hello, this is Caroline," she answered.

"I'm so glad. That's exactly the person I was calling," Roderick said.

"Oh, good morning. Or is it still morning?" Caroline looked at her father's clock on the table across the room.

"It is still morning, but the best part of the morning is gone."

"I hope you spent the best part in the trout stream," she said, looking at Angel and raising her right eyebrow.

Angel rose from her chair, smiled broadly at Caroline, and blew her a kiss as she slipped out the kitchen door. She knew when to make an exit.

"Could you hold for just a moment?" Caroline cupped her hand over the phone and told Angel they'd talk later. "I apologize," she said as she returned to the conversation. "Angel was just leaving, and I needed to say something to her."

"Angel? This is your neighbor?"

She twirled the phone cord around her index finger. "Yes, she and Sam own this property, and I live in the studio Sam built for Angel many years ago. She's an artist, but with some minor changes, this studio has become the finest recital hall in Moss Point. It's home for me, and they're like family."

"I'd like to meet them someday."

"I'm certain they'd like that. Sam's a retired judge and self-appointed protector for Angel and me."

"I'm sure that's so. You're fortunate to have a Sam and an Angel in your life."

"I am indeed. I'm curious: did you harm the fish population this morning?" She took the phone and sat down cross-legged on the sofa.

"You really know how to get quickly to the heart of things, don't you? And no. No harm done. But it didn't seem to matter until you asked me. I don't want you to think that I'm no fisherman."

"At least I know you're not a liar. Most fishermen would have lied and told me about the big one that got away."

"Well, I guess I could tell you about that one." He paused while she laughed. "Caroline, I've been thinking, and I've realized I may have been very insensitive about something."

"Insensitive?" Caroline grabbed a pillow from the end of the sofa.

"It came to me as I stood in the trout stream this morning that I've put you in a rather odd position. You had only wanted to play your piano again, and I asked you to come for several days and play a recital while you're here. You're a young, single woman, and you know nothing about me."

"That's true. But we're really in the same sort of position, aren't we? You know very little about me, only that I have a strong desire to play my piano again. I'm sorry—I said 'my piano.' It's your piano. And you don't know if I'm capable of playing a recital or not. And the worst part is that you've invited me to stay in your home, and for all you know, I could be the next Lizzie Borden."

Roderick laughed. "You mean the ax murderer? Maybe we'll put you in the apartment down at the stables just in case."

"No need to worry. It's nigh on to impossible to get an ax on board a plane these days."

"But you're flying in my plane."

"My, we are in a pickle, then, as my mother would say." Caroline paused. "Roderick, I was so driven by my desire to see the piano that I prematurely accepted your invitation. Then when I thought about it, I did have some serious misgivings. I shared them with Sam. He did some checking and decided you were safe. And frankly, I don't believe you would have invited me if you hadn't done some checking on me yourself."

I can't believe I'm being so transparent with this man.

"You're right. I made a few calls prior to contacting you. I knew of your study at the university and had someone do a little nosing around there. And then I had a conversation with Polly, your local florist. If you ever need an agent or a publicist, you should hire her."

Caroline grinned. "So maybe we're not in such a pickle."

"I'm very happy to hear you say that. The invitations were mailed a couple of weeks ago, the menu is planned, and I don't know how to play the piano. But you're sure that you're comfortable?"

"I think so."

"Would you be more comfortable bringing someone with you?"

"That's a good question. Could I think about that for a day or so?"

"Yes, it'll give me another reason to call you. But while I have you on the phone, I wanted to go over the plans again. Acer and I will fly down a week from Monday, arriving around noon. He's checked on the small airport there, and it's sufficient for landing and takeoff. Is there some place we could have lunch?"

"Oh, yes. Let me make those plans. Could I pick the two of you up at the airport?"

"That would be helpful. Renting a car in Moss Point proved to be impossible. Of course, I could call Polly," he said jokingly. "I'll call you from the plane before we land."

"I'll be here awaiting your arrival."

"We'll have a quick bite, and we should be back at Rockwater by three o'clock, which will give you time to get settled and play your piano before dinner." Caroline noticed he called the piano hers. "We'll make our plans for the week over dinner, subject to change, of course. I want you to have as much time to practice as you would like, or maybe to relax. And I do hope there'll be a few hours for walking or riding or fishing before we fly you home on Saturday."

"You'll be there for the week? No trips to London or Boston?"

"No, I've blocked out the week. I have an office at home, and with phones and internet, the world is atop my desk and just a few keystrokes away."

"I don't want to be a bother. I'm quite good at entertaining myself. Just give me a book and show me the way to the piano." Caroline pulled the sweetheart rose from the vase and twirled it in her fingers.

Roderick paused. "I called Sarah and told her about Bella. She and George are flying down for your recital, and you'll have opportunity to talk. I think Sarah will prove to be very helpful to you."

"I'm counting on her experience with children with autism to educate me."

"Sarah's written a number of papers and articles on autism. You'll find that she's quite respected in this field. She's anxious to hear your story and would jump at the chance to meet Bella."

"Hopefully there'll be more to tell before I speak with her. Thank you again for your interest in Bella. And here again, I've done all the talking. Today was supposed to be my day for listening," said Caroline apologetically.

"There'll be ample time for talking and listening. Well, I think all is set. Think about bringing someone with you if you'd feel more comfortable. And Miss Caroline Carlyle, I'm growing more anxious to make your acquaintance face-to-face."

"Why, thank you, Mr. Adair," Caroline said playfully, "and likewise."

"Goodbye, Caroline."

She hung up the phone with a decided smile on her face. She would be going to Kentucky alone, she decided right then and there.

Then her eyes settled on the framed photograph—the one of her with David when he'd received his master's degree. She picked it up and held it closer.

What would you think about this, David? You know how I have loved you, and I feel almost disloyal and unfaithful in even thinking about another man. Have I mourned long enough? Am I ready for this? Would you approve?

She placed the frame back on her desk and stared at it for another moment before returning to the piano.

After practice, her afternoon was spent reading and making her packing list. In between activities, she had time for a daydream or two, especially during the midafternoon rain shower. Just before sunset, with fingers curled around her teacup and towel in hand, she went to her favorite garden bench, dried off the seat, and planted herself there for a few minutes. She watched the water tumble over the stones into the pond and dreamed of a trout stream in Kentucky.

———·———

Gretchen called early Tuesday morning with news that Mr. Silva was on a run and would be gone for four or five days. Caroline immediately phoned Dr. Martin to make arrangements to bring Bella and Gretchen to the university. The timing seemed divinely appointed, and the meeting was set for Wednesday. They would go up and back on one day, and Caroline would have the weekend for last-minute preparations before leaving for Kentucky on Monday.

After Gretchen's call, Caroline and Angel left for Atlanta to pick up her recital dress and to do some last-minute shopping. She was glad for the distraction.

Mrs. Kramer greeted them at the shop's entrance, seated Angel, and excitedly went to the back for Caroline's dress. She insisted Caroline try it on. Caroline stood on the riser in front of the mirrors. The alterations had been done to perfection.

"Caroline, Gracie never came up with a new 'do, did she?"

"Angel, you saw it. Even GiGi thought it was awful."

"Well, I don't know how you're going to do it, but your hair has to be up. Not up severely, but just softly. The neckline of that dress just begs for it. Pull it up a bit so I can see."

Caroline did.

"Yep, I was right, it must be up."

"You're really a lot of help, Angel. First you talk me into buying this dress, then you send me to Gracie for a new hairdo that won't do, and now you tell me my hair has to be done up. Could you help me?"

"Me? You see my hair, don't you? Not one little thin white hair on my head longer than two inches. Maybe three if I stretched the curl. That ought to tell you what I can do with hair."

Caroline let her hair down. "Where's Betsy when I need her? She was always the one who fussed with my hair. I never gave it much thought."

"Call her. Maybe she could come for the weekend and figure something out. She'd enjoy seeing you."

Caroline walked deliberately to Angel and gave her a big hug. "You have the best ideas. I'll call Betsy on the way home. But we have a bit of shopping to do."

"More shopping?"

"More shopping. I want to buy a new dress for Bella and one for Gretchen for our trip to Athens."

"Now Caroline, that sounds sweet, but do you really think it's a good idea?"

"Perhaps it's a bit impulsive and maybe not the best idea, but it's something I really want to do. I think I've figured out their sizes, and I know what I'd like to get for them."

"Well, I have an idea. The way I'm moving these days, I will just slow you down. I think I'll stay right here in this chair. I don't think Mrs. Kramer will mind, and if she does, I'll just buy another muumuu. That'll make her and Sam happy."

"You're sure?"

"Why, yes! Get going."

Caroline did as she was told and quickly headed off to several of her favorite stores. In no time at all she'd completed her errands and returned to the dress shop to collect Angel. During the drive home, she reported in detail her recent conversations with Roderick.

"I was hoping we could do lunch at your house when he comes to pick me up. I can help with the preparation and the cooking, if that's all right. I want you and Sam to meet him."

"'All right'?" Angel's voice was almost shrill. "Do you think Sam would not finagle some way to meet this fellow? Of course we'll have lunch at our house, and Hattie will help."

"Will Hattie be back from her trip?"

"She's been back a week. You've just not seen her. I've filled her in on what's been happening since she's been gone."

Caroline, with packages hanging from both arms, and Angel, with one new muumuu, arrived back at Twin Oaks flush with plans. Caroline's optimistic mood faded, though, as she watched how slowly Angel walked up the stone path to the house.

She called Gretchen as soon as she got home. She wanted to deliver their packages, but once again Gretchen suggested they come to the studio instead. She realized that coming to the studio was a cherished outing for them and didn't resist.

They arrived within a few minutes of her call. Bella went immediately to the piano. Caroline and Gretchen sat at the breakfast table.

She felt a need to explain to Gretchen. "I know that our trip on Thursday is quite a big step for you and a big risk at this point, but I want so much for this to be a good experience for you and Bella. I've tried to think of anything that I could do to make it easier, but I can't."

"Oh, my precious friend, do not bother with thinking about this. Bella and I will be just fine. I'll waste no time wondering whether or not I'm doing the correct thing. I trust you, and I believe going to the university is what we should do."

"I'm so glad to hear you say that. But I did think of one thing. Stay here, and I'll be right back." Caroline went to her bedroom to retrieve the packages. She stopped at the door and turned to see Gretchen standing at the kitchen counter looking over into the room where Bella was playing. The language of Gretchen's heart was etched on her face as she watched Bella play.

Caroline returned with a large shopping bag in each hand—one for Gretchen and one for Bella. "Angel and I went to Atlanta, and I saw these things in a shop window, and they looked like you and Bella. I just couldn't leave Atlanta without them." She hoped God would forgive her for the lie. "I thought maybe you'd like to wear them when you go to the university."

Gretchen's face reddened, and she hung her head.

Caroline knew at that moment that Angel had been right. How thoughtless! If the packages would disappear and she could reel her words back in . . . But it was too late.

"Oh, Caroline. I have no way to repay you for all that you do for me and for Bella. I do not know what to say." Gretchen humbly and meticulously pulled the contents from layers of tissue paper to reveal a floral-patterned broomstick skirt in various shades of blue and green with a baby-blue sweater set to match.

"You can say something like, 'Oh, this is lovely. Let me try it on.' I thought the colors would be so beautiful with your hair and your eyes. And since Bella is almost your size, I got her the same skirt with a green sweater set."

With tears in her eyes, Gretchen said, "Oh, I haven't had anything like this in so long. It is so beautiful." She placed the clothes on the counter and embraced Caroline. The silence was broken by a whispered "Thank you. Thank you so much."

Caroline held her at arm's length. "You're so welcome, Gretchen. Now I have it all figured out. You can dress over here early in the morning before we leave, and then you can change back into your other clothes when we return. And if you like, you may leave these outfits right here in my closet until you want to wear them again."

"You have thought of everything, my precious friend. I like your idea very much." There was no need to explain why Gretchen liked the idea. Caroline already knew.

———

The morning arrived and so did Gretchen and Bella. Caroline took great joy in seeing Gretchen exchange her gray sweater for a new blue one. Gretchen dressed first and then helped Bella change clothes. Bella did not put on her new skirt and sweater as eagerly as Gretchen.

Gretchen twirled Bella around to see the skirt swish around her calves. "Look, Bella. This skirt makes you look like a beautiful dancer." Bella showed no change in expression, not the normal delight of an adolescent girl who's just been told how beautiful she is. She was a picture—her blonde hair tumbling in curls below her shoulders, her silver-green fixed eyes, looking always beyond what Caroline could see, and the slight blush on her young, unblemished cheeks.

Gretchen left their old clothes on Caroline's bed almost as if she were leaving more than old clothes behind. They walked arm in arm to the car. Caroline put her portfolio in the back seat with Bella, and they were off.

Gretchen's response to the drive was the response of one who had been confined for years. "Oh, look, the corn's been harvested, and the stalks are so dry." Then she pointed out the window. "Look, Bella, see the cows and the tractor?" Gretchen delighted in everything she saw—the bridges over the dry creek beds, the moss-laden oak trees, the farmhouses, the barns, all the things Caroline never noticed as often as she made the drive. Bella, in the back seat, acknowledged nothing.

They arrived at the University of Georgia half an hour before their appointment with Dr. Martin. Caroline drove them around pointing out certain buildings. "That's the dorm where I lived when I was a student here," she noted.

Gretchen's head swiveled from side to side. "Oh, Caroline, it must have been so wonderful, walking from building to building and under all these trees. Look at them—the students. They all look so engaged with life. And to think of all the learning that goes on here and what it can mean for so many."

It was timely for Caroline to see the campus through someone else's eyes, but she didn't mention the possibility that she would move here to teach and continue her studies. There was no need in planting that troubling seed. Not today anyway.

She parked on the west side of the music building and led Gretchen and Bella up the marble steps and through the entrance into the rotunda. "Here we are. This building is like my home away from home."

Bella remained very close to Gretchen and kept her eyes focused straight ahead. Even when Gretchen tried to point out something for Bella to see, Bella kept her focus, never veering. They walked down the long hallway lined by large wooden doors opening into professors' offices and music studios. When they reached Dr. Martin's office, the door was open. Annabelle was standing at the window looking out across the campus.

"Good morning, Dr. Martin." Caroline ushered Gretchen and Bella through the doorway.

"Oh, and a very good morning to you, Caroline. And I'm so happy you've brought your friends."

She introduced them. Gretchen was cautiously shy, and Bella remained expressionless.

Annabelle invited them over to her small conference table in the corner next to the window. Her desk was across the room. Her walls were a hodgepodge of paintings, posters, and photographs, all with the piano as their theme. A glass curio behind her desk housed her collection of little pianos and music boxes—many collected from travels and others as gifts from students and two that had come in gift boxes from Caroline.

"I've invited Dr. Wyatt Spencer to come over and meet you all this morning. He is a bright young colleague here at the university, a professor of psychology. He just phoned to say he's running a few minutes late, but we could have something to drink while we're waiting."

This gave Caroline time to tell about her meetings with Bella. In the middle of Caroline's description of hearing Bella play for the first time, a tall young man with an athletic build entered the room, not quietly but confidently. He wore khaki pants and a bright yellow pullover shirt with his sunglasses suspended from a string around his neck. His tanned ankles were visible above his deck shoes. He carried a clipboard and keys in his left hand and a tall mug in his right. His complexion and tousled light brown hair showed signs of hours in the sun.

He walked straight to Annabelle with a greeting. Then, giving her no time for introductions, he turned to Gretchen and introduced himself.

"Good morning. I'm Wyatt Spencer, and who might you be?" His straightforwardness took Gretchen aback. She shyly responded with her name. He then moved to Bella and said, "And if she's Gretchen, then you must be Bella. I've been anxious to meet you." He extended his hand to her.

Bella never responded, moved, or took her eyes off Dr. Spencer. He studied her for a few seconds.

Caroline remained in her seat, standing only when Dr. Spencer moved in her direction. She extended her hand. "Good morning, Dr. Spencer. I'm Caroline Carlyle, a student of Dr. Martin and a friend to Mrs. Silva and Bella."

"Good morning, Caroline Carlyle. Dr. Martin has told me about you and your wonderful talent. I'm very pleased to meet you, and I'm most grateful that you've talked Mrs. Silva into bringing Bella to meet us."

Caroline removed her hand and sat down. "You're very welcome. I was just telling Dr. Martin about my meetings with Bella and how Mrs. Silva has known for years about Bella's gift. Bella seems to have some characteristics of a musical savant. We're here to find out."

"Sounds like you're a woman on a mission. I like that. Dr. Martin has told me a bit of the background, and I can always get the details later from you, but right now I want to hear Bella play." He took the empty seat at the conference table.

"Do you suppose you could play for us now, Bella?" Dr. Martin rose from the table, holding out her hand to Bella.

Bella did not move.

Dr. Martin turned to Caroline. "Perhaps it would be better for you to coax her into playing."

"I think Gretchen might be better at that than I am."

Gretchen took Caroline's cue and rose to her feet, taking Bella's arm and lifting her from her seat. She walked toward the piano, assuming Bella would sit at the bench, but Bella stood exactly where Gretchen stopped. Gretchen whispered into Bella's ear. She still did not move.

Dr. Spencer wrote something on his clipboard.

After a slight hesitation, Caroline went to the piano and started to play. She noted that Dr. Spencer had stopped writing and fixed his eyes on her, but she locked her eyes on Bella. Continuing to play with her left hand, she extended her right hand to Bella.

Oh, please, dear heart.

There was more than one sigh of relief when Bella joined her on the piano bench. Gretchen picked up Bella's hands and placed them on the keyboard. Caroline gently slid off the bench, and as she did, Bella moved slightly more toward the center. She picked up Bach's Solfeggietto in C Minor right where Caroline had left off. Her body rocked back and forth as if the movement was choreographed into her brain before she was born. Gretchen and Caroline returned to the conference table. Bella never stopped.

As she continued to play, Dr. Spencer moved closer to the piano in stages. In between sliding his chair, he stopped to make notes. Finally, his chair was almost touching the piano bench. Bella never seemed to notice. He continued his writing.

Dr. Martin sat in astonished silence as Caroline and Gretchen smiled, glad for someone else to finally see what they knew to be true: Bella was rare.

This went on for quite a while before Dr. Spencer rose and returned to the table. "Remarkable, absolutely remarkable. I've read about musical savants. I've seen videos taken of them, but I've never seen one in person. You may be right, Miss Carlyle."

"Are you sure?"

"From what you have reported to Dr. Martin and from what I've observed today, I'm almost certain. However, there are some tests we'd like to do, but it would require spending more time with Bella here at the university. Or perhaps some of the work could be done in Moss Point." He turned to Gretchen. "Mrs. Silva, are you willing to move forward with this?"

Gretchen searched Caroline's face for assurance and turned to the professors. "Dr. Spencer and Dr. Martin, you are learning today what I have known for years. My Bella has a very special gift. Perhaps God couldn't give her a gift so big and so rare without taking some things away. It would not have been fair. There are things Bella cannot do, but she can make music. If what you are suggesting will help her to make her music, then I am willing to do it."

"Oh, that's wonderful," said Dr. Martin.

Dr. Spencer smiled and nodded in agreement.

Gretchen continued. "But you need to know that God has brought Miss Carlyle to us for a reason, and I trust her, and I will do nothing she doesn't ask us to do. So you must ask her."

"And what does Miss Carlyle say to this?" Dr. Spencer turned to Caroline.

"I say we should move forward with the next step."

He smiled and made a note.

Bella continued to play while they made arrangements for the next meeting, which would have to be after Caroline's return from Kentucky. Dr. Spencer pushed for sooner, but Caroline knew the delay would give her time to figure out what to do about Mr. Silva.

Finally, Gretchen pried Bella's fingers from the keyboard and led her to the door. Annabelle thanked Mrs. Silva and hugged Caroline.

Dr. Spencer extended his hand to Caroline. "I'm so grateful you've introduced us to Bella, and I'm very grateful to make your acquaintance also. I really look forward to working with you as we see what we can unlock here."

"Thank you, Dr. Spencer, for your time. We'll see you in a

couple of weeks," Caroline said as Dr. Spencer finally dropped her hand.

"Oh, by the way, what was that beautiful song that Bella kept playing? I was familiar with most of them, but not this one."

"I don't know which one you mean," said Caroline.

"The one that went . . ." And Dr. Spencer hummed the tune perfectly.

"I agree. That really was a beautiful song. I'm glad you asked," Dr. Martin said.

"That was 'David's Song.'"

"I don't recognize that one." Dr. Spencer jotted something on his clipboard.

"That's because I wrote it and it isn't finished yet." Caroline stepped abruptly away with Gretchen and Bella before Dr. Spencer could say anything else. They walked out through the long hallway, and down the marble steps to the car. They had taken the first step.

—·—

Caroline parked the car in the driveway, and before she could walk to the door, she heard Sam and Angel's back-porch screen door slam. She turned to see Hattie running down the steps and down the stone path. Hattie was like family to Sam and Angel. She had been housekeeper, cook, and companion to them through the years.

"Miss Caroline, Miss Caroline, don't go nowhere. Mr. Sam, he tol' me to stay right here till you get home. Miss Angel . . ." Hattie stopped talking and picked up the tail of her apron to wipe the tears running down her brown face.

"What is it, Hattie?"

"Lawd, it's Miss Angel. She's done gone and had a heart attack—a big, fat heart attack. Mr. Sam's says you s'posed to get to the hospital as quick as you can."

Chapter Twenty-One

Time to Dance

———— ✦ ————

*T*HE DREADED MESSAGE HAD BEEN DELIVERED THROUGH Hattie's tears. The doctor had sent an ambulance to take Angel to the local county hospital earlier this morning. Sam and Angel had been told a decade ago this day might arrive, but years of denial, medication, and watching Angel go on about her business had lulled Caroline into thinking the doctors could be wrong and that Angel could beat the odds.

She apologized to Gretchen for having to rush away and jumped into her car for the short ride to the hospital.

God, I had no opportunity to say goodbye to David. I simply cannot lose Angel that way. Please don't let this happen again.

She found Sam in the waiting room outside the intensive care unit. Strong Sam, greeting her with open arms, his own chin quivering as he wiped her tears with his handkerchief. She clung to his arm and remembered a conversation around their breakfast table just a few weeks ago—a conversation about Sam's handkerchiefs. Angel had pronounced handkerchiefs nasty, handed Sam a box of Kleenex, and vowed she'd never wash another handkerchief.

"How is she, Sam?"

"She's still with us, so there's hope. The doctors are still running tests, but the next forty-eight hours are critical."

"Have you seen her? Is she conscious?"

"They've let me in a few times, but they have her sedated. So we've not talked since right after the ambulance picked her up this morning."

Caroline started crying again. "Oh, Sam, I'm so sorry. And I hate I wasn't here. I should have known, and you've been here all alone."

Sam embraced her while she sobbed. "Shh, Caroline. There's not one thing you could've done. Why, you've brought more joy to that little woman than the law would allow, so don't you go feeling bad now. And besides, this place has been like Grand Central Station today. All kinds of comings and goings, and Brother Andy stayed all afternoon till I sent him home."

They sat together silently. The fading light through the narrow window was a prelude to the setting sun. Caroline encouraged Sam to think about going home. She would stay the night, and Sam could rest and relieve her in the morning. Sam agreed, but only if he could see Angel before he left.

The doctor came while Sam was with Angel. Initial reports confirmed that Angel had suffered only minor damage. The doctor was positive, hopeful, and said Angel was resting comfortably. Sam was relieved enough to go home. He was only five minutes away.

———•———

Sam stepped through the back door, gave Hattie the news, and asked her to take Caroline a change of clothes, her calendar, and a couple of books on her way home. Hattie always cooked, especially when she was upset, so a feast had appeared.

Exhausted, Sam ate quickly and went to bed, but with a new bedfellow—the reality of being alone. He had cuddled around Angel nearly every night for the last fifty-eight years. He could almost hear her saying, "Sam, the hair on your chest is tickling my left shoulder. Scratch it in a hurry." He would miss her squeaky little voice telling him good night and the feel of her soft white hair against his cheek. He prayed himself to sleep.

Caroline changed clothes and ate the plate of food Hattie had pre-pared. If something happened to Angel, Sam would need Hattie. Angel had known that, and she had trained Hattie how to take care of Mr. Sam. But no one had wanted to think of the possibility Hattie might actually be needed in that capacity.

Visiting hours were over, and the hospital was quiet. Caroline sat alone in the hospital waiting room. The room was pale yellow—the washed-out hue that comes from the passage of time and aging fluorescent lights. She curled up in a waiting-room chair—not cozy like a cat in a sunny window, but contorted into a piece of furniture that would neither cradle nor cuddle her.

I hate waiting—especially this kind of waiting where only You, God, know the outcome, and where You let life dangle on a frazzled string. I waited after David's accident. I waited for the authorities to be wrong. I waited for the floodwaters to subside. I waited for You to answer my prayer for David to be found alive. I waited for him to come through the front door. I waited while hours melted into days, and days into weeks. I've been waiting on something for the last six years, and here I am again, and where are You, God, while I wait? I need Your presence.

The doctor appeared in the waiting room. He quickly assured her that Angel was still stable and Caroline could go in if she would like. She followed the doctor through the double doors and into a cubicle where Angel lay hooked up to machines. The doctor told her to assume that Angel could hear her if she decided to speak.

When the doctor left the room, she pulled the chair up to the side of Angel's bed. The chair's chrome arm was cold.

Why does it have to be so cold in hospitals? She looks so helpless.

"Angel, it's me. I'm here, and I'm not leaving. You rest, and Sam and I'll be right here when you wake up."

She looked out the window to the streetlights. *There are folks just outside this window going on like nothing's happened—eating dinner, watching television, talking on the phone. Their lives don't stop. Just like when David was killed. The world did not stop turning. If he had to die, at least he died doing what he loved. He didn't die in a cold, sterile room like this.*

She shook her head. *I don't even really know how he died. I just know I didn't get to say goodbye. And nobody else's life stopped but mine.*

Nothing in this room was normal to Caroline. Angel's pallor, the beeping machines, the tubes and wires, the steady stream of nurses, the lifelessness—all so foreign. Just silence interrupted by the mechanical tones.

Caroline stared at Angel's still face. Angel—tough and tender, chopping down trees to create a garden and swatting at snakes while she built her pond, mixing oil paints on her palette and leaving a piece of herself on every canvas. She held Angel's hand and studied it. A womanly hand that crocheted beautiful pieces, arranged roses for the table, and yet could bait a hook and swing a hammer. Angel was thoroughly herself stepping in and out of the roles written by generations of southern women.

Caroline leaned over the bed to rest her head. She stayed there a long time, questioning, praying, remembering, and wondering what was happening to her simple existence. The unanswered questions haunting her since David's death reappeared like an apparition in the sterile room. Sometime between her fears and her prayers, she drifted off to sleep but woke when Angel squeezed her hand.

"Caroline?" Angel called her in a feeble voice.

"Angel? I'm here, exactly like I told you I'd be." She stood up, still holding Angel's hand. Her eyes searched the room for a clock—monitors, wires, machines, but nothing as simple as a clock. She looked toward the window. The night sky was drowned in darkness. "Angel, are you awake? It's Caroline."

Caroline watched Angel trying hard to open her eyes. She could see that her dry mouth made it difficult to speak. "Of course I'm awake," she said weakly. "I don't talk in my sleep. Why aren't you at home in bed?"

"Because I'm here to make certain the doctors and nurses do their jobs. Sam was here all day passing out orders, so I took his post for the night. How are you feeling? Can I get you something?"

"Never mind all that." Angel paused. "There's something I've been meaning to ask you, Caroline."

"Don't push yourself, Angel. Just rest. We'll have lots of time to talk." Caroline was desperate to be right.

"No, sit down. I've put this question off too long as it is." Angel's voice trailed off as the sedative took hold once again.

Caroline continued to hold her hand, sat down, and laid her head back down on the bed. *God, You can't take Angel now. You took David from me, and I'll never know why. Why must You take Angel now? Sam needs her. I need her. She's a good and giving person. Lord, I beg You not to take her.* She repeated these words until she fell asleep again.

"How long has it been since you danced?"

Caroline was awakened by a voice, but the room went silent again. She lay still and waited. Daybreak dimmed the streetlights and spread through the window. "Caroline, answer me. How long has it been since you danced?"

"Angel? What . . . Did you ask me how long it's been since I've danced?"

Angel took her time. "How long has it been?"

"Danced? Why, I don't remember." She squeezed her eyes shut, feeling wrinkles form on her forehead. *Why is she asking me about dancing? Maybe it's the medication.*

"That's what I thought—way too long. I'm glad and grateful for every dance step I ever took with Sam Meadows, and you have to dance sometime, too, Caroline," Angel whispered.

"Oh, Angel, who but you would talk about dancing at a time like this?"

"I'm not talking about dancing, Caroline. I'm talking about you."

"Me?

"Yes, somebody has to talk to you about you." Angel's determined voice was weak.

"I'd rather talk about getting you better and getting you home. Besides, some people dance, Angel, like you. You and Sam dance." Caroline remembered many times when Sam had taken Angel in his arms and sung "Moon Over Miami" while leading her across the kitchen floor as if it were a ballroom. "But I play the piano."

"But you play the piano all by yourself. When you dance, you have a partner."

"Then I guess I'll have to borrow Sam until you get well."

"I'll get better one way or the other," Angel said faintly. "You can count on it."

"I know you will, Angel. I just know you will."

"Just like I know you'll dance again." She paused. "When David died, you buried your music."

"What do you mean I buried my music? Angel, I make music every day."

"You make music trying to hear it once again."

Angel's words cut right through the veneer Caroline had created. She knew and understood exactly what Angel said. She had buried the music, the real music. Her faith had crumbled in a burning, angry heap, and questions arisen from the ashes. She was still the same on the outside—a disciplined, moral, church going young single woman admired by many. But inside, she was afraid—afraid of her questions, fearful of admitting her doubts about God, and petrified of change.

"How can you see through me?" Caroline whispered.

Angel fought to focus her eyes on Caroline. "We all lose the music sometimes. Oh, it's there. It hasn't gone anywhere, but we just can't hear it. Something has drowned it out. But Caroline, you've done all the right things. You've stayed close to people who can hear the music, and you've moved to their rhythms. And one of these days, your music will return. Not some big trumpet fanfare, but it'll drift back. It'll drift back like a feather on a breeze, softly but surely."

"We're not really talking about music, are we, Angel?"

"Yeah, the music I've heard all night—that kind of music."

"I love you, Angel." Caroline's tears dampened her cheeks.

"I love you, too, sweetie. Now you listen for the music, because it's time you danced." Angel's eyes closed slowly as she succumbed once again to the medication.

The nurse had stood in the doorway for a few moments, avoiding an intrusion on their conversation. After Angel dozed off and things were quiet again, she entered the room to check the monitors.

"She was just talking to me. Isn't that good? She was talking." Caroline wiped her eyes.

"I know, and yes, that's a good sign. I don't know what she said to you, but if I were you, I'd take to heart what a wise woman like Miss Angel says to you at a time like this. Now, why don't you go home? It's a new day, and you need some rest. I'm sure Mr. Meadows will be along any minute. I've known these two for a long time, and I know he won't leave Miss Angel alone too long."

Sam walked in as if on cue and went straight to Angel's side. After hearing how the night went, he sent Caroline home to sleep.

She leaned over and kissed Angel's cheek and released her hand. "I'll be back, Angel. You rest."

———•———

Caroline rested a few hours, knowing Angel was stable and showing signs of improvement. When she woke about noon, it was as if someone had punched her "take charge" button. She called her parents. She phoned Betsy to cancel their weekend together in Moss Point. She secured Hattie for the next few days to take care of the house and meals for Sam.

Now the phone call she did not want to make. *How can I possibly go to Kentucky? It's Thursday, and Roderick's flying to Moss Point to pick me up Monday. I can't leave Sam and Angel right now.*

She called Dr. Martin first to get names and availabilities of pianists to replace her for the recital. Annabelle suggested a young Brazilian pianist who was quite good and was available. She volunteered to contact him.

Just as Caroline put the phone down, it rang. "Caroline, it's Sam. Hope I didn't wake you."

"No, I slept a few hours, and I've been on the phone. How's Angel?"

"That's what I called to tell you. Angel's better. She's stronger and much more alert. The doctor says there's not as much damage as he first thought. I thought you'd want to know that."

"That's great news. I called Hattie, and she's at your house and will be there for the next few days, and don't you fuss. I know that's what Angel would want."

"I'm not fussin' about anything this morning. I'm just so glad my Angel is better. What in the world could I fuss about?"

"I need to make another phone call or two, and then I'll be back over. Do you need me to bring you anything?"

"Not fussin', and not askin' for anything either. I have all I need right here, and I'm holdin' her hand." Sam paused. "You wouldn't be callin' Mr. Adair, would you?"

"I'm about to do that in a few minutes. I'm waiting on a call from Dr. Martin before I call him. She is contacting a pianist who could play the recital next week."

"Now, Caroline, Angel will have a fit if she hears this. You've made a commitment for this recital, and you've planned this trip to Kentucky, and you're going."

"Sam, I'm not going to Kentucky. There'll be other times to go. But right now, my place is here with you and Angel. And besides, remember you're not fussing or asking today."

The call went through as Caroline prepared to express her regrets and make her apologies.

"Mr. Adair's office, this is Liz. How may I help you?"

"Hello, Liz, this is Caroline Carlyle. May I please speak with Mr. Adair?"

"Oh, Miss Carlyle. Could I take a message for Mr. Adair?"

"No, I think not. Is he unavailable to speak with me right now?" Caroline wished Roderick had answered the phone. Today of all days she didn't want to deal with Liz, whose past life had probably been as a prison guard. She imagined Liz in a gray uniform with a walkie-talkie on one hip, a night stick in her belt loop, and a ring of keys in her hand.

"He's very busy today."

"I understand, but I would not call if it were not very important. Could you please see if he'll speak with me?"

"I'll see, if you insist." Liz's voice suggested she wouldn't try very hard.

Caroline waited and decided she would not give Liz this information. She would simply wait for Roderick's return call.

"Caroline? I'm so glad you called."

"Thank you for taking my call. Liz said you were very busy, so I'll keep you only a minute." She sat down at her desk.

"Don't you mind Liz. She has her way, but I'll make certain to give her instructions about your calls. Let me guess: you've decided to bring someone with you."

"I wish that were the case. I'm afraid that I'm not calling with such good news." She looked at the number for the Brazilian pianist.

"Oh, I'm sorry. I don't like the sound of this. Are you okay?"

"Yes, I'm fine. But there is a bit of a bump in the road. Remember, I told you about Angel. While I was at the university with Gretchen and Bella yesterday, Angel had a heart attack. She's in the hospital here."

"I'm so sorry, Caroline. I know you're very close to her."

"Roderick, I just don't think I can leave Moss Point right now.

She's improving, but if I were gone, Sam would be alone. I am so sorry. I'm not one who doesn't follow through with commitments, but I can't help this one. Don't worry, though. I think I have a solution."

He paused. "No, you're the one who shouldn't worry, and you don't need to think about solutions. We'll simply postpone until Angel is better."

Caroline thought she detected a note of disappointment in his voice. "But I don't think there's a need to postpone. I phoned Dr. Annabelle Martin at the university this morning, and she has found a young Brazilian pianist who just performed his master's recital and would be available to perform for your guests next Thursday."

Years of boardroom meetings had obviously taught him the art of negotiation. "Caroline, I'm grateful you went to all this trouble, but could we do this? You said Angel is making progress. Could we hold off on a decision until early next week? Perhaps Angel will continue to improve, and we could fly down and pick you up even on Thursday morning. Would you be willing to do that?"

"But your plans?"

"The plans included you, Caroline. If you can't come, my friends will have a most delicious dinner, and I'll hire a local musician for a sing-along. But if you're comfortable to leave Moss Point by Thursday, then all is well. So, what do you say?"

"I'd say you are a most convincing man, Roderick Adair. We'll make a decision early next week."

"Good. Then it is settled. The Brazilian probably only plays Bartók, and he certainly wouldn't know 'Plaisir d'amour.'"

"You're about to make me laugh. I think it would be good to laugh right about now."

"Then laugh heartily, Caroline. I'll be checking with you, and if you need to call me, you won't have a problem with Liz."

"Thank you for being so understanding about everything. I'm headed for the hospital. Goodbye, Roderick."

She hung up the phone with a much lighter heart.

The weekend passed with tag-team trips to the hospital. Angel made steady improvements and convinced the doctor to let her come home on Monday. The plan was to treat her with medication for now. She was to follow a restrictive diet and limit her activities for a couple of weeks.

Sam was grateful to have her home, and Caroline was glad as well. But no one was happier than Hattie. Angel would be in good hands with Hattie—if Hattie could forgo the bacon drippings.

Fresh flowers graced every room and a bowl of freestone peaches sat on the breakfast table. There were even frozen strawberries floating in the lemonade when Sam brought Angel home in the car, parking out front to avoid the stone walkway in the back. Angel fussed about the wheelchair but finally gave in.

Hattie met them at the front door and nearly picked Angel up out of the chair she hugged her so hard. "Now, Miss Angel, ain't you a sight for sore eyes? I never did see so many ribbons and buttons on one dress in my whole life. You the most beautiful Angel. Ain't she, Mr. Sam?"

"She's got my vote." Sam wheeled her in the front door.

"Good heavens, Hattie, I didn't die, did I? You've never seen so many buttons and ribbons, and I've never seen so many flowers. Are these all from the garden?"

"Yes, ma'am. Mostly from yours, but I'll have to say some of the hollyhocks and hydrangeas come from my own little garden," Hattie said proudly. "I'm tellin' you right now, I don't want you going on to glory without Mr. Sam and me."

"Now you know better than that, Hattie. Why, if I had gone on to glory, all the widows in Moss Point would have already lined up from here down to the library bringing Sam their finest casseroles and homemade pies. You didn't really think I was going to let that happen, did you?"

"Oh, Miss Angel, I know you been mighty sick, but that heart attack didn't do no damage to that funny bone of yours."

Sam led Angel to the breakfast table. "Hattie, I think I see lemonade. Would you mind pouring us a glass?"

"Please do, Hattie, and I want us all to sit down and have a little chat. You, too, Caroline." Angel pointed them to chairs.

"And Miss Angel, how 'bout some poppyseed cake? It's jes' like you like it. Never mind, I'm gonna cut a big slice for everybody. Life's too short to pass up good cake." Hattie sliced the cake and put it on Angel's finest bone china and poured the lemonade into Waterford goblets.

When everyone was seated at the table and served, Angel took a breath. "You all know I'm glad to be home. And that's that. But it's Monday, and as soon as Caroline makes a phone call, we can expect guests for lunch tomorrow."

Caroline raised her right eyebrow. "Angel, are you certain you're up for that?"

"Of course I am. Now, Sam, you see to it that the grass is cut and the sidewalks are swept clean this afternoon."

Sam saluted.

"I'm about to change my way of eating per my doctor's orders. But I'm sick of Jell-O, and I want one more good southern lunch before all that starts, and Hattie, I'm counting on you." Angel continued passing out orders. "I know you've been cooking since I left here, but I have a special menu for tomorrow lunch. I want you to go to the farmer's market this afternoon and get some fresh vegetables. Tomorrow we're having fried chicken, cream-style corn, stewed okra, black-eyed peas, sliced tomatoes, and could you make some of that hoecake corn bread I like? Oh, and let's have some sliced cucumbers and onions in a little red-wine vinegar. And for dessert, I'd really like one of those chocolate cakes you make. You know, the kind with those thin little layers."

"Yes, ma'am. I'll have it all jes' the way you want it, Miss Angel."

"Oh, and we'll eat in the dining room, and set the table for six."

"Yessum. Who's gonna be here?"

"You and Caroline, and Sam and myself, and our two special guests coming from Kentucky." Angel looked toward Caroline, waiting for a reaction.

Caroline looked puzzled.

"And as for your assignment this afternoon, Miss Carlyle, unless you'd like me to, you are to call Mr. Roderick Adair and tell him that lunch will be served promptly at noon, and then you are to spend the afternoon packing, and I'll be down at four o'clock to hear your entire recital."

Caroline's mouth had dropped open. "But Angel—"

"No buts. Sam and I talked, and we even discussed it with the doctor, and I'll be fine. You're going. That's all there is to it."

Caroline looked at Sam. Sam just shrugged.

"But . . . Well . . ." Caroline turned again to Angel, who wasn't about to take no for an answer. Finally, Caroline laughed. "Well, only if I must."

"You must," Angel echoed with a decisive nod.

Caroline stood up straight, smiled big, brought her right hand stiffly to her right temple, and saluted the little general. "Angel's back." Then she went over, knelt at the side of Angel's chair, and embraced her.

"That's right. I'm back, and it's time to dance." She winked at Caroline.

Chapter Twenty-Two

The Way to a Man's Heart

———◆———

ONDAY AFTERNOON WAS A BUSY BLUR. CAROLINE MADE the call to Roderick Adair and learned he had contacted Acer, his pilot, to check the weather and establish a flight plan. All was set.

She knew Mr. Silva was still out of town and felt comfortable in phoning Gretchen about the change in plans. She accepted Gretchen's offer to come over to help her prepare for the trip.

Bella played the piano while Gretchen and Caroline packed. Caroline dragged her luggage from underneath the bed and began pulling clothes from her closet and from her dresser drawers. Gretchen folded and put them inside the suitcase. Giggling like adolescent girls packing for camp, they were actually having fun together—Caroline in anticipation of her trip and Gretchen thinking vicariously about Kentucky.

Caroline showed her the pink dress but didn't have time to try it on despite Gretchen's pleas. They made small talk before chatting about Bella and the return trip to the university, and Caroline told Gretchen all about Roderick and his sister, the psychiatrist in Boston. She invited Gretchen to stay and hear the recital at four o'clock when Angel arrived.

Just as the courthouse clock struck four, Angel and Sam knocked on the back door. Caroline was glad to finally introduce them to

Gretchen, and they even got to hear Bella play before Gretchen coaxed her from the piano bench. They made themselves comfortable, and Caroline took her seat at the piano.

For the next hour, Caroline played with little awareness of her listeners. When she finished and stood up from the bench, they all applauded, even Bella.

"Oh, how I wish I could be there on Thursday," said Angel, "but this was the next best thing."

"That is so true. I've never heard more beautiful music in all my life. Isn't that right, Bella?" Gretchen pulled Bella close to her. Bella clapped her hands again and went straight for the piano bench.

Angel agreed with Gretchen, then pointed to Caroline. "I hate to bring this subject up, but what about the hairdo? Betsy didn't come this weekend to help you, did she?"

Sam rolled his eyes and pulled at Angel's arm.

"No. I did have a few other things on my mind," Caroline said. "And besides, Betsy had babysitting issues." She hoped God wasn't counting her little white lies these days.

Angel turned to Gretchen. "Gretchen, your hair is just lovely. Do you suppose you could help her figure out what to do?"

Gretchen looked a bit puzzled but smiled.

"Have you seen her dress?" Angel asked.

"Oh, yes, it is the only thing that could rival her piano playing."

"But don't you think the neckline just begs for her hair to be up?"

"Perhaps it does," Gretchen said diplomatically.

Angel tapped Sam's arm. "Could you give me that little bag in your pocket?"

Sam reached into his pants pocket and pulled out a small, red, silk drawstring bag. He handed it to Angel, and Angel passed it to Caroline. "Now Caroline, these are for Thursday night. You know Sam is partial to sapphires, and these are pink ones. The pendant and earrings will be perfect with your dress."

Caroline slipped them from the bag. "Oh, Angel, they're

beautiful. I'll take good care of them and return them when I get back."

Gretchen was at her side. "Those are so lovely. You're quite right, they'll be perfect with her dress, Mrs. Meadows." She looked at Sam. "And Mr. Meadows, you have exquisite taste."

Sam smiled, put his arm around Angel's shoulder, hugged her to him, and said, "Why, thank you, and I picked this jewel out too."

Sam and Angel left. Bella continued to play the piano as Gretchen helped Caroline finish her packing and then played with her hair. She came up with something simple that Caroline could do herself. Finally, Gretchen looked at the clock and rushed away again just in case Mr. Silva called. Caroline walked to the street with them and watched as they walked hand in hand toward their cottage.

—·—

Tuesday morning came early—especially early—and Twin Oaks hummed with activity. Sam walked into the kitchen to see Hattie taking something out of the oven. "Smelling good and sweet in here mighty early. Hattie, did you spend the night in the kitchen?"

Hattie smiled. "No, I did not. Slept in my own bed but got up early to make Angel's chocolate cake."

Sam joined Angel at the breakfast table.

"Be kind to Angel this morning. She's in a bit of a snit since she wasn't up to doing all this herself. But she knows I want to help on this one. I mean that man comin' from Kentucky to pick up Caroline in his own plane? Why, I *woulda* spent the night in the kitchen to see that." Hattie delivered four one-inch-high cake layers to the breakfast table to cool.

Sam sipped his coffee and looked at Angel. "My Angel, you're not in a snit, are you?"

"Just a bit, but if you went and found us some fishing line, maybe I wouldn't be. Need some to slice these four layers to make eight. And I need it soon. Hattie is about to beat the icing, and by the time you get back with the fishing line, that icing will be light enough to float all the way to Hahira."

Sam gulped his coffee. "I'll have it right back to you. And I'll have a bowl of cereal when I get back." He walked outside and down the driveway to the shed. He was going through junk when he heard Ned and Fred arrive. He'd called them last night to come do the mowing, trimming, and manicuring before the guests arrived.

Waiting for them to find him, Sam grumbled to himself. "This is the dangedest mess I've ever seen. I just wonder what I'd see if I had ever put a light in here. What did I do with that tackle box? Fishing line. Who in the world ever heard of fishing line to cut cake?"

He saw Ned's shadow in the doorway.

"Mr. Sam, you all right in there?"

Sam came out of the shed flustered but with tackle box in hand. "Well, good morning, Ned, and you, too, Fred. I'm just fine. Just fulfilling my orders."

"We thought you was a-goin' fishin' the way you sounded."

"That would qualify as a winning idea, but not today." Sam plopped the tackle box on the garden table outside the shed.

"Too bad. The white bass are running up in the creeks right now. Papa used to take us boys when they're runnin' like that. Ma would make us pineapple sandwiches and leftover fried chicken and cold biscuits with some of her homemade mayhaw jelly."

"Well, that's quite a menu. But if you men don't mind, I have to find my fishing line." Sam continued rummaging through his oversized tackle box—corks, hooks, lures, swivels, pliers, but not one roll of fishing line.

"What you need fishin' line fer if you ain't goin' fishing?"

"Actually, I don't need the fishing line. Angel does."

"Now, from what we been a-hearin', Miss Angel ain't able to go fishin'. We been prayin' for her, Mr. Sam, and now she's done come home. Ain't God real good?"

"He is that, Ned. She's better, and I'm just certain that your prayers helped. But she's not going fishing. She needs fishing line to cut some cake layers. Why, here's that pocketknife I lost a couple of years ago." Sam brought it out, brushed it off, and stuck it in his pocket.

"Fishin' line to cut cake layers? Why, I ain't never heared of such a thing! Have you, Fred?"

Fred nodded his head.

"Ain't she got a knife?"

"She's got a drawerful of knives. It's just a woman cooking thing, Ned."

"Well, we for sure wouldn't know nothing about that, would we, Fred?"

Fred nodded again.

"Mr. Sam, I don't think there's an inch of fishin' line in that box of yours."

"I think you're right, Ned. Now what am I going to do?" Sam closed the tackle box and saw Fred walk away toward the pea-green truck.

"Don't you worry, Mr. Sam. I think Fred's done got it all figgered out."

Fred returned with the weed eater, pulled off about a yard of the heavy-duty filament, and got out his pocketknife to cut it.

"Why, Fred, you're a genius—a bona fide, certified genius, and you have saved my hide this morning." Sam realized this was the first time he'd ever seen Fred smile.

Fred nodded his head and kept grinning.

"Thank you for getting an early start this morning. Got to be done before noon. Extra-special company coming today—a man from Kentucky."

Ned pulled out his handkerchief and blew his nose. "He some sorta kin folk?"

"No. In fact, I don't even know him. He's flying down in his private jet to pick up Caroline, and she's going home with him." He started walking up the path toward the house.

"Must be some o' her kin folk."

"Nope, she doesn't know him either. She's going to Kentucky to play a piano recital on the piano she had when she was a little girl. It belongs to him now. Miss Angel wants everything just right for his arrival today. Got to get back to the house. Hattie'll be hollering any minute now. Thank you, men."

Ned took off his cap and scratched his head. "Mr. Sam, me and Fred are just about ready to start clearin' that land for your park. But before we go and do that, we gonna put you a light in this shed."

"That would be great. Just get the yard cleaned up first." Sam took off up the path to the house.

"Yessir, that's our first order of bus'ness," Ned called after him. "But you know, Mr. Sam, folks are mighty funny. You got a shed that ain't even got a light in it, got a tackle box and don't go fishin', gonna cut a cake with fishin' line, and Miss Caroline a-flyin' off with some man she don't even know."

"I'm with you, Ned, but I need to get back to the house."

Sam walked the pebbled driveway, but chuckled when he heard Fred mumble, "Some folks just strange, Ned. And he thinks I'm a genius."

—·—

Caroline wondered if she had slept at all. The *whats* and *what-ifs* had kidnapped sweet sleep. *What if the piano was in terrible condition? What did Roderick look like? What if her feelings for him made her more uncomfortable? What would the house be like? Would there be anyone else at the house while she was there? Would she finally meet Liz? What if Angel got worse and Sam needed her?*

She rose early, grateful for the hum of Ned's lawn mower. She liked knowing someone else was up. Jumping into some shorts and a T-shirt, she headed toward the big house. She knew they were up because she had heard Sam in the shed. She took the pot of coffee.

Hattie met her at the back door. "Good mornin', girl. You think we out of coffee?"

"I just wanted Angel to have a good cup this morning. We don't like the judge's sludge. Brought enough for you, too, Hattie."

Angel sat at the breakfast table slathering chocolate icing on the thinnest cake layers Caroline had ever seen. "Good morning, Angel. I'll trade you a cup of good coffee for a taste of that chocolate icing."

"Mornin', sweetie. That's a fair trade, but don't tell Hattie."

Hattie handed Caroline a spoon. "Tell Hattie? You think Hattie ain't got ears? Why, I got ears, and I got eyes in the back o' my head too! Have a whole spoonful, honey. They's a-plenty."

Caroline dipped the tip of the spoon into the icing and tasted it. "Hattie, how do you do that?"

"It's all in the butter, honey. Why, you can have the best chocolate in the world, but if you ain't got good butter, and you don't beat it until next Tuesday, then you ain't gonna have good icin'. That's enough. Hand me that spoon."

"I thought you'd be practicing this morning," Angel said.

She went to the sink to wash the spoon. "No, I closed the piano last night about nine and decided the next note I'll play will be in Kentucky. I just came to bring you some coffee and see how you're feeling this morning. I'm worried that you're doing too much too soon and that I won't be here to take care of you. You still sure you're up to all this?"

"I'm bright-eyed and bushy-tailed and confined to this chair. I'm just so glad to be home. I wouldn't have missed this for the world."

"We're all glad you're home. Twin Oaks isn't the same without you."

"That's the truth if I ever heard it." Hattie slammed the refrigerator door.

"Are you packed?"

"All packed—clothes, books, and pink sapphires. I have a few little things to do this morning, and I'm heading out to the airport about eleven thirty. Wanted to see you first, though. Oh, I don't think I thanked you for calling Mother Martha. It helped. I don't know what you said, but she's calmed down. Of course, I did get a call from Thomas last night, giving me his brotherly advice that I won't dare repeat."

"Oh, Thomas means well. He's just glad there's a man involved, and I am too. And I'm glad your mama's calmed down. Actually, I think Sam helped more than I did. He told your dad he had checked Roderick Adair out and thought he was first-rate. I guess we'll all get to see in just a few hours."

"Now, Caroline, I done heard lots o' tales about them Kentucky gentlemen. They're into either horses or mint juleps. I jus' hope he ain't short and fat. I guess he'll be okay, though, if he's got his teeth and hair." Hattie laughed out loud. "Missy, you jus' watch yo' step, and you keep him in his place."

"Yes, ma'am, Miss Hattie. Gotta go! I'll call you if we're going to be late." Caroline left with empty coffeepot in hand.

———·———

Sam walked into the kitchen and over to the table where Angel was smearing the last bit of icing on the cake. "Do I get to lick the bowl?"

"Do you get to lick the bowl? What if I said no?"

"Well, then, I wouldn't tell you that you're sweeter than Hattie's finest chocolate icing."

"In that case, here's the bowl and spoon. I'm all done."

Sam laid a folder down on the table as he took the bowl.

"What's in the folder?" Angel asked.

Sam grinned. "Something very interesting. Your curiosity antennae waving yet?"

"Sam, I know that look. What's in the folder?"

"It's something James just faxed me."

"James? Caroline's brother James?"

"Yes. He and I have been working on a little project."

"You have, have you? Is he helping you with the legal work on the park?"

"Yes, he's been helping me with that, finding out how we can deed this property to the city and still maintain some control over it. But what's in this folder has nothing to do with property."

She took the empty bowl from him. "I never did like to ask three times."

He laid the folder in front of her. "This, my dear, is a photograph of Mr. Roderick Adair."

Angel opened the folder slowly, almost fearful that Hattie's description was an omen. She smiled. "Hattie, I haven't known you to be wrong about much of anything in the last fifty years, but you're dead wrong about Mr. Roderick Adair."

Hattie stepped from the sink to the table and took a look for herself. "Lawdy, lawdy, oooh, Miss Angel. Miss Caroline's done into it now."

———•———

Caroline was sitting in her car listening to Mendelssohn when she heard the low-pitched hum of an aircraft and saw a plane in the distance beginning its approach to the runway. She looked in her rearview mirror to check her hair and makeup.

Her hair was in its usual ponytail with the loose fine curls misbehaving as they always did around her face. She wore white pants, a navy-and-white-striped shirt, and a bright yellow sweater with a nautical theme. Angel had picked it out. It had been a compromise—still Caroline's traditional tailored look with a bit of flair, as Angel had called it.

She reached for her cell phone to let Sam know the plane was landing, then got out and stood leaning against the car as the plane slowed to its stop. Sam had asked Ned and Fred to wash her car this morning. Clean, polished cars had never been high on her priority list. She kept the car's interior meticulously clean and neat, but never seemed to bother about the outside. Today she had no qualms about leaning up against it with her white pants.

Ray, the attendant inside the hangar, walked onto the tarmac to greet the Kentucky guests. The private jet flying into Moss Point had generated more excitement for him than the governor's plane did last September. Ray was beside the plane when the door opened.

Caroline's pulse sputtered a bit. She had worked since yesterday at denying the excitement she felt.

A lean young man, maybe thirtyish with sandy blond hair, dressed in khakis and a green pullover, walked down the steps and shook Ray's hand. Distance kept her from hearing what they said. He went back into the plane. She imagined something to be wrong. Ray stood at the base of the steps and waited.

A few moments later, another man appeared in the doorway of the plane. A bit older, he was also dressed in khakis with a sky-blue shirt and a navy blazer. He was taller. She guessed about six feet or slightly more. His hair, dark and curly, framed a tanned face. He pulled sunglasses from his coat pocket and put them on. Saying something to Ray, he continued to stand in the doorway, looking across the runway.

Caroline waved, but he didn't see her. As he came down the steps, she walked toward the opened gate in the chain-link fence. She waved again, and this time he waved back just about the time his foot hit the pavement. He shook Ray's hand and quickly made his way toward Caroline.

She extended her hand and smiled broadly as he approached. "Hello, Roderick, I'm Caroli—"

The touch of his hand catapulted her to Ferngrove and the night she'd met David. She remembered the wedding rehearsal and extending her hand to David as Mason began the introductions. David had taken her fingers and interrupted—"Wait, Mason"— before turning to her. "You must be Caroline, the wind-up kewpie doll who plays the piano. Do you take requests?"

She had looked at Mason with her right eyebrow raised before turning to face David. "It is my pleasure to meet you, David. Apparently, my used-to-be friend Mason has told you more about me than he has told me about you, and yes, I have been known to take requests." All the while, David held her hand—not in handshake fashion, but as though he were about to lead her onto the dance floor. She had not bothered to remove her fingers while she tried to decide which was more disarming: David's boyish, light-hearted smile or the depth of his warm, brown eyes only inches away from her. Regardless, she'd been somewhat charmed.

Just as she was now. Roderick held her hand just like David had.

Roderick looked at her and fumbled a bit for words, most unlike her phone conversations with him. "Well, hello, Caroline . . . You're so . . . You're so . . ." He paused.

She looked at him quizzically. "So short?"

"How about . . . lovely?" He chuckled.

"That's better, and thank you." She wondered what eyes hid behind the dark glasses.

"I'm so glad things worked out. And it is indeed my personal pleasure to finally meet you face-to-face."

Her cheeks flushed, and she removed her hand from his. "I'm glad, too, to meet you and to get to take a ride on that sleek silver bird." She turned toward the aircraft, feeling a bit awkward.

"Well, Acer has to do some paperwork for Ray, and then we can be on our way. I hope lunch isn't too much trouble."

Caroline laughed, thinking of Angel's instructions and Hattie's morning. "Trouble? Why, meals at Twin Oaks are pure pleasure, Mr. Adair!" she said in a mocking southern drawl. "I've been cooking for hours."

"You did the cooking yourself?"

She noticed the tilt of his head and his slightly graying temples. "Of course not," she said in her normal voice again. "It will be on the table when we arrive."

Acer joined them, made Caroline's acquaintance, and started toward the car. "Would you like me to drive, Miss Carlyle?"

"Okay, Acer, my name is Caroline, not Miss Carlyle, nor Miss Daisy, so I'll drive. But thank you for asking. You can fly high this afternoon, and I'll fly low on the streets of Moss Point. Wouldn't want you to get lost. Fair enough?"

Acer and Roderick looked at each other, nodded in agreement, and climbed in. "She has a sense of humor and a mind of her own, Acer. Better watch her."

On the drive through town, Caroline pointed out the Civil War monument, the Carter place with the treehouse in the backyard, the town square, the Methodist church, and finally the entrance to Twin Oaks. She parked in back next to the Pendergrass brothers' truck.

"We're here." She pointed to the studio. "This is where I live, in Angel's studio. Nesting in the middle of the garden is home for me. Normally, I'd take the stone path up to the big house, but I promised Angel to bring you in through the front door, so we'll enter through the gate over there and walk through the rose garden to get around front."

Sam met them at the front door and gave them a hearty welcome to Twin Oaks. He ushered them in to the sunroom just off the living room. Angel was holding court there.

Caroline pointed out Angel's paintings as they passed through.

Roderick walked directly to Angel. "And you must be the Angel I've heard so much about." He took her hand gently and winked. "It is indeed my pleasure to meet you, ma'am. And the food I'm smelling is the only thing that could smell better than the roses in your garden. You have created quite an Eden right here in Moss Point."

"You're a kind gentleman to say such things."

He removed his shades and Caroline finally saw his eyes—large and brown with depth and deep creases in the lids. They were quiet eyes, gentle eyes, not darting back and forth but present and piercing.

"Well, I would've prepared the meal myself, but I've been a bit—what shall I say?—confined the last few days. So Hattie, the finest cook in all of Moss Point, has prepared a wonderful meal for us."

"In fact, you might call it the Last Lunch," said Sam. "The doctor put Angel on a very strict diet, so she has ordered all her favorite foods for her last meal today before she starts seriously with her new way of eating." He helped Angel out of her chair.

"Well, I'm certain it will be the finest meal I've had in a while. I'm quite a fan of southern cooking. My mother was a southern cook, and as much as I have missed her food, I've never forgotten her fried chicken and blackberry cobbler."

Angel introduced Roderick and Acer to Hattie and directed them to their seats. When the platter of chicken rested in the middle of the table and Hattie had taken her seat, Sam said, "I think we should thank the good Lord for such a plentiful table and for such an occasion as this." He bowed his head, but remembered, looked up, and said, "And by the way, we hold hands around our table."

Caroline tried not to feel self-conscious as she took Roderick's proffered hand.

Finishing with a resounding amen, Sam entertained them through lunch with his history of Moss Point, interrupted occasionally by Angel reminding them what an accomplished young woman Caroline was.

Roderick put down his fork after one especially flattering comment and pointed to Caroline. "So this young woman is Mother Teresa, the winner of the Van Cliburn piano competition, and the university's homecoming queen all rolled into one?"

Caroline, pink cheeked, shifted the subject, asking questions of Roderick and Acer.

When the plates were almost empty, the front doorbell rang. "Well, who in the world could that be? Must not be from around here. Nobody comes to the front door." Sam excused himself, and in a moment Angel heard him greet their unexpected guests. "Well, hello there, ladies, what a surprise!"

"We just had to come by and see Angel. She got home before we could visit her at the hospital. These flowers are from all three of us, but Polly arranged them."

Angel immediately recognized the whiny voice of GiGi Nelson and sighed, making eye contact with Caroline. She wasn't playing GiGi's game today, so she excused herself from the table and joined Sam in the foyer to find not only the town's most infamous redhead but also Gracie and Polly. "My goodness, I see it took all three of you to bring this basket of flowers. They're just lovely, and as you can see, I'm doing just fine." Angel pointed for Sam to take the basket.

"We hope we're not disturbing anything." GiGi looked toward the dining room.

"Actually, we have guests for lunch."

"Oh, you mean you've only been home one day, and you're already entertaining guests?"

"This was already planned, and besides, Hattie has been a big help. Maybe you ladies could come back later this afternoon after I've rested a bit."

"But will your guests be here then?" GiGi pressed.

If Angel hadn't been so doggone irritated, she would have enjoyed this. "No, in fact, they'll be leaving just as soon as we can finish eating."

Polly strained to see the lunch guest who had ordered the bundle of irises for the recital. "Now, Mrs. Meadows, I know how much you love your garden, so I put together this basket with potted plants. You can enjoy it in the house for a few days, and then you can plant the flowers outside in your garden."

"Why, thank you, Polly. You ladies just thought of everything, didn't you?"

"Well, we just wanted to see how you're doing, Angel." Gracie tugged on GiGi's sweater. "Come on, GiGi, we need to let them get back to their guests, and we're glad you're doing so well, Angel."

GiGi pressed one more time to get a look at the dining table before Gracie tugged at her sweater again. With a last wave good-bye, they turned and walked down the steps.

Sam set the basket down while Angel stood at the door, smiling and waving like a fine southern woman even though she was spitting nails. Finally she closed the door and turned to Sam. She wasn't smiling now. "Can you believe that? Bringing me flowers to see how I am? Why, they still think you brought me to Moss Point on a turnip truck."

"Oh, they're just curious."

"And did you see those pink pants GiGi had on? Looked like somebody painted them on her. And whoever did the painting didn't tell her that wrinkled, age-spotted cleavage is not in this year."

Sam raised his eyebrows and grinned. "Looked pretty good to me."

Angel glared at him. He chuckled and took her arm to lead her back to the dining table, where they explained the interruption and continued with lunch.

———•———

Roderick talked business a bit with Sam only when Sam asked, and he was quick to inquire about Sam's career as a lawyer and a judge. He asked about Angel's paintings and poured out praise for the meal. He knew he was racking up points, but his flattery was sincere.

"Hattie, your mother taught you well about the way to a man's heart. But, Mr. Meadows, one look at Angel and I know that it was much more than fried chicken that melted yours."

"You're mighty right about that. One look at that woman and I was gone, and after fifty-eight years I'm still crazy about her."

"Now, gentlemen, this is bordering on way more than enough. And please don't start over when we serve you a slice of chocolate cake," said Angel.

As the last crumbs of cake were eaten, the courthouse clock chimed one thirty. Acer quietly reminded Roderick their flight plan called for a two o'clock departure. Hattie insisted on putting the leftover chicken in a box, and Caroline knew they'd find a few slices of chocolate cake when the box was opened later.

Roderick didn't resist.

Sam directed them through the kitchen to the back porch. They'd already made their front-door entrance. He would drive them in Caroline's car to the airstrip.

Roderick hugged Angel and Hattie and promised to take good care of Caroline. "By the way, ladies, I want you to know that Acer and I would fly back to Moss Point almost any day for a lunch like this one. It would only take about an hour."

"Our door is always open, and there's usually something good to eat," Angel said as politely noncommittal as she could. Obviously the verdict was still out on him until Caroline's return.

Hattie was noticeably more encouraging. "For sure, next time I'll fix you some of my famous chicken and dumplings. Why, I've made enough dumplings in my day to fill up two train boxcars, and Mr. Sam here has eaten his share of 'em. And I'll cook some greens and—"

"Hattie, you can start cooking, but I have to get these fine gentlemen to the airport," said Sam.

Roderick tried not to eavesdrop as Caroline lingered to hug the cooks and thank them for lunch. After a strong embrace, Angel took both of Caroline's hands, looked at them, and said, "Now, hands, you make beautiful music." She looked straight into Caroline's eyes. "And you, my precious one, you dance."

There was a story in those words, Roderick decided.

Caroline smiled, kissed Angel on the cheek, and bounced down the steps, leading the brigade down the stone path. Roderick followed. "Caroline, do we need to get your bags?"

"They're already in the car. Ned and Fred helped me with them this morning."

"Ned and Fred?"

"Um-hum, the pea-green truck." Caroline pointed to the driveway and smiled.

"I understand. Too bad we're so rushed. I was hoping to see your studio."

"Caroline, you have time to do that. Acer and I'll just get the car started. It's only one forty. That's three hours before rush-hour traffic." Sam laughed out loud, something he hadn't done in days—not even when he'd watched GiGi walk down the steps.

Caroline led Roderick through the side gate and into the garden to the back door. "That's where I would normally enter, but I'll take you around the pond and across the terrace to the front door." She pointed out her favorite garden bench and the irises that had stopped blooming. She then unlocked the terrace door and said, "Come in. This is where I live and work."

Roderick looked around. The room was like Caroline: lovely and comfortable, simple and unpretentious, and it smelled of flowers. "So, this is where all the music is made?" He stepped toward the piano. "I can see what you mean about the space, and I can imagine the sound. Time to play one little tune?"

"I closed the piano last night and decided the next note I would play . . ." The phone rang. She looked at it, then at him.

"Oh, go ahead and answer, I'll just look around."

"I'll make it brief." She picked up the phone on the fourth ring. "Hello, this is Caroline."

Roderick had heard her answer like that before. Now he would have a picture of her.

"Yes, you're welcome, and we were so grateful for your time also. It was quite a feat just to get them there, so it was good to make the most of the time." Pause. "You're right, Bella is quite a fascinating person, and I'm somewhat anxious about her future as well." Another pause. "I'm sorry, but I won't be here this weekend. I'll be returning on Saturday afternoon, but seeing Bella and Gretchen anytime over the weekend is improbable." Longer pause. "Perhaps it's best to just wait and stick to the schedule on our calendars." Silence. "I look forward to working with you too. Goodbye."

She hung up the phone. "Just the psychologist from the university who wanted to come to Moss Point this weekend. He's very interested in Bella."

Roderick said, "I see. Let's take an airplane ride, shall we?"

"Let's do."

As they pulled out of the driveway, he saw three heads duck down in a florist van parked at the corner under the big oak tree. Based on her grimace, Caroline had apparently noticed as well. The little town of Moss Point would undoubtedly be buzzing this afternoon.

Chapter Twenty-Three

Crossing Bridges

———◆———

ACER LOADED CAROLINE'S BAGS ONTO THE PLANE WHILE SHE and Roderick said goodbye to Sam. On board, Roderick surprised her with the announcement that he was the copilot and would be in the cockpit for the takeoff. He pointed out the lavatory and the monitor on the wall where she could track their flight until he returned to the cabin, then went to the cockpit.

"Miss Carlyle," his voice soon came from the cabin speakers. "This is your captain. Could you please pick up the phone in the arm of your seat?"

Caroline fumbled. *Which arm? Does it lift?*

"This is your captain again. Lift the top flap on the right arm-rest for the phone and mash the red button. Miss Carlyle, the red button—could you mash it please?"

She grabbed the phone, then saw the button and mashed it. *Of course, it always works if you mash the red button.*

"Ah, you found it. Anytime you wish to talk to the cockpit, just pick up the phone and mash the red button. Are you buckled in tight?" asked Roderick.

"Yes, I'm buckled in and ready to go, Captain."

"The flight will take a little over an hour. I'll join you in about fifteen minutes. Acer won't need me then. Prepare for takeoff."

Caroline put the phone away. The roar of the engines signaled their takeoff. Through the window, she spied Sam standing beside her car, his hand shielding his eyes from the sun. He grew smaller and smaller as the distance separated them.

What am I doing? she asked herself, fighting a sudden touch of panic. *I'm on a plane to Kentucky to spend several days at the estate of a man I just met today. I mean, really, after two months of phone conversations, and I'm flying, and he's the copilot. His world—not like mine. None of this is like me. I'm uncertain and confused, but it's too late now. I'm suspended midair between the reality of my everyday life, my sadness, and my daydreams.* She closed her eyes and took a breath. *Lord, help me. Don't let me fool myself into thinking I might be happy again.*

She retrieved a book and some journals from her tote bag. She was two pages into the article when the cockpit door opened. Roderick joined her, taking the seat across the table opposite her. He could view the trip monitor and see the cockpit.

Not counting the brief moments in her studio, it was the first time they'd been alone.

"Doing okay?" he asked.

She nodded.

He picked up the book on the table. "You're seriously focused on this savant thing, aren't you?"

"Yes, I am. Bella's so remarkable and so rare, and I still can't figure how she ended up in my studio."

"Well, that question might not produce an answer." He put the book down.

"I've had several of those in my life, but I have a way of dealing with them."

"Like Miss Scarlett, you just think about them tomorrow?"

"Hardly. When I realize the question is unanswerable, then I start asking questions around it—questions that will produce answers. Those answers can usually be acted upon. Then, after enough action, somehow the larger question is either answered or it just doesn't seem to matter anymore."

"That's quite a philosophical and practical way of dealing with tough issues. Ever thought of being a businesswoman?"

"You must be kidding! That requires a skill set I don't have."

"Like what? Musicians are good with numbers. You're a teacher, so you must be good with people and problem-solving. And you're a performer, so you know when the show starts and when it's over. Sounds like you're well equipped to me."

She closed the journal and put it on her bag. "You overestimate me. And besides, I really love what I do. I get instant gratification for most of it, and frankly, I like that." She frowned. "Sounds awfully shallow of me, doesn't it?"

"I think 'shallow' is hardly the word I'd use to describe you."

Her face flushed. "Let's see. What about . . . what about the schedule? What do you have planned?"

"We land in Lexington about three thirty, and then there's a half-hour drive out to Rockwater. I thought you could take a couple of hours to get settled, and we'll have dinner about six or maybe six thirty. And don't worry. I'm not cooking. Acer is."

"Acer cooks? He flies your plane and then cooks your dinner?"

"It's not exactly like that. Normally Lilah takes care of the house and cooks when I'm home. But when you didn't show yesterday, Acer and I went down to the stream and caught some trout. We thought we'd show off our catch tonight, so I gave Lilah the night off. But it wouldn't surprise me if she joined us for dinner. She's rather curious about you."

"You and Acer cook, and I'll make a friend of Lilah, and we'll do the cleaning up."

"Not this time. You're a guest, and you won't be cleaning up. No dishpan hands for a concert pianist. My job is to spoil you luxuriously this trip."

"Luxuriously? Never been spoiled that way." She paused. "Okay, that's tonight. What about tomorrow?"

"Tomorrow's up to you. You can have as much time at the piano as you'd like. Maybe between rehearsals I could show you around.

Perhaps a walk. Or if you want to go for a horseback ride, Acer would be happy to take you. I'm the rare Kentuckian who owns a horse farm in bluegrass country but doesn't ride."

"I think I'll join you for a walk. At this point I don't want to take a chance on a horse. With my luck, I'd wind up with a cast on each arm."

Roderick laughed. "You're right. Maybe just a long walk tomorrow. Do you play backgammon or Scrabble?"

"Yes, I do."

"Which one? Backgammon or Scrabble?"

"Whichever one is on the table, and the game is on."

"That won't endanger those beautiful little hands of yours."

Caroline embarrassingly moved her hands from the table to her lap.

He quickly added, "That is unless you beat me. Then I may break a couple of fingers—but I'd wait until after Thursday night. I'd prefer not to disappoint my invited guests."

She laughed.

"Now, Miss Carlyle, about Thursday? You set the schedule. Just let Lilah know when you'd like to eat and rehearse and rest. Or if you'd like a good invigorating massage, Liz can call someone for you. She offices at the house during the workday. Lilah has a cottage and lives on the property. By the way, I'm certain Hattie and Lilah are related."

"Oh, you mean she'll talk to a box of oatmeal?" Caroline giggled at the thought.

"Yes, and then cook it to perfection."

"Then I'll feel right at home." Caroline was glad for this information. "How many will be attending Thursday night?"

Roderick sat on the edge of his seat and put his palms together. "I think about sixty. Liz should have an accurate count tomorrow. They're coming for dinner at six thirty, and your program will start at eight o'clock."

"You're having dinner for sixty?"

"That's the plan. Lilah takes care of that with the caterer. Then after the recital, we'll have coffee and a chocolate dessert bar on the terrace."

Caroline imagined his terrace wasn't exactly like hers. "Sounds lovely. If I plan the day on Thursday, does that mean I don't get to plan Friday?"

"No. You may plan Friday also. Although I'll remind you that the stream is full of trout this year, and you said you like to fish." Roderick chuckled.

There was a playfulness about him when he laughed. She wondered if he did that much. "Why are you laughing?"

"I was just picturing you in my waders. Maybe you should let me know tomorrow if you're thinking about fishing. I'll get some waders your size."

The questions and answers flowed across the table for the next half an hour. She was growing more comfortable by the minute. Then came a call from the cockpit.

"Gotta go. Acer needs me. We'll be landing shortly."

"Yes, sir," she said.

He stopped at the counter, opened the refrigerator, and pulled out a small carton of ice cream with a wooden spoon attached to the top and tossed it to her. "Here. I think I heard Angel say you like ice cream."

She caught the carton and grinned.

"Good catch!" As he pulled the door to the cockpit open, he turned. "Oh, and if you get settled in time, some hushpuppies would be great with our trout tonight." He closed the cockpit door.

They landed at the private airstrip just outside Lexington. Acer secured the aircraft, unloaded Caroline's bags, and put them in the back of the dark green Bronco while Roderick did the necessary paperwork inside. It took just a matter of minutes. As they drove away, Caroline asked, "What about the airplane?"

"What about it?" Roderick responded.

"Do you just leave it there?"

"Well, we don't drive it home. Bruce will clean it up and move it to the hangar. It'll be ready for our return trip on Saturday."

"Oh, that's dandy," she said hesitantly. Her life was so simple. She was independent and accustomed to doing everything for herself, but the picture of how Roderick lived was coming more and more into focus.

The drive was different than the winding roads through the countryside around Moss Point. There were fewer trees along the roadside, and the grasslands were like green velvet covering rippling slopes of land divided by white wooden fences. "Why in the world do they call this the bluegrass country when the grass is so very green?"

"That grass isn't green. Can't you see how blue it is?" Roderick turned to look at her in the back seat.

She gazed out the window. "Blue, you say?"

"You arrived a few weeks too late. Had you been here six weeks ago, you would have seen blue. Bluish-purple buds appear on the grass in the early spring and give a rich blueness to the grass. That coupled with these wide blue skies make for Kentucky bluegrass."

"So, tell me, where are we?"

He pulled out a map and handed it to her. "We're driving out Route 68 going northwest from Lexington toward Paris."

"Paris? You mean when I get home I could tell my friends I've been to Paris and I wouldn't be lying?"

"I suppose you could, and if we had time to drive out east of Lexington, you could tell them you also went to Versailles." He turned in his seat to look at her. "But I seem to remember you told me you were an Anglophile. So was my dad. He preferred living in the English manor my grandmother had built in town, so we lived part of the time in Lexington. My sister owns that now since my parents died."

She folded the map and put it away. "Does your sister live in the house in Lexington?"

"No, she actually lives in Boston where she and George work, and they just come here for holidays and the summer and to get away from the city. But they're in the process of moving to the Raleigh-Durham area. George will be teaching at Duke, and they hope to start a family. They'll be here tomorrow. If their plans haven't changed, they'll leave Friday for North Carolina and house hunting. But I think they'll spend most of what's left of the summer here in Lexington."

"I can see why they'd want to stay here. What I've seen is more beautiful than I expected. So, tell me about where you live."

"Well, as much as my father loved everything English, my mother had a passion for everything French. So my father built her a French chateau in the countryside. I'm more of a Francophile like my mother, and I'd say I'm a country boy. I like my privacy, and I really like the trout fishing."

"But you don't care for horses?"

"No, I prefer cars," he said. "I've kept the stables and some of the horses, but I have no interest in riding them."

She noticed a change in his face. "I'm sure there must be a story there."

Acer slowed as they approached a bridge, and Roderick said, "Now look to your left as we cross the bridge. Up that stream about two miles is where we caught your dinner."

"Then we must be getting close to your place."

"Next entrance."

Acer turned left off the paved road a few hundred yards past the bridge. He stopped at the iron gate to punch in a code. There was no sign of a structure beyond the gate. Green grass rolled to the horizon, interrupted only by patches of trees whose size hinted they had seen centuries of life on these hills.

They came to a covered bridge. "Oh, could you stop? Please stop." Caroline moved to the edge of her seat.

Acer put on the brakes, and Roderick turned around quickly. "Are you all right?"

"I'm fine. I just want to see this."

"See what?" asked Acer.

"The bridge and the stream."

The vehicle stopped just shy of the bridge, and she hopped out and started toward the water. The banks were of clean, green grass right to the water's edge.

Roderick followed. She saw a large window-like opening in the covered bridge. She climbed back up the bank and walked toward the structure. "Why would anyone build a covered bridge over the stream?"

She noticed the change in Roderick's face—a sadness in his eyes and a slowing of his speech. "My mother loved to ride horses, and Rockwater's famous for afternoon rain showers. My dad built it for her in case she got caught out in the rain and couldn't make it back to the stables. She wanted openings on each side to feel the breezes and smell the rain."

"Your father must have loved her very much."

"He did. We all did. See the meadow over there?" Roderick pointed through the window toward the sun. "If you'd been here to see the bluegrass, you would've seen acres of yellow daffodils covering that meadow. Mother planted thousands of daffodils, and they still bloom every spring."

"It's so very peaceful and quiet here. I can understand why you prefer this over the city." Caroline leaned out the window and inhaled the Kentucky air.

"I'm glad you think so. It's home, truly home."

"Well, let's go see your *truly* home, but I don't think it could compare with this." She walked toward the Bronco.

They drove slowly through the meadow. The two-story house emerged in the clearing atop a slight hill. It was of brown and gray stone, but not cold stone; the ivy growing up its walls warmed its façade. The road veered slightly to the left and crossed another wooden bridge over a small creek. Roderick explained the house was positioned in the curve of the stream so the creek wound from the back of the house around the west side and across the front grounds to the bottom of the terraced gardens.

Beyond the bridge, the road appeared to head away from the house through a thick grove of trees. Just beyond this thicket, the road veered back to the right, and the house appeared again. The front gardens were terraced in three levels with winding walkways and raised flower beds lined with aged timbers. She spied two garden benches in choice locations, and a closer look revealed it wasn't ivy that covered the exterior walls. It was Carolina jasmine in full bloom. The fragrance greeted her as she stepped out of the vehicle.

"You'll find that my mother not only had a passion for horses, but she was obsessed with roses and daylilies. We'll take a walk later, and I'll point out some prizewinners. I think you'd enjoy that."

"I would. The garden bench is just beneath the piano bench on my list of desirable places." Caroline made a three-hundred-sixty-degree survey of the house and gardens before approaching the steps.

Acer retrieved her bags as Roderick led her across the stones and up the two steps to the oversized, curved wooden door. Its convex curve paralleled the semicircular shape of the stone landing. Large grayish-green junipers filled the concrete urns flanking the entrance. Roderick turned the wrought-iron handle and opened the door. "Welcome to Rockwater."

Caroline stepped onto the marble floor into a foyer larger than her whole apartment. Directly across the room in front of her, positioned in front of massive windows, was her piano. This thirty-foot wall of glass framed a scene of rolling hills. Mature hardwood trees filtered the afternoon light and silhouetted the piano against the backdrop of a manicured garden. The piano lid was up, and just in the curve of the piano sat a small table supporting a brass urn holding at least two dozen white irises. She wasn't certain if it was just the sheer beauty of the setting or if it was the sight of her piano again, but an unswallowable lump rose in her throat.

"And there, madam, is your piano."

She couldn't speak.

"Caroline?"

"Oh, I'm sorry. I'm just a bit overwhelmed. I never thought I'd see the piano again, and then to see it in this setting. It's as though the house were built for this piano."

"Perhaps it was. Would you like to play it?"

"You know I want to play it, but not now. That would be very rude of me. I'll get settled first." Caroline fought back not only her tears but her urge to feel its keys.

"Your choice, ma'am. Then I'll show you to your room."

"Lead the way." She took her eyes off the piano long enough to look at the white irises again. He had remembered.

"You have a decision to make."

"A decision? Is it an important one?" she asked with a smile.

"'Important' is a relative term, you know. It might be an important one—it's to decide on your suite. There is a guest suite upstairs and one downstairs, and you must choose." He turned to Acer. "Just leave her bags here, and I'll take them when she makes her decision."

"Then I'm off to the kitchen—things to do," said Acer. He walked toward the piano and took a right. Caroline saw the arched entrance to a very spacious dining room to her right and guessed the kitchen must be somewhere near. To her left stood the entrance to the gathering room and the staircase leading to the second floor. The arched doorway was symmetrical to the dining-room entrance.

"Let me tell you about the house. You see the dining room there. And the gathering room is here to our left." He led her to its entrance. "The piano is normally in that corner, but we've rearranged the furniture so the foyer and loggia could serve as your concert hall." He led her through the foyer and pointed to the right. "Down this way is the kitchen and morning room. I built my suite a few years ago. It's just off the courtyard behind the tall shrubs there." He led her to the window behind the piano.

Caroline could barely see the structure. "You don't live in the main house?"

"No, I wanted a smaller space with a tin roof. I like to hear the rain, and I didn't want to disturb the design of the house. So I built something for myself. I office there too."

"Your mother designed the house?"

"Yes, right down to the towels and washcloths. Now, down this hallway beyond the gathering room is the library, and just beyond the library is one guest suite."

"Roderick—I mean, Mr. Adair—could I speak with you for just a moment?"

They turned toward the voice. "Oh, hi, Liz. It's time you met Miss Carlyle. Caroline, this is Liz Hampton, my administrative assistant."

Caroline had never been more wrong in her life. Liz was not built like a gorilla, nor was she dressed in a gray uniform with a nightstick and key ring. She was a tall, athletically slender, brown-eyed blonde dressed in a camel-colored pants suit with an ivory silk blouse. She wore heavy gold jewelry at her neck and wrists. Caroline extended her hand to Liz and wanted to withdraw it when she saw Liz's long slender fingers covered in gold rings and her acrylic nails perfectly shaped and painted a deep crimson. Women like Liz made Caroline feel smaller than she was. "Hello, Liz, what a pleasure to meet you after these weeks of phone conversations."

Another necessary white lie.

Liz shook Caroline's hand and forced a smile. "Yes, it is indeed a pleasure." She turned away from Caroline to Roderick. "I need to speak with you."

"Well, speak."

"Here, in front of Miss Carlyle?"

"Yes, right here's fine."

Liz moved closer to him. "Your sister called and wondered if you had plans for tomorrow."

"Tell her I'll phone her later this evening." He took Caroline's arm.

"I could save you the call if you tell me what your plans are," Liz insisted.

"Thank you, but that's fine. I'd like to speak with Sarah myself."

"I could answer her question, and then you could speak with her at your leisure."

"That's one way to handle it, but it's not the way I will handle it. Thank you, Miss Hampton. Is there anything else?"

"No, that was all." Liz's face tightened.

Having dismissed Liz, Roderick led Caroline through the loggia to the left. The library was just beyond the gathering room. Caroline was beginning to envision the U-shaped design of the house. A glassed-in loggia lined the inside perimeter of the structure such that all rooms upstairs and downstairs opened to a view of the courtyard. French doors were positioned unobtrusively along the glass wall for entrances into the courtyard.

Caroline peeked into the library as they passed the door. The walls glowed a deep crimson with wood paneling beneath a chair rail. Built-in bookcases flanked the windows to the front of the house. Freestanding bookcases lined other walls. The furniture was large and overstuffed for comfortable reading. Occasional tables sat covered in books.

"Feel free to browse if you like to read," Roderick said.

"Thank you. I'll take you up on that. Are you a reader?"

"We're all readers. My parents were not fond of television, but stacks of books were always within an arm's reach. We read in the evenings when I was growing up." They continued their walk toward the guest room. "Here is your first option."

The spacious room with sage-green walls was inviting. Oil paintings of white flowers lined the walls: magnolias, lilies, roses, and peonies—only white. Next to the bedroom was a sitting area with a pair of green-and-white floral upholstered chairs and one large matching ottoman facing the stone fireplace. A crystal vase filled with white irises sat on the hearth. The same floral fabric covered what Caroline assumed was a window until Roderick pulled the drapery cords, revealing a French door opening to a walled garden.

More jasmine covered the stacked-stone walls of the garden, and moss crept between the pavers covering the ground. Urns held white impatiens and hanging baskets of asparagus fern created a canopy above their heads. At one end of the private garden sat a fountain built from the same stones as the house and an iron gate opening into the courtyard. A wicker sofa provided seating for the cool, almost damp, surroundings.

"This is very lovely. It's so peaceful and calms my soul. I think I would have liked your mother."

"Just like you, music and the garden were her passions. Shall we go upstairs?"

"Having seen this, I think going upstairs would waste your time. And after all, Acer may need you in the kitchen." She stepped back inside and glanced over the room again.

"Acer can hold his own. Besides, you need to know your way around. Let's go." They retraced their steps back to the foyer and up the winding staircase. "The other suite is directly above the one I just showed you."

This entire side of the second floor opened to a balcony over-looking the loggia below and the courtyard just outside. "My father's office . . . another guest room." He pointed them out as they walked passed the closed doors. They made a right turn at the end of the balcony. "Feel free to look around at your leisure."

Roderick opened the door to her second choice. Until Caroline saw this room, she'd thought white was white, but this room revealed shades of white. The walls were ivory with stark white wood trim and molding. The bed linens were a softer white and the white sheers seductively covered the windows, letting in the gold of the late afternoon sunlight and the reflections of the blue sky. There were touches of that same blue and gold in the paintings and accessories.

The room was laid out the same as the one below with the sitting area and fireplace at the end of the room. Instead of a matching pair of chairs, she saw a chaise lounge covered in a buttery yellow silk and an adjacent chair in a pale powder blue. Airy yellow and blue floral pillows sat on the lounge and chair. On the stone hearth, yellow irises filled what appeared to be an antique white bowl and pitcher.

Roderick left her gazing around the room and went to the French door beside the stone fireplace. He pulled aside the sheers and opened the glass door. She followed him. A private balcony just above the room below overlooked the walled garden and the courtyard. From here, Caroline could see Roderick's living quarters and then miles of bluegrass and trees stretching just shy of forever.

"How am I to choose? Do you have a quarter?"

"A quarter?" He fumbled in his pocket.

"A quarter, a nickel, anything that has heads or tails. Heads, and I spend my time in a sea of green with a private garden and direct entrance to the courtyard. Tails, and I spend my time right here overlooking it all."

"Would you like me to flip the coin?"

"Yes, thank you."

Roderick flipped the coin and without looking at it said, "It's tails, and looks like that pretty head of yours will be in the clouds." He made the choice. "I'll get your bags and be right back."

Caroline stood on the balcony until Roderick returned with her bags.

"You're welcome to join us at your leisure, but if you're cooking hushpuppies, then you should be down by six o'clock."

Caroline smiled. "I'll see you at six thirty." He was about to close the door when she said, "Roderick, thank you for the irises. They're quite lovely—almost as lovely as knowing you remembered."

"You're welcome. I wanted you to feel at home."

Caroline unpacked her bags and surveyed every detail of the room and bathroom, still trying to believe she was really here and that her piano was just downstairs. She pulled out her cell phone and called her parents and Angel to let them know of her safe arrival.

She next walked out onto the balcony to take in the amber skies. The sun headed toward the horizon on the other side of the house. She was glad, for it meant the rising sun would wake her in the morning.

Liz, briefcase in hand, walked across the courtyard below. They made eye contact. Just as she lifted her hand to wave, Liz turned her head abruptly and walked purposefully toward the gate. Caroline guessed she was leaving for the day.

When she could wait no longer, she went downstairs. She approached the piano looking at the familiar curves and scrollwork. She ran her hand along the edge of the raised lid and leaned over to see the tiny inscriptions and tuning dates her own piano tuner had made. She sat on the bench and slowly raised the lid covering the keys. The ivory was still in mint condition, and the warm tones of the wood shone through the polish.

She recalled standing excitedly on her tiptoes, looking out the picture window when the deliverymen had arrived at the Carlyle house with the piano twenty years ago. She remembered, too, seeing through that same picture window the white truck that had come to take the piano away years later. Parting with her piano had been like a death—but a death holding hope of a reunion. And here she sat looking out another window in a faraway, beautiful place, feeling its keys underneath her fingers again.

The piano and a picture window. She closed her eyes, breathed deeply, and began one of the pieces she had been preparing. After only a few phrases, she opened her eyes again to see Roderick standing in the courtyard, listening and looking at her. But it didn't matter. She was home again at her piano.

And so she played.

Chapter Twenty-Four

Condensed Versions

———•———

THE SUN WOULD NOT RISE SOON ENOUGH FOR CAROLINE. Lying in bed, she played the entire recital with the white matelassé coverlet as her keyboard.

She recalled a two-week bout with asthma when she was in the sixth grade. The illness had kept her from school and from playing the piano; nevertheless, she had kept up with her studies and had learned a Bach two-part invention studying the music and practicing the fingering on the bedsheets. She had played it near flawlessly when she was able to play the piano again.

When lying still became unbearable, she looked at the clock. Six fifteen. Surely the sun would rise before long. There was a tea box with an assortment of teas, a hot pot to heat the water, packets of honey and sugar, and a teacup on the wicker chest across the room. Lilah had thought of everything—or maybe it was Roderick. She slipped out of bed, reached for her robe and slippers. The night-light in the bathroom was sufficient so the stillness of the early morning was not disturbed with lamplight. She poured the bottled water into the hot pot and turned it on.

Minutes later, steam rose from the cup of Darjeeling in her hands as she walked to the window. She pulled the sheer away from the pane. The eastern heavens were a slight pink, and yellow rays shone across the heavy dew blanketing the bluegrass. Only four mornings in Kentucky, and she wouldn't miss a sunrise. She jumped into her sweats, brushed her teeth, twisted her hair up with a clasp, grabbed her teacup, and went out onto the balcony. She arranged the wicker sofa's cushions to her comfort and settled in.

The yellow sky gave way to blue, and untamed creatures woke to another day. The squirrels played chase in the large tree shading Roderick's quarters. The birds warbled, warming up for a day of chirping. A couple of hummingbirds heading for their first sip of the morning zoomed past her. The coolness made her glad for her sweatpants and shirt.

Across the courtyard through the windows, lights drew her attention. She felt like a visual eavesdropper watching Lilah moving around the kitchen to start breakfast.

The slamming door coming from Roderick's quarters interrupted the morning's quiet. It was Roderick, dressed in sweats.

"Good morning, Mr. Adair, and how is your world this morning?" Caroline cradled the teacup in both hands and stretched to see over the stone wall of the balcony.

He looked up to see her. "My world is mighty fine this morning, thank you, ma'am. I hope yours is too. Did you rest?"

"My world? Nigh on to perfect, I'd say. And yes, I rested. I was just too up-and-down excited to sleep. I didn't want to miss the sunrise over bluegrass that happens to be lime green."

"I see you have a cup of something."

"Made myself a cuppa tea." She rose and leaned over the balcony. "You know, we're not required to have this conversation long distance this morning. If you're going for a walk and wouldn't mind the company, I'd really like to go with you."

"Can you keep up?" He smiled.

"I'll try."

"How long will it take you to get ready?"

"How long does it take to come down these steps to the courtyard?"

"Depends on if you're stepping or sliding." He walked toward the steps to meet her.

She put her teacup on the wicker table and started down the stone steps to the courtyard.

"Be careful," he said. "Those steps are covered in moss, and it's damp this morning."

She attempted to tame the hair blowing in her eyes. "Should we tell Lila we're going for a walk?"

"Good idea. I'll ask her to delay breakfast for a little while."

"Wait just a minute. How far do you walk? And how long will it be before breakfast?" Caroline surprised herself with her boldness.

"Remember, it's your day as the tour director."

"Oh, that's right. Can we get to the trout stream and back in an hour?"

"In an hour, we can get there, take a twenty-minute swim, and walk back."

"If that's true, maybe Lilah could have breakfast ready in about forty-five minutes."

"I'll tell her." He disappeared into the kitchen. She could see them both laughing. He stuck his head out the door. "Want a cup of coffee to take with you?"

"No, thank you. One cup of coffee, and you'd send Acer back to Moss Point with me, and we'd be flying on my own steam instead of the plane's."

"By all means, skip the coffee, then."

—·—

The walk through the grounds revealed the stream that wound around the house and under the bridge out front. Flowers and herbs filled raised beds, and trees were pregnant with fruit to be harvested later in the summer. Roderick pointed out a swing under an oak tree and told Caroline how he and Sarah had played there as children.

"Do you always walk in the mornings?" she asked.

"No, I usually jog."

"Don't let me hold you up!"

"You're not holding me up. You're adding to my enjoyment of the morning." He meant it too.

"The morning is my favorite part of the day. I'm so glad it's morning somewhere all day long." She began to hum a sweet melody.

"I'll have to think about that one."

Caroline's humming gave way to lyrics as though singing to herself: "Gazing in the heavens in the dark of night . . . Every little twinkle gives hope of morning light . . . Heaven must be beautiful like sunrise all day long . . ."

"That's a lovely tune."

"Thank you. I wrote it for a student of mine a few years ago. Hadn't thought of him in a while, and then his mom called me not long ago."

"Lucky student."

"Not so lucky. He died with leukemia. But he did a lot of living in his short life, and he certainly taught me something about living and dying."

"I still think he was lucky—lucky to have you as a teacher."

Roderick asked questions about her childhood, and she responded with stories about James and Thomas and her solid-as-a-rock father and her good-as-gold mother. She told him about her parents' sacrificial provision of piano lessons and a college education for her, describing how she came to have the piano that now sat in his loggia.

When he asked about her college days, she described herself as a serious student determined to make her parents' sacrifices worth it. She told him about Betsy and their lifelong friendship.

He then asked the question he'd been building up to. "Surely, Caroline, there must be a young man in your life." Her delay in answering told him the question had moved her to a painful place.

"There was a young man in my life. We met at Betsy's wedding eight years ago. David was full of joy and big dreams for making the world a better place. We were different in so many ways, but we were on the same page with the things that really count."

"That's important." Roderick bent down to pick up a stick and tossed it into the woods.

"I guess you could say I was his anchor, and he was my sail." Caroline became quiet.

Roderick waited before asking, "You keep using the past tense?"

She stopped walking and turned to him. "David was killed in an accident in Guatemala six weeks before we were to be married."

"Oh, Caroline, I'm so sorry." He looked into the deepest blue eyes he'd ever seen.

"So am I."

Roderick wanted to brush the loose curls away from her face as if that would brush away her sorrow. He truly was sad she had been hurt, but he was glad she was here.

Caroline turned and started walking again. "My life really changed. David's death sort of disabled my motivating mechanism. Sam and Angel were longtime friends of my parents. They invited me to come to Moss Point. I had no other plans, so I went. That was six years ago. They've cared for me as if I were their own daughter."

"You've been there all this time?"

"Yes. Been playing the same phrases over and over again for the last six years—school starts in September, then the Christmas programs, church every Sunday, spring recitals, a summer break, and then it starts all over again. Sort of like visiting Aunt Maggie when I was a little girl. I loved listening to her recording of Van Cliburn playing Rachmaninoff."

She stooped to pick a dandelion. Roderick watched her twirl it in her fingers.

She blew the dandelion into the cool morning air. "There was this one spot in the second movement of the first concerto where the old long-playing album was scratched. Every time the needle passed this point, it would stick. I guess the needle deepened the groove through the years. I can still see Aunt Maggie walking over and gently bumping the lid of the stereo with the heel of her hand. The needle would magically jump to the next groove and the concerto continued."

"That's a good memory," Roderick observed.

"Yeah, the memory is better than living your life in such a groove. But with Bella, and Dr. Martin wanting me to move to the university, I think my lid has been thumped."

"Sounds like the second movement is about to start, but the question is, are you ready to get out of the groove?"

Caroline stopped and looked him straight in the eye. "Are you always this inquisitive before your first cup of coffee?"

Roderick noticed her raised right eyebrow. "And what makes you think I haven't had a cup of coffee already?"

"Well, I just assumed—"

"Assumptions will lead you to the ditch of delusions, ma'am," he said.

"Oh, my heavens, I never want to go there." A smile broke across her face.

"Wise choice. See those rocks? I think that's where you wanted to go this morning. That's the fishing stream, but we're taking the path over there and heading south just a bit. I want to show you something else."

Roderick surprised himself. *What is it about this woman? Her soul runs deep like her beauty. I've never brought another woman to Beckoning Rock, and yet I truly want her to see and know this place. I want to take her hand and lead her there.*

Slow down. Caroline's not a deal to be made.

They walked on talking, mostly Caroline commenting on the undisturbed beauty of this place. And him just listening and thinking about this woman whose hand he wanted to take in his.

"See the big boulder over there? That's Beckoning Rock and where my father taught me to swim. This was our swimming pool.

Mother wouldn't hear of putting in a pool at the house. 'It's just so unnatural,' she'd say. She didn't like chemicals and the noise of pumps running. So we'd come here for picnics and to swim." He climbed up a bed of large rocks to get to the top. "Here, take my hand."

Caroline accepted his help. "I'm hoping this will be worth the climb."

Roderick led her carefully to the top, unwilling to let go of her fingers.

"Oh, it's worth it. It's so clear and pristine. I can see all the way to the bottom. How deep is it?"

"I think maybe fifteen feet or more. It's safe to dive from here."

Caroline picked up a small stone and tossed it into the water and began softly singing:

> *"Toss a pebble in the pool, and what happens then?*
> *Ripples start to flow again and again.*
> *You can't stop the ripples—that's the ripple rule.*
> *So be careful of the pebbles you toss in the pool."*

"Do you know a song about everything?"

"Just about . . . and if I don't, I just make one up."

"Did you make that one up too?"

"Sure did." Caroline looked again at the water. "My dad taught me the Ripple Rule while we were fishing one day."

"Ripple rule?" *I'm feeling like that pool, rippling from the effects of this woman. She's right. I can't stop the ripples.*

"Yes, I'm sure you have one. You just call it something else. But Daddy taught me that all my actions have a ripple effect. It's a good rule, but I think it's why I have so much trouble making decisions. I can't predict or control the ripples."

Caroline plopped down on the rock with her legs dangling a few feet above the water. Roderick joined her, his arm gently brushing hers.

Caroline surprised him by taking his hand. She closed her eyes, inhaling deeply, and then opened her eyes, turning her head toward blue sky. "Good morning, Father. How kind of You to provide such a morning, and I'm enjoying it so. The rocks remind me of Your strength, the water reminds me of Your constant foreverness, the walk reminded me that I'm healthy, and my new friend here reminds me that You provide company for the journey. Thank you, Father." There was no "Amen."

As she prayed, Roderick studied her fingers draped across his own long, slender tan ones, wondering how these soft, diminutive, but well-formed hands could master a piano. It was only when he sensed Caroline removing her fingers that he realized her prayer was over. "That was a prayer?"

She paused and looked at him. "Yes, it was. Sounds like it surprised you. And honestly this spontaneity surprised me too. Don't think I've prayed so naturally in a while. But how could I sit here looking at all this and not thank the One who made it?"

"I've just never heard anyone pray here, and I haven't heard anyone pray like you pray before either."

"Sorry. I don't speak King James English. I don't know any other way to talk to God." They both laughed.

She was full of surprises, unlike the women he knew—predictable women all cut from the same mold, arrogantly rich, beautifully wrapped, and tied with silk bows of pretentiousness, with so little inside the wrappings. No woman he knew would have risen early, without makeup, dressed in sweats, and asked to walk with him. Caroline was different. She was real. No pretense, no games, and he guessed there was a real treasure underneath this packaging.

"Okay, Mr. Adair, it's my time to ask the questions. Tell me about your growing-up years."

Roderick described his childhood as a happy one, growing up with obvious advantages. He mentioned his family's wealth with sensitivity and discretion. He'd graduated from a boarding school in Virginia and then gone on to Vanderbilt, where he had done his undergraduate studies in business. His parents wanted him to continue his education, but he had no interest in further schooling. He was ready to leave the classroom for the business world. It had always been quietly assumed he would take over the family's businesses. Fortunately for him, it was something he really wanted to do.

"You like your work, don't you?" Caroline asked.

"I do. Oh, there are days I'd rather be trout fishing. But I like the challenges. I like to think that what I do makes a difference in a few lives anyway."

She picked up a pebble from between the boulders, tossed it into the water, and watched its ripples. "What is it that you like the most?"

"The sense of successful accomplishment—when the deal is done and when it worked just as I had planned."

"And what happens when the deal goes bad and didn't work according to your plans?"

He was impressed with her questions. "I just come home to Rockwater, sulk at least thirty minutes, and then turn my attention to something else."

"Sounds honest and healthy."

"So now you're Dr. Carlyle? And by the way, Dr. Carlyle, we need to head back."

Roderick picked up a small pebble from the boulder's crevice and stood up. He extended his hand to Caroline and pulled her to her feet. When they were both standing, he opened his palm and offered her the pebble, nodding in the direction of the water.

With both hands, she took Roderick's hand and coerced his long fingers back around the stone. "It's your turn. I've tossed my pebble into the pool."

Roderick didn't hesitate. "Let's see what kind of ripples I can create."

Caroline smiled.

Roderick had grown fond of the dimple in her left cheek when her face was happy. He liked thinking he had put it there.

They climbed down and started the walk back on a different path.

"Are we headed in the right direction?"

"Sure we are. Can't take the same path home. This way, you'll have something else to pray about when we get there."

When they had set their pace, Caroline surprised him. "Surely there must be a woman in your life?"

He paused. "Well, you were candid in answering my question, so I'll be candid in answering yours. There was."

"Past tense too?"

"Past tense. She didn't die, but still painful. I dated through high school and college, but nothing serious until my senior year. Her name was Julia Crownover. She was a smart and ambitious young woman, but I found out later her driving ambition was to marry well."

"Does it come with being named Julia? My sister-in-law's name is Julia. She certainly didn't marry James because he was from a wealthy family, but he was an attorney. To her that meant financial security and some degree of social standing in a small town. But James loves her, so our family has accepted her."

"My family accepted this Julia, too, but not without suspicion. I didn't listen and had to find out for myself that she was more interested in what I could provide than in sharing our lives."

"How long did it take you to find out?"

"Long enough. It was a quick summer romance that led to our engagement. She spent our senior year at Vanderbilt and most of my allowance on wedding plans. Remember assumptions and the ditch of delusion? I wound up there, and trust me: I didn't like it."

Caroline gave him a thoughtful look.

"About three months before the wedding, I crawled out of that ditch and called off the wedding. She quickly turned to one of my fraternity brothers, proclaiming she had loved him all along. They were married six months later and divorced two years after that.

But they had a child, and Julia and that child are set for life now." Roderick kicked a small limb out of Caroline's path.

"I'm sorry. Seems we've both experienced pain—for different reasons, but pain is pain."

"But you seem to have made for yourself a life in Moss Point, and you seem to be content."

"I guess so. No, that sounds ungrateful, and I'm not ungrateful for the life I have."

"So then we've established it: no significant man in your life."

"Oh, but there is. I have my father, my brothers, my nephew, and Sam. And you—what about you? Anyone since college?"

"I have a privileged life, and I'm grateful. The Julia jaunt made me gun-shy and a bit wary of female motives, though."

"That's understandable."

"Sarah's still trying to fix me up with women she knows. She's a psychologist, remember, and she has better discernment than I do. Put me in a boardroom, and I can't be fooled. But otherwise I count on Sarah."

"I can't wait to meet her."

"She'll like you, Caroline." These words slipped out of his mouth before he could stop them.

"I hope so. I'm bothered when people don't like me," she said with a grin.

"You commented yesterday that you have three goals for yourself, but you mentioned only your teaching."

"I must have gotten sidetracked. I do that sometimes. Just take an illegal left turn in the middle of the conversation."

He was convinced if she took a left turn it was because she wanted to, not because she was distracted.

"You're right. One goal was to finish a musical piece I started six years ago."

"Must be a tremendous work"

"Actually, it's not. It's only one song. Do you remember when I was telling you about Bella? I mentioned it then—the song she was playing. It . . . My surprise wedding gift to David was to be a song. I was in the process of writing it when he was killed. There's nothing so remarkable about the song. It's just that I need to finish it—for myself, I need to finish it."

"Is this the unfamiliar melody I heard you playing last night?" He thought he understood her need to finish the piece and bring closure to this part of her life.

"Yes, but I get to this one part, and the music stops. I've played and written down so many options, but none are right. I still get to the same place, that groove again, and the music stops. I can't tell you what snapped inside me when I was walking to my studio and heard that song being played on my piano a few weeks ago."

"I can only imagine."

"Now I know that it was Bella, but then I had no idea—only confusion. I even wondered if I was losing my mind. Well, finishing the song was my second goal. Not there yet." She shook her head in dismay.

The smell of bacon and coffee greeted them as they approached the door to the kitchen. Roderick stopped on the steps. "Do you want to eat or shower first?"

"Since I'm the tour director, I'd like to eat first. We shouldn't keep Lilah waiting. We're probably late, and I don't like being late."

He looked at his watch. "No, we're right on time."

"Do you mean it took only forty-five minutes to tell our life stories?" Her dimple appeared again.

"Hey, those were the condensed versions. What can I say? But wait. The third goal—you didn't tell me that." He stood on the bottom step looking up at Caroline

"The third goal was to find my piano and play it again. That one, sir, I can check off. So I have taken it upon myself to set a fourth one—that is if your offer still stands to locate some waders that won't drown me in the trout stream this afternoon."

Roderick laughed and followed her inside where Lilah had their breakfasts waiting. "So I take it you've set trout fishing in Kentucky as number four."

"Yep. What do you say about four o'clock we head for the stream, do a little fishing, and have a picnic?"

Lilah heard this conversation and popped into the morning room as Roderick and Caroline sat down to the table to eat. "I'll have the picnic basket ready at four, and then I'm taking off the rest of the afternoon and evening if that's okay with you, Roderick?"

"How could I say no to either of you?"

They talked through breakfast and then finalized their plans.

"Till four o'clock. I'll practice and do a little reading," Caroline said. "I might even mosey through the gardens."

"And I'll be going into town to find some waders that won't sink our novice little fisherman and wash her downstream." He looked at Caroline and noticed her raised right eyebrow again. "Lilah," he called through the kitchen door. "I'll check with you before I leave. And Caroline, if you need anything, Lilah's here, and Liz's office is through those doors right over there."

Caroline showered, dressed for the day, and found herself at the piano in short order. Feeling the ivory keys underneath her fingers was like settling in after a long journey. No instrument had ever compared to the way this one sounded or responded. The warm, rich bass and brilliant treble resonated throughout this large space and bounced off all the hard, reflective angles and surfaces of the loggia. This was the perfect spot for this magnificent piano.

She played for quite a while, unaware of time. When she stopped, she saw Lilah sitting in a chair in the hallway off the kitchen. "Hi, Lilah. Have I been playing too long?"

"Oh, Miss Carlyle, you could never play long enough. Why, you've brought music, real music, back into this house. Thank you."

"You're so kind." Caroline acted on a hunch. "Hey, do you sing?"

"Nothin' much I like better than singin', Miss Carlyle."

"Well, there's not much I like better than playing. So if you'll call me Caroline, I'll play and you can sing."

"Oh, Lord, Miss Caroline, I've never sung while someone like you played."

Acting on another hunch, Caroline said, "I've been the church pianist since I was fourteen, and I know all the hymns. Do you know a few?"

"Ohhhh, that's all I know. How 'bout 'Peace in the Valley'?"

"Goes like this?" Caroline started to play in a southern gospel style, catching Lilah off guard, from the look on her face, but bringing a broad smile as Lilah closed her eyes and sang and swayed. Her full voice filled the cavernous room with rich tones, and the freedom in her singing liberated Caroline as she accompanied her, adding her own vocal harmonies.

They were having a grand old time with one hymn leading to the next until Liz entered. She stepped up to the piano. "Excuse me, Lilah. Roderick is on the phone and would like to know if there's anything else you need from town. And by the way, aren't you supposed to be working?"

"You tell Roderick I don't need a thing, Miss Hampton."

Caroline chimed in, "And please tell Roderick that Lilah is doing a superb job of entertaining his houseguest." She winked at Lilah. "I think I need a break."

They both watched Liz's pencil skirt slither out of the room in a huff.

"You just make yourself at home 'cause your music and your smile are making this house a home again."

Caroline gave Lilah a hug and walked away. She selected a book from the library, picked up her journal, and headed out the front door to choose a garden bench. The pathway wound through each level of the terraced garden, where garden stakes identified prize-winning daylilies and roses named for horticulturalists and queens. She found a shady spot next to the stream at the bottom of the hill.

She read for a while before thunder in the distance alerted her to the approaching thundershower. Picking up her books, she headed back to the house, wondering if the afternoon storm would put a halt to their fishing and picnic. She needn't have worried. After a restful nap in her room while the rain fell, she rose to see steam rising off the bluegrass as the midafternoon sun shone. There would be fishing and a picnic after all.

—·—

Lilah had prepared the picnic, and Roderick had the fishing gear loaded in his vehicle. Caroline bounded down the steps in her jeans, a T-shirt, and her ponytail bouncing through the hole in the back of her university ball cap.

Lilah handed her a bottle of water and told her Roderick was outside ready to go.

"Do I need anything else?"

"Don't think so. Roderick has taken care of absolutely everything."

Caroline left through the kitchen door, but not before she heard Lilah say, "Liz, I'm done with my work for the day. Roderick is taking Caroline fishing and out for a sunset picnic. I know they'll be having such a good time that they won't be back till after dark. Please leave some lights on when you leave."

She guessed that Lilah had liked making that announcement more than she should.

Three hours and a picnic later, however, she knew Lilah had been right: she had enjoyed her afternoon more than anything she had enjoyed in a very long time. Now Caroline stood on the balcony speculating if the tiny flickers of light in the distance were stars or fireflies showing off. The night sky was wonderfully clear, and the distance from city lights painted the sky even darker. She felt relaxed and alive and realized how much she'd needed to get away from her routine and from Moss Point.

The long morning walk and the sharing of their stories, playing the piano, standing hip deep in a trout stream to catch more fish than Roderick, sitting on the big boulder to open a bottle of wine and have a picnic, all the talk about everything and nothing—it had truly been a good day. Her fears of being uncomfortable with Roderick had dissipated like the afternoon rain.

By this time tomorrow evening, her reason for coming here would be fulfilled. The recital would be over, and she would be winding down instead of gearing up. Her thoughts would turn again toward Moss Point. But for tonight, she could still look forward to tomorrow.

Chapter Twenty-Five

Surprise in Pink

———◆———

*R*ODERICK KNEW THAT THURSDAY WOULD BRING AN avalanche of activity starting early. Like an experienced maestro, Lilah would direct the caterer, the florist, and the men setting up tables and chairs. His plan was to stay out of her way.

While pouring himself a cup of coffee, Roderick saw Caroline drinking her tea on the balcony across the courtyard. He hugged Lilah and told her not to worry about breakfast. He would handle it himself. He walked out the door and across the courtyard. "Good morning, Caroline, and is your world—let's see, how did you say it?—still nigh on to perfect this morning?"

"You remembered; and to answer your question, it might even be a shade past perfect this morning."

"Would you mind some company?"

"Depends on whose it is."

"What about mine?" He stood in the middle of the courtyard.

"You mean you're not miffed at me for catching more fish than you yesterday?"

"I was, but I'm over it."

"Oh, I remember—when things don't go as planned, you pout for half an hour and then turn your attention to something else."

"Aha, you remembered too."

"We seem to be developing a pattern of early morning shouting matches across the courtyard." She patted the cushion next to her on the wicker sofa as an invitation.

"Is that your way of saying you wouldn't mind my company?"

She smiled and motioned again for him to join her.

He climbed the mossy steps. "I need to get someone out here to clean these steps," he mumbled.

"Oh, just think of the moss as part of Rockwater's charm."

"I think of it as a potential lawsuit." He leaned against the balcony wall, looking at her. "Well, today's the big day. How are you feeling?"

"I feel really wonderful, like I'd rather be here than Carnegie Hall. What does your day look like?"

"Like staying out of the way. Lilah has everything under control. Sarah and George are coming out about lunchtime, and they'll spend the afternoon and the night. We'll catch up on business and their activities. Would you join us for lunch? Sarah would really like to talk to you about Bella."

"I'd like that very much, and besides, I'm anxious to meet Sarah."

"And how do you see your day shaping up?"

"I . . . I think I'd like to practice this morning, and then rest some this afternoon. I'll *do* this morning and just *be* this afternoon. I don't get to *be* very often."

"Sounds good. What about some breakfast? I make a mean omelet."

"You're on." She followed him down the balcony stairs to the courtyard and across to the kitchen door.

Lilah was in the butler's pantry stacking dishes when she heard them come in. "Are you sure I couldn't fix you some breakfast?" She peeked around the doorway into the kitchen.

"Roderick just offered to fix a mean omelet. Am I safe?"

"You're safe, but he's not if he makes the kind of mess he usually does." Lilah laughed.

Caroline picked up the dishtowel. "You go on about whatever you're doing, Lilah. I'll clean up his mess."

Roderick and Caroline chatted as he broke eggs, grated cheese, chopped onions, and sliced ham. Caroline tried not to be too bothered when Liz appeared and offered to help. Lilah stepped out of the pantry just in time to hear Roderick assure Liz they had it all under control and instruct her to go on about her work.

———•———

When Caroline sat down at the piano to practice, she had a ritual of doodling. Like someone with a pencil drawing geometrical shapes and loops, she sat at the piano and allowed her fingers to move where they wanted to go. Often, her fingers played hymns or variations of simple melodies, or an improvisation of an old song—whatever came to her mind and fingers at the same time. This morning it was "David's Song."

And this time . . . new phrases came to her like the very first phrases had eight years ago.

Where did that line come from? It works even with the change in key. She repeated it, and another new phrase followed. *Where is my manuscript paper when I need it? I must remember these phrases and the key change. They work.*

She played and stopped, played and stopped, repeating new phrases, etching them into the groove of her memory.

When she finished, she played through the night's program from start to finish. The movers, the caterers, the florist, and Lilah stopped whatever they were doing and applauded when they were certain she was finished. Caroline thanked them and rose from the bench. She made it as far as the staircase before she stopped, turned around, and went back to the piano to play the new phrases in "David's Song" one more time before heading upstairs away from the activity.

Lilah came to her room about eleven thirty and knocked respectfully. "Caroline, Sarah and George are here, waiting in the morning room. Would you like to come down? I'll be serving lunch shortly."

Caroline opened the door and took Lilah's arm. "Let's go. I'm hungry."

"And Sarah's anxious to meet you. She's more than curious about the young woman here to play the piano."

Since Roderick was caught on an international call, Lilah made the introductions. Sarah looked so much like Roderick—thick brown hair, big brown eyes, and a smile that immediately put her at ease. She was slightly taller than Caroline and had on navy pants and a crisply ironed, tailored blouse like Caroline. George, of medium build, had light brown uncombed hair with graying temples and a graying moustache. He wore horn-rimmed glasses. She imagined him in a university classroom or at a patient's bedside.

———•———

They were deep into conversation when Roderick made his way into the morning room. "I see you've been waiting for me to introduce you." He shook George's hand and gave Sarah a brotherly hug and kiss on the cheek before smiling at Caroline. He felt inordinately pleased when she smiled back. "Sorry I'm late. Business called."

"We've been getting acquainted," Sarah responded. "And the conversation's been so interesting, Rod. We didn't even seem to mind that Lilah's quiche is getting cold."

"Oops." He grinned at Caroline. "I think that's my older and wiser sister's way of getting us to our plates."

The meal was served, and the getting-to-know-you conversation continued around the table until Sarah asked about Bella.

Sarah put her fork down. "Caroline, Roderick has given me some sketchy information about Bella and about how she entered your life. I'd really like to hear that from you if you don't mind."

"Oh, I want you to know every detail, and I'll be grateful for any insight or direction you have for me. I feel that I have been handed a rare gift, and I so want to treat it properly."

For the next half hour, Caroline explained how she had come

to know Bella. She described in detail Gretchen's story and how she and Bella lived their lives. No one interrupted Caroline with questions. In hearing the story, Roderick learned that kindness, goodness, and a strong sense of responsibility pumped through Caroline's veins. He heard it in the way she talked, and he saw it in her eyes, and he liked it.

When Caroline finished, Sarah asked, "And so, Caroline, how do you see yourself fitting into this picture?"

Caroline sipped her iced tea. "Do I need to lie on your sofa to answer this question?"

Sarah smiled. "Only if you'd like to."

"Well, honestly, that's the question I've been asking myself. All this came about as I'm contemplating a life-changing decision."

Roderick's antenna perked up. He had been fearful of probing too much too soon about the university opportunity.

Her face was serious. "I believe there's a reason Bella came into my life. I don't know what that reason is yet, but I know that Gretchen trusts me."

"How does this fit with the big decision you're considering?" Roderick knew that Sarah wouldn't miss his interest in Caroline's answer.

Caroline picked up her fork, turning it over and over. "Well, I've told you that I study piano with Dr. Annabelle Martin at the university. She's offering me a position in the fall to teach at the University of Georgia while I work on my doctorate. That would be a big change for me, and I was seriously considering the offer before I met Bella."

"You'd be moving from Moss Point to Athens?" Sarah asked.

"Yes. That's what makes this so difficult. I love my life in Moss Point, but I know eventually I need to make a change. I'm just unsure if the change should come this year. In some ways, it would be good for Bella. Dr. Martin has introduced me to Dr. Wyatt Spencer, a young professor at the university who's extremely interested in testing and studying Bella." She paused.

Roderick remembered Wyatt Spencer's call before they left Moss Point. Something about it niggled at him as he watched Caroline, and he imagined Dr. Spencer might be interested in more than Bella. The question was how Caroline felt about that, if it was true.

Caroline put her fork down gently. "This may be a way to get Gretchen and Bella away from Mr. Silva and to get her the help she needs. But these are heavy issues to solve in the next month."

Sarah sat quietly, listening to every word. "Well, you're right. You have some big issues and a mountain of details to consider in making this decision."

Caroline asked, "Any advice?"

"Just a word of caution. There are people—well-credentialed people—who would move mountains for an opportunity to work with Bella. Some are well meaning, and some are not, and they will use Bella to further their own careers—even to the point of exploiting her."

"I fear that, but I don't know what to do." Caroline's face showed her concern.

"Just remember, Bella is a person. A very rare person, but she's still a person. No one should treat her like a freak in a circus sideshow."

"Oh, and how will I know? I trust Dr. Martin and her recommendation of Dr. Spencer. He's young and extremely knowledgeable and anxious to start testing Bella. I'm sure that Dr. Martin has told him of the possibility of my being at the university in the fall. I just wish I had a clearer sense of what to do."

"Has Roderick told you we're moving from Boston to North Carolina?" Sarah asked.

"Yes, he told me George would be teaching at Duke."

"In fact, we'll be going there tomorrow to look for a house. I tell you this because I'll not be teaching full-time, and it will be a while before I can establish a practice again. I'll have time on my hands. And you know, North Carolina isn't that far. I'm not sure at this point what I can do, but . . . I want to help you and Bella," she said with conviction.

"Oh, Sarah, you're so generous. You just tell me what I need to do to get you together with Bella and Gretchen, and I'll do it. You can't imagine how this relieves me. Thank you."

Roderick had never been more grateful for his sister.

—·—

Caroline retreated to her suite. Sarah's reassurance made for a sweet, restful nap. When she woke, she tried to read. Too much nervous energy. A walk would be good. As she passed the library, she saw George stretched out in the window seat with pillows propped behind his head, either reading or napping. No sign of Sarah. She made it through the maze of activity to find Lilah in the kitchen. "Lilah, excuse me. Could I please get a bottle of water? I think I'd like to walk back down to the trout stream."

"Let me get a nice chilled bottle for you. You sure that won't tire you out too much?" Lilah headed for the butler's pantry.

"I actually think it would help get rid of some nervous energy and give these butterflies in my stomach a chance to fly away to a beautiful place. Would you tell Roderick where I went if he asks?"

"I will, for sure, just as surely as he'd be asking if he couldn't find you."

"Thank you for the water and for everything, Lilah."

Caroline walked out the kitchen door. After a quick meander, she reached the large boulder where she and Roderick had picnicked the afternoon before. Realizing the climb was easier holding someone else's hand, she took great caution, knowing that today was not the day for a fall.

At the top she looked all around her. *Green's never been greener. And you, old stream, you just never hesitate on your journey over those stones, do you? You just keep moving and reflecting the sky.*

She finally sat and opened her water bottle for a drink. Perhaps a Cherokee woman along this stream had drunk water from her cupped hands and settlers sipped from tin cups. And now here she sat, enjoying the same stream but drinking bottled spring water from who knows where. Knowledge and technology had made their impact, but human beings still needed water.

She thought about her own life and her own needs as she watched an oak leaf floating in the still water in the pool below. The current swept the leaf to the bank and then out into swifter water until it was out of sight.

My life's been like that leaf, floating, waiting for the current to pull it long. It's time to stop waiting, to make some serious, conscious decisions. I may get into rough water, but no rougher than I've seen. Couldn't be. And at least I wouldn't be drowning in stagnant nothingness. Better to be swept away. I'm feeling swept away.

So deep in thought she was, she failed to notice the sun-washed sky turning gray. A dark cloud loomed behind her, and the breezes whirling into strong winds blew her hair across her face and interrupted her thoughts. She rose quickly and started down the rocks and up the path to the house. The rain came, gentle at first and then hard. With only the distant rumble of thunder, she felt safe in sitting underneath the large hardwood tree to wait out the storm before walking home.

Car lights appeared in the distance. She got up to see. It was Roderick's truck. She waved, hoping he could see her through the rain.

He did. He stopped and opened the passenger's side door. "Need a ride?" He laughed at her. "Didn't your mother teach you to come in out of the rain?"

"What can I say? I guess I'm a slow learner," she said as she hopped into the vehicle and gratefully accepted the towel he handed her. "How did you know?"

"Lilah told me where you went. I own this property, Miss Carlyle, and I know about afternoon storms. You're my guest, and my job is to take care of you while you're here. Actually, I saw you leaving the house. When the clouds gathered, I figured there'd be a lovely damsel in distress somewhere down this way. I haven't rescued a lady in a long time."

"Well, I hope the last one you rescued wasn't as embarrassed as I am," she said, wrapping the towel around her shoulders and wiping her face.

"She wasn't." He took a right at the fork. "How about if I drive to the east side of the house and you can go up the courtyard steps to your suite and no one will know you've been playing in the rain except me and maybe Lilah? She's worried about you."

"Oh, thank you. What time is it?"

He looked at his watch. "It's four thirty."

"Good, I have time for a warm soak before I get dressed. I promise not to leave my suite until your guests arrive."

He pulled up to the side of the house. "Here you are, madam. Go through that gate. The stairs are to your right."

She was surprised when Roderick took her left hand as she slipped toward the truck door. "You're going to shine tonight, Caroline."

"Thank you, Roderick. You are indeed a gentleman." She got out and closed the door and looked at him through the rain-spotted window. She smiled.

I really want to shine tonight.

Caroline entered her room from the balcony door and headed straight for the tea chest. She plugged in the pot, chose a tea bag, and moved toward the bathroom. That's when she saw the box on her bed. It was about the size of the boxes she used to wrap the ties she gave her dad for Father's Day, only this one was sturdier and more elegant. It wasn't wrapped, only secured with white silk ribbon.

She pulled one end of the ribbon and lifted the lid of the box. Moving the tissue paper aside, she picked up a piece of rolled parchment paper tied with a gold ribbon. Inside was the printed program for tonight's recital. On the back were her picture and a biographical sketch. She had sent the titles for the program, but not this picture, nor this bio. It had been done without her knowledge but with the elegance she had experienced since her first introduction to Roderick Adair.

On the front of the parchment was a handwritten note:

Caroline, you will shine tonight.
Remember, there's music—when words aren't enough.
                                    Roderick

The water was boiling before she could put the printed program down. Her hot tea, her warm thoughts, and a half-hour steamy bath would prepare her to shine.

The hour passed quickly. She had finished her hair and makeup and was about to take her dress off the hanger when her cell phone rang. She heard Angel's voice. "Now, sweetie, I won't keep you, but I just wanted to call and say we're thinking about you. You just get all gussied up and be the beautiful woman you are, you hear me?"

"Oh, Angel, I wish you were here. I've done my best to get my hair up like you said, and the pink sapphires—what can I say? They're so lovely nobody will notice my hair."

Just before their goodbyes, Angel asked, "Have you danced yet?"

Caroline paused. "No, but does a picnic count?"

"That's progress, my precious girl. That's real progress. The dancing will come. Bye for now."

Caroline finished dressing and picked up the program one more time. It was six o'clock. She was ready and could sit no longer. She went downstairs to warm up before the guests arrived.

———

Roderick wondered if Caroline had opened the box. He was grateful for Angel's help with the picture and bio and her promise of secrecy. He guessed Annabelle Martin had helped Angel. Lilah had insisted the gift box would be a romantic touch. Romantic touches hadn't been his specialty in a while. He hoped she was right.

He pulled his tux from the back of his closet. There had been evenings like this when he was a child—evenings when his parents' guests would come all dressed up and have dinner and then sit and listen to his mother play the piano. He and Sarah would get all dressed up too. Their balcony seats, overlooking the loggia, were the best in the house. From there they could see her and all the guests enjoying themselves. He'd liked it best when his mother sang.

He adjusted his tie, splashed on the aftershave Lilah had bought for him, and headed to the main house. It was ten after six. His guests would be arriving shortly, and he didn't want to miss Caroline's entrance. He guessed she would come down around six twenty. But when he closed his door and walked through the courtyard, he heard music and saw Caroline through the window's reflection of the setting sun and the coral and lavender-colored clouds. This was more beautiful than the way he had imagined her coming down the steps. He'd been around beauties all his life, but Caroline was more than that. Much more.

He entered the kitchen, and as he did Liz stepped out of her office. "Good evening, Roderick. You're looking awfully debonair. I haven't seen you in your tux in a while." She came near and tried to straighten his tie that didn't need straightening.

"Thank you, and that's right, I haven't worn a tux in a while." He removed her hands and stepped away.

Lilah appeared as if on cue. "Roderick, everything is just lovely. Just like we planned. We're in for a grand evening!"

Roderick moved through the kitchen, leaving Liz in a huff and Lilah grinning. He stood at the end of the loggia. Before, he had seen Caroline through the window. Now he looked at her against the natural light of the sky's changing colors at dusk. The softness of her pink gown, her hair pulled high on her head, falling in loose curls, and the peace in her countenance—he wanted to remember this for a long time. He stood listening, only approaching when she stopped playing.

"Caroline, you are a portrait of perfection." He took her hand and guided her from the piano bench.

"Why, thank you, Mr. Adair, and you're quite handsome yourself. In fact, you look just as comfortable in this tuxedo as you do in your waders." She smiled.

"This gown was made for you—the color, the . . . everything."

"Thank you. Angel picked it out for me. She feared I'd wear my navy-blue suit, so she insisted on a shopping trip. Oh, enough about all that. But thank you. Is everything ready?" She moved from behind the piano.

"Lilah assures me everything is just perfect."

Roderick led Caroline around the loggia to see the tables and talk about the evening. The white linens were crisp, and crystal bowls, filled with irises, took center stage on every table.

They were admiring the portrait of his mother when Lilah brought the first guests into the gathering room to Roderick. He turned to greet them.

"Well, hello, Lawrence, and I'm so glad to see you, Beth. It's been a while. I'd like to introduce you to Miss Caroline Carlyle. She is our piano-playing angel who just landed here from somewhere in this pink cloud."

Roderick smiled as he saw Caroline's face flush and her left dimple appear.

—•—

A steady stream of guests arrived and found their places. Dinner was served. Caroline observed Lilah directing the serving. She felt as though she were on the outside looking in, watching Lilah's choreography of dinner courses, the expensive gowns and jewelry, conversations about recent trips to Paris—and not Paris, Kentucky. She overheard commitments being made for the next fund-raising event.

Roderick, the perfect host, made his rounds to all his guests, leaving her only for a few moments at the time. He'd seated her next to Sarah. Caroline had told Sarah at lunch about her dreams to start a Guatemalan Children's Choir. The choir would travel the States raising money to support the orphanages back in Guatemala. Roderick, hearing this, complimented her on her idea.

Sarah pointed out guests, discreetly explaining the social registry. "Caroline, do you see the older woman over there next to the gold satin chair? Remember her. She might be very interested in your Guatemalan Orphans' Choir idea. She could be very helpful.

Any other time, Caroline would have found all this very interesting, but butterflies circled in her stomach.

Coffee was finally served after the last course. Roderick stepped to the center of the room. "Well, my friends, I hope that I have welcomed each one of you personally by now, and if I haven't, please know that Sarah and I are warmly pleased you are here. You live in these parts, so you know the uncertainties of planning anything outdoors on a summer evening. Our plan was to have a chocolate buffet on the terrace, but you ladies are so lovely this evening, I dare not take a chance with the clouds that are gathering. But you're not to worry; your desserts will be served at your table after our musical treat. So please enjoy. I'll be introducing our stellar guest in just a few moments."

Caroline excused herself for a few private moments in the library. Sarah came to get her as Roderick started the introduction and led her to the curve of the piano, where Roderick took her hand. As he finished his introduction, he turned to look at her face and pulled her fingers to his lips. He kissed them. "Music—when words aren't enough," he whispered.

Caroline sat, making adjustments to the pink cloud of skirt, and closed her eyes as she dropped her head. She took a slow, deep breath, hoping to slow the rhythm of her heart as she placed her linen handkerchief on the bench beside her. She raised her head and opened her eyes to see Lilah standing in the distance. Lilah smiled broadly and folded her hands under her chin as though she were praying. Caroline thought she saw a tear.

She turned her head slightly to the right as she placed her hands on the keyboard. Roderick's gaze was intense.

Caroline began to play, quickly losing herself in the music. She was only brought back to this space and time by the applause of the guests as each piece finished. She knew she was playing well. The dynamic contrasts, the changes in tempo, the rise and fall of the melodies, the delicate passages—music she had internalized through years of practice flowed from somewhere deep inside her and out her fingertips. She and her piano were one again.

Only conscious of her music, she was barely aware the heavens were providing the guests with a fireworks display of lightning through the window and that the thunder had been resonating like a tympani.

When the last chord was played and released, she rose to accept her audience's generous applause. Roderick came to her side and took her hand again, raising it slightly and steadying her while she took a bow. By this time all the guests were on their feet. Even Liz Hampton was forced to stand. As they applauded, he turned to Caroline. "You are shining brilliantly."

"And you're too generous with praise and white packages."

He whispered, "'Plaisir d'amour'? You'll play and sing it? You promised, remember?"

She smiled and nodded in agreement. She reached for Sarah to hand her a glass of water, sipped, and sat back down to the piano.

"Friends," Roderick said, "you'll be pleased to know that Miss Carlyle will play and sing one more selection."

The room became quiet, and Caroline began to play again. She played through the introduction twice before starting to sing. Her voice soared with clarity, even on the nasal quality of the French vowels. At the finish, the applause returned. Roderick joined her at once.

When the room became quiet again, she surprised him by interrupting. "With my host's permission," she said, looking at Roderick, "and with your indulgence . . . I can't bear to end the

evening with a sad French love song bemoaning the bitter departure of the joy of love. Instead, I'd like to close the evening with an
original composition."

Roderick's look indicated surprise, and guests clapped in
anticipation.

She sat once again and lifted her hands to the piano. With
closed eyes and a deep wrinkle in her brow, she bowed her head
and took a slow, deep breath, inhaling not only the air, but the
remembrance of a familiar melody. She turned her head slightly
toward the window and opened her eyes. Raindrops that had pelted
the windows only moments ago trickled down the glass in slow
motion—small droplets meeting small droplets until streams were
formed, like years of her tears. They would slide away together until
the window was clear again.

Through the rivulets and the break in the clouds, stars twin-
kled and a full moon made its entrance from behind the mid-
night-blue curtain of thunderheads. One perfectly formed tear
escaped Caroline's left eye and rolled unseen down her cheek. Her
fingers, poised on the keyboard, coerced warm tones from her 1902
Hazelton Brothers piano.

The delicate melody was unfurling itself when a new and passionate melodic theme appeared. Both motifs were lyrical—the
kind the listeners would be humming tomorrow—yet even more
beautiful as a duet. Caroline was totally engulfed in the intensity
and the passion of the music. The melodies, entwined with the inti-
macy only understood by lovers, built to a tumultuous crescendo.

After the thunderous peak, the piano strings, vibrating and
resonating with each other, became abruptly still. The entire
room was silent. Nothing—not a listener's sigh nor a creak in the
wooden floor—dared intrude on that moment. Then the tautness
in Caroline's arms and shoulders relaxed, and the tension in her
face melted into serenity. Her right hand broke the silence, caressing the first, delicate melody from the piano again. A beautiful sadness blanketed her as she brought the melody gently to a satisfying

cadence. Soulful tears filled her eyes but did not spill out or blur the sight of the shining, full moon through the window.

This was her resolution, her benediction. Her journey back to wholeness had been a strenuous one. But there truly was light at the end of her passage through the long corridor of grief.

A holy hush settled as she lifted her hands from the piano and placed them in her lap and bowed her head. "Goodbye, David," she whispered. "Our song is finished. My gift to you for all time."

This time, the moment of silence was broken by an animated ovation.

The guests lingered and showered Caroline with garlands of praise and invitations to return for parlor concerts in their homes. She returned their generosity with her simple grace. This was not the most enjoyable part of the evening for her. She only wanted to sit in a quiet place and regain her strength.

Finally, the front door closed for the last time. The guests were gone. She and Roderick started toward the library to join George and Sarah to say good night.

Lilah made her way to Caroline and hugged her. "Thank you, thank you. I can't even speak. You have brought music back into these hollow walls. Thank you, Caroline." She walked away with a quivering chin.

On her way back to her office before leaving, Liz went to Caroline. "You play very well, Miss Carlyle. And your gown is lovely. I wore one very similar to that for my senior prom."

Caroline had already noted Liz's red, strapless, nearly painted-on dress and thought it her reward for eating celery and sweating at the gym. "Thank you, Liz. I'm glad to know we have similar tastes. You're very kind."

Liz walked away without a response. Roderick had heard the interchange. "And you, Miss Carlyle, you have class."

They walked together to the library and sat down on the antique sofa facing the fireplace, where they chatted about the evening—Caroline's performance, the dramatic backdrop of the storm, and the guests' sheer enjoyment of the entire event. Roderick and Sarah recalled similar childhood evenings.

Sarah looked again at the night's program in her hand. "I'm not complaining or suggesting, but I noticed you didn't play any of the twentieth-century repertoire."

Caroline was surprised. "Ah, you're an astute listener, and you're right. I didn't tonight, but I do play it when I must."

"Any of the atonal, avant-garde selections?"

"Honestly, no. I don't play it because I don't understand it. Maybe someday."

"Now, that's the beginning of another conversation," Roderick added.

Caroline turned to him. "A conversation about the music or perhaps my inability to understand it?"

"Ooh, I'd like to be in on that one, but we'll save it for next time." Sarah and George rose to excuse themselves, walking to where Caroline rested. She stood, and Sarah took both her hands. "You were brilliant, Caroline, just brilliant. I'm so glad you came, and I'm so happy you've become reacquainted with your piano."

"Thank you, Sarah."

They both smiled and hugged. "We'll say our goodbyes tonight since we're getting such an early start in the morning. I promise to stay in touch, my friend."

"Thank you for everything, Sarah. Something tells me I will need your help more than I know."

At long last, Roderick and Caroline were alone in the library. For the first time since her arrival on Tuesday, she felt awkward. The emotions stirring in her the last couple of days were like old friends she hadn't seen in a long time. She was sure she'd had them before, but time had almost erased their memory.

"You really did shine tonight, Caroline. I don't know when I've enjoyed anything more."

Caroline ran her nervous fingers along the embossed velveteen cushions of the sofa where they sat. "Thank you, Roderick. I would hang my head and run backward all the way to Moss Point if I thought that I had embarrassed you in front of your friends. I'm glad you enjoyed it."

"You're just full of surprises. You look like porcelain, even in a rainstorm." He touched the curl brushing her cheek. "You're so small, but you have such a big heart, and you make so much music. You return catty remarks with kindness. You're quite a mystery, Caroline Carlyle."

She turned shyly away. "Oh, mystery is good, I think. But I've never thought of myself as mysterious, just plainly simple and transparent."

"Maybe that's what makes you mysterious. I'm not accustomed to transparency."

"Well, then, we'll call it even. I'm not accustomed to private planes, secretaries and Lilahs and Acers, and trout streams and business ventures." She turned back to him. "And would you mind if I continued the list tomorrow? I think I should turn in."

As they walked in awkward silence from the library to the foyer, Roderick took her fingers. Standing at the base of the stairs, he lifted her hand and studied it. "Another mystery: your hands are too small to make that much music."

She gently pulled away. "Music comes from the heart, and mine is big. You said so yourself." She planted her feet on the first step.

"You finished 'David's Song.' When did you do that?"

She faced him. "I did, didn't I? I finished it this morning. At least I thought I had finished it. But when I played it tonight, I knew it was finished."

"It was beautiful, Caroline, just like the woman who wrote it. I'm glad for you that you finished it here at Rockwater on your piano. That was goal number two, I believe."

"It was indeed, and thank you," she said pensively. She lifted her skirt to start her climb up the stairs.

"Caroline." He paused as she turned to him. He took her hand again. "Caroline, may I kiss you?" he asked.

Caroline looked deeply into his eyes before responding, "No . . . and yes."

Roderick stood awkwardly still. She sensed he wasn't often caught off guard. "Well, Sarah's not here to interpret that answer. And I'm not trusting myself because I do not want to make a mistake, Caroline."

"Then trust me. 'No' means I don't want to be asked for permission. 'Yes' means when you don't feel a need to ask."

"I'll think about that one. But for now, I'll trust you." He kissed her hand and released it.

Caroline raised her hand to touch his face as she leaned forward to kiss his cheek. "Good night, and thank you for another perfect day, Roderick."

She knew he stood at the bottom of the stairs until the door to her suite closed.

Chapter Twenty-Six

Treasures Restored

———•———

CAROLINE WAS STRAPPED IN FOR TAKEOFF. WITH THE EXCEPtion of brief summer-afternoon showers, every day in Kentucky had been bright with sunshine; but Saturday morning brought fog and slick, gray skies. Yet only moments after takeoff, the plane pierced the gray ceiling of thick clouds and climbed to where the sun shone and the sky was blue.

Her life was like getting through this fog into the sunlight—first, the grayness of the morning drive and then penetrating the clouds to reach the light. In Kentucky she had come to a brighter place, a place where she could see and sense with more clarity.

She looked out the window. *I played my piano once again, and I completed "David's Song." Made some decisions, but I don't think I'll share them until I've had few nights to sleep on them. That's what Dad would do.*

But in spite of herself, her thoughts turned to Roderick. Even though he had treated her with sensitivity and kindness in weeks of phone calls, Caroline had sometimes wondered if he might be an arrogant aristocrat using his resources to spoil himself—a shallow person whose worth was in what he had and in what he could acquire. That had not been the case, something for which she was grateful.

He's warm and sincere, and he seems to handle well the weight of responsibility that comes with his wealth. Yes, he moves and works in global circles, and I don't, but he's grounded in Kentucky bluegrass and thirsts for the waters of his trout stream. Dad, James, and Thomas would like all that.

Slow down. I shouldn't be having these thoughts. It's too much and far too soon. But he sincerely appreciates music—not just being a patron of the arts because he's wealthy and has social standing but because he genuinely loves music. I like the way he spoke of his heritage and his family. He's such a gentleman. And the best part: he makes me laugh. David made me laugh. I didn't dance this trip, but Angel will be happy to hear that I laughed, really laughed.

And I think that she'll be happy to learn I've made my decision. Nothing like sitting on a boulder in a thunderstorm and a levelheaded conversation with Sarah to help clear up my thinking. I'm staying in Moss Point one more year. Time to do what I can with Bella, and time to see what other changes may come—changes I haven't even dreamed about before.

Roderick bounded through the cockpit door, stopping to grab a soda from the small refrigerator. "I have more chocolate, the kind you like." He reached into the snack cabinet.

"Can't say no to chocolate."

He sat across from her and handed her the candy. "I think I owe you an apology. I invited you to Kentucky, and the first time you set foot off Rockwater property was for the foggy drive to the airport this morning. No Paris or Versailles. I fear I kept you captive."

"Shackled with only bread and water. I can't wait to report you to the proper authorities." She unwrapped the chocolate. "Roderick, I had no desire to leave. You and Lilah were grand hosts, treating me like royalty."

"I intended to take you for a drive over to Paris and out to dinner last night to celebrate your wonderful performance Thursday evening, but it just didn't happen. Maybe next time."

She didn't miss the "next time" part.

"Normally on Fridays, I'm wrapping up all the loose ends of

a busy workweek and getting ready for Monday. Caroline, I can't remember spending a whole day talking like we did yesterday."

"Oh, but after Thursday night, I was emotionally drained and exhausted. That chair next to the window in the library hugged me all day. I hope it wasn't too much for you. I'm usually quiet. You can ask Betsy."

He smiled. "I trust you. I hope I didn't bore you with talk of business and projects." He pulled the tab from his soda can.

"Oh, no, I found it extremely fascinating. That's a new world to me."

"Well, as much as we talked, there was a very important subject we didn't address." He put down the soda can and wiped his hands on the paper napkin.

Caroline swallowed the last bite of chocolate. "Let's see, we covered everything except how to eradicate kudzu and how to get bakeries to make half loaves of bread again."

"You have a real knack for deflecting serious conversation with your humor, madam. But you're not getting away with it this time. We must talk about your compensation for the recital."

"Compensation?" she said before laughing out loud.

He did not join in her mirth this time.

"You're serious, aren't you?"

"Yes, businessman serious."

"Me too." She sat up straighter in her chair and put on her best I-have-to-be-serious face.

"Oh, but you're not really serious. You didn't raise your right eyebrow."

She laughed again. "You're right, I can't be serious about this. Roderick, I would have paid you for the chance to play my piano, and you're talking about paying me. That's why I can't be serious."

"I didn't expect you to take four days, come to Kentucky, and do a stellar performance for my friends without compensating you."

"Sorry. The recital was my gratitude for your allowing me

to play the piano. And you cannot repay gratitude with money, Roderick."

"I sit fully chastised and corrected."

"Besides, now I can say I've been to Kentucky. Let's just say we're even." She raised her right eyebrow and extended her hand for a handshake.

"Something tells me I'll never be even with you, Caroline."

Acer called for Roderick.

"We'll see about this later." He returned to the cockpit.

I hope there will be a later. She felt unexpectedly okay with that revelation.

The plane descended, and she could see the ground. As they neared the runway, she spied Sam and Angel leaning against his car at the fence just as Sam had when she left. Sam and Angel were the same, but Caroline wasn't.

———·———

While Acer took Ray, the airport manager, and Sam aboard the jet to satisfy their curiosity, Roderick took Caroline's bags to the car and greeted Angel.

"How can I thank you, Mrs. Meadows, for all your help? That copy you sent of Caroline's last university recital added quite a nice touch to the program and surprised the guest artist, I might add," he said, smiling at Caroline.

"Well, this precious girl has needed a few surprises." Angel hugged Caroline. "I'll admit, though, Sam threatened me with the duct tape. It's hard for me to keep secrets. Well, tell me, how did she play?"

"A notch or two above adequate," Caroline answered quickly.

"Shush, girl, I'll get your version later, and I already knew what you'd say. I'd like to hear Mr. Adair's response."

"Please, call me Roderick. And let's see . . . My version? Well, this heavenly creature floated in on a pink cloud, and she dazzled the entire crowd with her beauty and her music." He saw a hint of dimple and the raised eyebrow from Caroline again.

Angel smiled inside and out. "I knew it. I just knew it. I wish I could have been there myself."

"Enough about me. How are you doing, Angel?"

"Well, sweetie, I'm just as fine as frog hair, and you know how fine that is."

"You look good."

Angel wore her muumuu with all the ribbons and buttons. "I'm feeling stronger every day. Sam and Hattie are smothering me with attention, and the doctor says I'm improving right on schedule. Satisfied now?"

"Almost."

Acer interrupted their conversation, "Mr. Adair, we need to go. Ray says the weather is not improving up our way."

"Be right there." Roderick turned to Angel, kissed her cheek like he would have kissed his mother, and said goodbye.

Angel took her cue and went to the car.

Roderick stepped closer to Caroline.

She lifted her head and eyes to see his face, waited, and then extended her hand. "Roderick, thank you for making my world perfect the last few days. This has been a most unusual and fulfilling experience for me, and I have you to thank."

"You have brought music and laughter and warmth to Rockwater and to me—and to Lilah, I might add. I think your fan club might have a new president."

"She's a dear one, and so devoted to you."

"Don't know what I'd do without her. I know you're in limbo right now about your future, but I know you'll make the right decisions."

"A trout stream provides fresh perspective, you know." She wanted so much to tell him of her decision, but she knew not to let the words slip from her mouth. Once gone, she couldn't bring them back.

"I'll be in touch, Caroline, and until I see you again, you'll be lovely to remember." He kissed her hand.

"Thank you, Roderick. Thank you for everything."

With a last smile, he turned to walk away. He was halfway to the plane when she called to him. "Don't disturb the fish population too much, and take care of my . . . Take care of the piano." She waved and walked to the car, finding herself strangely reluctant to get in.

"Quick, before Sam gets back: did you dance?" Angel asked in an excited, adolescent schoolgirl whisper.

"In my heart, Angel. In my heart. But you'll be happy to know I laughed from the inside out."

Caroline watched Roderick climb the steps to the plane. He turned and waved one more time before closing the door.

Angel and Sam were nonstop questions all the way home, but something—perhaps caution—kept them from asking about Roderick. Caroline described Rockwater and told them of her activities.

"Well, you must know you've been the talk of the town," Sam said.

"I figured as much when I saw three heads duck in Polly's van Tuesday as we pulled out of the driveway."

"Yep, GiGi's been up to her usual. Of course, when Brother Andy explained your absence at choir rehearsal Wednesday night, he poured a little more fuel on the fire." Angel chuckled.

"Then Ray came down to the Café on the Square to drink coffee with the boys Thursday morning and told them about this private jet. And poor Ned and Fred, why, they've been worried silly about you. They even came by earlier this morning to see if you had gotten back home safely."

"Well, I'm back to reality in Moss Point." Caroline smiled with secret thoughts running through her mind.

"What about coming up for supper? Hattie has enough food in my refrigerator to feed Pharaoh's army," Angel said.

"You know, I think I will. I'll unpack my things and make a couple of calls. Then I'll be up."

Inside the stillness of her studio, Caroline put her bags on the bed and started the unpacking. It had been more enjoyable to pack, especially with Gretchen's help. She really wanted to call Gretchen but refrained, thinking that Mr. Silva might be home on the weekend. She would wait until Monday.

She opened her garment bag. On top was a plain white envelope with something handwritten inside. She opened it, hoping it was another surprise from Roderick.

Dear Caroline,

I write this Thursday evening, still in the afterglow of your recital. I asked Lilah to make certain this note was in your bag before you left. You were so drained that I decided to write these things for your reading when you were more rested.

You were simply dazzling this evening. I sat tearfully absorbing your music, remembering times when my mother's music filled the hallways at Rockwater.

Your warmth and vitality bring life wherever you are. Thank you for coming and for the gift that you've been to my brother the past few days. He needed to hear the music again.

I sense the responsibility you have regarding Bella, and I've heard your questioning. My offer to help is sincere. I have enclosed my card. Please call me when you'd like to talk further.

I have many reasons to think we'll be friends and that we will see each other in the days ahead. Thank you again for your music and for giving Roderick and me opportunities to remember sweeter times.

Warmly,
Sarah

Caroline read and reread the note. Her trip had been far more than she'd expected.

When she'd put everything away, she made herself a cup of tea and went to the phone to listen to her messages. Her mom and Betsy wanting full reports; Wyatt Spencer wanting her to call back as soon as she got in; Dr. Martin inquiring about the reunion with her piano; Delia Mullins wanting a return call; Brother Andy with some changes in tomorrow's worship service. She truly was home again. But home looked different somehow after her Rockwater experience.

She phoned her mom and Betsy and gave them abbreviated accounts. Betsy quickly halted Caroline's report and began asking questions. Caroline was cautious because Betsy knew her too well. There was an unspoken conversation between them that wasn't ready to be voiced.

Wyatt Spencer wanted to set a time to meet with her and Bella. Caroline had learned from Sarah to proceed with caution.

She simply was not ready to return Delia's call, but she had to. She didn't want to chance running into her tomorrow at church. She told Delia there was really nothing of interest to the Moss Point readers unless she wanted a copy of the recital program. Delia pushed and Caroline stood firm. Delia finally gave in and said she would just take a copy of the program. Caroline was home free. Few in Moss Point would read an article when they saw names like Beethoven and Bartók.

— · —

Monday morning's first call came from Gretchen. Eager to hear all about the trip, she and Bella were at the back door within minutes of hanging up the phone. Caroline greeted them, and all three headed for the kitchen to start the teakettle. She was surprised Bella did not make a beeline for the piano.

Bella carried a hatbox. Gretchen took it from her and gently placed it on the breakfast table. The box was covered in fabric pansies. The seams and edges of the box were outlined and decorated in a narrow, deep-purple ribbon topped with a gold braid.

"Oh, this box is beautiful. Gretchen, where did you find something like this?"

"Find it? I did not find it. Do you remember the day you dropped your favorite teapot with the pansies on it?"

"Oh, yes, I remember."

"And you told me that pansies were the symbol of friendship. I found this beautiful fabric and covered the box for you. Please open it."

Caroline nodded and picked up the box. "It's heavy. What's inside?"

"I made the box, but Bella made what is inside. Open with care."

Caroline untied the ribbon and lifted the lid. She carefully removed the crinkled-up brown grocery bags protecting the contents. Something solid sat in the center of the box. She lifted it and began unwrapping it. The last layer of brown paper revealed a remarkable work of art.

The sculptured piece, ten to twelve inches high, was a mold of a delicate hand holding a heart. With a more careful look, Caroline recognized shards of her broken teapot. She was stunned. Her questioning eyes forced Gretchen to speak.

"Bella loves puzzles, and to her, your broken teapot was like a puzzle she could put together. She made the mold of her hand from papier-mâché. I mixed the plaster for her, and she shaped the piece bit by bit, adding the broken pieces of china before the plaster dried."

"Oh my, I've never seen anything like it."

Gretchen took the piece from Caroline's hands and positioned it on the counter with the hand facing upward, showing the heart gently cradled in the palm. "This is how it should be displayed. Notice right here at the top and center of the heart, Bella put an opening. I didn't understand why, but there is no coaxing her when she is creating. A couple of days after the piece dried, I found flowers in the opening. She made the heart to hold your blossoms."

"I don't know what to say. I've never had a gift like this before. Not in my whole life have I been given such a treasure."

"You had the treasure all along, Caroline. It was a teapot, but it was broken and you assumed it was destroyed. But now it's been made into a new treasure for you."

"Yes, and it's more beautiful than it ever was," said Caroline as tears moistened her cheeks, "because it's been touched by your hands, Gretchen, and by your hands, Bella. It's such a treasure." She hugged them both.

"Did you hear yourself, Caroline? You said, 'It's more beautiful than it ever was.' Remember, that's how God works. He sweeps up all the broken pieces and puts them back together again."

The tears that had only moistened Caroline's cheeks now streamed down her face. The last few days had churned her emotions—playing her piano, completing "David's Song," and meeting Roderick. Her joy in what the future might hold had been clouded by fear and thoughts of her unfaithfulness to her love for David. It all seemed to erupt in this moment. "My life has been so broken. David disappeared in the jungle, and I disappeared in my music. I kept asking God why, and I never got the answer."

"That's because you're asking the wrong question, Caroline."

Bella stood quietly. Gretchen took Caroline's hands and moved her to sit at the breakfast table. Caroline wiped the tears from her cheeks with the palm of her hand. "But I still don't know why God would do such a thing."

"You're assuming He did it."

"Well, if He didn't, He surely could have prevented it."

"Yes, He could. Not everything that happens is caused by God, Caroline. Sometimes it is, but sometimes it isn't. Sometimes evil just steps in. But God's always present to pick up the pieces. Look around you. God gave you your perfect studio. He gave you Sam and Angel and your family and your students. You're not alone."

"I know, and I'm ashamed for not being more grateful." Caroline wiped her eyes.

"Do not be ashamed, Caroline. You've been broken, and I know about that. But remember, God is a potter and He takes the lumps of clay that we are and shapes them into vessels that can hold Him. When our vessels get broken, He just puts them back together again. It may take time, and it might not look just the same, but He'll fix it. Just like Bella. Look what she did. Your teapot's no longer a teapot, but it will hold beautiful flowers. Do you think God will do less with your life?"

"How did you become so wise, my friend?"

"Wise? Oh, not me. Whatever I know—it's from living and looking and listening to God."

"I want to hear Him again like I used to. I've just been in so much pain. I've stayed near people who hear Him and obey. I watch them and listen to them."

"You've been wondering where He went. Your heart was so full of sadness and your mind was so filled with questions that you couldn't hear Him. But He went nowhere, just waited for you to return. One day, when it is right, I'll tell you the rest of my story. Then you'll see how I know."

"You're such a gift to me—the two of you. Maybe God is using some of the broken pieces of your life to mend mine."

Gretchen smiled quietly as Caroline examined Bella's work of art once again.

"Bella, would you like to play the piano?" Caroline asked.

Bella flashed a huge, surprising smile and headed straight for the keyboard.

"Gretchen, would you like to sit and listen, or would you like to go out on the terrace?"

"I think I should like to have our tea on the terrace to hear about your trip."

The morning sun still hiding behind the magnolia tree provided shade for the terrace. Gretchen allowed Caroline to tell her all about the trip without interruption. She told her about Sarah McCollum. "I think that Dr. McCollum will help us, Gretchen."

Gretchen finally commented, "I think maybe Dr. McCollum is another answer to my prayer. I knew that God would provide in His time."

"We need to move slowly and very deliberately through the next few months. Sarah affirmed what we already know about Bella, and she also knows that as people learn about Bella, your life will change."

"Yes, I'm beginning to understand, but I don't know if Mr. Silva will ever understand. And we must help Bella. She doesn't take to change."

Caroline shifted in her chair. "There's something else I haven't told you because I didn't want you to worry."

Gretchen's face muscles tightened as they did when they talked about Mr. Silva.

"I've made an important decision on this trip. Dr. Martin has asked me to come to the university to teach and work on my doctorate. She has offered me a position starting in the fall."

"Oh, you'll be moving?" Hope disappeared from Gretchen's eyes.

"Eventually, yes, but not this fall. I've made my decision, and it feels good. The time in Rockwater helped me gain a fresh perspective." Caroline's eyes filled with tears. She paused and continued with broken voice. "All the time I've lived in Moss Point, I have lived a lie. I've been pretending, covering my deep pain. God forbid anybody pitying me or worrying about me. I have way too much pride for that."

She wiped her cheek with the back of her hand. "I have prayed and cried and prayed some more. I just couldn't let go of the pain. Every day I pasted a smile on my face while I was weeping, just weeping, on the inside. Every day I filled my calendar with things to do, but I would have preferred being in a fetal position in my bed. I filled my days with music students and church activities, but there was no music inside me. I felt it was buried in Guatemalan mud with David. I have silently grieved alone for the last six years, moving from day to day doing what fell into my lap to do, but I felt hollow inside—like part of me had died. Dead people can't make decisions, but I've made a decision."

"I know how that feels, Caroline. I felt that way for many years, but then I was given Karina and Bella. And as I gave life to them, they gave life back to me."

"It's like the treasure you gave me today. I felt like someone was holding my heart and now it's been handed it back to me, and it's beating inside my body again. My life is changing, and you've been a part of that. I can move forward now with making new plans. I haven't known that in a long time."

"Will you tell me what your plans are, my friend?"

"I'm certain I'm not ready to move to the university this year, but I'm ready to make plans. I really want to spend another year right here in Moss Point. I want to be with Sam and Angel, and with you and Bella, and see the Christmas decorations, and another spring of dogwood blossoms, and the irises out by the pond. Then, maybe next fall, I'll be ready to go. But I want to live, really live, every day for this next year looking at the people around me and seeing them as characters in my life journey and seeing myself as a character in their life stories. Am I making any sense?"

"Oh, yes, there is a brightness in your eyes and a new tone in your voice, my friend. And I must say to you, I'm so glad you'll be here for another year."

"Maybe we'll both make some changes together, okay?"

"Agreed."

"And I have something else to tell you. I finished 'David's Song' in Kentucky. I'm dying to play it for Bella."

"Then let's go inside. I'd like to hear it myself."

Caroline followed Gretchen inside and put away the teacups while Gretchen told Bella that Caroline wanted to play the piano. Bella took her seat beside the piano.

As Caroline played, she watched Bella rock back and forth with her fingers playing every note on the folds of her flowered dress. This song was as much a part of Bella as it was of her.

When she got to the new section of the piece, Bella looked startled and quickly turned her head and fixed her eyes on Caroline. Their eyes locked. Caroline finished the piece and rose from the piano bench. She went to Bella, took her hand, and brought her to the piano bench. Caroline played the entire piece once more with Bella sitting beside her. When she finished, she got up and Bella began to play. Caroline moved quietly to Bella's chair.

Bella played "David's Song" with perfection.

Playing the finished piece for her recital was one thing, but hearing Bella play the completed work made it real—like waking up and finding your treasure has been restored.

Chapter Twenty-Seven

Da Capo al Fine—
From the Beginning to the End

———◆———

ROCKWATER WAS QUIET AGAIN. SO WAS RODERICK. LIZ took phone messages, and he opened notes from his guests—gratitude, inquiries about this talented pianist, and questions about her return.

Roderick's treks for morning coffee weren't the same. He imagined hearing Caroline's early morning voice from the balcony. From the terrace table he envisioned her practicing the piano with the late afternoon sun shining on her hair or at the recital with the lightning flashing behind her and the soft glow of candles around her. He saw the fading white irises and her lifeless waders hanging in the mudroom.

Since Caroline, he found it difficult to focus on Adair Enterprises. He wanted to hear her voice morning, noon, and night. But he refrained from calling. He spoke of her with Sarah. When Sarah encouraged him, he listed all the reasons the relationship would not work—he was nine years older; she had deep roots where she was; she still grieved for David; he was too busy for a long-distance romance. Sarah refuted each argument.

He noticed Lilah's green gingham apron replaced her smile and song. She brought him a fresh cup of coffee to the terrace. "Here's another cup, Roderick. Looks like you been dragged through town backward and slapped with a buzzard gut. You need something to get you going."

"I look that bad? I need something to get me going all right."

"Uh-huh, and that something has a name: Caroline Carlyle."

Roderick put his cup down and looked at Lilah. "And what makes you think that?"

"Mostly your face and your voice when you talk about her. And then I remember how you were when she was here. You haven't been like that since she left. You just got a chronic case of the mully-grubs."

"None of this makes sense. I get word from this young woman who wants to play this Hazelton Brothers piano because it once belonged to her. I agree. I ask her to play a recital for my friends—something we haven't done in years. She's here for just four days . . . and . . ."

"Uh-huh, just long enough to turn you upside down and inside out. You're smitten, Roderick. Face it, you're just plain smitten. She brought some life and music back in this house. She made you smile, and she kept you from working while she was here. She's for real, and you know it. Not like the other women you know—plastic, just plain plastic."

"You think so, Lilah?"

"Yeah, I think so. But what I want to know is, what will you do about it? I'm tired of watching you mope around here."

"That's the question, isn't it?"

"You could ask her back to play the piano again. You could invite some different folks this time."

Roderick saw the sparkle return to her eyes. He knew Lilah thrived when she was planning a party.

"And besides, I know you bought that piano because it reminded you of your mother's. You bought and paid for it, but it's not yours. It may sit right here at Rockwater in front of that big window till Jesus comes, and the check that paid for it may have had your name on it, but that's Caroline's piano, Roderick. You know it. So you might as well let her play it, and I don't mean once in a while. I mean every day."

Roderick stood up, hugged Lilah, kissed her on the cheek, and walked briskly toward his quarters. He shouted to her as he went, "Thank you, thank you, thank you. You're just what I needed to get me going this morning. Lilah, don't you ever think of leaving Rockwater. I absolutely couldn't live without you."

———·———

A week passed. The summer heat in Moss Point was oppressive, with only the relief of an occasional afternoon shower. Caroline was restless. Angel was improving but still weak. Hattie was attentive, and Sam was tackling the park project.

Caroline talked openly with Angel about Roderick. "I'm a muddled mess, Angel. I'm not sure what I'm feeling. I'm so very fond of him, and I think about him. But he's older and from a different world. Maybe I should just settle down and think about being his friend. I mean, I'd like to be his friend so I get to play my piano again." She said the same thing a hundred different ways to Angel, and Angel's answer was always the same.

"Caroline, you're feeling things you haven't felt in a long time. You didn't get to marry David. Instead you married your grief, and I think you're feeling unfaithful. Just one day at a time, sweet girl. Look at all the doors that are open for you. Just one day at a time."

In the daily-ness of these days, she longed for the phone to ring. He had called twice to chat, telling her of another upcoming trip to London and wanting to know the latest on Bella. "You haven't asked," she'd told him, "but I'll tell you. I've made the decision to stay put here in Moss Point for another year. I feel so much peace about the decision. I wasn't excited about going back to the university, and when I leave here, I want to be headed somewhere, not just leaving some place." She smiled inside and out when he blessed her decision.

Caroline could no longer postpone the call canceling the trip to take Bella to the university. Mr. Silva had bummed up his knee and couldn't work for several days. Her sense of urgency about Bella was relieved since she was staying in Moss Point, but Dr. Spencer was agitated with the news and insisted on coming to Moss Point at the end of the week. Caroline gave in and agreed on Saturday afternoon, reminding him that seeing Bella was impossible.

After a sleepless night, she made the phone call early. "Dr. Martin, I'm so grateful for your offer to come to the university in the fall, but I am entirely certain I must decline. I am so sorry to disappoint you." Dr. Martin made one more plea, but Caroline stood politely firm. "Dr. Martin, I need this year with Bella, and we'll possibly be seeing more of each other now because of her, and I'll still be studying with you." She expressed hope that a teaching position might be available the next summer or fall. Dr. Martin made no promises.

The next four days of finishing journal articles and getting them to the editor afforded her little time outside her studio. She made a determined effort Saturday morning, but a sudden shower shortened her morning walk. She would have walked in the drizzle, remembering the rain in Kentucky, if GiGi hadn't blown her horn and stopped to ask her if she knew it was raining.

She spent the rest of the morning and early afternoon doing further reading about savant syndrome in preparation for Dr. Spencer's later afternoon visit. He arrived on time, and she greeted him at the door.

Wyatt Spencer, in his signature khakis, crisply starched blue-striped shirt, and sockless ankles, removed his sunglasses and entered the room. "And this is where Georgia's most talented pianist and composer lives?"

Caroline ushered him to the wicker sofa near her desk. "This is where I live. I don't know about Georgia's finest."

"I'm only repeating Dr. Martin. She thinks you're the best, and that you'll be a fine addition to the university in the fall."

"How about a cup of tea?" Caroline wanted to avoid this subject.

"Could you make it iced tea?"

"Of course." Caroline made her way toward the kitchen.

"Should I follow you?"

"Oh, no, just keep your seat. The kitchen is right there around the counter. I can see and hear you." She filled the teakettle. "Maybe you haven't spoken with Dr. Martin in the last few days, but I have declined her offer for this year."

"I'm really sorry to hear that. It's our loss."

"Perhaps it's my loss, but I'm hoping the offer will still stand for next fall. But you came here to talk about Bella." From the kitchen, she told Wyatt about how she came to know Bella and Gretchen. She served the tea and homemade snickerdoodles.

He took the glass of iced tea and reached for a cookie. "So along with this incredible talent, you have southern grace and charm."

Caroline blushed slightly. "My mother would just call it hospitality."

"Tell me about yourself. How did you come to be this Caroline Carlyle?"

She assumed she was being analyzed. "Is that a question that comes with your profession?"

"Ninety-five percent of the time, but this one's personal. I want to know how this beautiful young woman on whose sofa I'm sitting became so fascinating."

"Well, if I tell you my story, then I can assure you the fascination will wither, and I'll just be another southern cook who plays the piano."

She heard him laugh for the first time. She told him about growing up in Ferngrove and about her family. Before she got to the David chapter of her story, she glanced at the clock across the room. "My goodness, it's nearly seven o'clock, and the roast needs to come out of the oven."

"Wait a minute, I had thought to take you out to dinner."

"This is Moss Point, not Athens. I cooked."

"Embarrassed to be seen with me?"

"Quite the contrary. It's just there's no place that would be conducive to conversation." She refused to tell him she had kept the Moss Point tongues flapping enough the last few weeks and she couldn't feed him Mabel's cheeseburgers.

"I understand. But next time it's my treat."

While she got dinner together, he walked around the room and stood at the window overlooking the pond. She invited him to the table and sat down across from him. She served their plates with pot roast, potatoes and carrots, gravy, green beans, hot biscuits, and pistachio salad. Over peach cobbler and coffee, she asked about his background.

"Grew up in Tyler, Texas, and my upbringing was like yours—a stable, middle-class family with three boys. When we weren't on some ballfield, we were on horses. Learned more than my share about horse sense. I think that's why I've always been interested in human behavior."

"Are your parents still living?"

"Still live in Tyler on a small ranch, and both my brothers live in Dallas. This teaching position was the only thing that could have lured me away from Texas, and I plan to return after certain career accomplishments."

Caroline guessed that Bella might be one of those.

She enjoyed his humor and relaxed nature and found herself growing more comfortable with him in spite of the awkwardness of a man sitting across this table from her. It was the first time, and not nearly as comfortable as sitting across the table from Roderick at Rockwater.

During his second helping of peach cobbler, he told her how much he was enjoying the evening and how disappointed he was that she wasn't moving to Athens.

About ten o'clock an unfamiliar uneasiness lowered her comfort level, and she reminded him of his hour's drive back to Athens.

"I guess that's my cue to exit. But before I do . . ." He rose from the table and came to her side.

Her uneasiness turned to queasiness.

He took her left hand and kissed it softly. "Thank you. I don't know when I've had a meal so fine, ma'am. Reminds me of home and my mama's table."

She removed her hand, stood, and walked with deliberation toward the door. He followed.

"Thank you for coming to Moss Point. I have a better understanding now. We'll just see how things go with Bella." She felt like an awkward fifteen-year-old on her first date as she turned to face him.

"I hope we can see each other again. And let me make it clear—I hope to see you again, not just because of Bella. I really like spending time with you." He came closer and leaned to kiss her.

Caroline turned her head slightly. "Thank you, Wyatt, and good night."

He kissed her on her cheek. "And good night to you, Caroline, and I meant what I said." He turned and walked across the terrace to the driveway.

She watched his headlights turn to taillights through the kitchen window. Years had passed without a serious thought of a man, and now a Kentucky gentleman and a university professor had sent her head spinning. She went to the piano to clear her head.

———

Caroline ate Sunday lunch with Sam and Angel. She told them almost everything about her meeting with Dr. Wyatt Spencer.

Angel followed her to the door as she was leaving. "Sweetie, got any plans for Friday morning?"

"Don't think so. Why? Want to make some?"

"I really do. Could we go to Atlanta Friday morning? I need to go shopping."

"Well, sure. But it's not Sam's birthday or anything like that, so what's with this having-to-go-to-Atlanta?"

"I just need to get out of this house before I commit murder. I'm going to strangle Hattie with my bare hands. She's more help than anybody needs, and Sam won't tell her to just go home. By the way, do they put eighty-four-year old women in prison?"

Caroline laughed. "I think they do if it's premeditated, and you've just told me. I guess you'll have to kill me too. Maybe you'd better talk with that judge in the kitchen."

"Can't do that. He's the next one on my hit list."

"In that case, maybe we should go to Atlanta tomorrow."

Angel closed the screen door. "No, no, that really won't do. We must go on Friday."

"Friday it is, with one condition."

"Sounds good. What's the condition?"

"We take the wheelchair."

"Agreed. We'll take the chair, and I'll tell you if I need it. Honestly, sweetie, I'm growing stronger every day. We'll go early, take our time, shop a couple of hours, and I'm buying lunch."

"That's a plan. See you tomorrow. Going to get my hair trimmed in the morning."

"Have fun, and tell Gracie to do something else with Lucy's hair. She looks like her head got stuck in a purple cotton-candy-making machine."

"I think I'll let you tell her that. Bye, Angel."

———•———

Monday morning's visit to sit in Gracie's zebra-striped chair was the first since her trip to Kentucky.

"Mornin', Caroline. Come on back," Gracie said. "I'm dyin' to hear about your trip."

Caroline took her seat. Before Gracie could wrap her in the black plastic cape and reach for the scissors, four faces peeped around the wicker room divider—one in curlers, another in a plastic cap, and two wet heads. "So, how was it?" Gracie asked.

"Oh, it was fine. I went and played a recital and came home. Didn't you read Delia's column yesterday?"

"Yeah, I read the column. Didn't recognize half the names in it. And besides, you didn't play a recital from Tuesday until Saturday."

A squeaky voice from the other side of the wicker divider said, "Well, from what I read, she might have played four days—that was a lot of music."

"Yeah, she was playing all right, but it wasn't the piano." Gracie gave up on getting anything juicy from Caroline. "What are we doing today?"

"Just a trim."

"What about some wispy bangs? Or maybe some highlights? I've learned a new technique."

She needs to learn a new technique. Caroline had seen a few ladies in town with Gracie's bangs. They all looked like Buster Brown. And as for the highlights, she envisioned zebra stripes. "No bangs. Just trim the ends, please."

"Caroline, you've been comin' here for a long time and payin' me to trim the ends. I declare I hate to take your money for that, but I guess I will."

Gracie probed and Caroline sidestepped until Gracie asked if she was going back to Kentucky. Caroline answered honestly. "I have no plans to return to Kentucky."

She paid Gracie twice what the trim was worth, but the extra paid for the entertainment.

She headed to the Café on the Square for one of Mabel's cheeseburgers and a basket of onion rings that Sam said would make a rabbit spit in a bulldog's face. Then she drove around the Square. *Amazing how different this place looks now that I've decided to stay. It's like I've not really seen any of this before. Never noticed the monument in the morning light.*

Bo Blossom was on his late morning walk. *How could I have thought he was the intruder?*

She waved at Brother Andy going in the post office. *He'll make someone feel good today.*

She saw Tandy Yarbrough coming out of the library. *Probably a board meeting, and I'll bet she didn't make anyone feel good.*

Several of her students attending Bible school at the Baptist church waved at her through the chain-link fence. *Why do churches have fences—to keep folks in or out?*

She parked on the square as the courthouse clock chimed eleven thirty. She crossed the street to the restaurant only to find the lights off and a sign hanging in the window: *Gone fishing. Be back tomorrow if the fish don't bite.*

Clever of Mabel. Who can determine "tomorrow" with such a sign?

She looked across the Square. *How could I have overlooked these simple pleasures for the last six years? It's truly like I'm seeing them for the first time.*

———

After a grilled-cheese sandwich at home, she played the piano all afternoon. She hadn't even minded Ned and Fred's hammering. With the park project on the drawing board, she understood why Sam wanted a sturdy brick fence to separate Twin Oaks from the park property before Ned and Fred started clearing the land.

She'd heard Angel bargaining with Ned last week when she showed him the picture of the gazebo she wanted in the park. "You do the best you can to protect my roses while you're building this fence, and you'll get to build the gazebo. People will sit in it for the next hundred years, and I'll put a brass plaque with your name on it as the builder." So far, Caroline had not seen one broken rose cane or bruised petal.

She was at the piano late in the day when she heard a knock at the door. She opened it to Ned and Fred.

"Done for the day, Miss Caroline. Just lettin' you know we's headed home. May be a little late tomorrow mornin'. Mabel cooks pancakes on Thursdays. She won't cook 'em except on Thursdays, and me and Fred like her pancakes."

"Then you'd better pray the fish don't bite."

"'Fish don't bite'? Fish don't like pancakes, do they?" Ned said. Fred jabbed him hard in the ribs.

Caroline laughed. *Ned and Fred are as rare as Bella.* "I don't know if fish like pancakes or not, but Mabel likes to fish. I went to get a burger for lunch today, and her sign said she'd gone fishing and would be back tomorrow if the fish weren't biting."

"Oh, I get it now." Ned laughed hard. "We'll be on our way, ma'am. Sure have enjoyed your piano playin'. It's just plain beautiful. Yessiree, that's what it is—just beautiful."

"Thank you, Ned."

Before she could finish, Fred interrupted her. "Me too. Me too." He looked at his feet.

"And thank you, too, Fred. I'm working on a new piece—three movements, and I'm almost finished."

"And just think, we been right here while you been makin' it up. Fred, ain't that somethin'?"

Fred shook his head.

"Thank you, gentlemen. See you tomorrow." Caroline closed the door and went back to the piano. Through the window, she saw Fred slap Ned across the behind with his John Deere cap.

———•———

Ned stopped in his tracks and looked at his twin. "I'm done talking about being dumb. Yeah, we're dumb, but we're blessed, Fred. Think about it. We gonna be building a city park, started on the wall this mornin'. It's gonna be beautifuler than anything else in town, and we get to make it that way. Just two old dumb boys."

"Uh-huh."

"And figger on this: all the time we been aworkin' on that wall this mornin', we been listnin' to beautiful music. People pay money, big money, Fred, to hear that kinda music. I can see it now—Miss Caroline on a stage somewhere fancy with one of them grand pianos and a bunch of fiddle players makin' music like it's gonna be in heaven."

Fred stared at his brother like he was looking in the mirror. "You got a good 'magination, Ned."

"Yeah, brother, I do. But that park ain't gonna get built without somebody imaginin' it. And Miss Caroline wouldn't have one note of music to play if somebody didn't imagine that neither. And think about this." He took off his cap and swatted his brother's arm. "We got to hear Miss Caroline imaginin' all mornin', Fred. We's the first to hear that music, and I imagine it's gonna be somethin' beautiful."

He put his cap back on, and they walked down the driveway, threw their toolboxes over the pea-green picket fence around their truck bed, and left for the day.

—·—

The sunshine on Friday morning was bright and made folks at Moss Point glad the Dog Days of August were almost over. It was hot, but at least the drive to Atlanta wouldn't be through a rainstorm. Caroline poured a cup of coffee for the road. Standing at the sink, she saw Sam walking Angel down the stone path. She met them at the door.

Sam greeted her with his familiar hug and cautioned her not to let Angel get too tired.

She promised and asked, "So, what will you do without us today?"

"Oh, important things, very important things." He walked them to the car.

"Everything Sam does is important; didn't you know that, sweetie?"

"But it's Friday. I thought he took a break from important things on Friday."

"Not this Friday. Okay, ladies, get gone so I can get on to my business." He kissed Angel and helped her in.

Caroline cranked the car, turned the air conditioner to maximum, and began to pull out of the driveway. Angel rolled down the window. "If we can't find anything better to do, we'll be home by three o'clock. Remember, three o'clock."

Sam gave her the old "okay" hand sign, and the ladies drove off. Their conversation covered everything north of Ferngrove and south of Atlanta during the drive. Once there, Angel assured Caroline she was fine to walk and to leave the wheelchair in the trunk. In no time at all, Caroline was dropping her off at the entrance to the mall and going to park. They rendezvoused at Mrs. Kramer's dress shop. Angel wanted an elegant dress in burgundy. Mrs. Kramer seated her in the back and brought out several. Both Angel and Caroline knew the right one when it made its appearance. Mrs. Kramer reserved the keepers in the back—some kind of sales psychology, Caroline supposed.

Next they went to the bookstore. Angel wanted to surprise Sam with a new book on the Civil War. She looked at a low-fat cookbook for Hattie.

"I think you're going to insult her with that, Angel."

"Better to insult her than strangle her."

"Can't argue with that."

"Oh, I shouldn't be so mean about Hattie. She's just trying to take care of me. But that woman would fry butter breaded with biscuit crumbs."

Caroline grimaced. "Well, maybe the new cookbook is a good idea."

Angel looked at her watch. "Okay, one more stop before we eat." She wanted to go to the craft store. "I need a few tubes of paint and a canvas."

"Oh, you're going to paint? You haven't painted in a while, have you?"

"No, I haven't. Remember when I told you it was time for you to dance? Well, it's time for me to paint again. I have a couple of things in mind."

Caroline carried the shopping bags while Angel filled her basket with tubes of paint—mostly shades of pink—a linen canvas, and a couple of new brushes. They checked out and headed for the food court, where they chatted over lunch until Angel looked at her watch.

"Okay, we can go now," Angel said.

"You mean we have permission?"

"No, I mean I've done all I need to do, and we told Sam we'd be back by three."

"That's right. Then I suppose we'd better head for the barn. Can't leave Sam alone too long doing important things. We'll walk to the entrance together, and I'll get the car and pick you up at the front door. No more walking for you today."

———

Angel napped on the drive home while the third movement of Caroline's new composition ricocheted around in her head. She preferred composing at the piano, but the driver's wheel wasn't a bad second. She hummed the new melody, hoping it would help her remember it. She had already entered the first two movements into the computer and printed them out.

Stopping at the traffic light as they entered town woke Angel. "Are we here already? What time is it?"

"We're here and it's about quarter till three."

"Oh, we're early. Could we stop and get something to drink—a soda or lemonade maybe?"

"You don't want to get something at home? I have sodas, and you know Hattie keeps fresh lemonade."

"But . . . I think . . . I think I want something . . . maybe with ice cream in it."

"Oh, you mean like a real soda, an ice-cream soda?"

"Yeah, a real ice-cream soda."

"Is an ice-cream soda on your doctor's Angel-can-have-that list?"

"No, but maybe Harvey can make it with low-fat ice cream or sherbet or something."

"Or something? Okay." Caroline parked in front of Kimbo's Drugstore. "Should I get something for Sam?"

"No, I'll just share mine with him."

Their last-minute detour managed and with Angel sipping an ice-cream soda, they turned the corner to Twin Oaks. "What's with the big white van parked there?" Caroline asked.

"What van?"

"'What van?' What do you mean 'what van?' The one I just squeezed by turning in the driveway."

"Oh, maybe Mrs. Dickey across the street bought some new furniture. Lord knows she needs some. Those cats of hers have ruined everything in that house." Angel looked at her watch and opened the car door.

"I'll carry your packages up to the big house." Caroline got out of the car.

"I don't think I can make it, Caroline."

Caroline dropped the packages and ran around the car to Angel. Angel unfastened her seat belt. "What are you doing, child?"

"Are you all right? You said you didn't think you could make it."

"Yeah, my bladder is just about to go boom." Angel carefully swiveled around, taking Caroline's arm to get out of the car.

"Good."

"Good? So now you think a bursting bladder is good?"

"Beats a heart attack, I think. Don't you scare me like that anymore, you hear?"

"I think I can make it to the studio. Then you can walk me home."

Caroline, laden with shopping bags, followed Angel to the terrace. Angel turned the doorknob and walked in. Caroline frowned.

She was certain she had locked the door before she left. She said nothing and stepped inside just behind Angel.

"Well, it's about time you got home," said Sam in his judge's voice.

Caroline looked up. There sat Sam in the chair where Bella always sat.

And there sat Roderick in the chair next to him.

"Yes, we've been waiting for you." Roderick rose from his chair.

Caroline dropped the bags in surprise. Angel giggled, and Sam applauded.

Caroline wanted to run to Roderick, but instead she turned to Angel. "Did you know about this?"

"Of course I knew about this. You don't think I really wanted to go to Atlanta today, do you? You've been duped, sweetie, just plain duped."

Caroline went to Roderick and hugged him politely.

As he pulled away from her to look at her face, he moved his hands to her shoulders and guided her to turn around. "Yes, we've been waiting to hear you play."

And there was her piano—her beloved 1902 Hazelton Brothers piano that had supposedly found a home in Rockwater. It sat, as if on display, in the alcove in her studio.

"My piano?"

"Your piano, Caroline," Roderick said.

"But I don't have . . . I can't afford . . . And the piano that was here?"

"Let's just say we've made an even trade. Your baby grand is in the white truck right outside. The driver will take it back to Rockwater. That is, if you'll allow this one to stay here. Let's hear how it sounds. Would you play for me right now?"

Sam and Angel slipped quietly out the back door as Caroline sat down at the piano. Angel blew her a kiss before Sam closed the door.

Caroline sat there a moment, amazed. Her piano keys were

under her fingertips. Here, in her studio. And Roderick was in the armchair a few feet from her.

She began to play.

She played the first movement of her new piece. It was a simple, romantic melody—gentle and soft. Then, a moment of silence. Out of the corner of her eye, she saw Roderick move to applaud. But she wasn't finished.

She started again. This time the melody disappeared and reappeared several times in bold, dark, and vibrant sounds, like a summer night's thunderstorm. Again the music stopped to silence. Caroline breathed deeply and began the third movement, a variation on the first theme.

And then she stopped midphrase. She turned to Roderick with a smile that coaxed her left dimple to appear.

"I'm stunned. Caroline, what a lovely and powerful piece. But I've never heard it," Roderick said as he stood.

"No one's heard it. I'm writing it. It's the 'Rockwater Suite.'"

"But finish playing it. I want to hear it."

"I will finish it . . . someday. Trust me," she said as she stood and walked toward him.

—The End of the Beginning—

Acknowledgments

———◆———

As always, I am grateful for readers. Thank you for your time spent in the pages of this book. It is for you that I write. *Return of the Song* combines story and the metaphor of music. Both make my heart sing. With this book, I worked to create a space where you could visit and feel at home in Moss Point or at Rockwater. I hope that you will try on the skin of more than one of these characters as you read. See what he sees. Feel what she feels. If you can do that and maybe chuckle a time or two or feel a tear escape your eye, then I will have been successful. Thank you for your time in taking this story from the page and bringing it to life in your imagination.

I owe a debt of gratitude to Dr. Darold Treffert, world-renowned psychiatrist, who has studied savant syndrome for more than forty years. He has appeared on many television programs and has written extensively about savants and mental health. It was most important to me that I depict Bella, a musical savant, with absolute integrity and authenticity. Dr. Treffert graciously read this manuscript and put his stamp of approval upon it.

Piano teachers everywhere deserve our thanks. They are vital citizens in communities across our nation. They serve our churches. They teach our children. They provide entertainment. And they provide the gift of music for poignant times in our lives—times such as worship services and weddings and funerals. I salute you for the giving of yourselves and your music. Like me, you could write volumes about your personal experiences with your students and with your communities. I had the gift of a wonderful piano teacher who instilled in me the love of music and the discipline to develop the skill. Thank you, Mrs. Verran. You shaped my life.

A squad of professionals made sure this book ended up between its covers. Thank you, Gilead Team, for every big and little thing you do to publish clean fiction and to make it available to discerning readers. I'm so grateful you understand the value of words and the turn of a phrase and the importance of the story. Leslie Peterson, I am indebted to you. You know how to separate the wheat from the chaff when it comes to editing. And how blessed I am that you get Southern.

There would be no music and no stories without my Bill. As an artist, you've taught me to see. As a theologian, you've encouraged my faith. And as a philosopher, you have engaged me to think. And always, you've given me freedom to imagine. You are the music of my heart.

Phyllis Clark Nichols's character-driven Southern fiction explores profound human questions using the imagined residents of small town communities you just know you've visited before. With a strong faith and a love for nature, art, music, and ordinary people, she tells redemptive tales of loss and recovery, estrangement and connection, longing and fulfillment . . . often through surprisingly serendipitous events.

Phyllis grew up in the deep shade of magnolia trees in South Georgia. Born during a hurricane, she is no stranger to the winds of change: In addition to her life as a novelist, Phyllis is a seminary graduate, concert pianist, and cofounder of a national cable network with health- and disability-related programming. Regardless of the role she's playing, Phyllis brings creativity and compelling storytelling.

She frequently appears at conventions, conferences, civic groups, and churches, performing half-hour musical monologues that express her faith, joy, and thoughts about life—all with the homespun humor and gentility of a true Southern woman.

Phyllis currently serves on several nonprofit boards. She lives in the Texas Hill Country with her portrait-artist husband.

Website: *PhyllisClarkNichols.com*
Facebook: *facebook.com/PhyllisCNichols*
Twitter: *twitter.com/PhyllisCNichols*

The Rockwater Suite Continues in

Freedom of the Song

Coming Spring 2019

Get in the Christmas Spirit

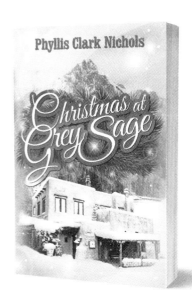 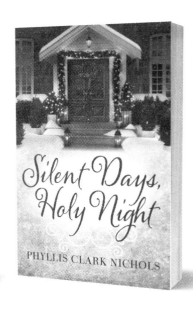

phyllisclarknichols.com

Read a sample from book 2
of the Rockwater Suite

FREEDOM
of the *Song*

Coming Soon!

ROOM 602 AT EMORY HOSPITAL WAS AS QUIET AS A RECITAL hall an hour after the concert. Caroline squirmed in a fake leather chair that stuck to flesh and whose cracks she had memorized. It was no more comfortable than when she arrived five days ago, not even for her petite frame. Sitting up straight and stretching her arms high above her head gave some relief. She pulled the hair tie from her ponytail and leaned over with her head between her knees, allowing her dark brown curls to almost touch the floor. The cracked linoleum had the look of a high school biology lab and had probably been doused with similar organic fluids and cleaning chemicals through the years.

Caroline massaged her scalp and brushed her hair with her fingers. Her unruly, wavy hair, inherited from her father, was the only undisciplined detail of her life. She sat up and tried taming it once again, pulling it severely to the top of her head and entrapping it with the hair tie. Tendrils escaping along her temples were beyond coaxing. She coiled into the chair and wrapped the blanket tighter around her.

Gretchen, free now of the tubes that had sustained her since the surgery, rested in the bed next to Caroline's chair. The bruising on her face and neck was migrating from a deep purplish-blue to green, and the swelling was subsiding. Prints of the brute's hands and fingers still encircled her neck—marks of evil, but she was beginning to look more like Gretchen. Her unblemished hand, like wax, rested on the white sheet. Caroline studied it, thinking of the gentle way Gretchen caressed Bella's hair. *How can one person's hand bring so much pleasure and another's so much pain?* Caroline could almost hear what Sam might say in his courtroom voice before pronouncing Ernesto's sentence: "Something wrong with a man who caresses his hound dog and kicks his wife in places where no living thing should be kicked."

The doctors did not know how long Gretchen's brain had been deprived of oxygen resulting from the attempted strangulation and the amount of blood loss. They'd know more when she could talk. Her size, her delicate features and porcelain skin, left them all wondering how she had survived such a vile attack.

Caroline's phone rang. She unwrapped the blanket and reached for her phone in her bag beside the chair, hoping not to disturb Gretchen's sleep. Roderick's number appeared on the screen. Since meeting him in the summer and playing a recital in his Kentucky home, Caroline looked forward to his calls. "Oh, good morning, Roderick, you can't know how good it is to hear your voice."

"Yours, too, Blue Eyes. How are things this morning?"

"Improving slowly every day. The doctor removed the tubes last evening, and we'll see how Gretchen does today. I just hope she can talk."

"And Bella?"

"Oh, she's more resilient than I thought. Her little face is healing and no permanent damage to the eye. She's with your sister and Dr. Wyatt Spencer. Fortunately, or unfortunately, this situation has given him the opportunity he wanted to observe Bella."

"And Dr. Spencer?"

"The professor from the University of Georgia."

Roderick interrupted her. "Yes, I remember Dr. Spencer."

"Well, he has permission to use the facilities here at Emory. So he brought in a few colleagues from Athens to take a look at Bella.

It seems his way of staking the university's claim on Bella. But I'm so grateful Sarah's here to monitor things."

"That's my sister, Sarah, the child psychologist coming to the rescue."

"And to my rescue. It's amazing to watch her with Bella. They're really bonding."

"That's what she's trained to do, and she's good at it because it's her passion."

"Passion. Oh that everyone's passion would lead to goodness." Caroline pulled the blanket tighter around her.

"So you're philosophizing this morning?" Roderick asked.

"No, just thinking. Had plenty of time to do that the last few days. Since I've known Bella is a savant, I've had to honor Gretchen's need to keep it secret. If Ernesto knew Bella and Gretchen had been away from the house and up to the University of Georgia, I fear there would have been more than a beating."

"Do you suppose he found out?"

Caroline's right eyebrow automatically rose. "Don't think so. All the testing and observation have been done in secret, but the secret games are over."

"You're right. Bella's free, and so is Gretchen. With Ernesto behind bars, their lives will be quite different. And yours too, Caroline."

What he said was true. Bubbles of change had been surfacing since last spring, since meeting Bella and since her trip to Rockwater. "When are you coming home, Roderick?"

"I leave London tomorrow. Acer's meeting me at LaGuardia with the jet. He'll fly me straight back to Rockwater, and weather permitting, he'll fly me to Atlanta early Friday morning."

"You're coming here?" Her pulse quickened.

"Yes. You don't think I'd leave you alone with Dr. Wyatt Spencer too long, do you?"

Caroline grinned for the first time in days. "You're worried about Wyatt?"

"Of course. I have to make certain that Dr. Spencer's making his professional mark with a young musical savant and not his personal mark in the life of the talented and beautiful pianist, Caroline Carlyle, who discovered her."

She hoped what she heard was a bit of honest jealousy. "I knew there was something more that I liked about you besides the fact that you like to fish. You're honest and straightforward."

"Oh, really? I'd like to think my business associates would agree. Although, they'd probably add that I'm cautious. But somehow with you, my caution heads downstream to wherever that big trout is waiting for your return to Rockwater."

She pictured Rockwater—the mansion, the gardens, the stream, and the view from the loggia windows. "Tell me, Roderick, what color is Kentucky bluegrass in October?"

"I won't tell you. If I do, perhaps you won't return to see for yourself, especially since your piano is now at home in your bay window instead of mine."

A bit of melancholy enshrouded her. She had met Roderick in July after discovering that he owned her beloved Hazelton Brothers 1902 piano, the instrument that had defined her and had been her place of joy and well-being during her childhood. Her parents sold the piano to pay for her college education. Selling the piano had been like separating conjoined twins, but playing this recital for Roderick's friends at his invitation had been like returning home again after a long and solitary journey.

The trip to Rockwater, the Adair family estate outside Lexington, had been magical. Roderick had stirred feelings in her that she was still sifting three months later, familiar feelings that had long been put away the way you dispose of a dead woman's clothes.

For six years since David's death, her life had been on autopilot, void of any feelings other than her pride in being Moss Point's piano teacher and charting the progress of her students. But meeting Roderick and his covert piano swap had disconnected her autopilot button. Roderick had surprised her by delivering her antique piano and loading her studio grand onto a truck bound for Rockwater while she and Angel were on a day trip to Atlanta. He declared it on loan, like a painting or a museum piece.

She and Roderick had spoken several times since the stunning delivery, but they had not seen each other. She wished it had been something other than this tragedy that brought him back to Georgia. "I'll be so happy to see you, Roderick."

"I'm sorry. Just when I could have been of help to you, I was away. But I'll see you Friday. I must go for now. Take care, my . . ." Roderick paused. "Take care, Caroline."

Caroline didn't miss his caution. "You too, Mr. Adair."

—·—

Gretchen stirred a bit. Caroline moved to her side. "Good morning, friend. You're awake."

Gretchen stretched her eyelids and attempted to talk. "Bell— . . . Bel-la?"

"Bella's just fine. There's so much to tell you. Do you remember anything I've been telling you?" Days of Gretchen's unconsciousness had not kept Caroline from talking to her as though she could hear.

Gretchen nodded her head.

Caroline saw her flinch in pain as she moved her neck. "You must still be sore. I'm so sorry, Gretchen. But everything's fine now. You came through the surgery, and you'll be back to normal in a few more days. Bella's great. She still has a sore nose, and they'll remove the stitches from her cheek Friday."

"Er . . . Ernes . . . ?"

Caroline took Gretchen's right hand. "Ernesto only had some bruises and minor lacerations. He's in jail where he's going to stay for a very long time."

The bruised woman struggled to speak. "I hit . . . hit him . . .my mir— . . . mirror." A single tear, maybe of relief or maybe of sadness, rolled down Gretchen's left cheek.

Caroline gently wiped it away with the corner of the sheet. She knew that Gretchen bore scars of other beatings. She also knew Gretchen had been long-suffering with Mr. Silva, forgiving him and making far too many excuses for him. She stayed with him out of gratitude for something in her past and because she was financially dependent on him. Perhaps soon Caroline would hear her story—the part of Gretchen's story that caused her to leave her family in Austria and marry an American soldier in Germany.

Caroline walked to the window and turned around to look at Gretchen. She could not conceal her excitement any longer. "I have a surprise for you. It's even a grand surprise for me too. Roderick's coming Friday. You'll finally get to meet him."

"He . . . he . . ." Gretchen's reach for her throat revealed the cast on her left arm.

Caroline walked back to the bedside and pulled her chair close. "It's okay, Gretchen, it's okay. Don't try to talk. The doctor says talking will be easier when the swelling goes down. Your left arm was fractured, and you'll be in a cast for a few weeks. That's the only broken bone."

Gretchen became very still.

"So let me talk now that you're awake. Remember, I told you about Roderick's sister who is a child psychologist, Dr. Sarah McCollum? I met her when I went to Kentucky for the recital. You saw the letter from her I found in my suitcase when I got home. Well, she and her husband just moved from Boston to Raleigh-Durham. He's teaching medicine at Duke, and I think she's taking some time off because they want children. When Roderick found out what had happened to you and Bella, he called Sarah."

Gretchen tried to nod again.

"Apparently Sarah meant what she said in the letter—I mean about helping with Bella. She called me right after she talked to Roderick and was on a plane for Atlanta the next afternoon. I don't know what I would have done without her, and Bella's so comfortable with her."

"Bella . . . where?" Gretchen strained to formulate her words.

"She's with Sarah now and Dr. Wyatt Spencer. Oh, let me back up a bit. I called Dr. Martin over the weekend to cancel my piano lesson at the university on Monday. Do you remember her? I took you and Bella to meet her when I first suspected Bella is a musical savant. And she introduced us to Dr. Spencer, the professor and psychologist."

Gretchen nodded. Her acknowledgment meant she could remember. Surely that was a positive sign, and Caroline would report it to the doctor.

"I told Dr. Martin that you and Bella were here in the hospital at Emory. So ten minutes later, guess who calls? Dr. Wyatt Spencer, insisting on coming over. He's been here since Monday to work with Bella and review the test results. Lucky for us that Sarah arrived on Sunday afternoon. I filled her in on his interest in Bella. So now she's Bella's self-appointed guardian—a professional one at that. Dr. Spencer has a group of experts observing Bella this morning."

Not even the soreness and discomfort could keep Gretchen from smiling.

"I know, I know, Gretchen. Now they're all going to see what you and I already know. Bella has a rare gift."

"Sarah?" Gretchen struggled to speak.

"Yes, and Sarah's there to protect her. I can't wait for you to meet Sarah and see Bella with her. She'll never allow anyone, not even the ambitious Dr. Spencer, to upset or exploit Bella."

Gretchen drifted off to sleep again. Her faint smile face hinted at a more peaceful rest.

———•———

"Okay, Bella, my name is Tom. Do you think you can lie very still for just a few moments? If you can lie really still, I have some candy for you when we finish." He covered her body with a thin sheet.

Mamá says, "No candy, Bella." Where's Mamá?

Bella lay on the metal table covered in a sheet for the CT scan.

Her body was still, her arms lay motionless at her side, but her fingers played the song in her head. *I'll come for you. Go, Bella. Not to the hiding place. Not to the safe place. Mamá said, "Go to Caroline's." Play the piano. Where's Mamá?*

Sarah stood beside her, caressing her arm, while the tech in bright blue scrubs made preparations. Sarah spoke to him of Bella's hypersensitivity to music and suggested that he turn off the CD player. He complied and described the procedure to her.

Sarah explained to Bella that she must leave the room for a few minutes.

Bella lay quiet and still as she was instructed. Lying still in the darkness was nothing strange to her. Only the cold table and the metal cylinder closing in around her were new. *Mamá says, "Go to your hiding place. Bella, be still and quiet so he won't hear you. Shhh, Bella. Be still. He'll go away soon. You're safe here, Bella."*

The test took only a few moments, nothing like the hours she had spent on the floor in the back of the bedroom closet. Her mamá kept quilts there to cover her.

Mamá says, "Bella, you were good. Tomorrow, we can go to the safe place." Good and quiet. Where's Mamá? I want to go to the safe place.

———•———

Bella's twelve-year-old petite frame was lost in the hospital gown and robe. Her grandfather's clumsily aimed kick left her cheek and eye area deeply bruised, but not even the awkward patch over her eye kept her from playing the piano with perfection. This morning, she had been hustled from a second CT scan, through an ungainly interview to a university conference room where a studio piano had been rolled in. Six professors sat in a semicircle of folding chairs around the piano observing her. Sarah was within Bella's reach, but not a part of this jury.

Bella played the last phrase of the Clementi sonatina. She hung her head and rhythmically rocked back and forth rubbing the palms of her hands together. "Mamá said, 'Go to Caroline's.' Mamá said, 'Go to Caroline's.'"

In his uniform of khakis, a blue-striped shirt, and a yellow sweater draped over his back with its sleeves tied in a loose knot just below his Adam's apple, Dr. Spencer was parked in chair number one. He sat casually, long legs crossed, exposing his sockless, tan ankles and twirling his pen between his fingers before pointing it at the pianist in the sixth seat. "Do you have something a bit less structured, say something from the Impressionistic Period, that you could play for her? I'd like to see what she'd do with that."

The pianist rose from her chair and approached Bella. "May I play the piano now?"

Still rocking, Bella was statuesque and unmovable. "Mamá said . . ."

The pianist looked to Dr. Spencer. He gave her the go-ahead nod. She moved behind Bella, placed her hands on Bella's shoulders, attempting to steer her from the piano.

Bella winced. Her rocking motion increased, and she rubbed her head around the bandage covering her stitches.

Sarah rose quickly from her chair. "I think this is enough for today. You seemed to have forgotten this girl has been traumatized from a beating less than a week ago."

Dr. Spencer looked at his watch. "But it's only 2:30. Could we give her a break and maybe start again?"

"I think not. She seems tired and a bit agitated. Perhaps tomorrow, you may see her again." Sarah put her clipboard in her bag and removed her reading glasses.

Dr. Spencer approached her but kept a respectable distance. "Do you know how important this is? We need this time while we have controlled access to her."

Sarah did not waver. "Yes, Dr. Spencer, I am aware of the value of knowing as much about Bella's abilities as we can discover, but this is bordering on something less than professional, and certainly has crossed the line of insensitivity, and I'll not be a part of it."

Dr. Spencer nodded. "Of course, you're right. I apologize for my… for my enthusiasm with this project."

"Might I remind you this project has a name? Her name is Bella."

"You're right again, Dr. McCollum. Please forgive me. Actually, this will give me time to talk with my colleagues about the test results and to send the data back to the university. I'd also like to review the tapes we've made today. Would you like to be a part of that?"

"Thank you for the invitation, but I, too, have had enough for one day. I do believe you will need signed releases before the video-tapes can be used."

"Yes, that's true. I'll have my secretary fax that document over this afternoon. Do you suppose I could get Mrs. Silva's signature?" He made a note on his pad.

"That, I will discuss with Caroline and Mrs. Silva when it's appropriate. Mrs. Silva is improving but is still quite sedated. Until proper documents are signed, I'd like to have the tapes please."

There was reluctance in Dr. Spencer's face, but she had him. He motioned for the technician to hand over the tapes to her.

She dropped them in her bag. "And I'd like copies of any test results also."

"Certainly, I'll be sure you receive those, and thank you for making today's work possible. I'm very grateful."

Sarah liked his more compliant attitude. Sincere or not? The future would tell. She took Bella's hand. "Let's go see Caroline. Maybe your mamá is awake. You haven't seen her in days. She is missing you."

"Mamá said, 'I'll come to you.'"

"Yes, she did Bella, but let's surprise her and go to see her."

Bella looked at Sarah and smiled. Nothing Sarah had seen or heard all day delighted her more than that one, simple expression. They walked hand in hand out the door and down the long corridor, leaving six stunned and energized professors perched like vultures around a silent piano.

———•———

Dr. Spencer pulled his chair in front of the five other chairs, sat down, and waited for the door to close and the sound of footsteps to fade before he spoke. "Well, ladies and gentlemen, there is no doubt. We have truly witnessed a savant this day—an autistic, musical savant, one of slightly less than one hundred in recorded history."

His colleagues agreed in unison. Dr. Purcell put his pen in his pocket. "So, what's the next step? I guess the real question is, what do we do after we have discovered such a rare individual?"

"I have some very definite ideas." Elena Daniels, in a mocha-colored suit and brown alligator pumps, stood and walked to the piano. She adjusted the leopard print scarf, which had been flirting with her cleavage all morning, and tucked thick strands of auburn hair behind her right ear. "We need to move quickly to claim this moment. Think what it could mean for the university and for our own careers."

Wyatt Spencer sat straighter in his chair as if to reclaim his seat of power. "Need I remind you we didn't discover Bella? That honor belongs to one Miss Caroline Carlyle, who is the key to the next step. At present, it would appear that Dr. McCollum has earned Caroline's trust. Our next step is to earn Dr. McCollum's trust. I believe what she says will determine what happens next."

Elena played with the gold chain around her neck. "Perhaps not."

"And what's that supposed to mean?" Wyatt bristled.

"What would happen if the press learned of Bella? Wouldn't that attention put this whole issue in an entirely different arena?"

Wyatt had no doubt Elena's beguiling smile had disarmed any number of men, including professionals, but he wasn't playing. "I suppose it would. But just explain to me how the press could learn of Bella when only a group of professionals who practice rules of confidentiality know about her."

"Oh, I can think of a number of ways. After all, her grandfather is in jail for beating her. That makes news, doesn't it, especially in a small town?"

Wyatt's palms were sweaty. The air in the room was heavy with ambition, and he was finding it stale and harder to breathe.